Shards of Empire

"*Shards of Empire* is a beautifully written historical . . . an original and witty delight."
—*Locus*

"At times heart-wrenchingly brutal, *Shards of Empire* gives an unromanticized picture of a violent, turbulent time. . . . Rarely have fantasy and history been interwoven with such skill. Shwartz is a remarkable writer."
—*VOYA*

"Decidedly superior, with a well-researched, persuasive, and engaging backdrop."
—*Kirkus Reviews*

The Grail of Hearts

"The most interesting treatment of the Grail theme in years."
—*New York Newsday*

"With careful scholarship and prose that sometimes sings, there is something to reward the reader on every page."
—Morgan Llywelyn

"*The Grail of Hearts* is one that you simply should not miss."
—*Amazing*

"The book is utterly fascinating, a seamless, inexorable working of myth and originality. I won't forget this book. Neither will you."
—Parke Godwin

Tor Books by Susan Shwartz

Empire of the Eagle (with Andre Norton)
The Grail of Hearts
Heritage of Flight
Imperial Lady (with Andre Norton)
Moonsinger's Friends (editor)
Shards of Empire
Silk Roads and Shadows
White Wing (with S. N. Lewitt as "Gordon Kendall")

CROSS
AND
CRESCENT

SUSAN SHWARTZ

TOR®

A TOM DOHERTY ASSOCIATES BOOK

NEW YORK

This is a work of fiction. All the characters and events portrayed in this novel are either fictitious or are used fictitiously.

CROSS AND CRESCENT

This book is printed on acid-free paper.

A Tor Book
Published by Tom Doherty Associates, LLC
175 Fifth Avenue
New York, NY 10010

Tor Books on the World Wide Web:
www.tor.com

Tor® is a registered trademark of Tom Doherty Associates, LLC

Library of Congress Cataloging-in-Publication Data

Shwartz, Susan.
    Cross and crescent / Susan Shwartz.
        p. cm.
    "A Tom Doherty Associates book."
    ISBN 0-312-85714-4 (hc)
    ISBN 0-312-86807-3 (pbk)
    1. Alexius I Comnenus, Emperor of the East, 1048–1118—
Fiction. 2. Byzantine Empire—History— Alexius I Comnenus,
1081–1118—Fiction 3. Military history, Medieval— Fiction.
4. Crusades—First, 1096–1099— Fiction. 4. Eleventh century—
Fiction.
    I. Title.
    PS3569.H873C76 1997
    813'.54—dc21   97-17580
                                                                                CIP

First Hardcover Edition: December 1997
First Trade Paperback Edition: July 1999

Printed in the United States of America

0 9 8 7 6 5 4 3 2 1

To Claire Eddy, patient and expert editor, who reminded me
about Bohemond

Acknowledgments

I would like to thank Harvard University's Center for Byzantine Studies at Dumbarton Oaks, Washington, D.C., for their research facilities, especially Dr. Irene Vaslev and Mark Zapatka for their forbearance and generosity. Any inaccuracies, infelicities, or just plain lapses in judgment are mine, not the Center's.

Special mention goes, of course, to the people of GEnie, especially the denizens of my topic on the Science Fiction Round Table, who may have distracted me, but helped me see this book through and provided unconventional insights on the trigonometry of siege warfare at Antioch.

SUMMER 1096
CONSTANTINOPLE

Byzantium *panted for breath in the late summer heat. The deep* green of the trees in the gardens wilted and sagged in the heat. The Golden Horn held a molten shimmer; sails bellied out, then collapsed. Even the statues, bull and lion, which gave the Bucoleon Palace its name, seemed to gasp: touching them burnt the careless hand.

A haze, more oppressive than the veil that clung to Anna's face, hung over New Rome. As much as the heat, apprehension and delight at her own bravery made her breath come faster.

She half expected the bull and lion guarding the palace to roar out that the Caesarissa Anna, eldest daughter of Emperor Alexius Comnenus and his wife, Irene, was stealing out of her home. When the creatures actually allowed her silent passage, she closed her eyes in relief and brief escape from the glare.

"You scuttle like a thief!" she hissed to make her maid hurry. She could threaten and swear the woman into obedience, even into silence, but not into composure. Obedience would do.

They turned away from the broad Mese that split and enriched the City into a side street. As the barrier of old houses blocked them from the Mese, the clamor of bargaining, theological quarrels, and political gossip that was Byzantium at work subsided.

Argument was as much a passion in Byzantium as racing; and, like racing or any other passion, dispute could turn deadly in the twinkling of an eye. Byzantium not only argued within itself, but about its enemies: Turks, heretics, or this latest wave of Western heretics, bandits, and tramps who had run riot in the suburbs. Anna's father, the Emperor Alexius, had taken his guard and his archers and put them down, then sent them on their way. They claimed to be pilgrims to the Holy Land; most Byzantines hoped they were on their way to hell.

The priests had compared the Franks or Celts or whatever they were calling themselves this year to a plague of locusts that swept across the Empire. Anna's own doctrine was sound; still, she preferred to put her trust in her father, his archers, and the tall, ax-bearing Varangians rather than in portents like locusts, shimmers around the sun, and eclipses of the moon. Still, the appearance of so many portents was a fact in itself. No educated person ignored facts, and Anna had received an education fit for the Empress she still dreamed of becoming.

The houses on this narrow street loomed overhead like weathered fortresses, many with jutting balconies that almost turned street into shadowed tunnel. Beneath the clinging silk of Anna's veil, her face cooled and her breath came more easily. Even though she and her maid were practically alone on this street, she did not dare to free herself from the veil's confinement. Not quite.

She could not remember how long it had been—if ever—since she had left the luxurious confinement of the Imperial palace, except for processions, which were simply walking imprisonment, studded with jewels. She would not count her move as a little girl, a child betrothed to the Imperial heir Constantine, to Maria Alania's palace so that the former Basilissa could raise her as a fit wife for her son. That was just more of the same type of life in a different women's quarters. Besides, it had come to naught, and with it, Anna's own hopes for the Purple after her father Alexius went—may the day be far off—to his undoubted and glorious salvation.

When news of her birth in the porphyry chamber had been proclaimed, how the people of Byzantium had shouted her name in the streets, she had been told as a child. And how quickly they forgot, this dark, volatile people so like her in looks and mood, who had shoved past her in the Mese, arguing, worrying, or denouncing the rabble from the West.

How long would it be before her absence was discovered? Gesturing at her maid to hurry, Anna tried to walk as swiftly as any of the men who had jostled her. She found the turn in the street just where the servant she had bribed told her a turn would be.

She scowled, her eyes filling with ready tears. She had been acclaimed not just as Caesarissa, but as Basilissa-to-be: she and Constantine. She was almost fourteen now and had reluctantly consented to another betrothal. The old longing stabbed at her even so long after Constantine's death. She had loved him as an intense, brilliant girlchild may adore an amiable, handsome boy conscious that he is older than she, but willing to smile at her and accept her adoration. Oh, he had been so charming.

The birth of Anna's brother Ioannes, that homely, interloping baby, had wrecked Anna's hopes. Constantine was no longer to be Emperor; and Anna, although still hailed as Caesarissa, realized that she would never be hailed as Empress. Constantine being Constantine, he hardly cared when they stripped the honors from him, but Anna cared for his sake—and for her own. She had cried in his mother's arms, and his mother had cried too. Then, it was back to Anna's parents for her: back to standards so rigorous that she might as well have lived in Old Rome, if it had had the blessings of Christianity.

Anna's father was the Emperor Alexius Comnenus. He could not be wrong. But he was very wrong if he thought she had forgotten that his eldest child shared his dreams of Empire.

She had been bred to rule, educated for it with the help of Michael Psellus, advisor to her grandfather, tutor to an Emperor: why would her father give her an Emperor's education if she were not to rule?

Perhaps, if she showed him how brave and devoted she was— *See, Father, I went to the Jews' market to find herbs for you!*—he would finally appreciate her as more than as a charming, accomplished eldest daughter and marriage pawn, and restore her birthright to her.

Heaven grant, though, that the time when she might grasp the diadem be far off. The City had weathered its plague of tramps. Now, it prepared to withstand another, this one composed of great lords, if you could call any of the Western barbarians truly noble. They would be hungry: when were the Westerners not starving for food, gold, land, anything they could snatch? How could they see the splendor of Anna's home and not covet it?

If she asked one of the aristocratic young officers of the Scholae what he thought, he would lie or try to curry favor. She did not know Nicephorus Bryennius, to whom she was betrothed, well enough to trust him yet. Perhaps, she should ask one of the Varangians, the tall Northerners with their red tunics and gleaming axes. They seemed to enjoy talking to their "little Caesarissa," and she liked them. They preened, and then they bent over double lest they tower rudely over her, a tiny lady, overpowered by her Purple, as she looked up to them, her eyes deliberately round and admiring. They told her stories, with frequent pauses to supply words or replace ones they knew her father would hate to have her learn and, because she was Anna, probably use at the worst possible moment.

One or two told her indulgently that she would grow to be like her father and her mother. Her father was only moderately tall, though he had powerful shoulders and eyes that could take you prisoner across a room. Her mother, Irene, was the beauty. Anna knew she would never look like her, so she must be wise.

Her grandfather Andronicus had fought against the Turks. Sometimes, she had nightmares about the dreadful day when an Emperor, even one as worthless as Romanus, had been taken captive, and it was only by the grace of God that the Turks had not rushed from Manzikert across all Anatolia to the Golden Horn.

When she was younger, the dreams used to make her wake crying. Then, Maria Alania would come and hold her and sing to her those strange songs from her native land. After Maria's son Constantine died and Anna had returned to her mother's care, the Empress Irene had schooled her not to cry at those dreams, but to kneel and pray until God—and not her mother—comforted her.

To keep the crescent from polluting the dome of the Church of the Holy Wisdom, to preserve her father's life until she could take up his work, Anna would do anything. If that meant paying lip service to John as Caesar, so be it: her time would come. If that meant wedding Nicephorus Bryennius, she knew she must marry at some point. It was her parents' wish that Anna marry—besides which a convent was hardly the ideal place from which to reach for a throne. The husband her parents had chosen for her seemed handsome enough. Calm, her mother told her. Mature. He would—what was the word?—steady her, be a steadying influence.

Anna snorted. Her veil fluttered briefly.

Her maid gestured: turn *here*. She did.

Anna had studied medicine along with the seven liberal arts. Her father's physician, studying her father's mood, indulged her. She knew where to find the true remedies, the Alexandrian cures. She would buy herbs and compound her own potions to lift her father's pain and her mother's burden of caring for him, even though as Basilissa she might have delegated the task to her maids. Then, her father would see, he would finally see that Anna—unlike the unspeakable, licentious women who had tried during Byzantium's long history to rule—was worthy of a crown and proclaim it, and the people of the city would shout her name once more.

As long as they acclaimed her, she would allow them to acclaim her consort too: an Empress could afford to be generous.

At the end of the street, sunlight and market noise struck her ears like hammers upon brass. The stalls of the perfume sellers in the Imperial quarter were very different from the tumult that sprawled out before her, all of it demanding attention, wariness, purchase, and *watch out, something's coming through here!* She smelled water and sweat, ships being unloaded and repaired, frying fish, and the lairs of exceedingly aggressive cats. Her maid coughed.

"The sooner I get what I want, the sooner we go home," she told her maid. Pressing her veil against her mouth, Anna picked her way through the filth into the market itself.

Gradually, clean-swept stones replaced the squalor. The stinks of fish, drying wool, and a thousand unmentionable objects gave way to the cool pungency of the herbs she sought.

She followed her nose and an increasing sobriety of robes toward a building in better repair than most. Here, the language changed along with the garments. Anna shivered with excitement and more than a little fear. The Greek she heard here was more strongly accented, as if the merchants had not grown up speaking it. Some indeed spoke languages no doubt drawn from almost the length of the great silk roads. Persian? Aramaic? How strange it must be to speak as one's birth speech the very language that Christ used. She was not certain at all that it should be allowed to unbelievers.

In the manner of merchants everywhere, these men gossiped about the war to come. The lords of the West were coming—the son-in-law of the Northerner who had conquered that island . . . she rather thought it was near Thule; a man with a name like an angel—Isangeles, was it?—married to a princess from near the Gates of Hercules. A prince of the Western church. And Bohemond.

The light seemed to dim as it lanced through the narrow windows whenever she heard his name. Marcus Boamundus. Bohemond, son of Robert the Wily. Fox and son of fox from a land of foxes, who had fought her father to a standstill and would not be satisfied with anything less than a throne to repay him for all the years he had been little more than a mercenary no decent *strategos* would hire. If, as the stories went, he had torn his best crimson cloak into tiny crosses to

adorn his kinsmen's garments in token of this madness the Westerners termed a pilgrimage, being Bohemond, he expected to be repaid
for the sacrifice—in Purple.

She wondered that the chain had not yet been stretched across
the Horn to close it. Her father had sent out a fleet. No doubt they
were waiting for its return and for the plague of human locusts that
would follow. And for Bohemond, who had once come close to de-
feating her father in a day that would have been as dreadful as a second Manzikert.

The churches of Byzantium rang with prayer. How frightening it
must be for the Jews, who refused the comfort and protection of
Christ. They looked frightened, these bearded men, who clustered together, their heads bent over scraps of parchment and papyrus. Occasionally, one would beat his breast as if in repentance; another
would lay hand upon his shoulder; they would nod, visibly gathering
composure, then separate, to go about their work.

Anna kept her head down, her steps tiny, a veritable icon of la-
dyship. She entered the building into which the most sober of the
merchants and bearded men who would have looked like priests if
they were not probably Jews vanished. In its shelter, her head came
up. It was scrupulously clean, and it smelled of herbs she could recognize, had put hand to, had seen her father's physicians use for his
aching joints and shortness of breath.

The long, polished rooms held nothing the merchants did not
need: a box could serve as well as a table and was scrubbed as clean.
Anna followed her nose and her instinct. Her maid followed with the
purse. Even through their veils, Anna could see how fearfully the
woman's eyes bulged.

The merchants whispered and drew away from her. And they
watched, always watched, from those dark eyes that, even more than
the Byzantines', were scholars' eyes. She had heard servants' whispers
that these people used the blood of Christian children in whatever
unimaginable rites her father and his predecessors had not suppressed.
She did not really believe that.

It was not as if her father had oppressed the Empire's Jews. He was
a kindly master. When the Jews' old dwellings near the bronze workers, the old Chalkoprateia, had burned, he had even helped them
find new homes.

Alexius's daughter put up her chin through her veils and swallowed. In an instant more, she would summon the courage to de-

mand that these . . . these clients of her father procure what herbs she required.

The men kept staring at her.

"A girl just that age," one of them whispered in husky Greek.

"Hundreds, all gone now. May millstones grind the bones of those evil men."

Perhaps Anna would need *two* instants longer.

Her maid put her hands on the purse she carried, a spectacularly stupid gesture that practically shouted "Come rob me!" and edged behind Anna.

"Caesarissa, what if they . . ." The maid's voice broke. Anna hissed pure fury at her. Thank God her mother had instilled in her the virtue of self-control.

The bearded men—it was impossible that they be taller than the Varangians; no one was taller than a Varangian—loomed up between Anna and the boxes and bales that had been her quarry. Three more stood in the door, blocking sunlight, sound, air . . . and escape. They still watched her, but now their eyes filled with what Anna realized was terror.

She had seen men stare and back away like that as if they saw a leper, the time they brought the son of the blinded Emperor Romanus before her father and his Varangians. People backed away until the traitor stood all alone. And then the guards closed in, bringing him to the prison where the brazier and the hot irons for blinding waited.

Now Anna and her maid stood isolated. The merchants stared at her and whispered in Greek and those older tongues, poplar leaves and branches rustling against each other. Sometimes, poplars fell on people, Anna recalled.

"I'll bring him."

Footsteps—rapid but a trifle uneven—pounded out of the hall. Anna forced herself not to crane her neck. It sounded as if the man who fled the hall might have a very slight limp. She would remember that when she was rescued. If she were rescued.

Anna waited. A moment more, and the footsteps returned, this time accompanied by others.

The princess touched her veils lest she be exposed in the presence of her enemies. She should cross herself, she knew. Instead, she reached for the tiny knife she had brought along. Her maid sank to her knees.

2

*T*he newcomers strode toward Anna. *One was the man with the*
not-quite-limp. He was no Jew. He could have been a tradesman
or a minor scholar or a kind of priest. Why was he here, and why had
he run out, as if fetching reinforcements?

The first of the two men he had fetched was . . . no, his hair and
beard were no longer fair, but silvering fast; and his massive height
seemed bent by long years of fighting. Her eyes widened at the sight
of a Northerner without his ax.

He must be in service to the third man, who looked so familiar
that Anna found him the strangest and most frightening of all.

Anna's maid rattled off whispered urgent prayers. Her breath
gusted somewhere in the neighborhood of Anna's back.

One or two of the younger men grumbled. The newcomer's eyes
blazed anger. "Even after all these years? The mood you're in, I bless
Theodoulos for bringing me right away. A wonder you didn't turn him
away, too. This is mine to deal with."

He gestured. The older men went back to their business, their
faces tense, even sorrowful. The younger men glared, then subsided,
not without a few glances at the old Northerner, who had not bent
an inch or thawed the winter in his eyes.

"If any of the ships bring further word—anything at all—I want
to hear. Instantly."

The stranger crossed the pale-scrubbed, echoing floor. Unfortu-
nately, it did not open up to swallow him or Anna herself. She forced
herself to look up at him. Taller than her father, he lacked her father's
breadth of shoulder. His beard and hair were grey. She thought he had
to be a few years older than the Emperor, though he moved without
the stiffness that plagued her father. Alexius's eyes sparkled with energy and wit; this man's eyes seemed more remote, as if he was used
to staring into the vast distances of the caravan routes or across time
into ancient texts. He was studying her now, and his eyes glinted
with . . . with what? For a moment, she had thought that he shared
the Jewish merchants' inexplicable sorrow, but now? Surely, he could
not think this was amusing!

She was the Caesarissa Anna, Emperor Alexius's eldest daughter, in danger of her life; and she was not used to being laughed at. Anna drew herself up. Her maid's prayers grew louder.

Then, he bowed to her, the exact depth that Imperial ceremonial accorded a woman born in the Purple.

"Caesarissa," he said, "you honor us, but your presence is an honor we may not survive."

His Greek was as fine as Anna's own, even to the accent used at court. Unlike social climbers as far back as Athens, he did not lisp, which Anna's tutors called a vulgar affectation.

Raising himself from his deep bow, he tried to peer through her veils at what she knew was her very puzzled face. He might dress like a wealthy merchant, speak with these men in their own language, and even have some power over them, but he was a Roman, not a Jew; and in the shapely boning of his face, the dignity of his carriage, Anna could trace something . . .

The man nodded. "They did not lie who spoke well of the Emperor's eldest child's wit—although perhaps not her prudence. Your father, may Christ save His Sacred Majesty, saved my life long before you were born. It has been years since we were close, but he was dear to me."

Anna realized she could name this stranger. There had been whispers of a Ducas who had turned on Anna's own grandfather that dreadful day at Manzikert. He had run mad, followed Romanus across Anatolia to his inglorious death, had disrupted holy services in Hagia Sophia, and almost drowned himself. Capping this madman's brief, but extraordinarily busy career, he had run off to Cappadocia to become a monk, but even they wouldn't take him. So he had married a Jew instead, heiress to a merchant prince whose riches, whisper had it, rivaled those of Solomon and Sheba combined.

"Good for Leo!" her father had exclaimed. "My mother, God rest her soul, always loved him."

Ice had sheathed the Empress Irene's beauty at Alexius's words, more so at his laughter. This Leo Ducas had even succeeded in organizing the remnants of the *akritai*, old veterans, youths, Armenians, and anyone else in Cappadocia who could fight against the Turks. Even though he had won, Anna's father had let him live.

Did Anna's father ever hear from this most disreputable of kinsmen? Judging from Irene's expression, she wouldn't have put it past him, and she didn't like the idea any more than she liked her husband's stubbornness on the subject of his choice of heir.

"Romanus blinded, his sons blinded, dead. The dreadful day at Manzikert cast a long, long shadow," her father had said. "Leo was some years older than I. If he's come into wealth, it's the first luck he's had, and God love him for it."

Her mother flared her nostrils in disdain. Ordinarily, that would have been enough to make her father nod and listen: the Emperor usually let himself be swayed by his wife's counsel, just as, years ago, he had bowed to the good advice of his mother, Anna Dalassena. Except in the matter of his son the Caesar, that unsightly child, secretive in the same way that her father was. Anna never would have suspected that he could keep sympathy for a man who had turned on his own Ducas kin.

On that note, Anna *had* been sent from the room. Her mother's lips had pursed, and Anna knew better than to speak the renegade's name ever again.

Now, she felt her lips part on it.

"You are right, Caesarissa," he said. "I am Leo Ducas, although I would not presume to call myself kin. I am not going to presume to scold, either, and say you shouldn't have come. It's true that you could scarcely have turned up at a worse time: still, you are here; and we must deal with facts. The question now is how can we serve you— then get you safely home?"

Had she put them all in danger simply by coming here? When Anna became Basilissa, she must care for all her people. This might not be, she realized, a particularly auspicious start.

Leo Ducas bowed again. This time, when he rose, his eyes were gentle. He even smiled at her, a smile so charming that Anna found herself constrained to smile back. She pinched her maid's shoulder: *get up*.

"You are frightening these people, Caesarissa," Leo Ducas told her, still in that gentle, persuasive voice. "They know their lives answer for your well-being, never more than now, when our news has been so bad. They think I have some power to intercede, so I have promised to take you off their hands. Come: you shall walk with me into the next room, where my own wife will find you what you desire."

Leo attempted to convey her, with a skilled courtier's gestures, into the next room, where all manner of thing even more unknown and more fearsome than a Jewish merchant princess might await. She planted her feet and tried to summon her wits.

Leo smiled at her. "Come now. It really does not do to frighten the merchants, Caesarissa."

Anna was not certain that she wanted—or that she ought—to see this . . . this Lilith of a woman her kinsman had wed.

Leo Ducas's eyes flashed into quick anger. "My wife, Asherah, is a great and kind lady, a woman of valor, as it is written in the Proverbs, her worth far above rubies. Even your august grandmother, who was my shield when I was a boy, thought so."

She pulled her veil away from her face. The unrestricted air against it felt like a release from prison.

"You have your father's eyes," Leo Ducas murmured. This outrageous creature actually seemed happy about it.

She supposed she should have resented the familiarity. Instead, her lips twitched. Only imagine: the sight of Anna Dalassena meeting the Jewish woman that a young Ducas had married. Seeing that would have been better than a spectacle at the Hippodrome. Her thoughts raced toward a conclusion as skilled as that of any adult logician: just how had the Jews of the city approached her father, anyhow? Through a man with ties to them and to the Empire. No wonder her mother had been furious.

Alexius would not expect his daughter to know. So, what Leo Ducas told her was valuable information. It might be equally valuable to meet this mysterious woman, gain her goodwill, and assure her of the friendship of a Caesarissa.

Leo's eyes warmed again, with comprehension and a wry affection, as if for the daughter of a friend or a very young kinswoman he found promising.

"I learned very early when to leave these people in peace, Caesarissa. Your father needs them. As you will learn, so do you."

He ushered her past him, then held out his hand to her maid. "You will be safe," he promised her more gravely than he had spoken to Anna herself. "Nordbriht here will guard you while my foster son Theodoulos makes sure that, when you leave, all is done with propriety."

The woman bowed to him as if he were still an intimate of the Emperor. She eyed the former guardsman with some apprehension, not unmixed with admiration. Now, the old wolf visibly unbent. Preened, even.

Did Anna imagine that her newfound kinsman winked at her?

Leo Ducas led Anna around piled boxes toward an unmarked door. He tapped on it, then pushed it open.

The room was small, haphazard, as if hasty workers had thrown up partitions, scarcely more than shelf space, between wall supports and only bothered to paint one of them, leaving the other dark. Light streamed in from a window, at which a woman stood, gazing as if her life depended on seeing what lay outside.

"Asherah."

Speak the word only leapt into Anna's mind. How young and joyous Leo Ducas's voice sounded as he spoke his wife's name.

"No word beyond what we had from the last ship, Leo," she said as if continuing an old conversation.

Tension stiffened the woman's shoulders, even through the shimmers and folds of the fine silk she wore. As Leo strode forward, his hands outstretched to clasp them and ease the strain from them, the lady Asherah turned. Her face was as drawn as those of the merchants—the other merchants—outside. But as she looked at her husband, it glowed with welcome.

Anna sighed. No one's face lit thus at the sight of her. And she had never been so purely glad of anyone except her father, who preferred her brother. And now she was betrothed to an estimable young man who would "steady" her. For an instant, she envied the unlikely pair, renegade and outcast though they were.

"My heart"—Leo's voice warmed the tiny room—"we have an august visitor, come to seek aid for her father. Caesarissa, I beg the honor of presenting to you the lady Asherah bat Joachim. Asherah Ducaina, if you prefer. My wife."

This Asherah, who bowed to her as gracefully as if she had lived at court her entire life, was older than her mother. She might even have grown children older than Anna. Yet, she was just as beautiful in her way as the Empress Irene. The Empress was a golden lily, shimmering in mosaics. Asherah blossomed like the deep-hearted roses Anna had always admired in the palace gardens.

Her smile had the same devastating results on Anna as Leo's.

Pay attention, Anna told herself, as the sonorous terms of court courtesy—Asherah's accent was as pure as Leo's own—filled the tiny room. She could respond to such ceremony in her sleep, and often had.

All right, so now she had met what her odd cousin insisted on calling his wife. What interested her more was the older woman's worktable, heaped with samples and accounts and yellowing books, some written in scripts she had never seen before. One contained drawings of a man, a woman, of planets, even a dragon, twisting about a central axis, within a starry sphere.

Medicine or philosophy? Anna wondered. Perhaps her cousin's wife really could help her to the herbs she sought or even better.

Asherah rose from the deep reverence Leo had probably taught her to perform. The Persian silks of her garments rustled about her and shifted colors with her movements. She put out a white, gemmed hand for the veils that she had evidently tossed across a box, then laughed at the folly of such ceremony among kin.

"Caesarissa, is your father dear to you that you venture here? Yes? Then, he is a lucky man! I would have done that and more for my father, blessed be his memory. If you permit, I shall tell you all I learned that helped him in his old age."

"The Emperor is younger than I!" Leo protested.

"Younger than you? Ah, Leo, when I look at you, I still see the young officer . . ." Memories flitted across Asherah's face. "Now, though, it is the Caesarissa who is the young one. August lady, you must consider this place as your own."

She touched her husband's hand, pushing it playfully away, when he would have drawn her to his side.

"Leo"—again that look, with Asherah's heart glowing in her deep-set eyes—"give the Caesarissa a chair. We must talk. Oh, she is too thin, she must have honeycake, fruit, whatever else a young girl likes."

Her words tumbled one over the other. She was speaking too much, too quickly, but the sheer music of her voice beguiled a smile from the reluctant Anna. Leo seemed totally besotted. Had he really been that way for more than twenty years?

It almost made sense, even to a very young woman and a devout Christian. Afraid and heartsick and at least as mad as Anna's family said he was, in his youth, he must have taken one look at this creature and lost his heart along with what remained of his wits. Oh, it was good that Jews had their own laws, their own dwellings, and that laws binding them were strict. Otherwise, all the Romans would pursue such ladies.

"Leo, I sent Binah to the docks. Don't scold, my love; you know she can protect herself. Will you find this child some food? Caesarissa, forgive me, you may be a woman grown, but you are still too thin."

Leo's laughter was a little forced. "Caesarissa—kinswoman—you are in the best care I can provide. I beg you to excuse me as I obey."

Anna edged down onto the chair he had given her and poised there, stiff-backed. Asherah darted to her worktable and her shelves, pulling down books, opening boxes, and piling them on the already-cluttered surface. Her fingers brushed a single curling sheet, torn, stained, and covered in exotic script.

Asherah drew her fingers back as if it burned her, then, visibly, forced herself to take hold of it and turn it upside down.

From a corner, she tugged a pillow that showed signs of being cut from a rug. When she dropped it at Anna's feet and seated herself, it was so wide and high that their heads were still almost level. She reached out her hands, allowing Anna to decide if she wanted to place her own hands within them. She was struggling with that decision when Leo kicked open the door.

Asherah started, her face going still. Her husband shook his head and held out a tray.

"No word yet, my heart. Honeycakes, watered wine, whatever I could quickly find. I shall keep watch, while you advise our little Caesarissa."

He set down his burden and quickly left.

"We shall not need the men, shall we?" Again, that irresistible smile.

Anna imagined that Jews had strange rituals or that they were too stiff-necked to eat with strangers, not that Christians really wanted to. Furthermore, was this food safe? At least, one knew one could trust the palace cooks. Usually.

Murmuring swift words, Asherah snatched up a cake, broke it in two, and ate half of it. Then she held out the dish to Anna.

She ate first to reassure me, Anna realized. The woman's rings gleamed with sapphires, an ancient specific against poison. Shivering a little, she reached for the half of the cake that Asherah had left and bit into it.

Asherah tilted her head. "Do you like it? In the palace, I suppose, you have cooks that make these cakes look like scraps, no?"

"My maid?" Anna whispered through a mouthful of pastry.

"I am sure Theodoulos will see she is cared for. He grew up among monks, you know."

Poison would be bitter, wouldn't it? The cake was sweet. If these people meant her harm, surely they would have more subtle ways of working it. *My father befriended these people! They will not harm me.* She ate another cake, and Asherah nodded approval as if Anna were her own daughter.

Whispering another blessing, the lady poured for both of them from the Persian silver pitcher, beaded with a coolness that made Anna realize how dry her mouth was. Asherah drank, wiped the rim of the cup, and handed it to Anna.

"I can add more water if you require it, or, if you care to wait, we can have sherbet made in the true Persian style."

Anna's eyes strayed to the books and herbs.

"We know you must return home soon," Asherah said. "But you really must eat. You will be wed soon, and you are much too thin."

Anna flushed. Nicephorus Bryennius was much older than she, a man in truth, where Anna knew herself truly to be little more than a grown girl. She reached for the goblet, finer even in a warehouse than anything the imperial children were allowed to use except on state occasions, and sipped cautiously. A noble vintage: that was to be expected. Leo Ducas had an aristocrat's training, and his marriage must have made him very rich.

"They say your promised husband is a good man," Asherah went on. "Do you like him?"

Anna shrugged. She blinked away a disgraceful tear.

"How should I not care? You are my husband's kin. My own marriage was so sudden I had no time to fear. But you, already you lost the one man, the young Caesar Constantine, whom you had known since you were a little girl. You must remember him, yet he is gone. Now, you sit among women in the palace, and they laugh and tell such stories that you do not know where or how to look. Doubtless you feel left out, perhaps a little afraid . . ."

"He is well enough, I suppose," Anna spoke quickly.

Not since she had lived with Maria Alania, who confided in her as if she were a child of her own, not a future daughter-in-law, had anyone looked at her as if her happiness, her feelings mattered. Anna approached the Basilissa for a respectful kiss almost as she would kneel before an icon—and only if she felt herself to be in a state approaching grace. This Asherah smiled at her, assuming that, as an almost-bride, she would have worries she would be ashamed to express.

"Just all right?" Asherah echoed softly. She put down a second honeycake and touched Anna's hand. "You are very young. I was older when I wed, and so was my elder daughter. I think it is better that way, but you are a good girl and do not choose, is that it?"

"I would remain unwed," Anna whispered. "But my father needs . . ."

Asherah misread the doubt on Anna's face.

"A marriage of state?" Asherah sighed. "Your Nicephorus—he is a Caesar, no?—is older than you. I have heard about him: respected and liked, a scholar and soldier. His father was no friend to my people, not as your father, the Lord of Hosts bless him, is. An arranged match is not all a young girl could wish, but if the young man is fine and steady—and I think your Nicephorus is—love can grow from such matches."

She would need all the love she could get, which wasn't much; and she would need it soon. The thought struck Anna like prophecy, and she drank again to conceal her shudder.

The attempt failed. Asherah nodded.

"We are frightened too. Look," she said, "I shall show you a book I received in the cargo of the last ship from Venezia, where many of my kinfolk live. The writer is one Master Donnolo, a philosopher and a fine physician, even though he was not born in Alexandria."

Were they truly frightened? Asherah and Leo seemed to have made their own world, coming and going as they would, bridging worlds and rules in a way unthinkable for Anna.

"Are you . . . all your people . . . merchants and physicians?" There! The question was out, and it did not sound too impolite.

"Not all, my dear. Some are wives and mothers, some go out along the caravans . . . My people do what every other people in the world do. And"—she drew a quivering breath—"we try to live and honor God. Your father . . . oh, when the Chalkoprateia burned, Leo dared to write. We had letters, messengers back and the favor of the Emperor."

Asherah's eyes filled. "We try to live," she repeated. "Oh, how we try."

Anna took her hand. Her own eyes filled in sympathy; her mother had once said she cried as easily as a good woman should pray, and then she had had that reproof to cry about as well.

"You are afraid. Why?"

Asherah's hand trembled, then clasped hers, hard.

"The news is very bad," Asherah whispered. "God forgive me for saying it, but I am glad my father did not live to see what I fear is coming. Only your father stands between us and growing evil. And he is ill."

The great lords from the West, Anna thought. Years ago, Bohemond had fought Alexius to a standstill in Italy. Her father was wilier now, older, and he sat on his throne surrounded by armies he had fought to rebuild, a battle almost as hard as any other he had won.

Asherah withdrew her hand, drew it across her face, and made herself smile.

"I am talking far too much," she said. "Leo would be furious at how I afflict a kinswoman and guest with my babbling. You must come back later, when the times again smile on us, and let us show you how well we treat our guests.

"Now to business," she said, pointing toward her worktable. "Your father's joints pain him, I have heard. After so many years on campaign, it is not surprising. But it sounds as if he has the start of the gout. He is young for that."

"But I have not begun to—"

"Tell me about your father? Now, you fear that we spy on him? Caesarissa, he and my husband are still kin; when you are older you will know that sometimes agemates compare illnesses. We have made sure the Emperor has the best possible care. I myself help mix the medications that his physicians use. But"—the lady eyed Anna shrewdly—"it is still no wonder that you fear and you wish to do more. It is frightening to see a man lose his breath. Now, as your father's physicians have told you, no doubt, we do not yet know how to cure your father's ailment, but much can be done to alleviate his pain. I used these herbs, steeped in hot, hot water—you have seen such decoctions?—when my father's bones ached. You shall have them, and this salve, and . . ."

Asherah pulled free, rose, went to her table, and wrote something in the script Anna had seen in the books strewn about. "You shall give this to your father's physician, who knows me, and he will explain anything you want to know."

Anna too rose and leaned over the worktable with its tempting array of books. She pointed at the one from Italy Asherah had said was a medical book, despite its picture of a dragon.

Asherah smiled. "I wish you read Hebrew," she said. "It is the study of a lifetime to learn it well, although Leo . . . he has learned everything so well. It is more than a language. It is a means of knowing. This book, *Sefer*, in our language, begins at the beginning, with how the world was formed."

"In the beginning . . ." Reassured by the familiarity of a religious dispute, Anna reached for another honeycake. She had not realized how hungry she was.

"I do not question it," Asherah disappointed her by saying. "Still, this theory may perhaps be new to you. You know how the universe is formed, how the celestial sphere circles around a fixed axis."

"But this is a dragon," Anna interrupted. "And dragons are evil."

"Not always," said Asherah. "In the Land of Gold—Ch'in, where silk first came from—dragons are a symbol of empire. Only the Emperor may wear certain types of dragons embroidered on their clothing." She reached over and picked up a pale green stone, intricately and curiously carved in the form of a strange creature, wings outstretched, claws gripping at the air.

"Here is just such a dragon," she stated. "But in this book, Master Donnolo teaches us about the 'tli.' "

Asherah placed the Ch'in dragon upon the drawing in the outspread book. "His theory is thus: When God created the firmament, He created it in the form of a great dragon, a great twisted serpent, and set it in the fourth heaven, the abode of the sun. He stretched it like a bar, from end to end, twisting it halfway about its length, joining the constellations and the planets and the luminaries to it. It moves and carries the luminaries . . ."

Anna glanced up rapidly. She had read of the heavens when she studied Ptolemy, and yet, what was this talk of dragons? "We cannot see this tli?"

Asherah shook her head. "It is fire and water. We can know the tli only through the learning handed down in ancient books—its power, its rule, how it was created, its good and its evil. Some say that there are *two,* dwelling within the fixed sphere."

Her eyes half closed, gazing into unimaginable vistas Anna tried to share. "The sphere turns the constellations, moved by the power of the tli; and all moves in accordance with the sphere. That is why it is written that the whole world depends upon the sphere—and the heart. For just as the world with all that is in it is ruled by the tli and the sphere, so is man ruled by the heart, for the heart rules the body."

Oh my, Anna thought. She set down the remains of a honeycake, lest it stain this precious, dubious treasure of a book.

"I would like to read this for myself," she said.

"Theodoulos and I shall translate it ourselves for you," Asherah declared. "A wedding gift to you, little scholar. And in earnest of it, this!"

She handed her the dragon. Its cool stone clung to Anna's hand.

"Since it is of Ch'in, it is not a tli at all, really; but it will serve as a symbol, just as our weak words do, of my promise."

Deep eyes met Anna's, fathoming her hunger for the knowledge and serenity Asherah possessed.

"Could I . . ." She had been taught to speak without her voice cracking like her brother's would, in a few years. "Could I come speak with you again?"

In knowledge was power—and perhaps advantage for an ambitious Caesarissa. Her freedoms would be greater once she was wed.

Her father cast his nets wide, she knew. She wanted so to think that these people—her newfound cousin who did not look nearly so insane now and this strange, cultivated lady—were part of them. They were wise, secretive, and they liked her. Perhaps they could help her to her heart's desire.

Clamor erupted in the street outside the warehouse, shouts that turned swiftly to wailing.

"Our Father, our King, protect us!" Asherah cried.

She leapt up. With movements so swift she must have planned them long ago, she slammed shutters over the window, dashed the contents of her table into a box on the floor, and turned—putting herself between Anna and the door.

"God have mercy," Anna prayed. "Christ have mercy." She reached for her knife.

Footsteps thundered outside, underlying rhythmic shouts.

Asherah quivered, listening. Snatching up a sword in a dusty sheath, she drew it with her left hand. Damascus steel.

"Stay behind me, whatever happens," she commanded. "For your soul's sake, do not speak!" She drew deep, rhythmic breaths, and her eyes grew distant. Her right hand moved as if drawing patterns in the air.

The doors of the warehouse burst open. A woman's voice rose above the outcry of the men, her quicker steps racing toward them.

Anna forced herself not to sink to her knees. Not when Asherah prepared to defend her to the death against God only knew what peril. Still, what approached might be a peril that only struck down Jews. In that case, it would be Anna who would save Asherah, and she must stay alert. She drew herself up. The Purple, she had been taught, made the best winding sheet.

Footsteps thundered outside. Had the Westerners already arrived—invaded? How could her father have failed, and failed so soon?

Her hand tightened on the tiny dragon, which bit into her palm. For good or for ill, she thought. God have mercy. Christ have mercy.

Maybe she could throw the dragon at her attackers. When they collapsed laughing, perhaps she and this lady, who clearly intended to
protect Anna with her life, could flee. That was stupid strategy. She
had been stupid to come here.

Anna's head spun. She commanded herself not to faint, but the
room was spinning like the tli in the heavens. Her breath came fast
and shallow. Her eyes must be as clouded as her wits; she would have
sworn she saw light dance on Asherah's right hand, rebounding in the
mean little room to fill it with a sphere.

The door of the tiny office slammed open.

A sherah leapt back, raising her sword and hand. The sapphires
of her rings glittered. Light seemed to pour from the gems, collect
about her hand, form into a ball.

Anna tightened her hand on her own weapon. *Into thy hands . . .*

"No!" cried the woman who rushed in. She flung up her own
hand, which clutched crumpled documents.

The light seemed to subside, collapse into itself, and vanish. As
it faded, Asherah sagged.

"Binah, oh thank God. Where are the others?"

"*They're* safe for now. They've taken the messengers to the empty warehouse where everyone can hear them. I took the letters and
came on."

The newcomer Binah caught Asherah in a sustaining grasp. The
older woman permitted it. She even let her head rest briefly on the
newcomer's shoulder. Then, she stepped free and sheathed her
sword.

"Caesarissa, this is my foster daughter Binah," Lady Asherah said.
Her voice still shook, and her eyes were dark with remembered
terror.

Binah looked past her foster mother toward Anna. Oh, she was
tall. She was much taller than Asherah, taller than Anna's grandmother, who was the tallest woman Anna had ever met. And she was
beautiful.

Terrible as an army with banners. For the first time in Anna's life,
she thought she understood what those words meant: this woman,

perhaps ten years at the most older than Anna herself, lovely, but stately as a fortress. Golden butterflies fastened her veils and adorned the heavy silk of her clothing—a purple so deep that it was almost black, so rich that, strictly speaking, no one but one born to it should wear it.

Anguish had turned her face with its strongly marked, symmetrical features pale and drawn, but the violet eyes that took Anna in could have inspired armies. A Jewish Helen, Anna thought. A wonder.

Visibly, Binah forced control upon herself. She inclined her head and poised for the deeper, ceremonial bow of ritual.

"Caesarissa, you might wish to sheathe your knife," she said. "I entreat you."

She turned back to face Asherah, whose gaze fell to the documents she held.

"You should have let me read them first!" Asherah cried.

"I had hoped to spare you," Binah protested. "Besides, you were busy." She gestured at Anna.

Asherah shook her head from side to side as if the younger woman brought word of some disaster. "You cannot protect me. You do not want me hurt, but I am still your mother," she said. "I have heard what you have. And I have made the same observations. It is dragon's breath, the tli twisting in its evil aspect to burn us. What did we ever do?"

"What you have always done," Binah replied. "As we both know."

Binah shook her head. "You know too what we must do now. We must all endure." Those extraordinary eyes closed. Her hand moved in the same sort of gesture Asherah had used.

Why, those were warding gestures, such as some magus of the Chaldees would make. And Asherah's talk of the tli and stars and cycles, her own gestures, and the eerie light that had glimmered in her hand so that Anna distrusted her own vision . . .

"You're astrologers," she blurted. One of her teachers studied the motions of the stars and their effects on human life. When she was older, steadier, she too might learn—though it was a grey area for one not warded by Faith. But these were Jews, not Christians; they lacked her protections.

"No, you're more. You're *sorcerers*." She had not meant it to sound like an accusation. The words cut the air with the deadly elegance of Damascus steel cutting silk.

"And how would a princess of Byzantium recognize a sorcerer?" asked Binah. Her voice almost hissed, and Asherah stiffened.

You shall not suffer a witch to live. She could charge these two with sorcery, she supposed, but would her own fortunes withstand the scandal? She could not become Empress with the taint of heresy, of witchcraft on her. Nicephorus Bryennius would not be permitted to marry her, which might be to the good. But it would break her father's heart.

"Binah, she's a child, she's Leo's kin. *Daughter, she could be the one to rule this land . . .*" Why was Asherah so frightened?

"You think so?" Binah eyed Anna.

Anna forced herself to stand as straight as her father's guardsmen. *I am porphyrogenita. I am not afraid.*

"I don't agree," said Binah. "I see a rash, rebellious child who might use what power she has to ruin people for a whim."

"Look closer . . ." said Asherah. "Beneath the clouds you sense."

Binah smiled. Her expression reminded Anna of some of the very oldest pagan statues she had seen, the lips carved in formal mirth that did not touch the dark, hooded eyes. It lacked the charm of Asherah's or even Leo's smiles. Anna had seen smiles at court that might as well be blows. Those smiles did not frighten her. Binah's smile did . . . almost.

She caught Anna's eyes and held them. The violet of her gaze seemed to deepen, engulfing Anna's consciousness as if she entered the dark places of the earth, where, as it was written in Job, gold and jewels were to be found.

Anna felt herself swaying toward Binah where she stood like a jeweled statue herself, toward those great deep eyes, deeper into the darkness, into the caves, the ancient silences where creatures of unimaginable power moved through history . . . dark-haired men and women wearing triple crowns; a golden-haired man from the West, his blue eyes fixed on vacancy; Leo himself, surrounded by frightened men; Asherah grasping a black knife, moving forward to stand before a laboring . . .

. . . what was that creature she attended? Was it an immense stone, or truly a woman? And was the child Asherah carried from that place a human infant or a creature from the caves beneath the earth?

Oh God, Anna would never escape this place alive.

I will not let these people be hurt. The voice seemed to echo in her head.

These people? Was this Binah not a Jew like her mother?

You will threaten no one . . . harm no one . . .

Witches . . . sorcerers . . . they were damned. If she were caught consorting with them . . . Dear God, she didn't want to be sewn up in a sack and thrown into the Bosphorus. Not even her parents could spare her. Or would.

You will forget . . . forget . . .

"Binah."

Asherah's voice made Anna start. Binah turned to look at her. Her eyes cooled.

"You have become much stronger," she told Asherah.

"Will I not need all my strength?"

"I congratulate you, but I advise caution."

"The stranger at our gates." Asherah's voice was firm. "Remember that. She is this Emperor's eldest child. And your father's kin. Just look at her."

"It is too early to know," said Binah. "She is young, angry, ambitious. It is a deadly lust, power."

"I told you, daughter, you dare not protect us!"

"What I can do, I will. See, she has already forgotten."

"Will it stay so?" Asherah's voice was a whisper.

Binah merely shrugged.

Anna shook herself. What were they talking about? Her attention had drifted, like that of an unschooled child. Everyone always said she was too young to understand. But she was a woman, soon to be wed; she knew enough of medicine to impress the lady Asherah, they said; and if lady Asherah treated her with respect, surely, then, her foster daughter, however beautiful, should too.

Binah bowed again.

"Caesarissa, I beg your pardon, but messengers have come to speak to the men. We have more news from the West, from Solomon ben Simson. He is family in the North—" she corrected herself, then shook her head. Her dark hair glistened in the light, the jeweled butterflies gleaming upon them seeming to move their fragile wings to hold the lavish coils in place.

Anna had the sense of having forgotten something—but not her manners. If bad news had come, clearly, it was time for her to take her leave.

"If the news is bad," Anna heard herself saying in her mother's most decorous tone of voice, "you will want to receive it in privacy.

In any case, I should leave before I am missed." She let herself look about for her wandering kinsman, who had promised that she would be brought safely home. "My thanks for your hospitality and for the herbs."

More commotion. Binah turned and looked into the warehouse. "They're coming."

Asherah nodded. She turned back toward Anna, who held out her hands. A jade dragon, carved in the manner of the Ch'in, rested in her left hand. Anna blinked. Had she taken it without permission?

"You admired it, remember?" Asherah asked. "Before Binah interrupted?"

"Oh. Yes." Like a much younger, more docile girl, Anna made as if to return it. How curious it was, and how precious. Why could she not remember?

"No, no, keep it. If ever you need me, send it, and I will know."

Surely it would be the other way around? As a princess, surely, her patronage might be worth something to these embattled, frightened people.

"If I can help you . . ." she ventured.

"I could be your go-between," Binah offered.

Anna smiled at her. Imagine Binah dressed in the style of the court. She was so beautiful! How people would stare! She herself would love to see it.

Binah swept up the herbs and salves that her foster mother had assembled. "I will carry these for you to the litter myself."

"Caesarissa." Asherah unclasped a bracelet from her wrist. "I am sure you will have finer gifts when you wed. Still, I would be honored if you accepted this. The sapphires come all the way from the Land of Lions, as they call it."

"I will value it because my new cousin's wife gave it to me."

Asherah's face went grave. "I pray that you always remain this innocent."

But that was silly; Anna would be a married woman, not innocent at all.

Asherah put her hands out and took Anna's face between them. "Will you accept the same blessing I gave my daughter as she stood beneath her marriage canopy?"

Anna knew better. Nevertheless, she bowed her head and let Asherah whisper and kiss her on the brow.

"Go now with God. My husband will escort you home."

"Better let Theodoulos do that," Binah suggested. The women's eyes met, locked.

Asherah reached forward and snatched the letters her foster daughter still held. She flinched even as she touched them. "After all these years among us, the old fears reach out to harm him. Arrange it as you wish."

Before Anna knew it, Binah had ushered her out of the tiny office and into the warehouse. At its door, she could hear the familiar accented rumbling of a Northerner speaking to Leo Ducas.

"Kirjalax's girl? Kyrios Alexios, I should say. Of course I shall guard her. The old wolf has a tooth or two in his head, and sharper fangs in his sword and ax."

Binah laughed, mirth that Anna was sure did not reach her heart. "Your father is well regarded even by old soldiers, Caesarissa."

"How does your father come to be served by a Varangian?" Anna asked Binah, just to have something to say.

"Nordbriht?" asked Binah. "He says he took back his word, his Emperor being dead after Manzikert. And then he met my father as he journeyed to Cappadocia. He was selling his sword to merchants, and my father wanted to be a monk. They fought Turks together and have never parted."

Romanus, defeated, taken captive, blinded, and dead after great pain, cast an even longer shadow than Anna had believed. Did her father know his cousin held a Varangian's oath?

A litter rested on the ground, old, but still of good quality. Its curtains parted, and Anna's maid peered out, uttering her thanks to several saints at the sight of her nursling.

"Theodoulos had my mother's litter fetched," Leo told Binah. That was right: even the poorest branches of the Ducas family would have a house in the upper city. His mother would have traveled in a litter as befitted her rank.

What did Asherah and Binah travel in? Anna wondered. Perhaps they rode on camels. Or horses, like the viragos of the West. Bohemond's mother, now: the story was that she donned armor and fought like a man.

"The house is in good repair," Theodoulos said. "I hadn't been there since the fires." He looked down at his hands.

"You worked as hard as any of us, son," Leo said, with a glare at the stubborn merchants. "This too shall pass."

Anna *had* heard Theodoulos named correctly. Greek, obviously Christian, he must have found it hard to grow up amid strangers. He could have been reared and educated within sight of Hagia Sophia, whereas Binah, his foster sister who was probably at least ten years younger than he, was as exotic as Asherah.

"Theodoulos," Binah murmured, "was raised by the monks of Peristrema. When they were killed in a raid by Turks, my father took him in out of Christian charity." Her voice took on a tinge of irony. "Well, it happened before I was born."

Anna regarded her in a way that had often proved effective in charming information from her elders. *Was* Leo still Christian? Anna promised herself that one day she would unravel this whole mysterious skein.

Binah shook her head with a look Anna knew meant *You have inquired too much already.*

"So, do we take the princess home, daughter?" Leo asked Binah.

"My brother does, and Nordbriht," Binah replied. "I think you should stay, now that the news has come from the North."

"You read the letters first?" Like his wife, Leo glared at the young woman. Binah stood unmoved as marble. Would Anna ever be able to withstand her parents thus?

"You will be needed," Binah said.

As if her words were prophecy, a wail of anguish resounded in the warehouse. The color drained from Leo's face.

"Go to her."

Binah laid a hand upon her foster father's arm, giving it a faint, but unmistakable push. Leo smiled distractedly at Anna, then strode off. Six steps later, he broke into a run.

"Here," she offered, "let me help you into the litter, Caesarissa." Her bow at parting could not have been improved. She let the curtains enclose Anna and her pallid maid, then gestured for the bearers to pick up the litter and carry her away.

"I should go back to assist the lady Asherah," Anna began. She drew breath to call to her bearers.

Theodoulos, walking beside the litter, bent over. "Don't you understand, Caesarissa? The news is bad. They do not want Christians to see them weep."

Anna twined her new bracelet about her wrist. Its catch was cunningly worked in the shape of a dragon.

A moment more, and the clamor of the markets of Byzantium swelled to drown the lamentations in the warehouse. Mingling with

the brine, the sweat, the frying oil, and the perfumes of the city came
the stink of fear from the West.

4

L eo raced into his wife's cluttered office. *She had kicked off her*
shoes and crouched down on the floor, clutching the letters she had
snatched from Binah to her breast. Asherah's voice keened upward,
then broke.

"Ah, Lord God! Wilt thou destroy all the residue of Israel?" Her
voice rose and fell in the desert-borne progressions of Ezekiel. Leo had
always loved the Hebrew chant, but it made him shudder now.
Asherah dropped the letters beside her on the floor and wrung her
hands.

Leo stared at those fragile-seeming, competent hands. The first
time he had seen her, one of those hands had rested, trembling, on his
arm as she stood, compelled to watch an Emperor's eyes burnt out.
Another time, gestures from those hands had summoned powers that
had saved Leo's life from assassins sent by his own people. Those
hands had clasped him close, restoring him to the world. They had
midwifed an ancient goddess, raised children, and calculated accounts
and horoscopes and the fortunes of her family. Those capable, white
hands.

Before Leo could stop her, Asherah tore at her garments. The
silk parted with a shriek of fabric, and her white skin gleamed. He
hurled himself to his knees beside her, gathering her close against his
shoulder, pulling the torn cloth back over her breasts.

He shook with the force of Asherah's sobs. She had not cried so
before he went off to war, the dreadful day she had miscarried, or
even when her father died.

Leo shifted her into one arm and reached with the other for the
letters she had dropped. He hated them already, and he knew he
would hate them worse once he had read them.

Now Binah knelt beside them. "Comfort, Mother," she whispered.

Now, was she speaking to Asherah or invoking her own birth
beneath the earth in Cappadocia as it trembled with the incomprehensible labor pangs of a creature who had been worshipped long before the coming of the Christians?

"I'll take care of her, little one," Leo told her. Absurd to call this creature, who looked like something out of Homer, "little one," but something in her still responded with the child's trust with which she had once clung to him.

Leo had guarded her birth and her first steps. He would die for her, but it was hard to be father to the likes of Binah; and as she grew to womanhood and powers beyond those of a woman and a scholar came upon her, it had become that much harder.

"You go out, keep people away. I'll bring her home as soon as . . ."

As soon as I judge it right to let anyone else see my wife. His Asherah was a poised, private woman: her grief should not be exposed before strangers.

"No one will stop me," Binah said, and smiled in the way that always reminded Leo of her mother beneath the earth. He had never seen Binah in a fury, her powers arrayed. He did not want to think of the goddess-child as anything but his own little girl.

"Emich!" Asherah cried. Leo had seen that name on copies of notes and bills of sale sent from the Rhinelands. "Volkmar . . . Gottschalk. Cursed be their names. Let their bones be ground up on millstones of iron!"

Leo shuddered. He had never heard Asherah curse anyone before.

The news from Mainz and Worms and Speyer, already bad, had turned catastrophic. Some of Asherah's distant kin and trading partners (which were the same thing, practically) in Mainz and Cologne had tried to pay for safety—which never worked. Matters must have gone tragically awry, as it did when warriors from the West mixed in matters of money and faith.

And I alone escaped to tell you. Leo remembered how messengers had found his Emperor, telling him how he had lost crown, fortune, armies, hope, and his life. It had been quicker for the Jews who died when gates were forced, when synagogues were burnt. Some had abjured their faith, and must be counted worse than dead.

What would become of a man and his adopted son, who had joined his lives to these endangered lives? Leo put that thought aside. He spread out the letters. The now-familiar Hebrew script blurred, then steadied under his eyes.

"Don't read them, Leo," Asherah cried. She tried to snatch them back, but he took unfair advantage of his longer reach to hold them away from her. At this distance, the letters became easier to read. Immediately, he wished they hadn't.

"*Kyrie eleison, Christe eleison,*" he gasped. *Tactless, Leo, tactless,* he chided himself, but how else could he pray?

"They said in Worms we drowned a Christian and used the water to pollute the city wells. Emich, may his name be blotted out, led a mob upon the quarter and killed them all. The bishop intervened and took in those of us who survived, but they forced it . . . they forced the sanctuary and killed five hundred!

"In Speyer, one woman slew herself rather than be violated," Asherah wept.

My God, what if someone touched Asherah?

Leo shook her gently. "Asherah, Asherah, we heard all this. What *else* happened?"

Asherah went on as if his words, his presence, could not touch her. "Mothers killed their children. Girls threw gold out of the windows to distract the mob while the babies died. Oh curse them, curse them, curse these . . . these *Christians.*"

Leo flinched at the hate in Asherah's voice. He had heard that depth of rage only once before, when Binah's mother turned against the men who violated her birthing chamber in the earth.

He caught her hands before she could reach up and scratch her face.

"In May. In Mainz," Asherah gasped. "It happened in Mainz. We knew Emich of Leisingen had attacked. Two hundred marks each in silver to the archbishop and the city's lord, they sent . . . you oversaw our part of the transfer of funds. Seven gold pounds to Emich, and he pledged he'd spare the community. The next day, Emich attacked the palace, and the archbishop fled with all his staff. All those Jews were slain."

Leo shut his eyes. He felt himself rocking in grief too.

"You can take pride in the city lord, Leo. He held firm, but Emich burnt his palace and everyone had to flee. Several Jews renounced their faith; the rest died. Two more days . . ."

"I know, Asherah, I know . . ."

"One man burnt down the synagogue to spare it from desecration, then killed himself and his family. Rabbi Kalonymos ben Isaac, you remember him? He read Theodoulos's letters, sent them to Rashi—that's Solomon ben Isaac, in France, who wrote back saying Theo could grow up and be a scholar, a veritable *gaon* among Christians? Rabbi Kalonymos and fifty friends fled to Rudesheim and begged shelter from the archbishop at his country place."

"Why, so then he's safe, isn't he?" Leo asked. At least one brand had been spared from the burning.

Asherah shook her head. "No . . . Rab Kalonymos and his people were so distraught that the archbishop saw his chance and tried to convert them all."

"Oh God, no," Leo whispered. He had liked Kalonymos, who had sent books to his father-in-law and written them when Joachim died.

"The rabbi . . . his mind just snapped. He seized a knife and threw himself at his host. The archbishop lived, but they killed all the Jews there, just when they were safe. All dead," she keened, "all dead."

"Asherah!" he whispered. He put his arms out to embrace her, then let them fall. How alien he felt in his good robes, the Christian garments he had put on to escort the little Caesarissa back to her palace. At least, she was safe for now.

His wife's eyes were glazed from the passion of her grief. Leo pressed the letters and his hand against his chest as if that could ease the pain that transfixed him.

These Christians, she had said. As if the very name were obscenity.

Twenty-five years bridging the gulf between worlds, he thought. Half a lifetime if you looked at it that way, and less than the blink of an eye if your history was as long as that of the Jews among whom he had made his life. Asherah had loved him faithfully, and he had thought he was as dear to them as he had been to Asherah's father.

Once, when he and Joachim had feared Asherah was dead in the collapse of the underground city that had proved a refuge against the Turks, Leo had offered actually to convert and Joachim forbade. It was not simply the matter of canon law, which was even stricter than Joachim. You loved what you loved; you believed what you believed; and truly, it did not matter.

Only now it mattered, he feared. Men Leo could not remotely imagine as brothers had turned his faith into a curse to his wife. So had all his life been a fraud, then? Perhaps, except for one thing: Asherah still clung to him. He looked down at the letters. Was this rage of language, these heart-deep curses truly what they thought of Christians, or was this the helpless fury of people driven temporarily insane?

A hand came up and touched his where it held the letters. It was a wonder his fingers did not blister. Why did the sky not darken before helpless people—mothers, old men, scholars—had reason to write such things?

"Leo," Asherah gasped, "Leo, don't read them. My people are in mortal anguish. They say terrible things." She sobbed once again. "These murders have taught my people—taught me—to hate."

"God have mercy on these poor lives," Leo whispered.

"They don't mean what they say. They don't know what they say. They can't judge all of your people by these."

Forgive them, Father?

He bent and touched his lips to her hair, yet kept turning over the pages, reckoning up his wife's dead, who had become his. The mother, found lying with her children in her arms. The people who had hurled themselves off a bridge. The others, burnt within their synagogue. The rabbi who attacked a bishop. Then, another name leapt out. *Menachem.*

Rest his soul. He remembered how, in Cotyaeum, after the Emperor Romanus had been defeated, Andronicus Ducas, the grandfather of the little princess he had learned today to cherish, had ordered Menachem to blind his Emperor. Menachem had wept, had complied, and had botched the job—and his own forgiveness. Troubled of soul, he had spent years in Jerusalem, had accounted himself healed, and taken up his duties—only to meet this!

"This last letter, Leo." Asherah reached out to touch the most battered of the letters. "You remember Menachem?" Asherah echoed his thoughts in the uncanny way she had always had. "That good old man. He was never well after that . . . In any case, he'd gone to Trier, God only knew why; but now we know too. To die.

"He saw the knights coming, he cried out 'Never again,' and then he said the *Sh'ma* and just stood there till they hurled him in the Moselle. *Kiddush ha-Shem*, they call it. Glorification of the Name. I don't understand, I just don't. Saul killed himself and they called it a sin, so how can it be right now?"

"He's at peace now, Asherah," Leo said. "No more nightmares. No more doubts. And—" He sought through the stained sheets, which seemed to cling to his fingers, for any comfort he could offer. "*These* scum have turned back," he said. "Volkmar disappeared. Emich fled. And Gottschalk was taken. Cast down by the judgment of God. Now, only the Franks come on."

"They are bad enough," Asherah wept.

"The messengers told me that this Henry who calls himself Emperor in the West has said that anyone who kills a Jew will have his head struck off."

"How much did we pay *him?*" Asherah demanded. "O sun and moon! Why did you not hide your light? *Why did the sky not darken?*"

Leo set the letters down and gathered his wife into his lap. So small she was, so beloved, and so valiant, as she had always been. Her torn garments fell away again from her breast. Selfless with his pity and his love, he covered her again and stroked her hair.

Asherah huddled in on herself, rejecting him; but he could wait. Life burnt so strongly within her that she would reach out to him again, she would have to. But if she did not grieve, it would consume her. Outside her office, merchants were weeping in the warehouse as the messengers told their stories. The torrent of grief flowed through the winding streets and into the shuttered houses that were guaranteed them—but for how long?—by the will of the Emperor. Mourning seemed to float across the waters toward the forces that massed upon Byzantium from the West.

When Asherah's sobs finally subsided to faint shudders, he raised her chin in two fingers.

"What are we going to do?" she whispered.

"This Emperor is our friend. My friend, once. He granted us Pera, didn't he?"

"We *paid,*" Asherah grumbled. "Oh, God of Hosts, how we have paid. Besides, you might say that because he is your kin, like the child who just left."

"You seemed to like her." Leo let himself chuckle at the stiff, precocious girl.

"She is charming, Leo. Just as she was schooled to be. But something hangs over her—that evil man Psellus who hurt you long ago. The likes of him would take her as a student; she is strong and might not bend, but she would twist for power, I know it. She called Binah and me sorcerers."

"And Binah did not strike?"

"I can still control Binah. But she laid a forgetting on her. Please God the Caesarissa never remembers."

"Binah was merciful."

Asherah shook her head against Leo's chest. He dared to stroke a lock of hair back from her brow. When she did not flinch, he raised it to his lips.

Leo had felt the lure of Empire in his blood and refused it.

Asherah, for all her strength, had refused even to consider it. Their own daughters had run on a far longer tether than even she had had, but none had ever played for Empire. Except, of course, Binah; and there was no telling, ever, what stakes *she* played for. Her mother had been a goddess beneath the earth, and the legacy burnt strong in her as it did not, thank God, in Theodoulos.

Our children are safe, out along the caravan routes in the East, Leo thought in silent thanksgiving. *The girls are wed, their marriages and their wits enriching our house. Our son—if his studies progress, please God, one day he will be a physician as learned as any in Alexandria.*

What of the elder two, however, their foster children? Binah remained near Asherah, her right hand and probably several fingers on her left, struggling with her powers and her at-times-dubious humanity.

Theodoulos? Leo had inherited him from the monks too late: scholar he might be, to a degree that scholars like Kalonymos, now slain, prized his letters, calling him a Christian *gaon;* but he had never quite adapted. Or been wholly accepted.

"I could move to the house," Leo said. Meaning his parents' house, which had come to him upon their deaths. "I can take Theo with me. Binah, for all her witchiness, works very well with you and the others, but Theo came to us too old. Too old to learn a trade, too old to learn the power that Binah wields as easily as breath. I'd send him back home to Cappadocia, but with the Emir there, it could be risky. Arslan—"

"Your namesake," Asherah murmured.

"—and young Kemal have taken over from their father, and there is no way that Theo understands horses or land the way they do."

"He's not much of a merchant," Asherah sighed.

"The others do not trust him. These days, they scarcely trust me. At least our other children grew up in your faith and bear no taint of me."

Asherah's head moved back and forth—*no*—against his chest. She had visited the old house so close to the palace twice. Once, when she had met Leo's parents, which had to be a meeting unrivaled for wariness since the beginning of the world, and again, after the fire, when Leo had opened it to families burnt out of their homes. Compared with the almost Persian splendors that had surrounded Asherah since her birth, the Ducas house was austere, even poor, though Leo remembered his narrow boyhood room as a haven of peace.

Asherah preferred to live among her own people. But *he* was "her people," wasn't he? He knew that if he retreated to the upper city, she would go with him, and it would blight her.

"I'd pack you all back to Cappadocia if I were sure you'd take no harm from the Turks," Leo said.

"You would leave me?" A new hurt quivered in her voice. Leo shut his eyes against the sight of her. Oh, this would tear them asunder. Someone might strike at her, and he would die of it. Or someone might try to kill him, leaving her defenseless. Or his heart would simply break.

Leo flinched. "We cannot let this drive us apart," he declared.

"Leo, in the name of God, *why?*"

"I must stay here," he said.

"That's not a reason."

Leo reached out and smoothed his wife's hair. "This is faith, my heart, not formal logic. I believe that I am meant to be a bridge between the nations."

"These wretched nations will be the death of all of us!" Asherah's voice was soft, but weighted with a controlled violence.

"Perhaps not," Leo mused. "The little one, I'd swear, was glad to see us. She is true to her blood. I'd wager the worth of the next caravan from Nisibis that she schemes now how best to use us. If *she* thinks that way, how must her father calculate? I knew him as a clever boy, but he's grown since then, my dearest, a thousandfold. He's not just an Emperor, but one of the great ones."

"No Emperor is really human. They haven't got kin, not really," Asherah said wearily. "I have prayed that we would build a refuge for us and all who would live in peace. Peace on earth to all men and women of goodwill."

Leo turned her face up again, looking deep into her eyes. Would her grief account it violation now if her Christian husband kissed her? He dared. Her lips tasted of salt. At first, she recoiled, and then she clung to him.

"This is no time to hide in caves, even the caves of home. This is a time to stem the tide. Not with shards this time, but with craft and faith and whatever else we have."

And swords, though I pray it does not come to that.

"We have kin to avenge," Asherah said.

Leo felt his heart leap at that "we." "Yes, we do. And as long as a saving remnant abides, we have won. Even if we fall, what we have built in Cappadocia may remain."

Believe me, trust me, he willed her. All these years, he had relied upon her spirit as she had trusted, he thought, his strength, his competence—feeble as they were. Now, for the first time since they had met, she needed his spirit to kindle hers.

If he burnt himself to cinders, Leo vowed, Asherah would have what strength of spirit he could give her. *Only let her trust me,* he prayed. She settled into his arms. He closed his eyes, thanking God for the private miracle of her response.

He cradled her while the light faded, quietly, joyously aware when she fell into a trusting sleep broken only by faint sobs, like a child who has cried herself to sleep.

The sunset flared one last time above the horizon and thrust a last ray through the shutters Asherah had slammed closed. The light splashed across the drawing of the dragon.

They would not be the first to attempt to harness the dragon and find themselves caught in its coils.

5

lexius Comnenus I, Emperor of the Romans, en Christo Autokrator, sat enthroned and unarmed in the courtyard of the Blachernae Palace. The thin April sunlight beat down upon the gold, the jewels, and the pearls that covered his crown, with its inset cross, and the robes such as angels were supposed to have given to the first Constantine. He should have been protected by holiness: not just his role as Autocrat in Christ, not just sheltered by the awesome height of Hagia Sophia; but by the day itself—Good Friday.

Instead, he was walled in by his courtiers, by his guards, who held up their great axes, by the walls of the palace, and by the massive walls of the city itself, some few hundred yards from the bridge that crossed the headwaters of the Golden Horn.

Together, they waited for the men of the West to attack.

What blasphemy! Anna thought. To shed blood on Good Friday! Still, what could you expect of barbarians?

She would have tossed her head in disdain and a great flash of the long, heavy ornaments that weighed upon her ears, but she must stand as motionless as the rest of her father's court. It was a small victory that she had been permitted to stand here at all. She had glared down her young husband, safe in Alexius's permission and his shadow.

They had come, the Westerners boasted, to free the Holy Sepulchre, but they would be quite content, Anna thought, if they could take Byzantium. Why should they not covet it? Not even Jerusalem the Golden could be more splendid or closer to God.

How still her father sat! Thank God, Anna thought, the medicines that the Jews had given her worked so well. Her father's brow was furrowed only by the weight of the heavy crown. His grip was secure and painless upon the well-worn sword with which, once, he had won his empire and with which he might yet have to defend it at the very end.

Nicephorus had not wanted Anna out here, so it was a victory for her simply to stand by her father: still, was that how her life would be squandered? Standing, if she were not kneeling, or on her back, doing what else was considered proper for a wife? She felt empty, dizzy—from fasting, she hoped, and not from fear, or even . . . She flashed a wary glance at Nicephorus.

Oh, she was still too young to be a mother! she protested.

Her husband Nicephorus caught her gaze and nodded grave reassurance. He had taken their vows and obligations seriously. He took seriously all duties, including hers. This duty of standing near his Emperor, who obviously favored him, struck him as an honor—one he had been reluctant to share with a porphyrogenita who had dwindled into a wife.

Alexius had named him Caesar, but not heir.

Imagine: her husband thought she was afraid. He didn't know her well yet, did he?

They waited. Anna strained to hear the army as it streamed across the bridge. If, with one swift move, it could take the palace, the whole empire lay within its grasp. Armed men glinted in the watchtowers.

Alexius leaned forward to speak to a messenger. "Tell this Godfrey," he said, "do not attack now. He should have reverence, for on this day God was sacrificed, refusing neither Cross nor Nails nor Spear. Tell him this: 'If you must fight, we shall be ready; but wait until the day after the Resurrection.' "

The messenger bowed, backed away from the Presence, and ran. One or two of the Varangians rumbled approval in their deep chests. Their axes trembled minutely. Nicephorus withdrew upon some errand or other, worry in his eyes.

"Go on," the Emperor had told him. "I sheltered my daughter long before she was your bride."

And then, to the unarmed courtiers, almost as if he schooled a horse, "Steady. If they have any shame, they will withdraw."

A flight of arrows, metal-tipped, whined upward, dipped, and rattled into the court. One struck an official who stood beside the Emperor. As the arrow's feathers quivered in the rich silk of his robe, he coughed blood, practically onto Alexius's knees, collapsed, and died. Five others broke, running for the shelter of the walls.

"Steady," repeated the Emperor. "What better day to die than today, armored solely in our faith? Look you: my daughter does not flinch."

Anna forced herself not to gag at the iron tang of blood in the air. She was sweating under her robes. Heavy they were; they were not armor. Another such deadly flight of those long, long shafts . . . she could see herself staggering, falling forward, perhaps screaming once before the blood gouted from her mouth . . .

Nicephorus Bryennius strode into the courtyard once again. Seeing her kneeling over the courtier, her hand poised to pull out the arrow shaft, he hastened forward toward her. Anna raised her chin, pointing at her father: *he* was the one who had commands for the young Caesar.

Nicephorus was the man, therefore deemed to be courageous. He was some years older than she, therefore judged the more enduring; but already she knew he lacked the steel that armored her spirit, if not her flesh.

She bent over the courtier, studying him to see if he still breathed. She held a wide, flat bracelet to his mouth. Blood stained it, but no mist.

"He's gone," she said. "God rest his soul."

She signed his brow with the symbol of their faith before wiping her bracelet clean upon his robe. Then she returned to stand by her father again. She, not her brother.

"These *barbaroi* mistake piety for weakness," Alexius mused as if to himself. "In that case, we must show them better."

He raised a hand, heavy with gems, and gestured. Bowmen mounted upon the walls.

"I would have no man aim to kill upon this day," Alexius said. "So, I command you, do not aim. Let the very sound and number of arrows themselves drive off these men."

The day wore on. The Lotharingians pressed on. The shriek of arrows overhead made Anna want to scream too. If she were not fasting, she knew which herbs would compose her. She schooled herself to patience. How could she learn to rule without learning war?

"They're near the Romanus Gate!" a man forgot himself enough to shout across the courtyard. Alexius waited until the man had approached, prostrated himself for pardon, and repeated his words. He nodded, then beckoned to Nicephorus. Her husband the Caesar had taken the time to arm himself. He looked magnificent. She was fortunate to be his wife, and if only he returned to her safely, she would welcome him back with all her heart.

"One company," Alexius said. "With bows and lances. Choose the best, but seek to kill horses only. Truly, I do not want to shed Christian blood. Not today."

"Open the gate!" the order came, and the massive gate opened. The Varangians growled and drew in more closely to protect her father. One winked reassurance at her.

Alexius gestured again. *Advance*. The armed, disciplined nobles marched forward. Slowly. Steadily. In years past, just the sight of the army of Rome had stricken the hearts of enemies. In years past, the sight of an Emperor had caused them to scream, "Run away! It is the Emperor!"

Alexius looked up. To Anna's surprised delight, he met her eyes. "Thanks to you, daughter, and your medicines, I am well today and can sit out this day's battle." She would have run to him, hurled herself, heavy brocades, clashing ear-bobs and all, at his feet and kissed his hand, but decorum forbade.

She could hear the whine of arrows, the screams of mortally wounded horses, the shouts of fighting men. The company pressed on. The Lotharingians paused, then kept on coming.

The Emperor's Western guest and "vassal" Uvos—Hugh, the name was, though Anna would never be clever with these wretched barbarian names—had told them of this Godfrey. He had gone to the camp outside the walls, embraced Godfrey, and sworn to take Jerusalem with him. Godfrey would go all the way to Jerusalem, Anna thought resentfully, but when Hugh invited him to visit the Emperor in the palace, the man refused.

Who was this Godfrey to think he could outfox an Emperor?

Anna tried not to shudder as the sun sank in the sky. She would think its decline into the West was a special omen. It flared like a burning city, which God avert. The sunlight flashed one last time, turning the armor and jewels of the men, women, and bodies in the court crimson before it faded.

"General advance," ordered Alexius Comnenus.

As the sun set on Good Friday, the Emperor rose from his throne. His guards saluted with their axes and closed in around him. The courtyard erupted into convulsions of signaling, running, shouting, drums, and trumpets. Byzantium advanced to war; the Franks retreated.

Alexius sank down again upon his throne, his dark-browed, bearded face resting upon his hand. Anna started forward, but her father gestured. His face was pale, the way it got when the pain in his joints started up, but he was smiling.

"We will pray first," said the Emperor. "Then, we shall break our fast, and perhaps my learned daughter will prescribe for me. Then, after we have broken our fast, bring my guest Hugh de Vermandois, called the Great, to me."

She hurried forward in case he required help—most of all, to conceal his pain.

6

I have never," said Irene the Empress, "been so appalled in my life."

Anna examined her conscience, which should have been clear, but never quite was.

Now what? She had married at her family's decree. It had brought her rather more in the way of wealth, little in terms of freedom, and less than nothing in terms of new power. She now had a husband, as well as parents, to whom she had at least to pretend to defer. Her brother John even remained a healthy child, which ought to be worth something in the eyes of Heaven.

Her mother waved her to a carved chair. Anna sighed with relief. Not a reprimand, then. It could not be a lesson: though she had much still to learn from Irene, she had scholars and a library of her own now. They sat in silence while Irene sent out the women, one to fetch refreshments, the others for privacy. Doubtless, at least three of them were spies. Guards came and went in the corridors outside: many more guards since the attack on the Blachernae Palace.

"Your behavior throughout Holy Week," began the Empress deliberately (Anna's heart sank again), "was such as to merit approval. See that you do not become overly proud."

Anna cast her head down at an angle just sufficient to denote modesty, but not childishness.

"Good: you behave like an intelligent woman. It is well that you are wed. It makes you a more serious claimant to the diadem. You and, of course, your husband."

Let anything happen to her *beloved* brother: well, Nicephorus was a trained soldier already, and she, born in the Purple as she had been, had the crowds not already acclaimed her once? Anna and Constantine, it had been. Why not Nicephorus and Anna, or better yet Anna and Nicephorus? Or, if he continued to plague her, Anna and someone else?

"Have you spoken with Nicephorus about this at all?"

Anna suppressed a smile of which her mother would not have approved at all. *In bed,* her mother surely meant.

He does not like to talk *in bed,* Anna wanted to confide. They had not selected him for her just because his father had been her father's rival for the throne. They had made what they thought was a good choice. He was cultivated, a patrician. But he was also a young, healthy man, while Anna was very young and lacked the skills of a Thaïs—or the experience of an Empress Theodora.

The Empress shook her head. "Anna, you have always been clever. Don't you listen to the women in the palace? If a wife does not make use of the power of her womanhood, she deprives herself of a powerful weapon."

"I wish to be Basilissa"—there, the dreadful words were out— "not a hetaira," she blurted. And waited for reproof.

"Silly girl," Irene chided. "In some ways, there is little difference."

Anna opened her eyes in amazement. Now that she was wed, the women who had frightened and repelled her before spoke more frankly. Now, she listened. A wife had to be moderately skilled at least so that her husband did not stray to a lady of no morals from an opposing faction (women of no birth counted for nothing).

Nicephorus might rarely take time enough to talk to her in bed, but he was considerate enough. She had to admit that welcoming him back after his troops had carried the day against the Westerners and his own skill with a bow had won cheers from all the Romans had been . . . interesting. The frantic confusion and some stirrings that one day might lead to more, even, perhaps, to pleasure, were the limits of her knowledge: enough to make her curious, which was enough to make her persevere. Her husband had no grounds for complaint. Anna had never failed in her duties.

She gazed at her mother Irene's serene face. Her lips parted on the question she longed to ask, then closed. Had Irene learned these same lessons of arms and legs, words and movements, to hold her father? She would no more dare to ask than she would think of such things while at prayer—although thoughts of which she was heartily ashamed did creep into her mind. She dared not talk to any of the women in the palace.

That strange kinswoman of hers through the madman Leo—Asherah, her name had been. Her medicines had eased her father's gout. Would she have spoken of lessons and controlling a man by talking to him in bed? Or more than talking? Remembering how Leo had looked at his wife, Anna knew the answer: yes.

Never mind that. Alexius had ordered a general attack on the Franks and driven them back so that, the next time he ordered this Godfrey to present himself, he did.

"They called the man Hugh a slave because he took oath to the Emperor."

"Then, may all Franks become such slaves," Anna replied. Her smile felt as wintry as the one on her mother's face. Civilized. Controlled. Good: she was learning.

"What did you think of this . . . Uvos?" asked Irene, her speech mangling the unfamiliar name.

Anna shrugged. "Too savage for a lord; too rich for a beast. If that—or this Godfrey they praise as a paladin—is the best they have to offer . . ."

There was Bohemond, she thought with a shudder. Bohemond, whose father had won a kingdom and thrust his son from it. Bohemond, who had fought her father to what would have been defeat in a lesser man. Bohemond, even now on his way to Byzantium. If Anna were indeed in favor now, she could at least expect to see this prodigy with her own eyes.

Empress Irene sighed. "I know you wanted to dedicate your life to Christ and scholarship, daughter. But now that you are married . . . did you hear the Emperor say that next campaign, he might leave me at home and take you along as nurse?"

She had exulted at that, but her father had promptly spoiled it by giving John more land. Not that a child his age could do anything with it.

Anna nodded. If she nursed her father well, perhaps she could increase her hold upon him. Could. He was clever past her abilities, yet. But, because she knew she must try, she had sent the tiny jade dragon back to the Bazaar. More herbs had come, together with a book: the Greek translation of the medical text Anna had seen and coveted. A wedding gift, Asherah had said. Along with the sapphire bracelet that Anna wore today.

Her mother raised her elegantly arched brows. It had been folly to think Anna could outwait her.

"If I am commanded to go, I am, as you say, a docile daughter. If"—she allowed irony to tinge her voice—"my husband permits, I shall accompany my father—"

"Your husband would do well to go himself."

"But truly, do you think it will be soon? I stood by His Sacred Majesty in this blasphemy of an Easter battle. The next ones—do you truly think he will go out with these Westerners to the Holy Land?"

Irene shook her head. "I think that someone must. He has been planning with Tatikios." She grimaced, never being one to trust a Turk, even a convert of long standing.

"I am not the one," Anna interrupted. "Me, travel with an army? I know how a crossbow works, it's true, but not how to shoot one. I could *never* lift a Varangian's ax, much less command him. Oh, I know some oaths in their language . . ." Her mother's glare caught Anna up sharply. "They didn't think I heard or understood, but I did. Nicephorus is an officer. But who needs me? I can barely ride, much less like one of the Western Amazons, that Bohemond's mother . . ."

She fell silent. The name she invoked echoed in the room.

"Bohemond is coming soon. Your father will want him bound by oaths."

Anna looked down, playing with her sapphire bracelet.

"I cannot believe my father lacks spies," she commented.

Irene waited her out.

"Not my father," Anna went on. "You."

"You and I, my daughter. You and I."

"Why?" asked Anna flatly. "After me, you bore a son. Surely that secured your place."

Irene's carved nostrils flared. "Let us say that I too weary of listening silently to men's boasts. A daughter, now, rather than a son upon the throne and I might have rather more to say. As you argue, you cannot ride with the Western hordes, and your Nicephorus is not yet fully broken to harness. I cannot blame a virgin bride for inexperience. Still, it leaves us—"

"Needing spies," Anna cut in, relishing the chance for once in her life to interrupt her mother. She had heard the westerners found spies disgraceful, which was another sign of their childishness.

The Israelites . . . Anna's fingers tightened upon her sapphire bracelet, the gift of a present-day Israelite, albeit in exile. It flashed in the light, the brilliant blue of cornflowers or the robes that her father chose when he was not forced to wear the Purple.

"Where had you that bracelet?" her mother asked.

Anna smiled at her. "Spies," she said.

"What spies?" Irene demanded.

That meant *What? Without my knowledge? Mother*, Anna replied inside her head, *for over a year I have gone my own way. You are a grown woman, a married one, as your mother has reminded you.*

Anna took a deep breath. She might as well be kneeling before a priest. She removed the bracelet, handing it to her mother, who examined it appreciatively.

"They are first-quality sapphires," Anna told her. "From the Land of Lions, where you find the best such gems."

"What merchant . . . I know you spoke to no merchants in the palace! And how you paid for this . . ."

"It was a gift, a wedding gift, from the same merchant who gives me the salves for my father. The ones that helped him hold out on Good Friday, and then win again."

"You went out . . . you left the Great Palace . . ."

Anna laughed. To her surprise, she was enjoying this. "It is all family, Mother. Yes, I slipped out to find medicines for my father. He has a Jewish physician who told me where the best physicians, those trained in Alexandria, Mother, as I am not and never can be, buy their medicines. I wore my veils and my simplest clothes, and I went there."

Her mother closed her eyes in horror and, yes, real fear for her.

Anna leaned forward and took her hands. They were cold. *She really does love me, not just wish to use me.*

"Alone?" From the way her mother drew out the word, she might as well have fled to Thule.

"I had a maid with me," Anna replied. "I suppose you will find out who, but it is not her fault. I commanded her. Besides, it was all family. I met your cousin Leo Ducas."

Irene's face chilled even further into a veritable icon of disapproval.

Anna found herself laughing. For the first time in her life, she had power, knowledge, and the opportunity to use them.

"This is not logical, Mother. You complain I went out alone and dealt with merchants. I tell you I went with a maid and met a kinsman. Who, I should add, greeted me politely, explained precisely what his relationship to our family is, took me aside, and presented his wife to me."

"The Jewess!" Irene's cry held real distress.

"My grandmother met her, Cousin Leo says. Met her and approved. She gave me the salves for Father, Mother, this bracelet as a wedding gift, and she blessed me as she blessed her own daughter when she married."

Anna leaned forward and retrieved her bracelet from her mother's motionless hand. "Lady Asherah gave me a token. When I need more herbs, I simply have it sent to her, and it is returned with what I need. No one has ever mentioned payment; it is all family."

Anyone less well-schooled than Irene would have wailed in dismay. Irene drew a sharp breath and shut her eyes. Calculating how to turn the lead of her renegade family connection into gold, Anna surmised.

"You think they would help you?"

"Leo Ducas says the Jews owe a debt to Father, who found them new homes when the Chalkoprateia burned. Father had him to the palace."

From the suppressed rage in Irene's face, Anna assumed she had not known this.

"Your tool is flawed, daughter," Irene said at last.

"He is? He has married well—for our purposes. His wife is wealthy. While I was there, she had messages from the Rhinelands. Private messages, carried on swift ships."

Irene was trying her usual stratagem of allowing Anna to talk herself into errors. This time, Anna would not permit it.

"You did not wish me to meet our cousin, I know. You sent me from the room whenever he was mentioned. But Father knows him and likes him, even now—and look at all I learned!"

"How long . . ." Irene asked faintly.

"Since last summer. It is easy enough to summon our cousins," Anna said, twisting the verbal blade.

"How?" her mother asked.

Anna thought of the tiny, precious jade dragon, so easy to catch up and take away. She thought of the codex that had also been a wedding gift, one she prized more than the bracelet, for all its fineness. And she smiled.

"Ah, let that be *my* secret, Mother dear," she said.

Irene shook her head ruefully, but, for the first time, her eyes registered Anna as an adult, almost an equal. "Leo Ducas betrayed my father; surely he might betray another."

Not Lady Asherah, Anna thought. She had seen how his heart shone from his eyes when he looked at her.

"They are Jews; they are twisty," said Irene. "But they live among us, and we can use them as we do the Turks. Even your brother is being brought up with a Turk as his companion."

As if dear brother Ioannes were not enough! Anna snorted in disgust. It was a graceless gesture, but her mother laughed.

"Oh, I have been waiting for you to grow up!" she exclaimed. "Now, about your informants. Are they presentable?"

"At court?" Anna blinked. "Your cousin is a Ducas still. He has a foster son and daughter. The one, Theodoulos, was brought up by the monks in Peristrema. He could be any minor logothete. As for Binah . . ."

"What sort of name is that?"

Anna shrugged. "Probably Leo's wife had the naming of her. She is . . . presentable." She would enjoy, she decided, the expression on her mother's face when Binah finally stood before her.

Irene sat, clearly balancing unpalatable alternatives. On one hand, ignorance. On the other, owing information to a hated renegade. On one hand, the security of dealing with family. On the other, knowing that the family dealt with Jews.

"We will have them summoned," Irene decided. "But do not let your father know. At least, not yet."

7

Anna's mother preached perfect amity between man and wife, perfect submission, at least on the surface—but woe betide Anna's father if he failed at least to hear Irene out!

He would not have liked to hear her now. Anna could have wished for at least temporary deafness.

"You bungled it. Summon them, I told you, without your father's knowledge. And, as I told you, just the *children*. Not *him*."

Anna's heavy gemmed skirts weighed her down like a ship heavy with cargo as she followed her mother down the long, gleaming corridors. A Frank, strolling by, bowed to them—courtesy of a sort, and better than that one lout's attempt to sit on the Emperor's own throne! There was only so much one could pass off with bland, deadly courtesy. At some point, the swords would come out, and there would be blood on the palace floors—not for the first time.

Irene slowed her angry footsteps, nodded icily in response to the Frank—faugh, you could *smell* him in the corridor down which he had walked—and allowed her much shorter daughter to walk only a pace behind. Anna felt her Caesar-mask freeze her features—chin elevated, eyes somewhat distant, face expressionless. Irene did it so much better, but think of all the practice she had had.

It sufficed for bumptious Franks. It sufficed for years of married life. It had even sufficed when Anna admitted she had dealt privately with Jews. But Irene's composure had shattered like icicles when she had heard from her usual eavesdroppers that her husband the Basileus Alexius had summoned to the palace a long-absent kinsman, one Leo Ducas.

"I did not tell him," Anna protested in a whisper. Head up, nod this way and that at the courtiers. Bow reverently to the bishop, wait until he passes, then move on, a little more rapidly. "I didn't!"

In favor, out of favor; if Anna were not careful, married lady or not, her mother would have her out of the palace, and she would never be able to see the next wave of Franks. Never see Bohemond, her father's great enemy; and her heart would break of vexation and thwarted curiosity, along with ambition. At least, she was being permitted to accompany her mother to a vantage point from which they could observe Alexius's audience with his kinsman.

"This way," Irene whispered without creasing that mask of imperial serenity. They turned from the main hall into a side passage, from there into a tiny room, kept almost completely dark. Anna heard her mother's skirts hissing across the floor. She paused at the wall. Then, a tiny panel in the wall slid back; a beam of light streamed into the room; and Anna could see.

Irene beckoned her to the tiny opening. All her life, she had lived in this palace or some other one; and she had had no idea this room existed.

She felt her mouth turning upward in a highly unprincess-like grin of pure delight. Irene went rigid, like a hunter spotting prey. Anna edged in beside her mother and tried to breathe silently.

The Emperor of the Romans had entered the room and seated himself in a chair that his choice transformed into a throne.

Do I really expect my will to prevail if I set it against his? Anna wondered. Almost, she despaired. But the woman standing next to her, supporting her, was Alexius's Empress, and her mother. She still had a chance.

Her father wore his favorite indigo, rather than purple, and few jewels; but for all that, he was truly imperial in bearing. He sat motionless as his guest entered, walked to the prescribed distance. Moving slowly in a grey formal robe that would have been austere had it not been tailored from the finest Persian brocade, he went to his knees and measured himself out along the black and grey mosaic of the floor. His prostration was a little stiff, as if he were unused to bending his back before anyone.

"Rise," said Anna's father.

Leo Ducas rose. Anna could feel her mother practically quivering with rage. He was taller, if much thinner, than her father, whom he watched, his eyes alight with a strange pride.

To her surprise, Alexius Comnenus rose. "Leo," he greeted the other man. A little shyly, the Emperor of the Romans held out his arms and embraced the family apostate. Then he gestured him to a seat and motioned toward the wine and goblets on a nearby table. Leo leaned over, poured for the Emperor, then for himself. Alexius drank without hesitation.

Leo sipped discreetly, glanced over his shoulder, then turned his look into a leisurely survey of the room with its high ceiling, its walls, inlaid with less elaboration but as much skill as those of Hagia Sophia, and its pleasant hunting mosaics. Sun poured in from a window, beyond which stretched a walled garden, fragrant with the spring, warded by trees. Children's voices shouted in the garden. Some of her brothers, no doubt, exercising between lessons.

"I wanted some time with you alone. It has been too long. So I ordered your foster son and daughter to await us outside," Alexius said. "That came as some relief to learn that they are foster children. Your . . . son is old enough to have children of his own. You were learning mathematics when you would have been of an age to get a son that age, and I doubt you could have gotten away from your mother long enough to do so."

Leo laughed, a little awkwardly. "That's Theodoulos. He was

raised by the monks in Peristrema. After it burnt, he just turned to me. We took Binah in after the battle for the underground cities. Asherah was midwife to her mother."

Alexius looked tactfully down as men tended to do when speaking about childbirth, the women's battle. *Not yet,* Anna prayed. *Not yet, please.*

"I'll have them summoned in a few minutes," Alexius said. "I wanted to talk with you first. Years, Leo, it's been years. I last heard from you—when? When the Chalkoprateia burnt?"

"His Sacred Majesty was good enough to permit my people to settle in Pera." Leo kept his tone formal.

"I'd have done so for my physician's asking, but your letter . . . I'll admit, it was like hearing from someone long dead. My cousin who was lost and is now found."

Leo eyed the Emperor warily over the lip of his goblet. The afternoon sun struck the wine, which glinted like the Purple—or like blood.

"You brought me," Alexius probed further, a careful surgeon, "only your two fosterlings. I would have been glad to meet your wife."

"You have guests here with allies from the Rhinelands," Leo replied. In all her years in her father's court, Anna had never heard such ice in a voice. "My wife is in mourning because some of your *guests* murdered her people."

"You know that was not by my will . . ."

Leo inclined his head. "You have been a good patron to us, especially in the matter of Pera, and I thank you."

"Still 'us'? My mother said that there was only one thing about your lady that she would change."

"Rest the August Lady's soul." Leo signed himself at the memory of Anna Dalassena. Anna's and Irene's hands moved by reflex in the same gesture. *You told me she was a domineering old tyrant,* Anna thought at her mother.

"She said the same thing to me," Leo went on, "and I told her that, without that one thing, my wife would not have been the same lady."

"We give Our word We would permit no insult to come to her."

"I would not have her even *see* them. Of course"—Leo had caught the shift from "I" to "we"—"if His Sacred Majesty commands . . ."

"I did not think anything would draw you from that kingdom of yours in Cappadocia. Do you know"—Alexius's voice turned into a spear that struck suddenly—"when they speak of you at all, they call you Leo Akritas? Like the border hero. Next thing we know, they'll call you twice-born, too."

Anna pressed her fingers to her lips at the sight of a man older than her father dropping from his chair to his knees. Leo had turned pale, almost as grey as his hair. In a minute, he'd be knocking his head against the tesserae once more.

"Sacred Majesty, that is not a kingdom, that is a trust. We wrote the City for help against the Turkmen, but we were cut off. So I defended my home as best I could. But God chose the right man as Emperor," Leo protested. "I have not the talent or, God help me, the desire to rule."

Alexius gestured, dismissing his words as modesty.

"Sacred Majesty, I remember you from long before you wore the Purple. You saved my life. Do you now wish the gift returned?"

Alexius laughed, letting Leo know he was safe, at least for now. "Oh, get up! The years have been kind to you, Leo," said Anna's father. "Even if you've gone grey—"

"Greyer for certain than I was before I came in here . . ." Remarkably, Leo interrupted her father, who, even more remarkably, did not seem to mind.

"But your hair had started to turn as early as when you returned from . . ."

Leo inclined his head. For all his humility, Anna could see how rigidly he controlled himself.

Alexius shook his head. "It's been too many years, Leo," he said again. He drank, and Leo refilled the goblets.

"Since I was thrust into the army? Since my Emperor was betrayed?"

Standing beside her daughter, Irene stiffened, even as she signed herself reflexively for the old scholar, who had died the year before. Her father Andronicus was the man who had withdrawn the rear guard at Manzikert, throwing the battle to Alp Arslan, sultan of the Turks, and the Empire to Michael Ducas.

"Or since you pulled me out of the Cistern and I exiled myself to Cappadocia?"

"You've done well down there . . ."

Leo laughed and dismissed it with a casual, gentlemanly gesture. "You have done better." Seated, he contrived a bow that looked half Persian.

Alexius laid his fingers over his lips, but not before Anna had seen the wicked smile her father allowed himself after he outwitted someone and took what vengeance he would—as he had done with Leo for his refusal to present his wife.

"Nevertheless, many years. Long enough to forget?"

"Some things you never forget," Leo said.

"Did you learn that from the Jews?"

"At my mother's knee," said Leo. "And at Manzikert. Nevertheless, let me reassure you: we tend your father-in-law's grave—and why was it placed in a Jewish burial ground?—with our own."

Alexius blessed himself quickly, instinctively, at the reference to his late father-in-law. Leo's hands remained at rest. He would not, Anna realized, bless her grandfather's memory.

Silks rustled. This time Irene raised her hand to her lips and stiffened.

"Burying Andronicus in the Jewish graveyard even after he'd taken religious orders—it is always ill-done to wage war against the dead. Even your father-in-law's grave deserves respect."

Irene turned on her heel and left her vantage point. Distraught or furious she might be: she took pains, nevertheless, to leave in silence. A loyal daughter would have followed her. Anna remained.

"I miss you, Leo. When I was a boy, no one else ever treated me as if I were already a grown man."

Leo smiled. "Majesty, even then, you stood out like a gem among pebbles." It was the same charming smile with which he had introduced himself to Anna, but now she saw another aspect of the man. He would defer to her father absolutely, but when the time came to resist, he did so without hesitation. Where had he learned such strength?

"Bring in your children." The Emperor clapped his hands for the door to be opened. "You have only the two here?"

"I also have a foster grandchild." Leo sounded almost boastful. "Theodoulos has a daughter, Xenia, living with the family of his oldest friend down on his lands outside Hagios Prokopios. His wife died young. Theo, as I told you, was raised by the monks of Peristrema. Asherah and I raised Binah."

"Where are your other children? They must be grown by now."

"Asherah and I have three living children to your—what is it?—six? Our daughters are married and settled out along the caravan routes."

"Adventurous, are they?"

Leo laughed. "They see themselves as very settled, very much burdened by responsibilities, but I tell them that their mother manages the whole network without a complaint. Our one son is in Alexandria."

"So . . ." Egypt lay in Muslim hands.

"He studies to be a physician," Leo said hastily.

"I would like to see his letters."

Leo raised his brows. "Those that do not compromise him I will send you. His mother wishes Manuel to be a physician, not a spy. I will not have him put at risk."

"Emmanuel, you said his name was?"

"Manuel. After your oldest brother. The name is close enough that it passes on both sides."

"Leo, you never told me. At the very least, I would have sent a christening gift."

Leo shook his head. "There would hardly be a christening. We only ask that you think of all of us kindly."

Alexius was master of half the world. Had Anna truly seen him outmaneuvered and interrupted by this quiet man?

The carved doors opened. A man and a woman glided in. Leo rose.

"I beg to present to Your Sacred Majesty my foster son and daughter." They sank into the prostration.

"This was to be an informal meeting," Alexius pointed out.

"It is fitting that they show respect. As His Sacred Majesty knows, Theodoulos is a scholar and my right hand. Binah aids my wife in the same fashion."

Alexius gestured as gracefully as his old friend and sparring partner. "They are welcome for their own sakes as well as their father's. Rise."

Theodoulos clambered up from his knees. He walked with an almost-limp, Anna recalled, from when he escorted her back to the Bucoleon Palace. Binah rose to her feet like a caryatid emerging from her native stone. She raised her hands, not to take the weight of a shrine upon them, but to unveil.

The Emperor's eyes widened. Just as well, Anna decided, that Irene had withdrawn. Even after only a few months of marriage, Anna knew that look. She eyed Alexius speculatively. Maybe the rumors about her father and the former Empress Maria Alania had been true after all.

"Binah, you say she is called? Not . . ." He paused, preparing his audience for a compliment. "Helena? I wonder that such a prize languishes unwed."

Did Leo wish a marriage arranged for the woman, who might, after all, come from Christian parents despite her outlandish name? The offer was implicit in Alexius's admiration.

Leo raised an eyebrow at his friend. Then, he looked at his foster daughter, who looked down. For a woman, silent modesty was always a useful protection, although Anna was surprised Binah would resort to it.

"Binah claims not to wish to marry, but to study and assist her mother. She has been a law unto herself since her birth. And, since we have means enough that she need not marry, we have not pressed her."

Binah glided forward, laid a hand on the back of her foster father's chair, and smiled down at him.

"When the right man comes along . . ."

Leo laughed. For a man his age, his face turned so tender that Anna could have laughed. Alexius did. "My wife also never expected to wed. Then I came along, even more unexpectedly."

Instead of laughing, Anna sighed. Nicephorus was as considerate as you could expect in a man of his age. But Binah had achieved Anna's dearest dream. And she was so tall and beautiful.

Binah glanced sharply at the wall, as if she could discern where Anna stood, listening. Anna paused, holding her breath.

"You are a fortunate man, brother," Alexius told Leo.

Leo chuckled. "We have both been blessed."

"Yours is the greater freedom, for you and your family. Your wife is a woman of valor, and your children do as they will. I wish . . . did you hear about my eldest girl? That's right, you met her, didn't you?"

"I had the happiness of serving the Caesarissa Anna one day and making certain that she returned home safely. Does she know that you discovered that adventure?"

Alexius laughed, then sighed. "My Anna is nobody's fool. She wished to study and serve God, but she is porphyrogenita and had the duty to marry early. I hate to see her dwindle into a wife, but what can you do? I swear, she has the courage of your namesake, the lion. Did you know that when Godfrey and his friends attacked on Good Friday"—anger at the blasphemy resonated briefly in her father's voice—"that girl of mine remained in the courtyard with me and tried to help the wounded men?"

"I am not surprised," Leo said. "A little appalled, perhaps."

Alexius sighed again and put his hand to the small of his back. "Please God Our son Ioannes has that sort of courage. He needs it. I have had to include him in an exchange of hostages."

Alexius and Leo signed themselves, followed by Theodoulos. Binah murmured sympathy. Anna's hands clenched into fists.

"I pray the Franks and Celts have more honor than I fear, for when he is grown, he will be Emperor after Us."

This time, Binah's glance at the wall behind which Anna hid was followed by her foster brother's. Brother and sister looked at each other, then nodded. Awareness kindled in their eyes like the fire in fine gemstones.

"My children are all worthy of empire," Alexius said. He rose, signaled the other to remain seated, and tried to pace. "But these are wicked times, and I cannot, will not, dare not, leave the Purple to a daughter, however worthy, or even to a son-in-law while I have a son born in the porphyry chamber and acclaimed as my heir."

Anna shook with fury. Her father knew she listened, he had to; and he took this means to punish her.

Alexius turned, starting back across the room. Abruptly, he paused and gasped, bending almost double. He tried to take a step back toward his chair, but he staggered.

Leo Ducas and his son reached the stricken Emperor at the same time. Boldly, Leo caught hold of him and held him up.

If Anna ran to him, he would know she eavesdropped. She was furious at him. Let him stagger. Let him fall. Let him will the crown to her brother. *Holy Bearer of Burdens, let her beloved father survive this!*

"Get the Emperor settled," came Binah's low, rich voice. "Most Sacred Majesty, will you permit me?" She reached within the heavy splendor of her garments. "I am never without some medications, and these are simples that I have supplied your daughter. Majesty, you will recognize their taste, dissolved in wine."

Binah took a grave risk. If she failed and Alexius died—which Christ avert—the lives of every Jew in Pera would be justly and painfully forfeit.

"Or," she added, "we could call for your physician. He is the best we have."

"No," gasped Alexius Comnenus. "I will take your drugs. No one must know."

"Hold on, brother," Leo murmured. He was older than her father, yet he moved like a much younger man. "Just a few steps more. Half a step. Down . . . easy there, Theodoulos, don't drop His Sacred Majesty like a sack of grain into his chair."

Binah came forward with a goblet into which she had shaken a mixture, the sight and smell of which Anna did indeed remember. Catching the Emperor's eye, she drank from it—*did she think the Emperor didn't know about Mithridates and how he immunized himself to poison?*—and held the goblet to his lips. He turned it so his lips rested on the place from which she had drunk. Binah flushed and bit her lip.

"He'll be all right." Laughter and relief trembled in Leo's voice.

"Drink all of it, Majesty," Binah urged. "All of it. Shut your eyes and rest. Draw strength up from the earth itself, which you protect. Theo, prop his feet; you know how from when your own leg aches."

Kneeling at his old friend's feet, Leo Ducas took the empty goblet from the Emperor's hands.

"His hands are hot," he muttered.

"That's part of the ailment," Binah told him. "His physician really should see him quickly."

"No," Alexius repeated. "No. This is a bad time. He's coming. Bohemond is coming here."

"You'll need all your strength to deal with him."

"That's right. My doctor will put me out, or muddle my wits to kill the pain; and I don't dare. I'll offer it up. I need all my wits to deal with Bohemond. Old pirate he may be, like all the Sicilians, but he is a younger man than I. Just as I was younger than his father. God help us all, when I wrote to Urban asking for help against the Turk, I never guessed . . ."

"Steady," Leo urged. "You have always prevailed."

"He threw me into retreat once, did you know that? He saw my back, and then I thought, 'We cannot go on like this,' and turned and rode back and spitted the first man who charged at me. And now, he's coming, he and these others your wife is right to fear . . . Leo, if I fail, we won't just have these wolves in the palace; they'll gobble up the Empire."

"We'll help as we can, Alexius," Leo said softly.

"No one must know."

"No one will," Leo assured him. "Binah?"

"The Caesarissa already knows these drugs. There are others I could teach her, and certain motions . . ." She was on her knees, easing the Emperor's scarlet shoes from his swollen feet. "She is clever, thoughtful. I can teach her, if the Basilissa permits."

"You had better be called Helena Ducaina, if you come to my court," Alexius said. "Not Binah, daughter of Leo, or however else you're known. What is your mother's name?"

"My wife's name is Asherah," Leo reminded Alexius.

"Maria," Binah said softly. Theodoulos's shoulders shook.

"Same as your mother's, Leo. That will do well." The Emperor's voice grew in strength. "A little more wine, please, lady, and then I shall do well enough for now."

He drank, then handed the goblet back.

"Leo, this should work: your daughter travels between your people and the palace. People will think I have found my Anna a woman teacher so she can further her medical studies without reproach—not that anyone would dare. Her husband will never object, and as for her mother, who tends me from time to time herself, she could benefit too. Will that suit you?" he turned to ask Binah.

Binah bowed her head. The sunlight upon her dark hair glinted almost purple.

"What else can I do for you, Leo? I am much in your debt."

Leo laughed a little sadly. The sunlight coming through the windows slanted and dimmed; the afternoon had worn on.

"Sacred Majesty, I am no better than all the rest. I seek a place for my son—be quiet, Theo. You have been drifting since your wife died, and you know it."

"I could return to Cappadocia . . ."

"What then? Young Ioannes—my man, not your son, Majesty—has our lands well in hand, he and Kemal's sons. Pera is no place for you now. Sometimes I wonder if your mother's people will, at the last, turn against me too . . ." Deep unhappiness quivered in Leo's voice. "The Jews have known Theo more than half his life, but they fear him now because of the massacres in the Rhinelands. Binah—Asherah brought her up and she is a girl . . . only a girl, they are stubborn enough to think. But Theo is as I was—in need of a place and a future."

"You're thinking of a place as a secretary to me, perhaps a logothete? He is old to enter the Civil Service."

"Theodoulos knows the languages of Persian, Turk, Egyptian . . . yes, and Jews. He even knows several of the languages of the Franks, including their sacred speech."

"Does he indeed . . ." The purr of calculation returned with the strength in Alexius's voice. "He is, as you say, Christian?"

"Brought up by the Holy Meletios himself," Theodoulos replied.

"I may not need such a secretary at court, but when the wolf pack runs eastward, I shall send a *strategos* with them. A man with your son's talents would be worth his weight in gold."

"Dear God, Majesty, I cannot ask my son to put his head in the wolves' jaws!"

"No?" asked the Emperor. "You cannot, or will not. But I can. I can *command*. And I will. I need someone I can trust. Someone who knows the land to the East and its secrets. Boy, you have been to the Holy Land?"

"Twice, Most Sacred Majesty."

"How I envy you. I shall never see it, but if I can liberate it from the Muslims . . . will you serve me?"

"Majesty, yes!"

Theodoulos threw himself to his knees and bent his head until it touched the mosaics.

He raised it long enough to see his father's anguish.

"Sir," he appealed to Leo, "you know I've come to naught. You yourself say so. You found manhood earlier than I when you sought refuge in Peristrema. I remember. My sainted master forbade you to shave your hair, but you found tasks and a life. Can you deny me my chance?"

"But this may be death, not life!"

"Luring the Turks beneath the earth was life? Is that what you call it?"

Alexius laughed. The strength had fully returned to his voice. Thank God.

"He pleads to be allowed to risk his life in my service, and I am minded to let him. Leo, *I have no choice!*"

Leo Ducas bowed his head. "This is why you are Emperor and I am a merchant. Be it as my son wishes."

"I give you my word, Leo, they will be well treated. Do they need housing in the palaces?"

"That is too much favor," Binah put in subtly.

Leo nodded.

"We will open the house. My old one—you remember it?"

"I remember how your mother threw me and the other Leo—you know, he came to a bad end?—out of your room." Both men laughed. For a moment, Anna's father looked years younger.

"All the court needs to know is that some distant Ducas cousins have taken it over. We have only stayed in it once since my marriage. Asherah finds it cold and shabby, but the children don't object to it."

"And what if I fall ill while they are living there?"

"Binah *least* of all will I permit to live in the palace." So Leo had seen how Anna's father's eyes had lit at the sight of her and disliked it.

It was pleasant to think that Binah would become her companion. She would be a teacher to Anna, perhaps a friend, like the mother who had given Anna honeycakes, books, and a bracelet, and kissed her more gently than her own mother did.

"I give you my word no one—not even my wife—will insult your girl, but they will plead with me to give her in marriage."

Leo frowned.

"Leo." Alexius made his voice persuasive, although he might simply have commanded his old friend and kinsman. "As you point out, they are man and woman grown. They can take care of themselves, and my hand is over them—yes, I know. Discreetly. I cannot promise their perfect safety, but who among us is safe? Their lives shall be upon my soul."

Leo turned a nod of assent into a deep prostration, then rose.

"We should leave you now," he said. "Will you . . ."

"I shall do well enough," the Emperor said. "Get home while yet you might."

They bowed deeply, then backed from his presence. Alexius Comnenus sat facing the wall until the light faded and servants came in with lamps. Only after he left the room did Anna venture forth from her hiding place. So, he thought he could move her about the board just as he had manipulated his old friend and his children?

If she were a chess piece, she would be queen and king combined. For once in his life and after it, the Emperor of the Romans would be proved wrong by his eldest daughter.

"My worthy Theodoulos! I could have used your help yesterday evening at Cosmides."

Theodoulos turned so quickly that the folds of his ceremonial robes caught in his legs and made him feel as if he were a crippled lad again. Just in time, he turned his clumsiness into a passable bow to Tatikios, the general to whom he had been assigned as a secretary. Despite his embarrassment, Theo came up from his deep bow grinning. How odd it was to hear the accent of the City coming out of a face that was pure—or half-blood—Turk. Tatikios's square head and stocky build reminded him of Kemal, who had lost his last battle with what had been truly epic bad luck several years ago. To the surprise of most of the people in Hagios Prokopios, his death had left a vacancy in their lives.

"Theo's not *crippled*," Kemal had told the old women who tried to cosset him even after he emerged from the caves, miraculously healed of the limp that had blighted his childhood. Thanks to Kemal he was an even better rider and archer than many veterans.

Theodoulos's fondness for his foster father's old companion had made him greet his new master with immediate liking. That was probably more than Tatikios got from many of the City's family-proud nobles, although not from Alexius himself or the *strategos* Butumites, who would also escort the Franks at least as far as Nicaea.

Tatikios laid a hand on Theo's shoulder, turning him to one side for more private talk. Theo had not been a good merchant. His wife had died. He was an adequate scholar, but his learning was not such that Christians would accept, and he himself was no longer fully acceptable among his foster mother's people. Being secretary to Alexius's chosen officer would simply be another role to fail at.

Every time he had filled his hands, something had emptied them. He would probably leave his bones on the plains like Peter the Hermit's rabble. *Thy will be done*, he had learned to pray at Father Meletios's knee. Perhaps the saintly old man would intercede for him.

"I was unworthy to accompany our worthy guests"—Theodoulos kept his voice light and brittle on the honorifics as several tall Franks in long capes, each adorned with a cross in the Western style, swept by—"to their lodgings in the monastery of Saint Damian and Saint Cosmas."

"You should have seen him," the general told him. His dark eyes danced with mirth. Byzantium might be rife with Franks and Celts—the haughty Baldwin; that Godfrey whom they treated as if he were a fragment of the True Cross himself; Hugh, who almost behaved as if he were the Emperor's own errand boy; and the older man, one-eyed Isangeles, who companied with the Western bishop, Holy Urban's own envoy. Nevertheless, "he" always and solely meant Bohemond, who had defeated Alexius years ago at Dyrrachium and meant to do it again.

"I *have* seen the worthy Count," Theodoulos replied. "He stared at my lady sister as if he would bid on her."

It was probably indiscreet to mention his sister at all, but he thought that Tatikios would respect a display of spirit.

"Bohemond is staying there, he and his armsmen," Tatikios said. "You should pay the holy monks a visit before we leave the city. They're close enough to the Horn that they've got a view, and close enough to the Blachernae Palace that they're prestigious. His Sacred Majesty keeps a suite of rooms for *very* important guests like Lord Long-legs of Sicily and his ten armsmen."

The "armsmen" were what the Westerners called "knights," and therefore possibly of patrician blood. Still, it amused all of the Byzantines to treat them as if they were mercenaries, of far less worth than a noble in one of the regiments of cataphracts. "You should have seen the horses they rode!"

Kemal to the life, rest his soul.

"It came time for them to dine. They had actually even washed, when an upper servant opened a door to show them a table already laid with more food than you can bet that they had seen in all their months of travel."

Theodoulos nodded. Then he bowed so deeply that any more courtesy would have had him on his belly in full prostration. A fragrant splendor of ladies swept past, young Caesarissa Anna leading them. How that slender girl could walk in the pearls and amethysts and gold-stitched silks that weighted her, he did not know, unless pride served her as a second backbone.

Binah followed in Anna's magnificent wake. She was in full role as Helena Ducaina today, her eyes downcast, her dress deliberately restrained as befitted a minor noblewoman who was practically a scholar-nun in her aspirations. Theo suppressed a smile. His sister was not that demure, not that shy: no one who had worked since she was ten as a midwife could possibly be—but she was a good actress. Almost as tall as most of the Frankish lords, she was accompanied by sighs as well as the sweep of skirts and robes.

Even Tatikios watched her with appreciation. The general was not a Muslim, Theo reminded himself. He already had a wife. And Binah had always been a law unto herself.

You are too timid, she had accused him when she grew out of the adoration of him that a child scarcely walking grants an older boy. *You have the land sense from our mother, if you would only care to use it.*

Watching Binah's sure progression in the wake of the imperial ladies, Theodoulos tried. Listen to the land: did it tremble underfoot with the weight of invaders? Would it tolerate them or throw them out? It had thrived under Alexius. What about these newcomers?

The effort made him dizzy. Tatikios watched him strangely. Time to recover.

"I was watching the court, sir. It is more splendid than I dreamed of. I beg your pardon."

"Ah! The palace is overpowering, if you are not used to it. As I was saying, it came time to feed the Franks, and the majordomo showed them their feast. No one moved. So the majordomo—this had all been planned beforehand, you know—said he quite understood if Bohemond preferred to have his meals prepared rather than eat those offered him by His Sacred Majesty. And there, on a tray, was a whole selection of uncooked meat."

Theodoulos shook his head, genuinely shocked. "What a guest!"

"It gets better," Tatikios told him, taking an instant to nod gravely at a hurrying logothete. "Although *he* would not eat, he allowed his guards to cook the meats, and he went to bed. Next morning, he asked how they felt. 'I really thought the Emperor might have poisoned the food,' he told them (we had listeners posted, of course), 'after all the terrible wars we had fought.' "

"So much for all his oaths on the Crown of Thorns," Theodoulos said.

"Just so. His Sacred Majesty has some other tests for him today. Come watch the game."

"They say Count Bohemond's got himself a new cloak," Anna could not resist observing to Binah. At Clermont, he had torn up his best scarlet cloak into crosses before coming east, ran one of the many stories that followed the man.

"He never paid full value for the cloth," Binah—no, Helena—whispered. "If he paid at all."

They moved their lips as little as possible. Silence while awaiting the Emperor was correct; and in the presence of these ill-mannered Franks, correctness itself became a weapon.

Binah smiled so briefly Anna thought she had imagined it. Already, she had proved her worth. Even the Empress had to admit she had made herself useful.

Odd to think of even a Ducas's fosterling as a merchant; odder still to think of her as a subordinate, even for Anna, who had a keen notion of her own position. Some at court called her an Amazon.

Count Bohemond's father's wife was said to be one such: she even rode in armor. But Bohemond had been dispossessed. *You want an inheritance?* his father Robert, another of Anna's father's dearest enemies, had asked, in effect. *Seize Byzantium.*

And here he came, ready to snatch the diadem and anything else that was offered. He had been her father's enemy at Larissa and Dyrrachium, Bohemond had himself admitted. But now, he had come of his own free will as the Emperor's friend.

Emperors had many "friends."

The Franks' boots clattered on the tesserae. Binah flinched—at the damage to all that artistry? She actually closed her eyes in pain. Were the great lords of the West wearing spurs? Anna wouldn't put it past them. One man—not Bohemond—had actually sat on her father's throne. Just as astonishingly, he had been rebuked by the lord Baldwin, who probably craved it for himself. And then there was Tancred, who had hurled himself at one of her cousins and had denied Anna's father the oath of homage that was the right of an Emperor, reserving obedience—assuming Tancred bowed the head to anyone—for his uncle Bohemond.

Godfrey, after the blasphemous Good Friday attack on the palace, had called her father's guest Hugh a slave for taking such an oath; but he had, inevitably, sworn. Doubtless, things would be different for the old man, the one married to an Iberian princess. He traveled in company with a prince of the Church; he had the Pope's confidence. But the time had come, Anna knew, for her father to bring his most spirited adversary to heel—and those heels wore spurs inside the palace.

"They're coming!"

"Hush!"

Anna had never seen an asp, praise God; but she imagined that they sounded much like the whispers that subdued the women of her following into blank-faced, hieratic order. Long, splendid cloaks brushed the floor, hissing, sweeping after the long strides of the immensely tall Franks. And now Anna could see Bohemond, new cloak and all, walking not as far behind her father the Emperor as Alexius— and his guards—could surely have wished.

As much as the splendor of the fabric that Binah attributed to plunder, light swirled about the tall Norman. To Anna's astonishment, Bohemond wore it consciously, just as her father did. As much as the Emperor himself, Bohemond became the center of attention. For there to be two centers of one circle violated geometry: that, as much as faith or land, was what this meeting, this war-to-come, was about—who should be the center.

Alexius nodded greetings at the assembled Romans. His eyes sparkled with the gratified malice that showed he had another test for his "friend."

Suddenly, the Emperor's face turned color. He put a gemmed hand up to his face to hide a cough. His shoulders heaved once, but only once. He widened his eyes, as if noticing a man across the room, a man with important business, requiring the immediate attention of an Emperor.

Alexius Comnenus left the room. He didn't even stagger.

Anna started forward: her father was ill; she must go to him. A hand caught her by the wrist and held it, pinching almost to the bone. Suppressing a cry of pain, she turned just enough to see that it was the Augusta who had stopped her. Her mother's face was paler even than usual. She smiled, but as if the gracious movement of her lips was an iron mask, heated until it burned her.

"No one would miss me. Shall I go, Augusta?" Binah whispered.

No. Irene held Binah in her place by force of will.

Let the Franks know that Alexius was ill, and any oaths they took would vanish like the breath on which they had been spoken. Anna breathed deeply. *Kyrie eleison, christe eleison.* God help her father. God prevent the Franks from knowing.

Bohemond swept by, his nephew Tancred at his shoulder. He was tall, easily the tallest man in the room, even though he leaned forward a little, as if he were about to leap forward to snatch prey. He kept his face motionless, though his pale eyes flicked across the room, across the motionless, splendid Romans, as if he assessed how much it would cost him to buy or take them.

His eyes touched Anna's and widened as if . . . as if . . . she had seen a faint cousin to that look once or twice in her husband's eyes. Bohemond paused.

Christ in glory, he was magnificent. She had expected a certain crude splendor, like a Varangian on parade. This man's smile was wider and broader, and so hungry—wolf-hunger restrained by fine manners—that it took all her discipline not to step backward. His eyes were not pale, but a brilliant blue when he smiled, and he wore his hair short, shorter even than the other Franks did. So his helmet would fit, he explained; but it might also be to show off the strength of his neck where it flowed into those shoulders, so much broader than his hips.

Anna's Caesar was handsome, tall for their people and dark-haired. Serious. Thoughtful. Their marriage had been arranged, but Anna would give parents this: they had chosen for her as best they could a man she might find attractive—and she supposed she did. But looking at this outland pirate, she found something else—an understanding of the women's knowing laughter that her mother had bade her listen to. This new awareness prickled down her spine and touched within her.

Despite the weight of Anna's ceremonial garments, she shivered.

Anna knew she should not study Bohemond as if she were a woman other than a wedded wife and princess. An unexpected sound caught the man's attention. His nostrils flared. Profit? Danger? Glory? Where? The light seemed to wreath him with a kind of passionate intensity. Fine cloth and fine features were only an aristocratic mask that dropped away at the merest hint of excitement; beneath, Bohemond was all predator.

"I warrant, he puts on his garments just as any other man does," Binah whispered. "Even if he does not pay for them."

She should not be talking, but her words were like a pool of cool water on a hot day. Bohemond was magnificent, but Binah had lived in Persia and seen magnificence before. She was not impressed.

An attendant came forward, bowed, and gestured to Bohemond: Behold. He laid hand to paired doors that sprang open as if hurled wide by servants within. There would be no room, ever, for servants within that room. No one would possibly walk in it, for it was filled with treasure from floor to ceiling. Brocades spilled across closed chests and silver basins. Other chests gaped open, showing heaps of gold and silver coins. It was more treasure than Anna herself had ever seen heaped up in one place.

Had Bohemond's father not intended Byzantium for his pirate son's patrimony? The wealth that crammed the room could be a first installment.

Bohemond backed up like a cat sprayed with perfume. Eyes glittered, and he wet his lips. "If I had such wealth," he observed, his voice husky, "I would long ago have become master of many lands."

The man drew himself up and smiled thinly. "All this is yours today—a present from the Emperor."

"Give the Emperor my thanks," said the Frank. "Or I shall, to-morrow."

He smiled with satisfaction; he glowed; he visibly expanded as he swept from the room. It meant food for his men, fine horses, payment for his army, which was the smallest of any of the lords there, as he had been the least in wealth and resources.

Anna watched the Westerners' backs disappear. Wealth they wanted, and wealth they had received. Was that all there was to her father's strategy? It made sense; poverty had soured Bohemond and made him even more ambitious and dangerous. Perhaps this would send him on his way to the Holy Sepulchre rejoicing.

She could not believe it.

"There must be another round in the game," she mouthed to Binah.

Binah's smile, more than ever, reminded her of a statue she had seen, the weathered stone keeping its artist's thoughts to itself for eternity.

 9

The door of the bedchamber Anna shared with Nicephorus Bryennius burst open. Light exploded in her eyes. Voices erupted in the corridor, forbidding, protesting, pleading.

"The Emperor commanded it, do you doubt me?"

Anna knew that voice, remembered the flint underlying the dusky softness that Binah cultivated as assiduously as she groomed herself. Nicephorus's arm, flung across her as he slept, pinned her to the bed.

"You need not expose the Caesar and Caesarissa to every servant in the hall, you know. Close the door." The door closed: it would be a formidable servant indeed to withstand the ice in Binah's voice.

"Caesarissa?"

Binah advanced calmly across the floor. A single flame rose from the lamp she carried.

Nicephorus's arm tightened on Anna, all but hurling her from their bed on the opposite side from the advancing woman. Snatching the sword he kept by his own side of the bed, Nicephorus leapt up, drawing steel and casting the sword's sheath across the room.

"What's wrong?" Anna cried.

"Get down and stay down!" her husband cried.

But it was only Binah! Anna wanted to protest. You never argued with a man carrying steel, she had learned young.

Fabric tangled about her feet, and she reached down for it: Nicephorus's bed robe, shed that night. She, at least, had managed to retain her shift, and she pulled it down, decently, over her legs.

Binah had said the Emperor had summoned her.

"What's wrong?" she cried again. Her mother, perhaps? Surely, they would not wake her to tell her her brother had been murdered by the Franks.

She began to tremble.

"Your father is ill, Caesarissa," Binah told her calmly. "Your mother thinks you may be of service."

She stood very still, neither eyeing Nicephorus nor showing undue fear. You would have thought Binah had been menaced by naked men with swords every night of her life! Anna clapped a hand to her mouth to keep from hysterical laughter or tears.

She tossed the robe to her husband. "I beg you, cover yourself," she said, which was something she wished she could say when he bedded her. Impressive: he caught it in midair and covered himself without lowering the point of the sword he held.

"You can't leave here like that," he protested.

"Is His Sacred Majesty very ill? What do I need?"

"It's being readied, don't worry about that. Only you must come quickly." Binah darted a look at Nicephorus Bryennius that should have wilted steel or anything else.

"Put that sword down," she said.

He opened his mouth on what had foolishly started as "I forbid . . ."

"Father's physicians?"

Binah shook her head. "And he forbade the Augusta to send for a priest, too."

Nicephorus reached out to restrain Anna, but she dodged him.

"Let's go!" She snatched up a robe of her own and struggled into it as she followed Binah down the hall. How cold the tiles were on her bare feet.

"How did you know?" she demanded, already half out of breath and shaking from fear and the shock of a too-sudden awakening.

"I beg you, never mind that now. Just come!" Binah ignored her question as Anna thought she might.

One day, I am going to get some answers, Anna thought. The woman had a house of her own: what was she doing prowling about the palace at night? So short a time the woman had been coming to the palace: had she already found a lover? Worse thought yet . . . no, Binah had mentioned the Augusta.

The doors—and the guards—outside the Emperor's bedchamber seemed no different than they had always been. *He wants no uproar.*

Impassive at the sight of a violet-eyed woman and a half-dressed princess, the guards admitted them.

Inside the Emperor's room, all was chaos.

Alexius sat up, red-faced in his bed, the Augusta supporting his shoulders as he coughed and choked. Not the gout, but his asthma, a disease Anna knew could turn deadly. It was so frightening to watch her father gasp and whoop and fight for every breath. Incongruously, Binah bowed. Anna ran to her father's side.

"Father!" Anna cried as if she were a much younger girl. She was the eldest; she could usually persuade her father to anything—*except making her the heir,* she thought even then, with a twinge of angry guilt. "Let us call your physician!"

"*No.*" Alexius's voice was a strangled wheeze.

Binah rose from her bow. Hastening over to a table near the Emperor's bed, she nodded approval at the steaming basin Irene had ordered placed there. "Well done, Augusta," she told Irene, who, for a miracle, did not glare.

From a bag slung around one shoulder, Binah removed packets and tiny phials.

"Caesarissa, don't let the lamps smoke," she commanded. "It hurts his breathing."

Like a good servant, Anna trimmed the lamps, then joined Binah, who had laid out the medications she had brought.

She bruised herbs in a mortar and tossed them into one basin of water. "This will help the steam aid his breathing," she said. Fumes rose from it to scent the room, making the air seem somehow fresher. She chose a phial and reached for a cup.

"Use this," Anna thrust a goblet at her. "It's wider."

Binah nodded approval. "No wine with this," she said. "You and the Augusta, make His Majesty drink this. All of this. It will ease the strain on his heart."

How could he drink while he coughed and whooped? Anna wanted to ask, but Binah had turned back to the table. So calm she was, so calm while enemies lay within the cities and the Emperor— Anna's beloved father—might be dying.

Tears ran down the Augusta's face. "Not even one priest here," Irene moaned.

"Augusta, imagine the scandal if *I* fetched one," Binah asked.

Alexius shook his head: *no priest*.

Anna sniffed at the goblet, recognizing the herbs. To be safe, she tasted it, as she had tasted many drugs as her father's physicians watched. She wished she had the sapphires that had been Asherah's gift to her to test further. No, that was foolish; her attendant served Anna's father as if her life and her family's lives depended on it— which they did.

"Help me," she asked her mother.

With hands that scarcely shook at all, Irene held her husband steady as Anna tipped the goblet toward his bluish lips between spasms of racking coughs.

Binah swooped down, holding the basin where the Emperor could breath the fumes—assuming he could breathe at all. It was heavy; it must be hot: she handled it as if it weighed no more than an empty goblet. Anna set the goblet aside.

"Another?"

"A little while," Binah murmured. "See how he reacts to this dose. Watch his breathing."

Irene had begun to pray loudly.

"Majesty." Binah's voice was perfectly respectful, but it silenced an Empress. "The Emperor feels your agitation. I beg you, calm yourself. It will stir up the humors. Talk to him, or pray calmly. Majesty, if you could breathe in rhythm to the Augusta's words? Try, please!"

Anna leaned over and wiped Alexius's face with a cloth. His eyes were bulging with the effort to breathe. Binah held the basin directly under his nose. "Breathe deeply," she murmured. "In . . . out. In . . . out. Like the tides. Calm as the tides, unchanged, eternal, never fading . . ."

Her voice grew softer and softer. Irene drew a deep breath and prayed more calmly; and still, Binah's voice whispered on into the night.

Gradually, the Emperor's gasping subsided. Binah set aside the now-cooling basin and brought the Emperor an empty one and a soft cloth.

"Better?" she asked as easily as if she spoke to a family member.

He spat noisily, then allowed himself to subside against his wife's shoulder as if exhausted. Binah bent to wipe his mouth, but the Au-

gusta gestured her away and did the task herself. Binah smiled thinly
and moved a decorous step away from the bed.

At a gesture, Empress and daughter piled up pillows behind him.
Binah brought over another goblet, holding it toward Anna so she
could test it. "There's honey in there too," she said. "At this point, we
must avoid anything that could make him gag."

Before Irene could protest, Binah approached the Emperor and
tilted the dose into Alexius's mouth.

"This will ease your throat," she said. "In a little while, you will
rest. I wish you would let me send for the physician. Sabbath or no,
he would come for you."

Alexius shook his head around the rim of the goblet and gestured
for Binah to take it away.

"No," he whispered, his voice husky. "No one must know."

Anna and her mother both raised eyebrows. How had Binah
known?

"I had been speaking," she said with some constraint, "to some of
the Augusta's women before I went home. Then the doors crashed
open. Your mother came running out, and I heard the Emperor cough.
Since I knew what to do . . ." She shrugged.

You expect me to believe that? Anger and suspicion flickered in her
mother's eyes. Binah met them unflinchingly.

Alexius yawned, drawing the women's attention.

"Majesty." Binah spoke to him as she might have spoken to Leo
Ducas. "You have overspent your strength. You must rest."

Alexius shook his head.

"I . . . I cannot . . ." he said. "Do you know what he did?"

"He" being Bohemond, once more.

"Sent back all the treasure?" Anna asked a little too brightly.
She did not think her father should be talking, but Binah did not object. Maybe speech would relieve some of the strain that burdened
him.

That won a smile from her father. "My wise daughter," he whispered. "When servants unpacked the treasures at Cosmides, he had already changed his mind."

"Like a sea polyp," Anna breathed. "What a pirate he is!"

" 'I never thought I should be so insulted by the Emperor,' they
told me Bohemond said. 'Take them back. Give them back to the
sender.' "

"My convent of Theotokos Kecharitomene or your monastery
could use such wealth better than that pirate," Irene said.

Alexius settled himself more comfortably against his pillows. He pressed his wife's hand.

"You surely do not think he sent it all back?" Alexius asked. "He is mischievous, but it will rebound upon his own head."

Alexius coughed again, and Binah brought another basin, steaming with herbs, to his side. He breathed deeply and sighed with relief. "My servants began to repack the treasure. That did not please my lord Bohemond . . . oh no, not at all. So he smiled and said he had changed his mind."

"An odd notion of honor, surely," said Irene.

"What a rogue," Anna said. "He had never seen so much treasure in his life!"

"The rogue has asked to be Grand Domestic in the East," Alexius murmured. The drug was taking effect. He smiled benignly at Anna's cry of outrage. Let Bohemond win supreme command, and who knew how he might manipulate the other nobles from the West.

"If I granted *any* man that title, it might be he who companies with the Holy Bishop—how do you call him?"

"Isangeles." Anna could never shape her mouth for these barbaric names.

"The count Raymond of Saint-Gilles," Binah put in.

"And he wants naught of me, so proud he is, determined to call no one but God his lord."

"So you told him, Father . . ." Anna prompted.

"I told Master Bohemond that the time was not ripe for that, but 'with your energy and loyalty, it will not be long before you have even that honor.' "

"Oh, well done!" Anna applauded. He had his wits; he had his breath back; and now Anna could breathe again herself.

He smiled, and Anna saw in his eyes the old zest of the man who had fought Bohemond and his father even before he had become Emperor.

"None of this," Irene told Binah, "none of this is to be known outside this room. Do you hear me?"

Binah bowed her head, her shoulders stiff.

"She would not betray us," Alexius said. "No more than her father . . ."

Binah came to kneel at his feet. "His Majesty saved my foster father's life," was all she said.

Alexius accomplished what seemed to Anna to be another remarkably well-timed yawn.

"His Majesty should sleep," Binah said. "I think he is ready to. Sir, could you rest now?"

Anna dimmed the lamps in the room, dousing all but two. Above their mellow light, the shadows closed in, as comforting as heavy robes on a cold night.

"Majesty," Binah said to Irene, "may I watch for a while? When he falls asleep, I shall leave."

"You cannot go home now," Irene said, shocked out of her usual disapproval.

Binah shook her head. "It is not long till dawn. When the sun comes up . . ."

She did not look tired at all—unlike Irene, whose delicate skin seemed bruised with shadows, or Anna, who felt herself ready to drop from weariness. Calmly, Binah carried empty goblets over to the table. She pulled up several cushions. Settling herself on one of them, she pulled a tiny book from some fold of her garments and began to read in a low murmur.

"What's that?" Irene demanded.

Binah smiled. "A medical treatise."

Anna glanced over. Seeing a sketch of a dragon within the text, she suppressed a smile.

"The Caesarissa knows of this book," Binah went on. "And that there is no harm in it."

Anna walked over to sit by Binah. She did her best to look knowledgeable, reassuring, composed—although she almost cracked her jaw in the next moment with a yawn.

Asherah had translated the book for her into Greek. It was not Greek that Binah was reading, but her voice was too soft for Irene to know of that. Anna's mother left Alexius's side and knelt on the bare floor, bowing her head in prayer. For a long time, the room was tranquil, except for the murmur of the women's voices.

Anna felt herself dozing. How still Binah sat, curled up on her cushions. She had probably learned to sit that way in Persia. Anna tugged at a cushion, rested her head on it, then stretched out. She was so tired that the floor itself was better than a bed.

The lamps dimmed. The shadows hovered closer. Binah's voice eased them all. The Emperor slept. Irene looked up from her prayers.

"Thank God," she whispered. And then, because she prided herself, if she prided herself on anything, on being a just woman, "Thank you," she told Binah.

Binah smiled and bowed her head. "It was my privilege," she said.

Anna dozed. From time to time, she looked up at the faces of the others in the room: worn as her father was, even asleep he looked as if he could spring to his feet. Her mother's beauty, like a golden lily, seemed to glow in the light, while Binah was all twilight and mystery.

"What's that?" Irene cried.

Measured, assured footsteps, down the hall outside. Anna flushed.

"Presumably, your lord has finally found time to dress," Binah whispered.

Anna forced herself back onto her feet, stumbled to the door, opened it a trifle, and admitted her husband.

"His Sacred Majesty is resting easily," she whispered.

"I came to bring you back," Nicephorus told her. Then, as if he finally listened to her, he blessed himself at the news.

Anna glanced over at her mother. Go, her mother pointed with her chin at the doors. *Your place is with your husband.* Anna sighed, reluctant to leave.

"We will all leave, shall we?" Binah asked, tucking her book away once more and rising effortlessly.

The room jolted sideways. Anna felt herself swept up into Nicephorus's arms as Irene gasped.

"I'm fine," Anna protested. "I can walk. See, you've waked him."

"Still a little girl?" Alexius's voice was very sleepy. "Son-in-law, you should carry your own children to bed, not your . . ." He broke off, laughing a little.

"Sir, you should be treated by a physician, not your daughter."

"They must not know." Alexius's voice was an exhausted whisper. "Too many Franks, all of them here. My son's life is in their hands."

You have had other heirs, Anna wished at her father. *Constantine. Me. Why not Nicephorus, too?*

"Many are called, but few are chosen," Alexius mused. "I have been chosen by God to be this land's guardian."

Why didn't Binah urge him to rest? Anna opened her eyes. To her astonishment, Binah watched him raptly.

"Go to sleep, husband," her mother's voice urged.

"Yes, Augusta." Laughter trembled in Alexius's voice.

Go now, mouthed Binah.

Nicephorus turned and left the room, Binah following, shutting the door behind them.

"Will you be safe?" Nicephorus asked Binah. They were much of an age, Anna thought, but Nicephorus had always held aloof. Now, it appeared as if Binah had won his approval.

"Of course," she said. "The guards have heard you ask about my safety, and they will watch for me."

Nicephorus paused, ready to argue the point. He had to be prodded, Anna already knew that. If she let him argue himself out, she would still have been in their room, and her father might have coughed himself to death. Ostentatiously, she yawned, and Nicephorus laughed intimately.

Yes, Anna thought. Even that again tonight, if it gets us away from here now.

Not quite *now*, perhaps, gurgled a mischievous voice within her head.

Binah withdrew, settling herself with ease upon the floor.

"Bring the lady a chair," Nicephorus ordered a guard. For once, he would have the last word.

He turned away.

"I can walk," Anna whispered.

"You don't have to," her husband said. "Let people talk."

To Anna's surprise, his arms felt good around her.

"What was it that you did in there?"

She was too tired to be discreet: best not to discuss it, even with her husband. Perhaps *especially* with her husband. Whom would *he* tell?

"Will he be all right?" asked Nicephorus. A little fear quivered in his voice. It softened Anna toward him.

She rubbed her face against his shoulder to beguile him, and his arms tightened about her. She suppressed a wail of sheer exhaustion.

Servants, carefully not watching them, opened the doors to their room. Nicephorus carried Anna within and set her on a bed that had been put hastily to rights. She burrowed into the pillows, listening to Nicephorus pulling off his clothes and tossing things about the room with less than his usual degree of awkwardness.

She felt his weight settle down beside her and sighed. He rested his arm protectively over her body, drawing her in closer to him.

"Go to sleep, little one," he whispered. "I won't bother you."

That made her open her eyes. He met them, smiling a little ruefully.

"Oh, Anna, Anna. Everyone says how wise you are, how learned. But so very young. I wish your wisdom taught you a way of growing up all the way overnight," he said. "Your father gave me one of his greatest treasures . . ."

Look what he gave Bohemond! Anna wanted to comment, but she was too tired, and the expression on her husband's face too tender for the joke.

". . . but I do not want treasure; I would rather have a wife who would stay with me as the Augusta stays with *him*. And you are so very young . . ."

He bent lower, looking into her eyes. *You promised to leave me alone!* She bit her lip on the undutiful words. Why, Nicephorus was looking at her as if she were as beautiful as Binah. He looked at her the way Leo Ducas, old as he was, stared at Asherah—or . . . Tears filled her eyes. Nicephorus wiped them away.

"Sleep, my dearest," he whispered. "But try to grow up quickly, will you?"

She let herself relax in his hold for the first time.

"I will try," she whispered.

As the shadows and her husband's warmth enfolded her, Anna mused on her father's words. *Many are called and few are chosen.* She had long ago chosen herself. And, since Nicephorus seemed likely to prove as dear to her as he was eminently suitable, what if she chose them both?

"I promise I will try," she murmured against his shoulder, and closed her eyes.

1097
FROM CONSTANTINOPLE INTO ASIA MINOR

 10

A change in the air, as if a thunderstorm had scoured earth and sky, woke Theodoulos. He gazed wide-eyed into the darkness, then attempted to reach down into the earth for reassurance.

Let yourself go limp, Binah had repeatedly instructed him. *Imagine yourself sinking into the earth. Feel what it feels.* The last time Theodoulos had come close to success, the sense of being trapped had engulfed him, and he had struggled free, as near panic as he had ever been since his boyhood when Father Meletios ordered him to limp through the lightless caves of Peristrema.

The caves had cast him out. Although what he knew of them had saved his life, gaining him freedom and family, he preferred not to think about the places and powers that came so naturally to Binah.

Or perhaps it was the land sense that he could not escape, crying out in revulsion at what oppressed him. Binah was not here to coax him into trying again. Soon, the sky would grey toward dawn—at least he knew that much; and he must shortly be on the move with the armies of Byzantium to Nicaea.

He was secretary to a general now. Leo had begged the post for him, but Theodoulos must rise or fail—fail again, doubtless—on his own.

Alexius had given them gold, arms, siege machines, his officers, and his best craft. Please God, let it be enough.

Theodoulos gave up on sleep as dawn crept in through the narrow windows. Except for the quick, vicious raids in Cappadocia, this was his first campaign as a soldier. He did not fear the road east. But, at nearly forty, to ride in the Emperor's army for the first time . . . *Kyrie eleison.*

The light grew stronger, turned golden. The air freshened, harbinger of an easy crossing into Asia. A butterfly flew in at the window, danced by his face, then out again. *Sister, do you choose this means to comfort me?*

Theo smiled and rose with an odd lift of heart. Long before the command to move out was shouted, he was ready and armed. A priest led the soldiers in prayer. It was odd to see Tatikios, with his Turkish features, kneel, rather than scrub himself with sand, then prostrate himself on a battered rug like the one Kemal managed to hang on to until his death. For that matter, after years among Asherah's people, Theodoulos found it odd to be part of a group of Christian men praying publicly.

After prayers, Tatikios nodded at him.

Ready? He raised an eyebrow.

Theodoulos nodded, trying to stiffen into some semblance of military bearing.

His master swung with Turk-like agility into the saddle and gestured his men forward. Silent, disciplined, they started toward the harbor.

On horseback, Theodoulos had not been "that poor crippled lad who serves the Holy Father," but a boy like any other; he had always loved to ride. He kept his back straight and his head high, trying to look like a man fit to ride in such close companionship with one of His Sacred Majesty's most trusted officers.

Tatikios grinned at him, remembering their many conversations. *You know Nicaea, don't you?* Better yet, Theodoulos knew the palace, had spoken with the sultan while Binah had displayed silks and gold in the women's quarters of the palace. Theo had been proud he could answer all of the general's questions.

Horse hooves clopped down the streets to the harbor, the smells of manure warring with the water smells of tar and boats and fish, and the earliest baking of bread from ovens all over the city. Men and women who had already been hard at work for hours broke off, lining the streets as they had when the Franks rode out. After all, they could always hope for some new sight or perhaps some copper and silver coins thrown to coax a cheer from them.

Theodoulos had seen the Franks ride out: huge men made all alike by those curious, masklike helms and the crosses stitched to the long capes that swept the flanks of horses that dwarfed even the steeds the heaviest cataphracts rode into battle. The Franks sang as they rode out—a deep-throated exultant hymn that for a brief, treacherous moment had made Theodoulos pray that they proved victorious. What a feat it would be to return Jerusalem to the embrace of Christendom!

The sun had kindled on Bohemond's hair, flourishing still, though he was now at an age when a man might think of grandchildren on his knee, stories of old victories rather than winning new ones, and a fire on the hearth. He sat his horse as if it were a throne, and his eyes blazed.

The crowds had cheered the Franks, enjoying the spectacle as well as the chance to see the back of their antagonists. Saying farewell to troops of their own was different. Many cheered, but more blessed themselves and fell to their knees as the banners passed.

Over here!

The cry seemed to explode in his consciousness.

A man and a woman, no longer young, stood in the center of a knot of other workers, all waving with energy they would regret squandering later in the workday. Insignificant enough, Theo mused. Then, the woman darted forward, baring her head with a girl's impulsiveness as if she meant to use her coarse veil to wave farewell to her boy in the army.

It was, or would have been, a touching sight.

It was also Asherah.

She wore not the rich, sober fabrics of the merchant and scholar she was, but the clean, shabby "best dress" of a poor woman, perhaps one who received gifts of food and clothing in times of hardship from the holy nuns. One arm drawing her back into what safety his tradesman's dress and deliberately inoffensive posture might afford him, Leo Ducas stood beside her. As Theo's eyes met his foster father's, Leo drew himself up proudly. He saluted quickly, then stood firm as if before his Emperor. His jaw was set, his eyes shone, and tears rolled down his face as he watched his son ride off to war.

What need had Theo of drums and banners and singing *barbaroi* when he had *that?*

Asherah held up a hand she had smeared with dust to make it look sufficiently work-worn. She blessed him, while the workers nearby nodded respect at her piety. Only her husband and foster son would know her gesture was not a Christian sign at all. Light blossomed about her, glowing with the dawn, spreading out from her outstretched hand into a sphere that grew and grew until it seemed as if it would swell and ward the entire city.

As the light touched Theodoulos, Asherah's hand dropped as if virtue went out of her. She sagged against her husband for support, and people standing near her murmured sympathy. A butterfly hovered nearby, touched her cheek, then flew away.

Sunlight struck the Horn, turning it the molten gold of its name. Theo turned back to see the city shine as if guarded within a sphere of power, like a pearl Saint Michael himself admired so much that he took it up into his own hand.

Had the Exodus out of the land of Egypt, out of the house of bondage, been this confused?

Theodoulos shook his head. Exodus might have been this hot, but it had been on flat ground—or the seabed—until the children of Israel reached Sinai.

Theodoulos's crippled land sense had made him reel as he stepped off the gangplank and sensed how the land flinched under the heavy tread of this latest interloper army.

One of the Westerners steadied him.

"You weren't on board long enough to get your sea legs, were you?" the man had asked. His Greek was atrocious, but it was something that he'd tried at all.

Theo had grinned at him and turned to help with the horses. They had made a less pleasant trip than the humans—the warriors, families, priests, and the rabble of camp followers and profiteers that inevitably followed any host. Horses couldn't vomit, thank God for small or not so small mercies. Horses had never cared that he was lame.

It was sixty miles overmountain to Nicaea. The route would not have been particularly troublesome to a merchant caravan, especially those of Asherah's family. They had everything of the best. She made sure of that, like her father before him. Joachim had always been kind to him. Perhaps if he'd shown real aptitude for the merchant's life . . .

This was not a caravan. It was an army, and it accompanied pilgrims. This . . . this undisciplined, prayerful straggle would travel as slowly as the slowest among them. Some among them were old, some infants, some poor knights as well as those like My Lord Godfrey, whom all the other *barbaroi* pretended to defer to, who went magnificently mounted. The huge beasts they favored were good for carrying these taller, more heavily armed barbarians; but they went through an unholy amount of water and grain, and the Bearer of God only knew how they'd survive the heat of the Holy Land.

Theodoulos secured his burden and swung back into the saddle. Up ahead, a party of scouts emerged from the scrub oak, passing the engineers on their way to mark the route with crosses. The scouts merged into the line of march, which promptly disintegrated and started shouting as the rumors fanned out.

Theodoulos reined in his horse, awaiting orders. The man who had steadied him at Pelecanum waved jauntily, spurring ahead. A knight of the West he must be, despite the leather-bound volume in one saddlebag. Other knights rode back and forth, attempting to keep order, to close up the column.

The shouting grew louder, taking on a note of outrage and even horror. Theo stood in his stirrups, leaning slightly forward to hear better. He shut his eyes . . . and sagged against his horse's neck. Something . . . something *wrong*.

He edged his horse nearer Tatikios, whom he should be following more closely in any case. The Christianized Turk narrowed his eyes at him.

Go and see. Meaning, of course, *Go and eavesdrop*.

Here the land was rock and scrub oak; but he had ridden in the rain near Cotyaeum where the rock was milky-white.

What were those piles of white up ahead? And why were those armsmen weeping?

A shabby man riding an ox, though he wore sword and spurs, shook his fist at Theo, even as his eyes raked jealously over the fine horse and fine arms that were his.

"Damn you and that twisty gold-buggering liar back in the City! You killed these saints!"

There might be advantage in pretending to be ignorant of the man's speech, Theo reminded himself. He made himself look about vaguely: the Byzantine secretary now in arms and out of his element.

Again, that sense of wrongness twisted at him. It was a wonder his horse did not stumble.

The heaps of white up ahead were not rocks, but bones. Some still bore shreds of flesh. Theo pulled a fold of cloth, desert-fashion, up over his mouth and nose to protect them against the flies that still buzzed at their dreadful feast.

"Jesus wept," said Theodoulos.

Alexius had fed Peter the Hermit's army, clothed them—and sent them off to be slaughtered in the hills. And yet Alexius was the man whom his foster father trusted above all others and who commanded Theodoulos's obedience.

Theo still had nightmares about scurrying through the tunnels of Cappadocia as they twisted in the land's anguish. His mother's anguish. There had been women and children in Peter's army, determined to conquer by faith what *these* great ones sought to take by force of arms.

He dismounted fast, pressing close against his horse lest the beast, which had never seen or smelled death, panic and start a stampede.

Did he really have reasons to guard his life? Ioannes's wife raised his little girl. Asherah and Binah had done their best at the birth; and their best went so far beyond what most physicians knew that it might as well have been magic and (seeing who the midwives were) probably was. Still, his wife had died, and his daughter had been so fragile that they sent him away lest he become too attached to a little one who would die.

We feared for your reason, Asherah had explained much later. It never quite healed *You sent me away.*

The bones up ahead must receive Christian burial. A good thing the sappers had all those crosses to mark the way. They would serve to mark a mass grave as well.

Up ahead, a horse screamed—the full-voiced rage of a warhorse goaded past its limits. Proud of his beast, one of the knights might well pay for his pride with his life without benefit of Turkish arrows. As Theo rounded the bend in the trail, he saw the knight who had assisted him at Pelecanum attempting with knees, hands, and voice to soothe his frightened mount. It teetered perilously near a drop steep enough to shatter man and horse alike.

"Stay," Theo breathed to his mount and dropped the reins onto the ground. In Central Asia, he had had horses that could be ground-tethered.

He walked forward steadily, calling to the stranger's horse, holding out his hands, as if he had brought it the most tender spring shoots to eat.

"Easy . . . easy . . ." Theo advanced further, attempting to reach down into the earth for the sense of calmness that he had always found in prayer.

This is my caravan. He was a scholar, not a merchant, but the instinct was strong, waking the land sense.

The horse could probably feel the earth give under its feet, clods and gravel scattering downslope as it shifted perilously close to the edge. *Steady. The earth is steady beneath you. Steady,* he wished at it.

It tossed its head, whipping the reins from its rider.

If the knight hurled himself clear, and left the brute to its fate, he might well be trampled. Or fall with it.

Theo advanced again. "There . . ." he crooned. "There . . ."

The world narrowed to him and the frightened horse. Ropes of froth spun from its jaws, and dark patches matted its hide.

"Come on back here. Come," he urged. "Nothing will harm you."

God account it to him as a kindly lie.

The horse dropped its head. Its legs began to bow. It could still topple. If Theo caught its reins, it might pull him over with it.

He is of my caravan!

The reins trailed in the trampled earth. Slowly, his gaze never leaving the horse's eyes, Theo bent to retrieve them. The horse responded to his steady pull. Briefly, Theo shut his eyes: *master taking charge, master taking care, safe herd, safe safe—*

Then three other men secured the animal, which stood trembling. Its rider slipped out of the saddle. For a moment, he clung to his horse, either to comfort it or steady himself. He gave it an affectionate pat, opened his saddlebag, nodding with satisfaction as he patted the wad of parchment that tried to escape, then turned back to Theodoulos.

He had checked to see that his book was secure. His *book.*

An educated Westerner. Heavens. And Theodoulos had saved him.

"You repay good with better, friend," said the man in his accented Greek. "I owe you not just thanks, but my life."

"Repay me in Jerusalem," Theodoulos said in the tongue of the Franks he thought most likely to be the man's birth speech. "After we take the Holy Sepulchre."

The cheer that went up at his words nearly staggered him.

So did the clap on the back from a Frankish knight.

"Well said! Who'd have thought one of you perfumed easterners would have a man's heart in you!"

The man Theodoulos rescued dropped to one knee. Theo turned to see whose arm rested as heavily on his shoulder as if they were sworn brothers and whose rough praise still echoed in his ear.

It was Tancred, Bohemond's nephew and commander of this entire column.

You wanted another future, Theo, something commented wryly inside his skull. *How about the favor of a lord of the West as the first step?*

"*Good man!*" *Tancred approved him.* "*An officer?*"

"I have had some small experience with weapons, my lord," Theodoulos replied smoothly. "I am logothete to the *strategos* Tatikios—"

"Speak so a plain man can understand you, Greek. You mean you serve that *Turk?*"

"He enjoys the Emperor's confidence," Theodoulos replied. *And is a better Christian than you are,* he thought.

"So you serve him as . . ."

"Logothete—you would say secretary or clerk."

"My uncle's man Raymond should meet the two of you," Tancred said. "He's forever scribbling away. We could have a whole—what do you call it—scriptorium? on campaign, though God only knows why." Another idea hit him, and he brought it out with the same bluntness. "Are you in orders, then? In that case, should you be brought to the notice of His Grace Adhémar?"

Adhémar, Bishop of Puy, Theodoulos remembered. The Pope of Rome's own legate and confidant.

Almost as big a man as Bohemond, not reputed to be as shrewd, Tancred was: still, Theo judged it best to answer with as much truth as possible.

"I was brought up by the holy fathers in Cappadocia," he replied. "But I am neither monk nor priest."

Another clap on the back almost sent Theo reeling. "Like Rainault here, who stripped the skin off half the sheep in Europe so he'd have wherewith to scribble his history of my uncle Bohemond? Join us tonight after prayers. Eat with us! Drink! You can answer me some questions. With my lord uncle back in Pelecanum"—Tancred pointed with his chin in the direction of Pelecanum and, presumably, the Emperor—"I need some answers."

It would be a lie to say it would be Theo's pleasure, so he bowed deeply and kept his head down as Tancred strode off with a final order to "do something about those damned bones!"

As the turbulence of Tancred's cavalcade subsided, Rainault, Theodoulos, and the others stared at one another, then at the bones that had once been pilgrims. The buzzing of flies intruded on their attention.

"They're not *damned* bones," whispered an armsman. Under the grime, he looked as young, Theo remembered, as he and Ioannes the first time they fought under Leo Ducas's command. "They're practically relics."

"We can't bundle them up and take them with us," said Sir Rainault. His hands twitched as if they ached to write a description of what he saw.

"It's *him*," whispered another knight. "That twisty, crowned bastard. He sent them off to be slaughtered by Turks."

"Hush! That's one of his spies. Do you want him hearing you and running back to his masters?"

"They'll all run back soon enough. Leaving us for the Turks to pick off, like those bones."

"You have engineers," Theodoulos pointed out, ignoring the whispers. "Why not use them for burial detail?"

Engineers always complained they got the hardest jobs. For once, they'd be right.

"Evening prayers any moment now," another man put in. "If they worked by torchlight, we could have that lot buried by dawn."

"It isn't right just shoveling them in, is it?" the armsman ventured, hesitant in company so much above him. "They ought to have a priest."

"Worried about their souls, lad? They died on their way to Jerusalem. If that isn't state of grace enough for you, what is?" Sir Rainault asked, with a kind of rough kindness. "The priests hover about the great ones. This time of day, our chances of getting a priest over here . . ."

"What about you and the Greek?" an older man put in. He was dressed not as a knight, but not poorly either. "You're scholars, aren't you? You can say the holy words over them."

Sir Rainault and Theodoulos eyed each other, doubts of the orthodoxy of each other's faith surfacing like bubbles in muck.

"Come on, sirs. If a word or two's different, the bones won't mind."

"God," Theo muttered, dropping to his knees and trying not to gag.

The fat flies buzzed. *Go away*, he wished at them. *Go back to your master Beelzebub. Die, damn you.*

Astonishingly, the buzzing subsided. *Did I do that? Did I even try?*

The man whose life he had saved eased down beside Theo. "Just gnawed and thrown away, a whole army," Rainault said. He started to spit, then reconsidered. "Lord, shall these bones live?"

"Not before the end of time," Theo muttered. Best not pray in Greek among the Franks. Or in the Aramaic and Hebrew that had been the tongues of prayer he had heard most often since he had joined Leo's household.

Lord, shall these bones live?

A long sunbeam struck the heap of bleaching bones, dazzling Theodoulos's eyes. Perhaps it was not sun dazzle at all, but tears at the thought of his own little daughter, safe in Ioannes's home. What if she had been here, her feet perhaps bleeding on the rocks, her belly swollen with hunger, lost, and frightened in a crowd? *I would die to protect her.* He had almost died in leaving her behind. She would grow up to think of Ioannes as her father, and that broke his heart; but she was safer where she was.

No, it had not been much of a life for these children. The least they deserved now was decent care . . .

A mother's care.

Face in his steepled hands, Theo hid from the sight of the bones. He remembered Asherah, venturing into the Christian burial service for Xenia, his wife, gently dropping a stone upon her grave. Asherah had begged Theo's forgiveness at her failure to save her. His own mother . . . and the mother of God, though: they would serve.

"Here are brothers and sisters of mine, Mother. Take care of them. Please." His voice broke, and the hot tears in his eyes simultaneously burnt and cleansed them.

Heat washed over him, not the fire that had reshaped and healed his leg, but akin to it. He shuddered, or was that another tremor in the earth?

Come and see.

Greatly daring, Theodoulos looked up. The scrub oak that over-hung the largest pile of bones seemed to waver, but that might have been the tears in his eyes. He blinked furiously. The tree shimmered. Its leaves glowed a deeper green. It grew before his dazzled eyes. The network of its roots spread, branching out, covering the bones of children. The tree's crown expanded, the leaves glowing until they shone like emeralds, and the light from the setting sun seemed to dart in patterns from branch to branch.

The patterns grew brighter and stronger, their light engulfing Theodoulos's consciousness.

You could climb that tree, he knew. If your faith and your strength were great enough, you could follow those patterns of light that flashed from mercy to strength up the middle pillar like a trunk that stretched into the heavens and set its roots deep within the earth anywhere you chose, anytime you chose, for on the Tree, time and place became eternally present. Binah, he knew, explored those paths; but she was daughter of their mother, not cast out.

Theodoulos looked up beyond the tree into the heavens, where the earth spun on its axis and the dragon, the tli that spread its wings over heaven and earth, mantled overhead.

Brother! What's happening?

Sister, he thought. As a child, Binah had known truths and secrets toward which all his scholarship had barely enabled him to struggle.

Later, he promised. *I will tell you later.*

She had been right. His *was* the power, from their common mother, if only he had the strength and will to use it.

Theodoulos stared at the scrub oak. Oh, those bones beneath it would live, all right. And his life would be changed. The tree shimmered again, dwindling from the manifestation of the Tree of Life that had dazzled him into a mere scrub oak. But he had seen it change. He had sensed what it could do, and what he could do with that knowledge. And he knew he could call it up again. If he wished to be other than human.

"A miracle!" the older man cried, his voice husky. Prayers rose behind them. Theodoulos blinked again. They did not look upon the oak tree, but at the hillside itself. Where the bones had lain was covered now with soft grass.

Struck dizzy by exhaustion and awe, Theodoulos let himself fall facedown upon the ground like a priest preparing for consecration. He pressed his lips to the earth as if it itself were a holy relic—or his mother's hand.

* * *

Theo laid aside a well-gnawed bone, looked for napkin or basin of water, then resigned himself to wiping his greasy mouth on his sleeve. He took a deeper pull than he wanted on a skin of sour wine.

"None of that Greek swill! You know, they actually put pitch in their wine?" The lord Tancred had approved the wineskin when he received it in his turn. One or two knights rolled their eyes in Theo's direction, but would not gainsay their lord.

The firelight cast reddish shadows on the faces in the circle of feasting men who lounged near Theo. In that moment, they looked their true age, which was less than Theo's for all that his dark hair, sturdy bones—*and decent physicians!* he thought ruefully—made him seem closer to them in age than to Tancred's uncle Bohemond.

"Ho, Herluin! Don't throw that joint away because it's burnt!" Rainault cried, working the words out around a mouthful of coarse-baked bread. "You may be glad of it tomorr—"

He fell silent, as if choking on words or bread.

Theodoulos managed not to raise an eyebrow. Was their progress so slow that they were running out of food?

"I'll take it," Theodoulos offered. It was always best to eat one's fill when one could.

Herluin threw the meat across the fire to him, without the agency of a servant. Considering that the servants seemed even less clean than the nobles, he was relieved. He bit down on the meat, eating as noisily as among nomads far to the east. The knights grinned approval at him and passed him the wine yet again. How they would rise before dawn for prayers and another day's journey, he did not know. But they were young.

He had always been a boy among men, since his earliest days in the monastery at Peristrema, then in Rab Joachim's caravans. He was used to quiet, orderly dinners on the caravan trails or the almost ritualized meals of the homes in which he had lived.

Still, when Rainault held out a hand for the wineskin, hefted it, and laughed at him for the way his last pull at it had lightened it, Theodoulos made himself laugh back.

At long last, he judged it polite to stand, bow, give his thanks, and wander off into the night. The night wind rose up: this far into the mountains, the nights were cold. Would even the red crosses on the marchers' shabby cloaks keep them warm?

His general knew he had to feast among the barbarians; Tatikios would not expect him back before dawn.

The area behind the tents smelled like a latrine, and he moved rapidly beyond it, climbing upslope until the entire camp lay exposed to his vision. He wrapped himself in his cloak and composed himself as if to pray.

Instead, he tried to visualize the Tree he had seen only that evening: its gleaming leaves, its gemlike fruits, and light racing in patterns from one to another, a greater light gleaming overhead. He too was light, he saw that now. He stepped out of the flesh that bounded his consciousness and approached the Tree.

A silvery strand joined him to the dark shell of his body. Well enough. Now for that Tree. As a boy with a crippled leg, he had never taken to tree-climbing.

But it was so simple!

With a thought, he climbed into the patterns of light. They filled him, more exhilarating than wine, and carried him along until he found himself carried up to the Tree's highest branches. Now, he could see not only the camp but the folds of mountains in the land, the sheen of seas, and the gleams of cities and villages, each flickering light a single life, the whole melding into great fires. It would be the task of a life, or several lives, to study this, he thought.

Brother!

The light grew more . . . *vivid* was the only word he had for it.

Binah! You walk this way?

Always, but I am surprised to see you here, after all these years. What . . . ?

Did you see the bones? he asked. *All those bones, scattered on the hillside.* If he had had "hands" in this guise, he would have blessed himself. *I buried them.*

I felt it. So you take up our mother's power after all?

Theodoulos turned his thoughts aside from the question. *How goes it with you, sister?*

Well enough. The little Caesarissa is an apt pupil, when she is not throwing up. Another shrug. *If he—*Binah sent an image of red hair, great height, confidence, and a persistence that she clearly found objectionable—*see if I do not scorch him.*

He has the confidence of his men. If he knew they were running out of food . . .

What is that to me? Our mother's people in the Rhinelands will never eat bread again. The light solidified. Cast out onto the surface of the earth, Theodoulos had been raised in a gentler mode than Binah, who possessed the flintiness of the creature under the earth who bore her and the long, passionate memory of the human mother who had raised her. Cast out, Theo had embraced humanity.

There are innocents here . . .

Innocents died there too. Binah flared at him. *What are these people to you, brother?* Her "voice" was baffled, almost plaintive at what struck a goddess-born as weakness, inconsistency.

Friends, perhaps. It remains to be seen.

More than that remains. Binah's light almost stung. Her light drew back, as if contemplating him. *But you falter; you are not used to this. Return to your body, Theo. Now!*

Theodoulos awoke shivering. He drew his cloak more closely about him, grateful for its warmth and for the fact that several others lay in his packs. Perhaps one of the poorer knights might accept a gift.

He glanced up the hillside. No sign of the Tree remained. He had not expected it: it was not of this world at all. His belly, which was all too much of this world, rumbled.

There might be food enough in the Greek camp. He would tell Tatikios that food was scarce among the Franks. Perhaps His Sacred Majesty could send help.

Why do you care? he asked himself, echoing Binah's question.

I like these people, the answer came.

God only knew why.

13

Theodoulos lightened a packhorse's load.

"What if we made up packs?" he wondered aloud. "We could load up everyone who's not a fighting man . . ."

"Man, you can't expect knights to act like beasts of burden!"

Theodoulos shrugged. Merchants who stood on points of pride never returned from their journeys. Perhaps this horse could survive the day's travel. If not, they would have horsemeat this evening. Stringy, it might be, but it would be food, even if the Franks despised the idea.

Theo slapped the packhorse on the dulled coat of its neck and started forward. Some of the Frankish knights followed his example. They were all hungry. If only Tatikios had not detached him to ride with the Franks . . . *You wanted this post*, Theodoulos reminded himself. *You wanted to succeed. Isn't self-respect worth an empty belly?*

At least, he had his general's promise that his letters would be sent on to Byzantium, where, after passing through many layers of logothetes and spies, Leo would ultimately read them. *And probably that little princess he seems to be so fond of, too*, Theo realized. It might mean favor. It also might mean involvement in a fight for the succession.

Before you borrow trouble, concentrate on surviving this campaign, he warned himself.

"Well," said Sir Rainault, "when we get to Nicaea . . ."

Nicaea had temporarily replaced Jerusalem as the focus of their wants. Nicaea would provide food, treasure, horses, everything an army might want.

"You don't care about Nicaea, friend Theo?" asked Rainault. "Almost as rich as Antioch, they say, or are you so rich, like many of these Greeks . . ."

Testing. Always testing.

Theo flung up a hand. "Nicaea has always been a center of the Church. The Creed. How should I not care? As for wealth, when I was a lad, I traveled east with merchant caravans. I still care more for wealth than I should: not having any, I suppose that's natural."

Rainault laughed. "My lord"—he meant Bohemond—"says that God will favor us if our courage holds. We could come out of this with great fortunes, men bowing to you and begging you to marry into their families."

"I *have* a child," Theo replied to the question Rainault had been too courteous to ask. "A little maid." She was the age of the Caesarissa, who was already wed, Theodoulos realized in shock. Had he truly lost all those years as well as her mother's life?

"You could dower her like a princess."

Theo shrugged. "As God wills."

"Do you suppose," another man said almost to the noisy air, "Jerusalem really is paved with gold?"

"It's not paved with gold," Theo said softly. "But its stone has gold flecks in it."

"You've seen Jerusalem?" How strange to see these large, scarred men widen their eyes like children offered rare gifts.

"I served a priest," he reminded them. Let them think he went on pilgrimage.

"Watch out!" The packhorse stumbled to its knees.

"Tell us of Jerusalem," Rainault asked. The other knights clustered around. For now, a tale was as good as dinner—but for how much longer?

The packhorse died that day. They ate it that night and, the next day, pulled their belts tighter.

"My lord Count!" Rainault cried. Like a much younger man, he colored up as Bohemond rode past. *He* had never missed a meal, Theodoulos thought to himself. Easy enough, when Butumites rushed up supplies to the Westerners, for Bohemond to claim as much of the credit as he could. Traveling more slowly, some of Butumites's forces brought up the Emperor's own siege engines.

Now Bohemond paused near Rainault, who had resumed his tasks as the Count's historian.

"You," he said, shocking Theodoulos. "I saw you at court."

Theodoulos bowed in the manner of the Franks.

Bohemond nodded, his blue eyes shrewd. "My nephew Tancred speaks well of you."

Theodoulos felt himself flushing at the praise and at his companions' mutters of agreement.

Bohemond drew breath. "I've just ridden back from the head of the line. Beyond this bend, you'll see Nicaea!"

Joy erupted as if Nicaea's gates already lay open, the Sultan's treasure laid out in glittering heaps. Despite the narrowness of the path, Bohemond made his warhorse rear. And then he was off again, taking all the color and the light in these mountains with him.

Now their way sloped down, a much gentler way than the path they had climbed. For the first time, Nicaea's basin and the city itself lay before their eyes. Built by the Byzantines on Roman foundations, the city had walls easily forty feet high, with . . . "My God," muttered Raymond, who rode with Theodoulos, "there's more than a hundred towers."

Four great gates, closed now, stood at the city's compass points. Half of the city's walls were further defended by a double ditch, while the other half was guarded by the vast Ascanian Lake. Nicaea's west wall rose like a cliff from its bank. To the east, the basin widened into a wide, gently sloping valley. To the north, the land rose sharply.

"Boats," breathed Rainault. "We'll need boats."

"At least we've got siege engines," Raymond commented.

Alexius had tried twice before to take Nicaea and failed both times. *He hasn't given us much in the way of reinforcements to take it for him, has he?* Theo wondered.

"Master Theo!" shouted Rainault as Theodoulos rode away from the Greek camp outside Nicaea. "Where in hell is Khorasan?"

"It's hellish enough come high summer," said Theodoulos. Here it was only late May. "Khorasan's to the east. Way to the east as the caravan trudges."

A train of baggage carts lumbered into camp. Now he saw bags, baskets, and a cart, much like the ones that held supplies. This one, though, held coils of rope that spilled over its sides and cluttered the trampled ground by the catapults. Some of the men-at-arms had crammed themselves into scaled leather shirts that Theodoulos iden-tified as armor belonging, or formerly belonging, to Turks.

Theodoulos raised an eyebrow at Sir Rainault. "Why worry about Khorasan, in the name of God?"

"You must have slept like the dead, man," Rainault told him. "Didn't you hear? We ran into a Turkish relief force, little army of jokesters, you could say. They had this cart, filled with rope to tie us all and take us to Khorasan as slaves."

"I gather you frustrated their plans," Theodoulos said.

"My God, can they shoot! Arrows flew like sleet! We took some of their bows, and I only wish our bowyers could match them. Battle, after all this time, and you had to miss it."

Theo shook his head. He must appear to regret it too. "Least you can do is tell me what I missed." He dismounted and joined the Frank in yet another leisurely surveillance of the city's walls.

"The Count of Toulouse . . . bless the man, his troops held like iron. The Turks attacked, and his people took the brunt of it. Those archers! They ride light, wearing almost nothing in the way of armor and those little round shields, but they can shoot at anything and not miss. My lord Baldwin Count of Ghent was killed."

Rainault crossed himself, and Theo followed suit. "Still, we won," Rainault added cheerfully. "And we killed a *lot* of them, see?"

He kicked over one of the baskets. Heads, black-haired, blood-smeared, staring-eyed, goggled up at Theo, buzzing with flies.

"That'll teach them not to make jokes," he said.

Theo made himself punch Rainault on the arm. "A victory in-deed. I wish I had been there, but my lord had commands for me."

He wished some way could be devised to speak without breathing.

The sight and stink of the rotting heads—on top of sweat, horses, and the dung of an army—made his gorge rise.

He gestured. "I wouldn't have thought knights would bother taking heads," he observed.

"My lord Bohemond plans to cap the Turks' jest." Rainault laughed grimly at his pun. He gestured at a distant, gleaming figure, which set spurs to horse and raced toward them. With a leaping dismount and a shout, Bohemond was at their side.

"Master Theodoulos wants to know why we collected the Turks' heads, lord," Rainault asked.

"No one jokes with me," said Bohemond. "Not about my men's lives. I'll give them something to laugh at. Save out a few of those heads, some to stick on spearpoints, and a few for the Emperor at Pelecanum to thank him for the food. He's got perfumes enough to cover it if they get a little high in this heat. But we'll keep the cream of the joke for ourselves."

He held up a mailed fist. "Are you ready, men?"

The roar of assent echoed off Nicaea's high walls, scarred now from bombardment.

"Load catapults!"

Men formed a line, tossing heads from one to another. They were lighter than the catapults' usual shot.

"On my command." Bohemond's eyes glittered with mirth. "One . . . two . . . NOW!"

Some of the heads splashed into the moat, while others smashed against the walls; by far most of the loathsome shot fell inside the city. A cry of sheer horror rose up from within.

Bohemond dusted his hands. "Next time, they'll think twice before they jest with me. It is an affront to God."

Did he even know the difference any longer? Judging from the look of worship on his men's faces, some of them had long since forgotten.

Theo had heard stories from Hind of great hooded serpents whose gaze could entrap their prey. He gasped a little as his own eyes met Bohemond's wide blue stare. He could fall into that bright expanse and, if he emerged, it would be as Bohemond's creature, not his own man.

Why try to charm me? Theo wondered. The answer came in a moment. Theo was a Greek, high in the favor of men close to the Emperor; therefore Theo was to be won over. He had probably tried that with Binah as well, with the added reward, if he succeeded, of her womanhood.

No, Theo thought. No. And yet, the force of the man's belief in himself drew like lodestone or amber rubbed with silk.

Within the city came the sound of bells and semantrons.

"Let them pray," said Bohemond. "We will crack those walls like a nut."

"Sir, those are Christian churches," Sir Rainault ventured.

"Heretics," Bohemond cut him off. "Like our friend Master Theo here. They will learn the right of things, and if they do not . . ." He patted his sword. "Now, just because you're out of heads, don't let those catapults stand idle!"

Men leapt to his command; and Bohemond leapt to horse.

"Think of what I said, Master," he ordered Theo.

"May I ride with you, my lord?" Rainault begged, eager as any squire longing to prove himself. "I will need to see, if I am to write a history of your deeds."

"*Our* deeds, by the grace of God," said Bohemond. "I'm riding toward the south of the city to check on the Kneeling Tower. Our sappers have been huddled under their tortoiseshell for days now, gnawing away at its foundation. It could collapse any hour now. Ride with us, Master Theo. See what men of the West can do."

It was threat, then, as well as seduction. Theo bowed with the same degree of formality as he would have accorded Bohemond in the Emperor's palace.

As they rode toward the tower, the earth trembled underfoot.

"So, boy, soo . . . easy . . ." Bohemond soothed his dancing, lathered horse. "You see how busy they are?" he ordered. "That tower will fall by sundown!"

Again, the rumble within the earth. Not the sappers this time, but a kind of counterspell, binding land and stone, the work of nature and mankind, together.

Bohemond was an optimist, surely. The tower would not fall by sundown. Sooner or later, however, it would fall.

His officers dismissed, Tatikios stalked about his tent, then turned to transfix his secretary with a glance as sharp as a Turkish arrow. "You saw this throwing of heads over the walls?"

"I saw, sir." Theodoulos ordered his pens, his cake of ink, his notes as precisely as if he were an Egyptian scribe.

"Barbarians," snapped Tatikios. Then he grinned. "But *useful* barbarians. They shouldn't have carried those ropes with them: God punishes overconfidence."

God, Theodoulos wondered, *or Allah?* Orthodox, Tatikios was, but he was Turkish-born, and the fatalism that was in his blood occasionally emerged.

"That prank will serve us well, not just with the Sultan, but with the emirs and the city garrison. As supplies run short, they will be afraid. The sultan, riding back from Melitene, will try to protect his city and his family. The emirs within will seek to save themselves and what they have." He barked out laughter. "And we will let them."

"Can we stop the Franks from sacking the city, sir?" Theodoulos asked. He had read enough history to know how naive his question sounded, but what one read and plotted out on a map and what one saw hurled over city walls were two different things.

"If they break through the walls, no, we won't be able to hold them back," Tatikios answered. "Yes, I know, His Sacred Majesty certainly has shown his trust in us. Any more trust, though, and we may not come out of this alive ourselves. Which is"—he turned from a highly questionable line of reasoning—"precisely how the emirs within the city must be thinking too."

Theodoulos knew he must look like a fool. Tatikios sighed.

"We know that the Christians within are ours," he explained. "Now, let's work it out. You!"

He snapped the word at Theo.

"Yes, sir?"

"You are, let's say, a Christian in Nicaea. Who would you rather have rule you, a pagan Turk"—the general's grin was sardonic—"or the Emperor of the Romans?"

"The Emperor, of course." Theo could respond to catechism when he heard it.

"Very good. Take it one step farther. Now, let's say you have not one but *two* Christian forces. You're Orthodox. Whom would you wish to surrender to? Other Orthodox, or these oversized barbarians who throw heads—even enemy heads—over city walls?"

Theodoulos nodded.

"We must move fast." Tatikios took another turn about and came up close to Theodoulos, almost breathing in his face. "I'll know your loyalties in this, Theodoulos. Ducas spoke for you and the Emperor gave you to me, but you like these people, and that troubles me."

Theodoulos hoped the sweat that broke out did not show. "They're brave. They've treated me like a friend."

"Ha! They are not kin. I will know where your loyalties lie, or, so help me, maybe your head will be the next one to fly over the city walls."

Theodoulos drew his dagger. Lamplight gleamed in the watery patterns of its steel: the blade had belonged to Asherah's father Joachim, but Theodoulos had borne it more than twenty years. "If you distrust me, why wait?" he asked.

Tatikios snatched up the dagger. Theodoulos braced himself for the stroke. Then the *strategos* cast the blade down upon a table, laughing as the fine metal twanged.

"Because you have powerful friends. And because," he cleared his throat, "I like you. Let's admit, we all have weaknesses. But, swear on your mother's soul you will speak of this to no one, or you will not leave here alive!" he commanded. "And," he added, "you will never know what our plans are."

A punishment, clearly, worse than death.

His mother's soul? Tatikios didn't know what he was asking. Theodoulos blessed himself. "I swear," he whispered.

"Let them have their towers and their catapults, their toys. We have *minds*," he hissed. "You know that Butumites is bringing boats up overland—oh, nothing large, but big enough to carry troops across the lake? His Majesty has told my colleague that there are those within Nicaea who will open a gate. It won't be anything huge, but it'll admit more supplies and *our* troops. Let the Franks attack—when they scale the walls, they will find our banners flying from them."

Theodoulos laughed. "If they die of the shock, who will take Antioch for us?"

"Ha!" Tatikios clapped him on the shoulder. "We shall see. Actually, you'll be the one to see it if you ride with these people as you're supposed to."

That was news to Theodoulos. "All the way to Jerusalem?" he asked.

"If you are spared," the general said gravely. "You have leave, if it grows too bad, to seek rescue from your family's caravans."

"The Jews don't think they're my family, sir." Theodoulos hated himself for sounding sullen as a boy. "Not anymore."

"Don't be a fool. You broke bread with them for twenty years. You were practically raised by a princess in their tents."

An odd turn of phrase, that, Theo observed.

"If the Jews serve the Emperor, what would they not do for you?"

What they did. Whisper. Look coldly on me. Turn away.

"Did they actually turn you out? They were angry, frightened, and it made them unkind. Would the lady Asherah turn you away after caring for you all these years? Would she let anyone else?"

Theo's eyes flared, and the general grinned whitely in the shadows. Tatikios was still Turk enough to know he should not be speaking of a lady of another man's family.

"I was sure that would get a rise out of you. I need to bind you to your service."

"How?"

"I know of that family that took you in, you see. I know *much* of them, including the lady whom you call foster mother and the one who is a sister to you."

In a moment, Theodoulos would regret that the general had not struck him down with Joachim's dagger. "They serve the Emperor."

"*They serve the Emperor,*" Tatikios mimicked him. "You're playing for time. The Emperor trusts his boyhood friend. I trust his boyhood friend. It is not every man who turns down what might have been a road to the diadem, as your Leo Ducas did. But I have more eyes and ears than in my head, and I turned them loose in Cappadocia.

"You know what I found, don't you? Knowledge."

"It is generally known," Theo parried, "that my foster mother and her daughters are scholars as well as merchants. Her son is even a physician in Alexandria."

"They are *mages,*" whispered Tatikios. "They have *powers*. And your lady sister serves the Caesarissa, too. Do you think they know what she is?"

Binah says the Caesarissa is an apt pupil. Theodoulos would rather have died than confess that. He picked up his dagger, looked at the patterns in it as if they spelled counsel for him.

"Whom do you plan to use it on? Me? That is treason. Yourself? Suicide is the deadliest of sins. Put the knife away, Theo. Put it away. I seek but to know how much of this . . . this scholarship you share."

"I have no aptitude," Theodoulos whispered. Then, because he feared Tatikios in this mood, he added, "Or very little."

"You were there when the bones of that first rabble-army changed. You are no dullard, whether you happen to believe that or not. You have access to knowledge that I need and that I will have. I need *you,* a Greek who does not look at me and see a barbarian. So, dullard or not, you are about to return to school."

He glanced at the Damascus steel Theo held. "Put your blade away," he repeated gently.

Tatikios poured wine from a pitcher into two battered cups.

"Drink it down," he advised. "Never saw a man need a drink more."

The wine had resin in it, Theodoulos noted as he gulped it.

"Can you use this . . . this knowledge to send messages?" Tatikios asked.

"Now, I can."

"I may need that of you. To Pelecanum. Or even Byzantium itself. Your ladies are clever; they can think of a way to pass a message on, if need be."

"I beg you," Theo interrupted, "leave my kinswomen out of it."

"Your family cast you out, did they? You act as if they hate you. And then you beg *me* to spare them? Not very consistent, are you?"

Theo could only shake his head at Tatikios's ruthless logic.

"Have some more wine. Lord have mercy, I'm sorry to have given you the scare of your life. I'm not going to betray them to the priests or to His Sacred Majesty. But I need to use you, use you as miners take tiny birds down into the pits with them to test the air."

"And if there's magery about, I choke and die, is that it?"

"If power's about—thaumaturgy or a village witch's spells, I don't care which—you guard yourself and tell me! My lads are already talking spells and djinn, as if they're any guard against good engineering.

"I heard a story, Theodoulos," said the general. "Before you joined up with Ducas, you served a priest, didn't you, in Peristrema? And you had to bring him out of there?"

Theodoulos nodded.

"The place was full of raiding parties. How'd you get through? You rode fast and lightly armed. I know that. But I would wager my immortal soul, that wasn't all you did—was it?"

Father Meletios had been afraid. He had all but begged Leo not to make him use powers he hated and feared. Theodoulos had helped tie his beloved old master to his saddle, had trembled as power crackled from his hands and voice and light itself had twisted to shield them.

Theodoulos looked down. "I can't do what he did."

"I warrant you can learn, a bright man like you?"

"For the empire, yes," said Theo.

Tatikios smiled again. "And for your kin. Learn this, and you will be one of those who enter Nicaea with Butumites. Your reward will be great." He held up a hand, forestalling Theodoulos's angry protest that he needed no reward.

"Think, man, of how many lives you can save!"

"How long do I have?" Theo asked.

"I hope you're a quick study. Until moonrise."

Theodoulos rose and saluted the general, civilian though he was.

"Ah, you wish to be dismissed, do you? Where do you go now, Theo?" asked the *strategos*.

"To school, sir. Back to school."

He let the tent flap fall behind him and stepped out into the night. A wind blew down from the mountains, for once mercifully devoid of the stench of siege and camp. It eased the burning in his eyes. The stars seemed to dance in their orbits. Again, a gust of wind, and the sky darkened, as if some vast wingspread overhead had blotted out the light. The stars were gone in an instant. Shouts rose from the Frankish camp. There would be talk around the fires.

Theodoulos headed back to his own tent and the knowledge he had dodged for far too long. Sheer panic, as well as the wine, made it hard for him to concentrate. When trance came, though, it struck hard. His spirit erupted from his flesh onto the Tree, the light piercing it as though it were, in truth, fire and pitch. He made his need into a cry of distress and knew when Binah jerked upright in her bed—was she alone?—then settled back.

Bend the light, came her voice. *Bend it. Shape it around your hand, and remember.*

He thrust his "hand" into what appeared to him as a pool of brilliance. Yes, he could still see it. With his other hand, he reached for the light and heaped layers of it over his hand until he could no longer see it: the light *bent* . . . and cast him from the Tree back into the body twitching and muttering on his cot.

A lamp burnt down nearby. He filled it to try again, in this world. The flame leapt, grew bright.

Taking a deep breath, he plunged his hand toward the fire and twisted his thoughts—just *so*. When he withdrew his hand, he saw nothing. *Couldn't have all burnt off, or I'd have felt it,* he told himself.

Now, try without the fire. Even the little princess can do this.

Moonlight. Starlight. Even no light at all. Staggering from the effort, Theodoulos lay back down to rest. He had, the *strategos* said, until moonrise.

A silent guard beckoned him out. Butumites, dark-cloaked, waited for him in his general's tent. As they hurried toward the city, Theodoulos prayed and cast the light about Butumites and his men. All about, Franks hammered, shouted, swore, and prayed—but saw nothing.

He was sweating by the time they reached a small, secret gate. The gate cracked open, and they entered Nicaea. He could hear chanting from the churches of the city. God have mercy on the souls within them. The people who knelt, sobbed, and prayed were the ones who would suffer if this plan failed. Up those stairs, past that ramp. Into that basilica . . . no!

"What . . . what's that?" cried a soldier, passing and seeing a shadow, but no body. He leapt, drawing his blade—but Theo had seen him, had drawn steel, and cut him down.

Blood gushed out, and a body that had been living just moments ago sagged, kicking faintly against him. *He never saw what killed him.* He eased it gently to the pavement and signed it with a blessing.

Outside, the sappers continued to scrape away at the city's great towers. But the true conquest of Nicaea had begun.

 14

Seven weeks into the siege, the Kneeling Tower finally collapsed into the moat. The tumult of its fall was drowned by the cheers of the men who had brought it down.

"We did it!" Sir Raymond shouted, clapping Theodoulos on the shoulder.

They must know I report to my general, he wondered as he always did. *Why do they welcome me?*

They like *you, fool of a brother.* Words that he had not expected almost spun him around. *My princess heard of you from your general the Turk and attempts to question me. I say nothing, of course, and she tolerates it—or no more lessons.*

Again, the ground rumbled. Men erupted from beneath the tower as if freed from the Pit. What was that story he had heard once from one of the islanders who had come East to take oath? Dragons, found beneath a cave, a red and a white, erupting overhead? Were they the tli, its benign and its malignant aspect, writhing around the world's axis? He needed Asherah to tell him, but Asherah had turned her back on him, on all Christians . . . The earth underfoot grew unsteady, and Theo reeled.

"Master Theo, are you all right? Theo?" Rainault, his particular friend among the Franks, was supporting him, trying to ease him to the ground. "Damn them, did they—"

"Something I ate . . . a touch of fever . . ." Theodoulos lied clumsily. He accepted wine that tasted of old leather.

"Sometimes siege work gets to you like that." Rainault forestalled his apologies. "By the time we reach Jerusalem . . ."

Would they truly bring down the high walls of Jerusalem, the navel of the world? He blessed himself and saw the others copy the gesture in their heretical way.

"Ah, we'll make a proper Christian out of you yet!" Rainault said. "Look you, Count Bohemond's been to approve the work!"

Bohemond, his fiery hair matted to his head with sweat, strode up from the ruins of the tower.

"Dawn," he said, drawing out the word as if planning a tryst with some much-desired lady. "We attack at dawn. Now," he said, his eyes transfixing Theo's, "you will see. If you want, you may ask your general if you can come with us."

Now that was an honor of a sort that Theo could have done without, but fatal to refuse it.

Spurning the cot that a general's secretary might claim in his master's quarters, Theodoulos wrapped himself in a cloak and stretched out upon the earth, his hands pressing against it, his face turned to the sky.

No dragons flew, but the stars were very bright. Could he trace in them the pattern of the Tree? Lightnings exploded within his eyes, and his spirit rose, joining the flow of energies on the Tree, from mercy to severity to the high road between them, until it found itself at the uppermost branches. Theodoulos dared a glance upward, then shrank down, dazzled by even the hints of a white brilliance he knew he could not bear yet.

You claim to like these people, brother? Even after what you've seen and facing what you fear?

Binah? You here?

I sensed the earth in pain, Theo. The light did not as much dim but turn barbed. Theodoulos stretched out his awareness, down into the violated depths of Nicaea's foundations. He sensed Binah's fury: very like the creature who had birthed her.

That creature, manifesting under the earth as a stone image with pulsing gem for a belly, had been his mother, incongruous and terrifying as the thought was. Binah: he had taught her songs and wiped her face. He had marveled as she grew into a towering beauty, glared at young men who came too close, and learned to withdraw before her towering rages—*perhaps for too long.*

Hold off your earthquakes, sister mine. There has been enough loss of life.

More than enough, came Binah's "voice." *Like it or not, I take a hand now.*

As I have done?

The light sizzled, almost striking him.

Watch.

Again, he extended his awareness to the city walls.

Thus.

He shuddered as Binah—he had no words for it, even in this state between heaven and earth—wrested energy from that whiteness overhead he dared not fully contemplate, thrust it along the patterns of the Tree, and out along its roots into the wounded land.

Be thou whole! her thought was.

There! His sister's voice was weary, but content. *Did you doubt me?*

Never. What shall you tell the little Caesarissa?

He "heard" weary laughter. *Oh, she has spies of her own, better far than I. You shall tell her yourself, perhaps.*

Theo rose and stretched. Voices rose in the camp, hymns, prayer, gradually replaced by shouts. At first, the shouts were sheer exultation.

Theodoulos ventured from the tent. Not even the forest of siege towers could conceal that the Kneeling Tower stood again, stronger and taller than before. Rainault spotted him from afar, gestured, and hurried over.

"The boats!" someone shouted from the Greek camp. "Butumites broke up the blockade!"

The sunlight made the Ascanian Lake flash as if its bed were filled with mercury, not water. Drums beat and trumpets pealed as the ships sailed forward to assault the sheer city walls. The ships bristled with flags, each flying as many banners as it could to make it seem as if more ships than the small fleet that the *strategos* Butumites had had carried, with effort almost as agonizing as the construction of the pyramids, from the City.

Someone howled frustration at the ships. Hearing it, a sailor turned and dropped his drawers in contempt.

"Like to take a shot at him," Rainault muttered. "Right up his . . ." He glared at Theodoulos. "Did you know anything about this?"

Theo managed a shrug despite the armor.

"What everyone else did."

"She ran!" the commander of a "wing" of cavalry exulted. "Put not thy trust in princes. Or emirs. Or barbarian counts."

"Do you ride with us?" Rainault asked.

"I must beg permission." Theodoulos raised an eyebrow as he headed toward his *strategos*.

"I thought you were a great one for hearing all the news, Theodoulos," Tatikios said. "Last night, the sultana fled the city. She had a fast boat—a wonder it didn't sink, with all the gold she'd piled on it. Butumites is sending her to Pelecanum. Let the Emperor dry her tears."

Likelier, Theo mused, the task would fall to whatever ladies were present. What would the Caesarissa Anna make of a sultana, and how would Binah explain that "Helena Ducaina" could speak with her?

That was not his problem. He explained his problem to the Turk turned *strategos*.

"Ride with the Franks?" Tatikios asked. "Good work, man!" He slapped Theodoulos on the shoulder—high favor, signaling him to go forward and take the place Tancred held for him.

"They've got *mages* there! Demons!" someone shouted.

"Oh hush, man, they've got nothing of the sort."

"They're all sorcerers," the man persisted. "How else . . ."

"Must have worked on it all night," one of the Byzantine engineers muttered. "Christ, they're *good*."

"It's a filthy cheat," Theodoulos heard Lord Tancred mutter, his hand on his sword hilt.

From within the city came the sounds of thanksgiving.

"By God, they'll pay for that," snarled the count. "And soon." He showed his teeth in a grin that reminded Theodoulos of stories of tiger hunts in Hind.

As if belying Tancred's boast, the walls bristled with Nicaea's garrison, making a brave attempt at holding out.

"Kilij Arslan"—Rainault butchered the name, if not the sultan— "can never return in time. What are they waiting for?"

"Forward!" the command came.

"*God wills it!*" roared from thousands of throats, as armed pilgrims started forward. The sunlight glinted off the grappling hooks of the towers. Not much longer, not long now . . . *Kyrie eleison, christe eleison*, Theodoulos prayed; nor was he the only man whose lips moved in prayer. He was glad his helm concealed most of his face, lest his prayers be mistaken for trembling lips.

The front ranks stopped. Stopped dead, Theo would have said, except that the men stood in their positions so that some of the next ranks bumped into them.

The drums and trumpets rang out from Butumites's fleet, to be joined by clamor from the walls. Overhead, banners rose, flaring out across the dawn sky: purple, the *Chi Rho*.

The banners of Imperial Byzantium flew over Nicaea.

"What a cheat!" Tancred shouted. "What a stinking cheat!"

15

Anna, daughter of Alexius, scowled. *Her father's health was far from strong, yet now he must prepare for a battle of wits (if you could call it that) between the Empire and its great enemies. She put a final touch to the herbs and salves she thought he would need. She should be grateful to the herbs, she thought ironically. They were, after all, the only reason her father saw for her accompanying him to Pelecanum: kind nurse, dutiful daughter.

Although the Emperor at times ringed Anna about with such restrictions that she felt as if she had escaped the prison of the palace for a prison in this camp, campaigning agreed with her. As a woman, she would never be a general as an Emperor should—as an Emperor must. But a woman who would rule must understand the ways of the armies.

You will not like being on campaign, her mother the Basilissa had stated. *I do not.*

Of course not, Mother, Anna thought at the absent Irene. *If a convent would allow you to rule and wear purple, you would be perfectly suited.* It was a wonder that Irene and the Emperor had ever had more children than Anna—a pity that they had.

The pestle with which Anna had been grinding herbs suddenly slipped in her hand. She laid it aside and breathed deeply. *Care for yourself, take your rest, eat as I require, and I shall not tell*, her dictator of a companion had warned her. If her father knew—never mind Nicephorus Bryennius, Anna thought, with her usual pang of guilt at having to dismiss her husband—he would pack her back to the City, and she would *never* be free again.

She much preferred the excitement of the camp. Why, only days ago, the sultana of Rum had arrived with her children, under heavy guard. Anna had won praise by coming forward to take her by the hand and offer her hospitality. Anna spoke no Arabic, the Sultana little Greek: thank God for Binah. Still, Anna would be relieved when the Sultana and her children were sent back to Constantinople until they could be ransomed. The Blessed Virgin only grant that she was not sent with them.

"Daughter?" Only one man in the world would call to her that brusquely. Anna ran out to help her father seat himself, to fuss about him with goblets and offers of food, warmer clothing, servants, until he waved her offers aside, smiling.

"So good to me, daughter." Alexius smiled at her, and she smiled back. Why could he not see that, of all his children, she understood his mind and his plans best?

"Don't stand too long," she warned him. "And don't let those fool barbarians lure you to walk or ride out to see what they consider a prodigy. They are twenty years younger."

Except for Count Bohemond and the Count of Toulouse. Both of them were practically laws unto themselves.

"Babes in arms, daughter. Like you, yes?" Alexius's dark eyes warmed as he teased her. She would have tossed her head if not for the heavy earrings she wore. Alexius preferred that she dress to suit her station, especially now that she had the care of the sultana, the Emir Chaka's daughter.

"Why not come and see me follow your orders?" Alexius asked her with a mock salute.

"May I, Father? Oh, thank you!" Grateful; guileless—that struck the right note. Her father grinned like a much younger man. Another pang struck Anna. Her husband would be glad of such a delighted response and seldom earned one. Still, when she presented him with the diadem, perhaps he would forgive her; and if not, it would not matter.

At least, Anna had her reward for good behavior. She could accompany her father, and all would see her stand behind his chair: Caesarissa Anna, a favorite, if not the heir. How prudent she had been to dress suitably.

Prudent? Alexius's gaze upon her turned skeptical. He had found her not so much prudent as predictable, that look told her; yet it pleased him to indulge her. She let her smile turn knowing.

"Both of us must keep our wits sharp," she said.

She smoothed her face into the feminine equivalent of a Caesar mask and put up her chin. Escorted by the usual Varangians, she followed the Emperor to where the pilgrims from the West awaited. A quick glance showed her Helena Ducaina, companion, spy, and God only knew what else standing protectively between the Emperor's warriors and the sultana.

Leo Ducas slipped into the huge tent. He might sketch a bow in the direction of his august cousin, but his eyes were all for his foster son, returned alive, thank God, from the victory at Nicaea. Anna liked her outcast cousin, his thoughtfulness, even his willingness to descend beneath his station and serve as a kind of aristocratic quartermaster.

Anna stiffened her spine as the Franks crowded in. They seemed to stride, to sprawl, to take up more than their share of room, causing the Romans, trained to more decorous courts and camps, to draw in as if under a siege of their own. And they were so noisy with their comments and their needs for constant translation. Her father arranged his best beneficent smile upon his face, and spoke.

That much gold for Stephen of Blois? The man was practically made of gold, and her father had just added a veritable mountain to his store. He had his hands between her father's almost immediately and would, Anna thought, have done far more had no one been watching and had it been required.

Leo Ducas caught her eye and winked. She supposed her father knew what he was doing. (It were better, Binah had commented that morning while brushing Anna's long black hair, to keep this Stephen's wife, the princess Adela, daughter of the English king and the power in that marriage, happy: and Anna had sighed in envy.)

"Oath?" the lord Tancred asked. "I have taken oath—to my uncle, the Count Bohemond, and I shall serve none other. But"—he gestured at the pavilion in which they now stood and grinned, showing surprisingly well-kept teeth—"let the Emperor fill this tent with gold and give it to me, with as much more gold besides as he has thrown to all you others, and I shall put my hands between his and be his man."

"Sir, this is hardly how one speaks to the Emperor!" her cousin Georgios Palaeologus exclaimed.

Tancred erupted from the knot of Franks, strode over to Georgios, seized him by his fine silk robe, and shook him.

Somewhat to Anna's surprise, Leo Ducas started forward, shaking free of his foster son's grasp.

Looking half amused, Alexius rose, one hand going out for attention or to stop the two men from fighting. With the other, almost imperceptibly, he signaled Leo to stop.

Watch this. The lesson was for Anna, too.

Keen as hounds in at a kill, Franks and Greeks watched Tancred pummel the shorter noble. The Varangians tensed and drew close to their Emperor. Binah turned to reassure the sultana, but need not have bothered: she was royal, and her control held. Anna rested a hand on the back of her father's chair where she could touch him. His heartbeat was strong, steady. Well enough. Let the charade be played out.

The knot of Franks parted. The muscles of her father's back relaxed as he sighed in pure pleasure, as if a contest on which he had bet was won.

Count Bohemond stepped forward, drawing the light in the pavilion with him.

"Fair kinsman."

Tancred half turned, his hands still digging into Palaeologus's arms. Bohemond strolled over to him, as if the two of them were alone.

"Who equipped you for this pilgrimage?" Bohemond asked in a voice of deceptive moderation.

"You, my lord."

"And to whom do you owe service?"

"You only, Uncle."

"Then, sir," said Bohemond, "release this man." He dropped his voice almost to the purr of a great cat, but Anna had no doubts at all that he meant his words to be heard by Frank and Roman alike. "If I do not scruple—"

That is the truth of it, Anna thought. *Bohemond has no scruples at all.*

"—to give my promise to the Emperor, our benefactor, I hardly see why you should object." He put out a hand to rest on Tancred's where it had bunched the fabric of Georgios's robe at his throat. Although he had reached an age when many men thought themselves too old for active fighting and Tancred was in his prime, it was the younger man who dropped his eyes. And his hands.

Palaeologus fought to keep his breathing level. He smoothed his silks, while his eyes smoldered with resentment.

"You will . . ." Bohemond ran eyes over Tancred, who bristled. Clearly, the older man reconsidered what might have been his demand that Tancred apologize. "You will take the oath—after me. And you will hold it in the same regard in which I hold my own oath. Is that understood?"

Tancred nodded. Bohemond knelt, recited the oath as easily as he would have swallowed cool water on a hot day, and accepted Alexius's thanks—and gifts—with composure. A hand on Tancred's shoulder, Bohemond brought him before the Emperor. The hand tightened, emphasizing, but not actually to the point of coercion. Tancred knelt and held out his hands for the Emperor's and the oath. Give him this much: he managed to force out the Latin and the Greek words with less sullenness and more grammar than Anna had expected.

Some of the Varangians remained tense. One actually *growled* at the Franks. Alexius turned his head slightly, and the man fell silent.

Conversation eddied away into the familiar bargains: how much gold for this one, how much gold for that one? How much gold did the Emperor have to lavish on these people? It had been cheaper bargaining with the sultan.

"I must see to my guest," Anna murmured to her father. "Do you require me?"

Alexius gestured indulgently. He had almost forgotten her already. One of the guards detached himself from attendance on the Emperor, to follow her—guarding, watching, or both.

Deftly, Anna made her way through the crowd, which parted before her. Nothing showed yet; nothing would for months, given the concealment of the heavy court robes she wore. Binah had cautioned her to expect backaches and unsteadiness as her balance shifted, but she still felt as lithe as a girl. A girl with a secret, with many secrets, only one of them being the child. *If I am not Emperor, perhaps a son . . .*

Or even a daughter.

Binah eyed her as she approached. Anna shook her head minutely. Nothing hurt. Simultaneously, she and the Sultana greeted each other. Anna supposed she would have to return with this most unwelcome hostage and spend time admiring her children. Royal children—as her own would be. She eyed the woman with somewhat more interest, and the Sultana brightened visibly.

The Varangian nearest her beamed approval. She had listened to them often enough to know what they appreciated in great ladies, whom they called weavers of peace. Well, if silk was the province of the Gynaecium, why not peace? Anna held out her hand for the Sultana's, to lead her away.

A shadow fell across her path. Binah stiffened, and the Varangian stepped forward, not beaming at all now.

Count Bohemond laughed. Binah glared at him, curling her lip and turning her shoulder in disdain.

"Call off your watchdog, I beg, Caesarissa. Both of them, I should say."

You should not, Anna thought and held her ground. She found her eyes were at about the level of some incomprehensible device or other on the Count's chest and reluctantly raised them to meet his, which shone with admiration. Humility, even.

If the Count is sincerely humble, surely the Resurrection must be at hand.

Bohemond smiled the surprisingly charming smile that had won him so many followers, even his sullen brute of a nephew. "I have forced my kinsman to swear to your father. Does that not merit thanks? Will you not give me some token of thanks?"

Nicephorus had asked for nothing beside her prayers—and her acquiescence in their bed. She had managed more, and he had been happy, or at least as happy as he ever was.

The sultana's attention seemed caught by this byplay. All the Muslims loved songs and stories, the more improbable the better. *He is your* enemy, *fool,* Anna thought at the veiled woman.

Binah actually fidgeted, eager to be away, eager to be away from Bohemond, Anna realized. How tall they were—one golden, one dark—and how well matched. Her mouth quirked up in mischievous speculation. Her breath came more rapidly; some hazard of her condition, she imagined.

Behind her, her father rose from his chair: best she leave with him, and these ladies with her. But he stood where he was, and his conversation with some of the western "princes," as the uneducated called them, drifted into talk of strategy, the lands they would cross, the enemies they could expect, and how best to fight them.

She turned to go. The count Bohemond remained in her path, visibly awaiting a reply. She could not leave without appearing to snub him, and such a snub would be—just as he calculated— disastrous.

What did she have on her person that she could spare? A jewel was too much and too personal. What did the stories recommend? Ah! She had it now. She produced a gauzy square of silk, so fine that the light shone through it. Bohemond smiled into her eyes so directly that Anna could not help but flush and look down. Shyness would hardly do, however: she made herself look up and meet those fierce blue eyes, which regarded her intently. He received the token from her hand with a bow lower than he had accorded her father, backed away several steps in mock-homage, and withdrew.

Binah stiffened, and the Sultana's dark eyes crinkled with amusement. *He acts as if he is chosen to rule this land,* Binah had told Anna once.

I wonder, Anna thought. *She is so divinely tall, so beautiful, for all she dresses almost like a nun: I wonder, did he try to back her into a corner and manage only to offend her? It would be like him.*

Only Bohemond would be madman enough to try—and warrior enough to escape unmarred, she thought. Now Binah glowed with her anger like some giant amethyst held to the noonday light.

As herself, as Binah, the taller woman would be the Count's natural enemy. As "Helena Ducaina"—why *had* Binah never married? Certainly, she had opportunities enough, especially if she did not insist on a man of the highest family or greatest fortune. Binah, of course, said nothing: like keeping company with a caryatid when her personal affairs were mentioned—except her resentment of Bohemond.

"You gave him *purple*," Binah hissed at her. "Purple of the finest quality."

Anna's belly chilled. She laughed, high-pitched and unsure, like a fool of a girl. Not a wife. And certainly not an Empress.

"You return to the City at His Sacred Majesty's command?" Theodoulos asked. There was no appeal from such a summons.

Leo Ducas shook his head. "Not even at the little princess's. Her behavior, by the way, has been exemplary, has it not, Binah?"

His foster daughter shrugged. "Some folly at today's court with the red Count," she said. "He outmaneuvered her and, rather than snub him visibly, she gave him a token."

Leo sighed. "He is wily, that one."

"Will you not ride with us and keep an eye on him yourself?" Theodoulos asked.

Leo Ducas chuckled, busying himself rolling documents too important for him to leave to even the most trusted of his servants into neat tubes and packing them away. He took up a letter, his fingers almost caressing the bleached parchment.

Gently, Theo's foster father folded it and slipped it into his clothing against his heart.

"My foster mother is well?"

"She wants me home." A smile of relief and love took ten years off Leo's age.

A light had emerged from the rubble after the earthquake. It had been Asherah, improbably wrapped in gold brocade, decked with gems, and carrying a child whose amethyst gaze was both ancient and ageless—just as it was now. Leo had run to her and embraced her before everyone.

Theodoulos looked away. So long as Leo's world held his Asherah at its core, all was well with it. Her fury at the massacres in the Rhineland, which had reached out to encompass all Christians, had hurt Theodoulos, but it had stricken Leo more severely than anything since the betrayals at Manzikert. He had lost more than his freedom and an Emperor at that battle. He had lost faith in his entire world until Asherah restored it to him.

Thank God Asherah had at least reconciled herself to Leo. Theo had always had a half-awed, half-admiring regard for the lady he called foster mother—she was a Jew, and therefore strange; she was Leo's wife, and therefore to be cherished. It could not have been pleasant for her, as a young wife, to acquire a foster son less than a decade her junior and one, worse yet, who had been raised by monks. He loved her as if she had been his own mother.

But then, it was somewhat difficult to love an idol beneath the earth.

Leo met Theodoulos's eyes. "Tell me, if your wife were alive, tell me truthfully that you would not do anything to obtain her forgiveness and her trust again."

Theo shrugged. That grief was old now, more a memory of pain than the open wound it had been.

"I would do anything," he said. "If I could go where my heart is, it would be with my daughter in Cappadocia."

She would be ready to think of marriage soon: God forbid she turn into a hoyden like Binah—regardless of how much Theo loved his sister. He was surrounded by turbulent women.

"So go back home!" Binah challenged him. "Ioannes is doing a fine job as deputy, but you are *family*."

"Family?" Theodoulos felt his eyebrow go up as cynically as any noble's, bred to court intrigue. "They cast me out. They cast . . . I have two mothers who threw me aside, then, don't I . . . sister?" he asked. "And reasons for loving and forgiving both of them. It is not *they* who bar me from our home. Besides, think of it . . ." His eyes lit as he remembered the longing in Rainault's eyes as he had spoken of Jerusalem. "To reclaim the Holy Sepulchre . . ."

Binah shrugged. Reclaiming the Holy Sepulchre did not interest her in the slightest, save as it impinged on what *did* interest her—the lives of people she cared about and the welfare of the land itself.

He turned again to Leo. "You could be of such service if you rode with us."

"Who is 'us,' son Theo?" Leo asked. "Tatikios or . . ."

"The *strategos* wants me to ride with my lord Bohemond's men. I have made friends with the count's . . . he is not his secretary, but a knight who is lettered. All Rainault's heart is fixed upon Jerusalem."

"The more fool he!" Binah interrupted. "Why must you squander yourself on these fools?"

"They are strangers in a land strange to them."

"Good!" she exclaimed. "Then let them go home."

"But I can help them." Theodoulos felt himself turn pleading. "I know the routes, know the languages, I can ease their way. And if any on the caravans remember me, I can even—"

"They will slaughter you for being a spy!" Binah exploded. "What if they turn on you?"

"I grew up among men and women who turned on me," Theodoulos retorted.

"You like these people," Binah accused. "You *like* them."

Whatever she was, she was too self-assured by half. She had never been cast out and orphaned as he had been. Loving arms had received her from her mother . . . their mother. She had all the flinty nature of the creature who had borne them both.

Binah had worshiped him when she had been a child, but had speedily outgrown her adoration and damned near everything else.

"Aye, I like them," Theo conceded.

"How can you? Look what they did to your mother!" Binah flared up.

Asherah is not my mother, not really. And she's not yours.

"Who held your daughter at her birth? Who closed your wife's eyes?" she went on, seeming as always to read Theo's mind. "Your mother!"

"Binah . . ." Leo tried to cut in. "My child . . ." Even when she had defied Asherah in the turbulent years when the girl-child transformed herself into a woman of such spectacular, dangerous beauty that she frightened them all, her father had always been able to bring her around.

"It's different for me," Theo mumbled, half ashamed. "I was older than you when I . . ." He gestured, feeling like a youth, not the man only a few years younger than Count Bohemond himself.

I must find a value for myself, must do something of worth, and I must do it now.

"Don't you see what I have become?" he demanded of Binah. "I fit in every place, and no place at all."

"What makes you think that *these* will not turn on you?" Binah retorted. "At least, our mother's people did not slaughter innocents. Don't you feel how our mother, the earth, cries out under their feet?"

The violet of her eyes deepened, and Leo reached out, drawing her against his shoulder. They were almost of a height.

"My child, my child," he whispered to her. "How often have I spoken to you about building bridges?"

Her glare cut across Theodoulos's: *Yes, and see what it has brought you.*

Leo shook his head, extending his free arm to touch Theodoulos on the shoulder. "I won't have you fighting. Outside our family, all is chaos—"

"And inside?" Theodoulos interrupted. "They cast me out. How if, next, they cast *you* out?"

"Theo, be quiet!" Binah snapped. "That is your anger speaking. Our father has deserved better than you would ever—"

"Both of you, stop it!" Leo ordered. "Right now!"

Binah and Theodoulos faced off, their eyes flashing. Binah's anger was dangerous: rocks had a way of falling, walls of cracking.

"I beg you, no more. I do know what you love me too well to say. I build bridges. Let me tell you about bridges. Being what you are, born of what you are, you will understand me in your very souls. You build a bridge with stone and mortar and sweat and, more's the pity, the lives of your workmen. It is not enough to set a keystone in a bridge. It was not even enough to secure it, as they did in ancient days, with a blood sacrifice. You cannot build a bridge unless you are willing to hurl yourself, a living, hurting human keystone, across the void to complete the span."

"And so they undermine you or ride over you," Binah complained.

"I have built my bridge. And my faith is that it is all worthwhile. Asherah shares my faith. We have tried to bring the children of our bodies up in it—"

"They are out of harm's way!" Binah cried.

"Shoshonna is in Jerusalem even as we speak. If what Theo says is true, it is a city that may soon receive an army that I do not trust, I do not trust at all.

"I offered to send you away, child of my heart. You would not go, remember? The time may come," Leo told her, "when 'harm's way' could reach out and touch the entire world. If that time comes, we will need all the bridges we can build. Are you with me, daughter? You, Theo?"

"I love you, Father," Binah said. "I love you. I think you're wrong, but you have set me this task, and I will not prove false to it."

"There's my girl!" Leo said and kissed her hair. "Daughter, daughter, there is an Empire to be sheltered . . ."

"Beneath that, there is the *land*, and only the land."

"Close enough," he said. "You should go and pack. Help the Sultana. There is a bridge of sorts for you there as well as with the Caesarissa. Kiss your brother, now; don't let him set out on his journey with the two of you still angry. Come, do so to please me!"

Binah obeyed, but only just. Her lips on Theo's cheek felt like polished stone. She flung her arms about Leo once more, and then she was gone.

"My son," Leo asked, "you are truly resolved upon this?"

"Tatikios has asked for me. And there truly is a welcome for me among my lord Bohemond's men."

"Then," Leo said with a heavy sigh, "God help you. You know the family codes and signals. We shall all pray to see you safely home."

Tears prickled in Theodoulos's eyes. "You understand, don't you? I have to have something of my own, make something of myself."

He had always thought his foster father looked like a sadder version of the Roman fighting saints, and never more than now.

"It was easier for me," Leo said gently, "being so much younger. And my Asherah—praise God, my Asherah lived. If your heart had waked again . . ."

Theodoulos flinched.

"I think we are all riding the dragon's back, no one more so than my Emperor, but like Binah, I have a land to protect."

Theodoulos dropped to his knees. "Bless me, Father?" His voice cracked as it had not since he was fifteen and shouting in his first battle. Leo's fingers spread to cup Theo's head, bowed for the holy words.

"I thank God for you, son," Leo told him. "And I will thank God again if He spares you. God send that the world's navel prove not the world's trap."

"Amen," Theo said and left. He knew Leo stood looking after him but dared not turn around.

16

Summer became a torment as Theodoulos and his strange friends ascended to the high plain of Anatolia. Ridge after ridge they climbed, as if ascending wave after wave of a harsh sea preserved in stone. After crossing the Sangarius, they struggled across a magnificent desolation—rock spires, cliffs, silences, grass browned by the late summer sun—that reminded Theodoulos of home.

"This blanket's worn thin," Rainault said. "I can't imagine being cold again—let's leave it."

Theodoulos shook his head. "Even in high summer, the nights get cold. Keep it."

They lifted the saddle from the horse whose foreleg had snapped. With the saddle strapped on his own back, Rainault walked alongside Theodoulos, who led his mount.

"What happened to your black?" Rainault asked.

Theo shrugged. "I gave it away."

"Gave it away? You *gave* away a perfectly good horse. Theodoulos, you've been out in the sun too long."

"I gave it to a lady. Saw her trying to help along two children, so I dismounted and put the children on the horse. She thanked me, and I found another mount."

"God's own mercy that you did, or you'd be walking along with your betters, you know that?"

Theodoulos snorted.

"Not much eating on this one."

Horses died; knights died; and those men unhorsed inherited from them and rode once again. The poorest of the pilgrims had begun to die: the children born on the journey, the eldest come merely to lay their bones down in holy land, and those too ill to withstand the hardships of a land so different from their own.

"Ho! Rainault! What happened to your horse?" said Raymond of Aguilers.

"Broke its leg," said the knight.

"Does that mean we're finally rid of your endless scribblings?"

Rainault showed his teeth, remarkably fine for a man from the West. "The Greek here offered to carry my writings. You'll thank me when we're famous all over France and Italy."

"I'd thank you both," said Raymond, "if you had some decent wine. Or some indecent wine, for that matter."

"Don't let my lord Bishop Adhémar"— someone signed himself—"hear you say that or he'll declare another fast."

That provoked a groan.

"Greek, you had a black horse, good enough for a count. Now you're walking that nag alongside us. What happened?"

"He gave it away!" Rainault said. "To a lady."

In the eddy of laughs, suggestions, and resentments that followed, he whispered to Theodoulos, "Do you recall her name?"

"Adela," Theodoulos said. "She said she was some sort of niece to the Bishop."

Rainault walked in silence for awhile. "Tall for a Greek, but not a Frank, light-haired, plain?"

"Name of God, man, I didn't study her face!" Theo burst out. "Those children wouldn't have made it till sundown."

"No offense meant." Rainault waved a hand, thinner than it had been and ink-stained as usual. "I know who you mean. Old Berenger's daughter. Bastard, I think. He named her after the child of William of Normandy—another bastard, if one with a crown . . ."

"Better not let anyone else hear you say that."

"Anyhow, this Adela's named after the King of England's daughter, not that she got much in the way of baptismal gifts out of it. She's a widow now, I think. Married to . . . oh God, these damnable heights blow the name out of my head. She signed over her lands when she came east with her uncle. Probably, she'll take vows. Did she say?"

Theodoulos shook his head. What the lady had said was closer to "Well, Greek, are you going to ride like a prince while these children stumble and die?"

"She should stick closer to her uncle," Rainault said. "Otherwise someone might mistake her for—"

"I don't think so," Theodoulos replied. "She had a sword. And quite a way of looking after herself."

"I'll believe that if she lives to see Jerusalem. If any of us do."

Jerusalem was all their dream, but they had a nearer goal: Antioch, and on the way, Dorylaeum.

Before the army had split asunder, Theodoulos had observed Godfrey of Bouillon, austere, unlike his brother, now intriguing with the Armenians (and much luck might he have, Theodoulos hoped, with that shrewd, ancient people), but prone to outbreaks of violence. He had countenanced the slaughters in the Rhineland. Then, there was Stephen, too indolent to ride without complaints; too proud to make them; fond of his wife and writing to her—quite under her thumb or some worser part of her frame. Alexius had paid him, but would he stay bought?

Theodoulos had knelt once nearly at the feet of Adhémar, the lord Bishop of Le Puy, during these Westerners' heretical Mass.

The land they struggled through seemed deserted, although air and land prickled with expectation. The only other time he had had such a sense that something was coming, lightning had seared through a clear sky and struck the ground. Tatikios's scouts had seen Turks. Worse yet, they'd learned the raiders were led by the Sultan, returned to claim his own, and that he was reinforced by the Danishmend emir he had been off fighting.

Some storm indeed.

Even you *have enough land sense,* Binah had flung at him.

How can I sense anything with this crowd about me? he asked his absent foster sister. God only knew what she was up to, or the Caesarissa. At least Leo was happy. Perhaps when they reached Antioch, there might be letters brought from the ports, reminding Theo that once he had had a home and family.

"What do you think of this ragtag?" Tatikios had snapped at him only the night before.

"I wouldn't call fifty thousand people ragtag," he had said.

"You've led caravans. If this were in your charge . . ."

Leo had overstated his credentials: Theodoulos had never quite led a caravan of his own. But he knew the answer: too big and too scattered.

July 1, and they were nowhere near the fortress. Armies traveled far more slowly than caravans, it seemed. Too slowly. They could be surrounded and cut off.

"Up ahead." Theo pointed. "Rainault, you wanted to see green grass. There you are!"

"A river, praise God," said his friend. "Maybe we *will* all live after all."

"Not if you drink the way you did at the last one," Theodoulos scolded. "Camels can drink enough to hold them for weeks in the desert, but that can kill a man. You saw."

"Theo's croaking again," Rainault commented. Amiably, several of the Franks croaked back, and Theo made himself laugh. The time might come when they would be glad enough to eat frogs.

"I heard from Fulcher that he and Ralph saw Turks a few hours back," a man muttered.

Rainault unstrapped the saddle from his back and tossed it aside. "I suppose I'll find another one day."

He laid hand on his sword. "Better look to your own weapons, Theodoulos. Are you ready to fight?"

Theodoulos shrugged. His armor was good enough, though he suspected that the Turkish bows could pierce it.

Now he could hear the screams—*Allahu Akbar!* plus the howls and shrieks that were the Turks' first weapon and that could panic an entire army.

"Make camp!" one man shouted.

"Here comes my lord Count," someone shouted.

Armored and helmed, Bohemond rode his laboring horse past the line of march. "You on foot, pitch camp now! The rest of you, follow me!"

Theo slapped Rainault on the back. "Take my horse."

The man's eyes lit, then narrowed, and Theo could read them before he slammed his helm upon his head. "You're a trained knight, and I'll fight better on foot."

Rainault shook his head. "Crazy Greek."

"Up with you!" Theodoulos helped boost him into the saddle. Rainault reached down and clasped his arm for a minute. "God be with you."

"You too."

Theodoulos slapped the sweating horse on its flank, and it leapt forward. He turned to the task of pitching camp in a hollow square, then helping bully the troops and dismounted knights into some semblance of a battle line. At least the marsh afforded protection along one side of the camp.

They waited. "Like sheep waiting for the slaughter," Fulcher said.

"Now, who's croaking?" Theodoulos snarled. Surely the Turks

would pick off the stragglers first, then perhaps the messengers he had seen dash off to the main force. You didn't send a fighting man as a messenger in this country: you sent a boy, a light-armed man, burdening the horse as little as possible. *He* should have gone, twisting the light about him until no one would see.

He turned, as if a horse would suddenly appear and let him mount and redeem himself by a mad dash to fetch aid. He saw the women rushing to fetch water, kindle fires, assemble what supplies and arms they thought the fighters might need. One woman burst into tears and plucked at her dress, attempting to twitch it into some better array.

"Think they'll spare your life if you're beautiful?" came a voice Theo remembered. "What do you think they'll spare it for?"

Adela slapped the woman, then shoved a pot into her hands. "Fetch water," she ordered. "And when you're finished, don't even think of hiding. I've got my eye on you."

Spotting Theodoulos, she waved a cup, then ventured forward to offer water to him and the others standing guard.

"Where's my horse?" he asked.

"You gave it to me," she replied reasonably enough. "And I passed it on to one of the messengers to my uncle the Lord Bishop."

A prudent woman, one with her wits about her, witless as she was to venture this far forward . . .

"Here they come! It's the Count . . . They've been driven back!"

"Ambush!" came the cry, followed by a wail from the women and children who lacked Adela's resolve.

"God help us." Theodoulos blessed himself, not caring that the pilgrims saw him do so in orthodox wise. He pushed the woman away. She dodged him nimbly, seized her vessels, then withdrew.

Knights and Turks broke through the ranks of guards into the camp. Theo's sword was wet to the hilt, and his shield arm ached. At least the archers had no room to draw.

Like a fool, Theo tripped over a discarded helm—no, it had not been discarded, it still had a head in it—and toppled. The footmen leapt over him.

"Get up before they ride you down!" someone shouted at him.

A rumbling beneath the earth. Oh God, had it too rejected them? Nordbriht had shown him how to listen to the earth for hoofbeats; and now he heard them.

"They're coming!" he shouted. "The Bishop, the princes—they're coming!"

The line re-formed and braced itself for the next attack. Up from the river darted the quickest of the women, bearing water to the men on foot. Some of the boys followed, carrying knives.

A volley of arrows, and at least three of the children fell.

"Get them back!" Fulcher cried. He had lost his helm. Tears and sweat streaked the grimy mask that was his face.

Bohemond and Robert had regrouped their knights before the camp and hurled them forward, counting on the Western horses' greater size. A Turk turned to flee on foot, pursued by a knight. The Turk turned, shot the man, and as he fell dying from his horse, darted forward to take it.

Arrows sleeted from the camp at the Turkish horsemen. "See, they're not the only ones who can shoot!"

Had all Alexius's advice, all Tatikios's warnings gone unheeded? Would they all die because of *stupidity?*

Now, the knights were massing before the camp. Heavy cavalry, if it made itself the smallest possible target and stayed in formation, could disperse Turks—but for how long?

"They're coming!" Fulcher screamed. He fell to his knees so abruptly that Theo seized him to look for wounds. But Fulcher laughed and wept and pointed. "See there?" he asked.

Light erupted from the rounded hills, blinding the men fighting in and around the camp. Many in camp fell to their knees, praying and weeping in thanksgiving. No more, surely, than the last rays of sunlight striking polished metal, Theo reasoned. But it was hard to hold to logic when the men around you were bawling about the appearance of the Archangel Michael and when a bishop in full armor appeared at the crest of a hill.

Again, the light flashed. Some fool screamed St. Michael had ascended into the sky to combat the great dragon.

"St. George and St. Demetrios!" came the shouts from Tatikios's troops. Wheeling, they turned to reinforce the bishop Adhémar.

As the Turks turned to face this new menace, Adhémar charged straight at them. Again, the Count of Toulouse pressed forward—and the Turks fled.

"Follow my lord Archbishop!" a knight shouted.

"God wills it!"

"Uncle!" Adela's voice was higher than the rest, which was how Theo must have heard her. From somewhere, she had acquired helm, sword, and bloodied armor of the cheapest sort. Theodoulos grasped her by the shoulder.

"You're not going out there," Theodoulos said. "Get back, or we'll waste a man making sure you're safe."

"No one's safe," she spat. "I did not come on pilgrimage to be *safe*. I came for Jerusalem!" Her eyes flamed with the light that Nordbriht's transformations had taught Theo as a lad to distrust.

Do something, he ordered himself. The light. Yes, that was right. He drew breath, summoned what little he could remember in this uproar, reached up, and *twisted* the last remaining daylight into a shield far wider and subtler than those that mere armies used.

"Angels . . . they're here . . . they walk among us . . ." gabbled a footman with a wounded leg. He screamed as someone pressed forward and stepped on him.

"You're more use dragging out the wounded," Theodoulos told Adela.

"Be a good wench . . ." Then Fulcher turned and saw to whom he spoke. "Lady, your uncle would put the ban on us for risking you. Get you back!"

"It's my right!" Adela flared.

"And those children you saved? My black horse?" Theodoulos shouted. "You owe me. Get *back!*"

Normans, he heard, loved a bargain and even honored some they made. Adela withdrew, pulling the wounded footman with her. He screamed to high heavens, and she paused to hit him on the jaw with the pommel of her borrowed sword, then tugged until his body rested on her back and she could stagger back toward the center of the camp.

The battle frothed and crashed about the camp like a deadly tide. And, like the tide itself, there came a point when the waves broke at lower points upon the shore, when their force diminished, and when the roaring of the water subsided. And there was silence, broken only by the plaints of the wounded and the weeping of those whose courage had been strained past bearing until the knights arrived.

Bishop Adhémar rode in, his armor stained a darker red than the cross he bore, and many fell to their knees. His niece—would that woman *never* stay where she was safe?—wept with joy, thanked God, and ran forward to bring him water.

The sickness that had been growing on Theodoulos since the battle twisted in his belly. He staggered, hastening to the camp's perimeter by the marsh. Some of the servants had dug a latrine pit; already, it was foul beyond belief.

"Don't go far, Greek!" an armsman shouted at him. "You're dark enough someone might mistake you for a Turk!"

Laughter.

"Greek or not, he fights like a man!"

"And pukes like a girl or a woman with child, does he?"

Anger slashed him.

Bad enough to fight, Theodoulos thought. *Do I have to listen to these animals equate men with brutes?* Sometimes, the Franks compelled his admiration—and sometimes . . . thank God, the Turks had had no women with them, and that they had not won the day.

The idea of the women and children of their camp the prey of enemies brought him gagging to his knees, his bloodstained hands reaching for purchase in the earth.

Then he heard sobbing.

It is Rachel, weeping for her lost children, he thought at first. It had been a day of prodigies: why not? He rose. Perhaps someone had been wounded and crept away.

The weeping changed to the unmistakable sound of someone trying to vomit.

Theodoulos slipped the cloak he had created for himself and let his footsteps be heard as he drew closer. "Lady?" he asked softly, not at all surprised to find Adela.

She looked up at him, her eyes swollen, her face blotched, her hair in strings: a valiant disaster of a woman.

"First time in battle?" he asked gently. "I heaved my guts up first time I fought."

She breathed deeply, fighting for control. He offered her a bottle of wine mixed with water, safer by far than the standing water of the marsh.

"I've assisted in childbirth," she whispered. "That is bloody. But it's *life*."

Not always.

"By the Virgin, lady, this is no land of milk and honey, no easy jaunt, singing psalms, all the way to the nearest church. Go back home," he urged her. "No one thinks less of you for trying."

"What home?" she hissed. "I signed over my husband's land for gold enough to come. My uncle's protection is on me now: how long would I keep that if I fled?"

"It's different for you . . ."

"I am no soft City fawn, but a Norman, not like that fool I slapped before the battle. An arrow got her. I helped bury her. I managed my husband's lands and did it well. This should be no different. Our Lady stood at the foot of the cross. I can withstand this. I can offer it up. I can."

Her anger had burned away her sickness. She took his bottle, rinsed her mouth, and spat. Then, after a careful mouthful of water and wine, she wiped the bottle and handed it back. "But you have eased me, sir, and for that I thank you."

She started to rise and did not slap away his helping hand.

"I will conduct you back to my Lord Bishop's camp," he said, not offering her the choice. Inclining her head as if they were at court, she permitted his escort through the lines of guards. She even smiled as she thanked and dismissed him.

Neither Asherah nor Binah would ever have allowed themselves to be seen that disheveled, Theodoulos mused, then astonished himself by smiling.

Late that evening, Rainault staggered into the camp, his sword arm crudely bandaged.

"Let's see that." Theodoulos bent to check the wound.

"Never mind the wound. It'll heal or not as God wills. Greek, did you save my history?"

"It's here, it's here. Right with this soft cloth. This *clean* cloth. Now, do you let me dress that wound, or do I turn you over to the women?" Theodoulos demanded.

"I have seen another miracle—" Rainault yawned and sat down with such suddenness that it jerked a grunt of pain from him. "A Greek secretary turned nursemaid. I want my history, Theodoulos. I want it now. Then I'll let you see the arm." His eyes, glazing over with fatigue, turned cunning: a bargain, a bargain!

"Let me write it for you," Theodoulos offered. "You might bleed on the parchment."

Rainault yawned again. "No, no wine till I finish this. God, I could sleep until Judgment Day, and damned near did. You won't like what I have to say, man."

"What difference does it make? If you really wanted this story of yours to last, you'd write it in Greek."

I do not wish to admire these Franks as much as I do, Theodoulos told himself. Wine and water blended stood nearby; he used them to wet the ink—who knew but that it might yield a reddish color?—and began to write, his neat scribe's letters a contrast to Rainault's crabbed, abbreviated hand.

"Write this, then: Of all the warriors in the world, only the Franks and Turks have the right to call themselves knights. They would be right noble, if they were Christians."

Theodoulos laid Rainault's parchments carefully aside. "There it is," he said. "And not in Greek, either. Now, redeem your side of the bargain. The arm."

Rainault extended it. "It's a flesh wound. Bled itself clean, but see for yourself. And you'd better not handle me roughly in return for what I had you write, either."

In the dark, they tended such wounded as they could, more by prayer than by medicine. In the dark, their guards waited in case Kilij Arslan and his newfound ally attacked again. In the dark, they snatched such rest as they could. They would wait to bury what dead they could until dawn.

 17

W e can't eat victory," Rainault muttered.
        Indeed it seemed as if they would eat little else.

Beyond Anatolia rose the mountains. The land seemed bare of life, except for the thornbushes that they could not eat and the brackish water in the occasional marsh that they dared not drink without falling ill of a flux as deadly in its way as Turkish arrows.

"You think My Lord Raymond will live?" whispered one of the youngest knights. His spurs had been shiny when he set out from France. They were bent and dulled now, and he rode an ox.

"The Bishop of Orange gave him Extreme Unction today, I heard. The Sacrament will save him."

Theodoulos blessed himself. The Count of Toulouse would be a sad loss for the pilgrims—and for the Emperor. Tatikios even sent his own physician.

Their horses that had made the mountain crossings died, and many more knights walked, or if they could not bear the thought (or were too ill) rode oxen. Sheep, goats, and even large dogs were yoked to carts until they too were eaten, along with the few falcons that had not flown free.

"I hoped to dine," Count Godfrey commented, stripped to the waist and sweating with pain as his surgeon cleansed the claw marks as best he could, "not to be dinner." The princess of the West put the best face on it that they could: the bear was a sad loss.

"At least, some of the great lords remain with us," mutterings were heard. Theodoulos knew that the Emperor had plotted to use the army to drive wedges into Anatolia and down into the south, into Theodoulos's homeland of Cappadocia.

On a day so dry that some pilgrims walked with their mouths open, hoping for a breath of fresh air, Theodoulos, walking his reclaimed horse beside Sir Rainault, came upon Adela. She knelt over a woman who had collapsed by the side of the road.

"You must get up," she urged through cracked lips. "We cannot leave you here, Alais. Get up!"

"Let us help," Theodoulos urged. Adela's eyes lit, but they were all for the black horse that she remembered.

He and Rainault tried to turn the woman over.

"Alais!" he too called her name.

She struck at him.

"Do not call me that," the woman whispered. "My name is Hagar."

She wore what had once been a grey smock, stained now with dirt, blood, and what looked like fluid at the breasts.

"Alais, I thought . . . you bore the child already?" Adela exclaimed. "I had told you, call me, and I would attend you."

"Before dawn, lady," the woman said. "Why trouble you?"

Tears poured down her filthy face, and she licked at them as they filled the corners of her mouth. "Not to see the death of the child. No . . . no . . . I dug a trench in the earth . . ."

"Sweet Jesu!" Rainault exploded. "How can you bear to touch her!"

Adela's eyes flashed. "And what would you do?" she demanded.

"We could ride back and look for it."

"Him," the woman muttered, her attention drifting.

Theodoulos touched her brow. "She's burning up!"

"Are you surprised?" Adela asked. "You'd give your mares clean straw and water, but she . . . Alais . . . Hagar, this was not right. You know that from Hagar's son Ishmael, God promised that a mighty line would descend."

"Yes," the woman retorted. "And they're killing us. All of Ishmael's sons . . . no . . . no . . ."

With a dreadful compassion, Theodoulos started to lift the woman to the saddle, but she thrust him off, then fell.

"Let her be," Adela said. "I do not think she could bear to sit astride—"

"She will not live out the day," Rainault hissed.

"She will not survive her son," Adela whispered. "And I will not leave her."

"We can't just leave you here," Theodoulos said.

"Leave me the horse." Adela flicked a weary smile at him. "Leave it with me again. If I can persuade her to mount . . . well and good. If not, I shall return it myself. I daresay you knights are used to walking by now."

Adela returned the horse that night. She refused to answer questions. She wept, and Theo with her.

"What is this?" cried an immense voice. All around the fire, men forced themselves to aching feet.

"My lord Count!" Adela gasped, and withdrew somewhat behind Theodoulos.

"You should ride with your uncle, lady," Bohemond told her. "I shall have an escort take you to him. The rest of you, listen! The priests are singing. Sing with them. Sing with all your hearts!"

Bohemond waved his arms as if with the rhythm of the hymns, urging his knights to their feet as he bellowed out the words. Rainault, his eyes bright with loyalty, or perhaps the remnants of a fever, joined in the song. After a while, so did the others.

"There!" Bohemond exclaimed. "That's better for you than tears. Now, I brought a gift of wine. Don't even *think* of tainting it with the wretched water hereabouts. Lady, you shall have some, and then it is back to my Lord Bishop with you."

The Count passed the wine around. He was as shabbily dressed as any knight among the host, except for his burnished sword and a touch of purple, like glass long baked in the desert, from a silken square he pulled from his tunic and used to wipe Adela's eyes.

"I beg you, Count, let me conduct her," said Theodoulos.

"Why? So you can weep together again? I have heard stories about you—Greek secretary fights like a man, writes like a scholar, plans like a merchant, and weeps like the lady here. Ducas, aren't you?"

"My foster father is Leo Ducas."

"I met him at Pelecanum. And so your sister . . ."

Theo felt his spine freeze.

Bohemond laughed. "I meant no harm, sir secretary," he said. "Here! Why do you not drink? Our wine does not suit you?"

Theodoulos shook his head and drank the wine Bohemond offered him. "I did not know if your invitation included me."

"What? Not share wine with a man who has helped my people so? Let all my own knights serve me as well! Why do you weep? Because a woman died? More women will die. Perhaps all of us will die. You've looked death in the face, haven't you, Greek?"

Theodoulos nodded bleakly.

"Then no more of this weeping. More would die without your help. If you wish to lead, you must expect this."

Then I do not wish to lead. He looked up at the vacant sky for inspiration and got only a question in response:

If you do not, who will?

You have that much land sense, Binah had told him.

He fought for it, prayed for it, struggled to wrest or coax it from the earth. And after several nights of screaming nightmares that made him highly unpopular, memories began to wake: which herbs brought down fever or slowed the flow of blood; which, packed into a wound, helped it to heal without the fatal rot you could smell from yards away. Small and homely magics, his land sense brought him, not Binah's instinctive mastery or Asherah's long study of magery. They were more than he had expected; and if they saved fewer lives than he hoped, they helped. Day after day, Theodoulos found himself thanking Bohemond for the harsh comfort he had brought him.

Day after day, these Franks surprised him. They were a stubborn lot, but this was more than one people's refusal to be beaten or the desire of their leaders for victory.

This was faith. Each comet that streaked across the sky, each exhalation of night air, each trick of the sunset was seized on and judged a miracle. The hymns sung each sundown seemed to nourish many of the pilgrims far more surely than the scanty food. Perhaps God's angels *would* descend and feed this tribe of exiles with His manna: it was no more implausible than that they had survived thus far.

And as each one said, it had happened before.

I do not want to like these people, Theodoulos had said months ago. *I do not want to respect them. I do not want to love them.*

Life grew a little easier after Iconium. Friendly villages taught them to make waterskins and sold them food. They even had a few days' rest in Heraclea, after taking the city.

Tatikios reclaimed his secretary to dictate letters to him that could be carried to the Emperor. "There is a pattern," he said, as Theodoulos bent over his writing. The general began to pace as he spoke. "Many of the cities in our line of march have expelled their Turkish garrisons and welcomed us."

He paused, and Theodoulos looked up, to exchange wry glances with his superior. "I have intelligence from My Lord Stephen of Blois that the army there has turned on the Emir Baldajii, called Hasan. Your home, Theodoulos?"

He nodded.

"Let me go on. Write: 'This emir held power in Nicaea before Kilij Arslan retook it on his escape from prison after the death of Malik Shah. As we move toward Caesarea, the man Simeon's advice will become of the greatest help. Should God favor us, we will give the land to him to hold. I have heard Comana is ready to surrender into our hands: may we travel thus far!' "

"Is that all, sir?" Theodoulos asked.

Tatikios paused, as if unsure of whether to reply.

"Make another copy for Caesarissa Anna."

Theodoulos looked up.

"She is very keen on military matters, you know."

And, in case her brother dies or is otherwise . . . displaced, you mean to indulge her, don't you?

Tatikios took a risk in telling Theo this much; he would pay for the information, and the general would pay for Theodoulos's silence. Somehow.

There had to be more news, Theodoulos thought. Tatikios surely had more detailed accounts to send.

Not by your *hand,* he realized.

"Theo, I assume you have letters of your own to send," Tatikios observed. "You may include them with mine."

Ah. The reward of discretion.

"I shall bring them," Theodoulos said. "Thank you, sir."

He assumed that even his letters to his foster father would reach the eyes of the Imperial ladies: probably, that insured his standing with them as well as with the Emperor. As they neared Antioch, if he chose to bypass his general, doubtless he could arrange other couriers for his more private correspondence with Leo Ducas.

You know how you can communicate with Binah, he reminded himself. The family owned ships that, with fair winds, could bring a letter to Byzantium in ten or twelve days. He could reach her sooner.

She would, he knew, trade that information with the Caesarissa for whatever Binah judged would benefit the family most.

Theodoulos shut his eyes, visualizing the energies of the Tree of Life and his sister's presence on it.

"Now," Tatikios ordered, "leave me. Tell my guards to send in the Armenians. And request my lord Robert of Flanders to attend me here. Use all the proper flourishes—you know the terms these barbarians call courtesy."

Such, of course, as he thought they were. Hadn't he traveled with the Frankish army long enough to have more value for them than that?

"You do not wish me to return?"

"I will not want formal records until all the princes meet. Your presence will be a sign of our good faith." Interesting. So Tatikios trusted him as he trusted all his allies—this far, and no farther.

Theodoulos left Tatikios's quarters and tracked down Robert of Flanders. The guards waved him through with a grin—he had splinted the arm of one, and it had not rotted.

I build bridges, Leo Ducas had told him what seemed like years but had only been several months ago.

Father, Theodoulos hurled the thoughts into the night sky, *is this what you would have me do?*

"Mountains of the Devil, these are," Rainault grumbled. "Sweet Christ, will you look at that—"

Someone shouted as a fully loaded packhorse plunged over the edge, taking another one with it. They could not hear when the beasts hit ground.

"Did the groom fall too?" Theodoulos asked.

One of the knights shrugged. "He wouldn't be the first. Damn, we could use those supplies."

"Hush!" whispered Theodoulos. He pointed. "Look up there, the way the rocks are balanced. Move too fast or clumsily, make too much noise, and you could bring it down on all of us." He had seen rockfalls in the eastern ranges that were the very roof of the world. They were instant terror and death: the only thing that frightened him worse than rockfalls were the vast, deadly cataracts of snow toppling down from the highest peaks of the mountains, carrying with them boulders and trees.

"Here," Theodoulos said, pulling a coil of rope from the cart in which he had stowed it. "You may not like Greeks, but now you're going to be roped to one. Let me get a hold on the rocks, then start across."

Sister, he thought. *Binah, have you forsaken me? These rocks are our bones. I should do better than this. Advise me!*

His thoughts were useless as the prayers of the damned: he dared not expend the strength that might let him speak mind-to-mind with his sister or risk leaving it unguarded while he climbed, in heart and soul, the Tree of Life. Any exit from his body might be permanent.

He had his wits. He had his experience on the caravans. And he had whatever land sense he could draw upon. It was more, perhaps, than the others might have.

"Christ, what a land." Rainault welcomed Theodoulos as he made his own traverse. "No wonder you people turn out twisted."

Theodoulos coiled his rope into a neat loop and thrust it into one of the surviving carts. "Remind me of that next time the trail narrows, won't you?"

Rainault actually smiled. "Half the trouble is that even if you *could* kindle fires at these heights, there's nothing to burn," he grumbled. "I'd even be glad of some of those damnable thornbushes. You can't eat them, but they ought to burn well. We should have loaded up before we started climbing."

"There is a solution," Theodoulos said, coming up from where Tatikios and his officers were encamped.

The knights started. "Make some noise, will you, Greek? You move like a cat. Do you still fear bringing the rocks down upon us?"

Theo shrugged. "Rocks or bandits. But if you're looking for something to burn, burn dung."

"Burn *what?*" demanded one of the knights that evening.

"Dung," said Theodoulos. "You Franks all value your horses so much, I don't see why you should object. Good dried dung—in the East, they follow the camels and scoop it up. They say it flavors the food."

One or two of the older knights eyed him to see if he were joking.

Fulcher dropped his head into his hands. "Lord have mercy, five hundred people died today. And more won't see the dawn."

"Fewer would die if they could get warm. Maybe they'd even be able to sleep."

"You fall asleep in this weather, you don't wake up," Aimery, from the south of France, complained. "How did the twelve peers manage in the Pyrenees?"

"They all died, remember? Killed by pagans."

"God, what a country," Rainault repeated. "Sit down, Greek. If we're to burn dung, you might at least get your share of the stink." He actually managed a smile.

"When I was a boy, the man who brought me up told me that when the Children of Israel wandered in the desert—"

"God send we too do not wander for forty years!" cried Rainault, and "Amen!" agreed the others.

"—they were fed on manna. The desert itself was swept and polished the way a careful housewife cleans her platters. And the manna fell like snow."

"Do you think it will snow tonight?" asked Fulcher. It was one more thing to fear.

Each morning, tiny bodies were lined up for the priests to bless. Theodoulos thought he saw Adela once, kneeling on the rock beside them, but the wind made his eyes water so much that he could scarcely tell.

One of the older men had pressed one hand to his chest, gasped for breath, and simply died, unable to force enough air into his lungs.

Some of the knights had abandoned their armor, the better to climb, unburdened. Theo saw several marching as close to naked as possible in this weather. You could count their ribs as they strained for breath. One tall man, skeletally thin, wearing filthy sackcloth, clutched a scythe. The land seemed to shudder beneath the stranger as if it, not his feet, bled at every pace.

Theodoulos stepped forward instinctively, but the stranger's eyes bore such a glare of hatred of all comfort that Theo recoiled again. He did not even check his footing, a folly that could have cost him his life. The madness in the other's eyes showed him clearly that he valued not comfort nor health nor life itself so long as he achieved whatever inhuman goals he set himself. Yet he too sought Jerusalem.

Theodoulos signed himself. The madman loosed his grip somewhat upon the scythe and grinned approval like a grey skull turned over in the waste by a careless footstep. Drawing a deep breath, Theo warded himself.

Rainault struggled up beside him at that moment, panting. Theo forced himself not to flinch at the resemblance between what was almost a friend and that madman. They were both Franks, and if one could so abandon his humanity, then it stood to reason that Rainault, too, who called him "Greek" but guarded his back at need, could abandon it too.

"Never saw Tafurs before, did you?" asked the Frank.

He nodded at the madman, then clapped a hand on Theodoulos's back, as if taking him in charge. The creature gestured with his scythe—why, that was a salute!—and moved on, as if reassured.

"What was *that?*" Theodoulos asked, low-voiced. They had passed the region where rocks might fall: he feared echoes and the keenness of the madman's hearing.

"I didn't think you'd seen them before. First time's always a shock. That was a Tafur, one of the poor of God. Usually, they keep to themselves."

Theodoulos wanted to spit, but decided it would offend the Frank.

"At that, you were lucky. You saw King Tafur. Must have come to speak with Count Bohemond. If they follow anyone, they follow him." Rainault grimaced. "They're shock troops. Useful, in their way."

"*Kyrie eleison,*" Theo whispered. He reached for the flask of wine and water he tried to fill each dawn and found it empty. No point in hurling it away: at some point, years from now, wine and water might once again be his for the asking.

"Water is running low," Rainault reminded him.

"If it snows, we could melt it," Theo pointed out. "At least they'd be able to drink. You can live a lot longer without food than without water."

Day and night blended together. Though he was still able to snatch some sleep each night, it brought him no rest, while the days brought only a return to fear and toil. The ranks of pale bodies, stripped of every rag that might warm the living, grew longer each dawn.

We're not going to make it. When had the counsels of despair sneaked into his thought? It was in the eyes, he realized, of everyone he passed, even the dulled, dispirited gaze of the surviving animals.

That night, a comet streaked overhead. Prayers and hymns assaulted the sky as hopelessly as the army had dared the cliffs, their echoes taunting in the darkness.

Theodoulos lay on his back, staring at the darkness where the comet had so briefly glowed. They were tired. They were hungry. They were frightened. But they believed, sweet Bearer of God, how they believed.

Eyes open to the cold sky, he forced concentration upon himself, marshaled his awareness, and summoned his vision of the Tree. The green and gold and blinding white of it nourished him almost as much as . . . no, do not think of lamb, of bread, hot from the oven, of olives, or cakes dripping with honey. Think only of your needs: for care, for safety, for guidance . . . ahhhh, there the answer was.

Long ago, deep beneath the earth, he had recited that psalm to comfort men temporarily under his care. And they had been healed of fear. Now, he drew strength from the rock beneath his back and fashioned his illusion, robed in white, compassionate of eye, carrying . . . a staff, was it? Or was it a lance? Shepherd or soldier, he hardly knew which: but when his creation looked back at him with eyes that seemed to pity all the world's pain . . . *thy rod and thy staff, they comfort me* . . .

His head spun; he was weary enough that his spirit was almost ready to escape his flesh in any case. He allowed just enough of it to animate the robed figure, and send it walking forward through the camp, regarding all, stopping for none. The figure walked to the head of the long, ragged train, and gestured with its staff, *follow me*, then disappeared into the shimmering lights that had made the past nights frightful. The crowd's exclamations of joy warmed Theodoulos.

He woke to find people kneeling over him, Rainault praying, the lady Adela chafing his hands and scolding anyone fool enough to suggest that "the Greek" be left for dead.

"You saw the joy on his face. You know he saw the Shepherd. He had to. Greek or not, heretic or not, he shares our dream," she said. "That makes him our brother. Now, give me that blanket!"

Rainault held out the ragged cloth they had almost discarded days ago, and Theodoulos was grateful for its extra warmth.

That day, the sun seemed warmer at noon. The night was not so chill. Not quite. Not quite so many died by morning, and their scouts swore on their very souls that their path finally led downward.

In the distance, they saw a valley. After the waste of rock through which they had passed, it was shockingly green, lavishly watered by the Orontes. Rising from it like the image in mosaic of a city being presented by an Emperor to God towered the high pale walls of Antioch.

LATE 1097
THE SIEGE OF ANTIOCH

 18

Adela had managed to transform a small space of fires and plundered carpets into a tiny island of comfort. Beyond her fire, the camp outside Antioch reeked of blood and burning; from her hearth, though, rose the fragrance of food.

"I will never forgive myself for missing the battle," Rainault lamented again outside the walls of Antioch.

"Will this console you?" Adela refilled his bowl with the ladle she had used to indicate the order of her uncle the bishop's battle.

Rainault grinned at her. "Go on," he mumbled through a mouthful of fragrant, fresh bread.

"The Turkish archers shocked our men."

Theodoulos forced himself not to wince. If he allowed his land sense to awake, he would feel every man falling wounded or dead to the suffering earth. He took a deep breath, steeling himself.

"Then, our army made a tortoise." Adela gestured, arms above her head, to indicate the moving fortress of wood and leather used to protect themselves from archers. "And they pressed on until they won the day!"

"Ah, lady!" Rainault stretched like an untidy cat. "A tale of battle that would have done the Emperor Charles the Great's twelve peers proud. And a fine meal too!"

The Lady Adela inclined her head with incongruous stateliness and insisted once again that no one had eaten nearly enough. Theodoulos sighed, remembering his foster mother's opinions about how much people at her table should eat.

She eyed the valley as if it were a keep she must provision. "The harvest is mostly gathered. You wouldn't believe how low prices were for lamb and goat."

"You paid?" Theodoulos raised an eyebrow—a gesture he had acquired from Leo, he realized. Rainault wasn't the only homesick man sitting around Adela's hearth fire.

"Theft is a sin," Adela reminded him primly. "God's army *pays*. My uncle made a point of settling that."

"Easy enough, lady, to strike a good bargain when armed men stand at your back while you count out the coin." Rainault got the words out between mouthfuls of stew, scooped up with slabs of the local flat bread.

"How long before we eat the place bare like a plague of locusts?" Theodoulos asked.

Beyond the camp so quickly thrown up loomed Antioch's great walls, Justinian's work, with their four hundred towers.

"Yaghi-Siyan can quarter a whole army inside those walls," Theodoulos remarked. "And Antioch has water, pasturage, and gardens within."

"You've seen it, Greek?" asked one of the bishop's knights, eyeing Theodoulos narrowly.

"How could I?" he asked. "After the Turks won Antioch by a trick from Philaretus, Yaghi-Siyan held it for ten years. I but know what every Greek knows."

"Antioch," Adela mused. "I don't know what I expected. More holiness and less war, perhaps? Here, where my lord uncle preaches, St. Peter founded his first bishopric, and here we—all of us—were first called Christians. Yet, the first thing we do is plan how to destroy it."

"We are an army of God, lady. Armies fight. But, I beg you, say on," Rainault urged. "After the Iron Bridge fell, what happened next?"

"My lord of St. Gilles urged his men forward to storm the walls," Adela took up her tale. " 'Surely,' he said, 'God who had protected us so far would give us the victory.' "

"Take a fortress like that, worn out as we are?" Rainault asked. "We'd do better to wait for Tancred to ride in from Alexandretta, I'd say."

Eyes skewered Theodoulos. Hopes were that Alexius himself might be on the move, bringing gold and troops and those excellent siege engines that had helped the Emperor seize Nicaea.

Alexius's capture of Nicaea had been the rehearsal for Antioch, the biggest prize of the East—apart from Constantinople and

Jerusalem. Bohemond, who saw himself as a king without a kingdom, must surely crave it for his own.

"You, you over there," Adela called out to some people who hunched staring at her cooking fire, "are you hungry?"

"What brought *them* out?" Rainault muttered.

"You're the one who should know; they serve Count Bohemond, as much as they serve anyone but King Tafur," Theodoulos retorted. Only the cookfires and the fragrant pots masked the stink of six of the Tafur king's subjects.

"Are you hungry?" Adela called to them again. "We have more than sufficient. Here . . ." She jerked her chin at her women. At her command, they edged forward to serve the Tafurs. A two-year-old who had survived the mountain crossing without fear sent up a wail.

Came a wordless shout, and the Tafurs scattered, driven away by a taller man, the light of sunset bloody on his scythe. King Tafur himself, no doubt on his way to confer with Bohemond. The count ruled him the way a man rules a hungry leopard: only while the beast permits.

"All of us cannot together restrain King Tafur." Rainault shrugged.

"It is going to be a *long* siege," Theodoulos sighed.

"I still cannot believe this stupidity," Tatikios complained as November turned chill and the harvests seemed to disappear. "Your precious barbarian horde ate their way across the valley without a thought for winter."

"We're expecting relief, aren't we?" Theodoulos asked. Surely, those letters on the table, weighted by a sword, were from the city.

"Yaghi-Siyan's forays are getting bolder," one of Tatikios's officers said slowly. "I heard Antioch was full of spies, Armenian, Greek, and Syrian Christians, whose rumors made nothing of siege or city walls."

"Urban—after two years!—sends arms and reinforcements. Which our allies cannot feed. Theodoulos, what other news about the Franks?" Tatikios shot at him.

Theo took a deep breath. How much could you tell, without betraying friends? How much could you conceal without proving yourself a traitor?

"They'll have scoured the place by Christmas," he admitted. "Talk is of another foraging party, a big one up the Orontes Valley toward Hama, led by Bohemond and Robert of Flanders."

"Keep your ears open," Tatikios instructed Theodoulos. "Now, off with you."

So he was not to be trusted to know what those letters from the city contained, Theodoulos thought. He took his dismissal with as much grace as he might. Well enough: now that St. Symeon and Alexandretta were open, he had letters of his own from home.

> The Emperor plans a journey to Philomelium, and I (Leo wrote toward the end of his letter) will accompany him in hopes of seeing you, if I do not contrive other means. Doubtless, you have found merchants willing to deal with the camps of what I still consider most dubious allies. There is a man, I am told, he is called Firouz, now that he has made submission to the Turks' prophet: avoid him, as your life depends upon it. The city is filled with spies. Keep yourself safe; destroy this; farewell.

The very handwriting seemed to ease his hunger, whether for food or home, he scarcely knew. It hurt to throw the letter into a nearby fire.

"Spies?" Bohemond's bellow of outrage made him whirl around. The Count strode past him, drawing a trail of armsmen and knights after him.

"Spies? I can use a few spies. I can tolerate a *few* spies. But this veritable plague of spies—it is a plague of locusts, not men, and I will burn it out!"

The camp began to boil like a pot in the long-ago days when pots could be filled so full with grain that some could splash over the rim to be wasted in the fire and no one would lament.

"Bring me out those spies we took!" Bohemond ordered. "And fetch my cooks! Wake the lazy bastards up, I've work for them!"

Theodoulos heard men in the camp begin to laugh, bloodlust underlying their mirth. Tafurs' grey shadows flicked at the very corner of his vision—Bohemond's jackals, if not Christ's.

"Build up those fires!" Bohemond shouted. "Put your backs into it! I want to see you sweat!"

The count stalked back and forth in front of hearths turned almost into bonfires, his hair shining. Bohemond's blood was up and he wore his widest grin. Theo remembered Leo's friend and armsman Nordbriht, a former Varangian who used to turn into a beast at the full moon. He had accounted it a great curse. Bohemond probably would have enjoyed it.

Pikemen prodded the latest coffle of spies forward. Theodoulos shut his eyes in dismay. He knew that man, had traveled with him to Aleppo.

He started to step forward to plead for his old associate, but the man jerked up his chin. *No.*

Oh God, and now Bohemond had seen him, was waving Theodoulos over. He looked despairingly at the bound man. If they stripped him, they would know that he was no Christian. Maybe they would think he was a Turk. The doomed man's lips moved. *Hear, O Israel . . .*

No one would hear in this world. Perhaps he would have better luck in the next. Theodoulos would have to tell Leo as well as Tatikios. Thank God, it would be Leo who would have to water the story down to tell Asherah.

"Two problems with one blow, eh?" Bohemond shouted. "Greek, come stand by me and watch. Tell your precious Emperor how we handle spies." He laughed again. "I learned it from *le roi Tafur*. A veritable *feast* of spies. You, there, Thierry. Cut me that man's throat!"

The armsman stared at his lord, appalled. Bohemond bounded over to him and sent the armsman sprawling. "I am surrounded by idiots! If I want a thing done, I must do it myself."

He drew his knife and bent over the bound spy. Mercifully, his tall body blocked what he did—but not the kicking legs of the dying man or the spurt of blood from his throat.

"Pity you didn't think to bring a pot to save the blood for sausage," Bohemond remarked. "Remember that next time. Now, you cooks, butcher me the rest of them. You know how to dress meat, don't you? When you're finished, truss them up on the spits. Make it fast. In an hour or two, we'll have a feast fit for a king."

"Right," Rainault's voice buzzed in Theodoulos's ears. "Fit for a king. King Tafur."

He spat. "I don't think I *get* this hungry."

Theodoulos shut his eyes. Years ago, his foster parents had watched a general blind an emperor. Could he do less?

"Now, what's the Count doing?" Bohemond had summoned KingTafur. The man's sackcloth, if possible, was ripped more indecently than when Theodoulos had first glimpsed him in the mountains. His scythe's blade was notched. But he had polished it, and his laughter was even louder than the Count's.

"Giving him wine from his own table. What a waste!" Rainault complained. "There's my lord Godfrey. He looks sick."

"Well he might," Theodoulos retorted, speaking low so that the screams of the dying spies would drown out his words. He looked his disgust at Rainault: *How can you follow him?*

Bohemond turned from his grim cookery and roared laughter at Theodoulos's distaste. "So, Greek, you have a delicate stomach? Don't you believe King Tafur when he says spies taste sweeter than pork?"

"*Voici Mardi Gras!*" someone shouted behind them.

Theodoulos shut his eyes on the hideous preparations. Already, the fires had started to crisp the spies' skins as they turned on the spits reserved for sheep and cows, when they *had* sheep and cows to cook. To his horror, his mouth was beginning to water.

Theodoulos's gorge rose: little enough in his belly now remained that he could afford to waste it. He recoiled as someone jostled him: a Tafur, come to crouch near the fire, one of many, waiting.

Tears rose in Sir Rainault's eyes.

After a deed like this, how could they dare think of Jerusalem?

Caves yawned beneath the City of David with its golden domes, dazzling in the sun and the sky, the color of turquoise of Marakanda. Tears rolled down Theodoulos's face. "If I forget thee, O Jerusalem . . ."

That noonday city was not for him. The caves were for him. A beam of sunlight danced off al Aqsa, pointing the way below, bright gold against the paler tint of the stone. He walked downward, the shadows easing his eyes, comforting his soul. He turned to ease the people who followed him, for he was not alone as he had been for so many years. A child perched on one shoulder, a woman whose face he could not see marched at his side. His heart swelled with content to know that she was there. The people looked to him, hope in their eyes; and he was not "Greek," not failure, not weak—but their leader.

The child whimpered with thirst. Setting it down, Theodoulos advanced to the rock and spoke gently to it. Water jetted forth from the sandy stone, and the child put its lips to the rock and drank.

"Wake up, Theo!"

Someone thrust at Theodoulos, and he uncoiled from a cocoon of cloaks and spare garments.

"Yaghi-Siyan's attacked north of the river."

"St. Gilles is up there." Theodoulos struggled his way into his mail. "He'll fight, if they didn't kill him already. Do we reinforce them?"

One last twist of his body settled the chiming rings about his shoulders. He snatched up his sword.

"Why should we?" one of Tatikios's officers shot at him.

"Count Raymond's good," Theodoulos said, running after his *strategos* to where the horses were tied. For a mercy, his was still there. "He's not just good, he's a little mad. What if he turns the whole thing around? They're all crazy, these Franks. Perhaps, sometimes victory needs a little madness!"

With the ease of long practice, Theodoulos hurled himself into the saddle before any of the knights. Tatikios pounded after Theodoulos toward the bridge, which resounded like an anvil in hell from the hoofbeats of Raymond's knights.

Rainault had promised him a sight of knights in full charge, but Rainault was away, foraging with his lord Bohemond. The knights shouted their war cries, their faces hidden by their helms, their voices magnified.

Trumpets and Count Raymond's voice slashed across the tumult of battle. Pale banners flickered like ghosts in the night, and the knights charged once more.

"My God, they've made it to the bridge!" a cavalry officer marveled.

"If we're not a part of the victory, *you* explain to the Emperor!" shouted Tatikios. *"NOBISCUM!"*

Yelling, he rode forward as wildly as any of the Turks who opposed him.

Theodoulos stood in his stirrups. He thought he could see what was happening, a bolting horse, a more general panic—but the stampede had reached him, and he must ride with it.

The Turks shrieked and pressed forward in their turn again.

"A bloody rout!" someone screamed beside Theo.

Another instant, and the man fell, blood spouting from one eye where an arrow quivered.

"Back!" Count Raymond screamed. "Back! *Sauve qui peut!"*

The Turks pressed the Franks until they reached the bridge of boats. Let the Turks burn that, and they might as well turn around and ride home.

A scream went up. *Le roi Tafur* ran out toward the Turks. Immensely tall, thin, he wielded his scythe with the deadliness of the sword he had once carried when he owned name, knighthood, and more wealth than the rags he wore. His followers hurled rocks at the horsemen as they charged. Many fell beneath their hooves, but reinforcements ran up, feet splashing in their fellows' blood.

Some of the Turks fell back in sheer horror before them.

Trumpets and drums erupted. The Turks wheeled, withdrawing across the bridge behind the walls of Antioch.

"Ho!" Theodoulos fought to bring his mount under control, then reined in. He recognized that face, bloodied and twisted with the mortal agony of its defeat: Guy, who had been standard-bearer to Adhémar himself. Dismounting, Theodoulos snatched up the body and flung it over his saddle, screaming for the lord bishop, for his own general, for anyone he knew.

 **19**

D*ay after day, the camp dwindled as death and desertion stalked* outside Antioch.

Tatikios himself had to intervene when Theodoulos lost his temper with a Syrian merchant for his prices—seven gold bezants for a donkey's load of grain!—and drew his sword. "You are beginning to *act* like a Frank," the Turk rebuked him.

"Not I." Theodoulos defied his superior. "I do not desert."

Theodoulos knew some of the knights had laid bets on when the Greeks would withdraw. At least they did not gossip about them in his presence. Not that they could: desertions, as much as fevers, stalked the camp. The man-at-arms who cursed you for a crust of bread today was gone tomorrow, vanished into the countryside, perhaps taking his wife and children with him.

And not just the poor: William the Carpenter, he of Melun, and even the so-saintly Peter the Hermit, fled, to be dragged back by Bohemond. Bohemond kept William of Melun standing all night in his tent before reading him a lecture that, had it been whips, would have skinned him. Theodoulos, there as a witness for the Greeks—and for William's greater embarrassment—could only take notes and read over Sir Rainault's shoulder:

> *We were thus left in the direst need, for the Turks were har-*
> *rying us on every side, so that none of our men dared to go outside*
> *the encampment. The Turks were menacing us on the one hand,*
> *and hunger tormented us on the other, and there was no one to help*
> *us or bring us aid. The rank and file, with those who were very*
> *poor, fled to Cyprus or Rum or into the mountains. We dared not*

*go down to the sea for fear of those brutes of Turks, and there was
no road open to us anywhere.*

Bohemond had no need, at least, to prepare another grisly ban-
quet. A rumor went about the camp that the Tafurs found new uses
for the bodies of the Turks they slew, digging them up from the city's
cemeteries. In obedience to King Tafur's demands for poverty, they
left the gold funeral ornaments with which the men were buried lying
by the opened graves.

"I cannot bear this," Bohemond was heard to remark. "My men
and my horses are starving to death. Out of our whole army, only
seven hundred knights are fit. I cannot bear to see them suffer."

Anna heard Binah's voice, low as a stringed instrument, speaking to
the guards in their own barbarous tongue. Her voice was husky. The
guards spoke in the tones people used after someone had died.

"I thank you," Binah said, effortlessly changing languages with
none of Anna's faults of pronunciation, "and I would be glad of any
news you have."

"You always have our . . ." one of the guards said.

"Yes, I know, and it is good to know." Someone set hand to the
door, pushing it inward.

Heavy footsteps echoed on the stone floor outside.

Binah entered the room. With one hand she lifted the veils she
had worn to speak with the guards. Pale as marble down to the lips,
she held her head "far higher than a woman of her parentage has a
right to," the Augusta remarked rather too often. For all Binah's pallor, her eyes were dry.

Of course, Alexius chose right then to kick and wail. Sometimes,
he could be the most aggravating baby. Anna's maids ran to him,
crooning and exclaiming. One fool brought him to Anna as if she
were what he needed. He needed his clouts changed, that was for
certain. And then he needed the breast.

She felt like providing neither, but she was under observation,
under the damnable constant observation that she had hoped to escape with her marriage, but that had only intensified now that she was
a mother. Yes, she knew what a wonderful mother Irene was. None
better. She knew that Irene had nursed all her own children. Anna
was thinner than her mother, though, and it *hurt*.

"The maid you gave me is packing the rest of the supplies you ordered for His Sacred Majesty's next campaign, Caesarissa," Binah told Anna. "I must also thank you for the guards."

Her voice took on a sort of flinty irony that, as much as Alexius's suckling, made Anna flinch. Binah eyed her.

"You could use some herbs yourself," she remarked.

"The guards were not my idea," Anna said, "but the Augusta's."

Binah raised her eyebrows in what would have been challenge to anyone but a princess born in the porphyry chamber. Anna knew no insolence was meant. Between Binah and the Empress was the most ceremonious deference and scant affection, hostility masked by fine manners. Only last week, Irene had commented that Helena Ducaina (she flinched at the name Binah) had begun to look like a woman of decent background and less like—whatever it was that Binah looked like. Her namesake, perhaps, for whom cities had been sacked.

Word had come to Binah of the Augusta's comments. Wide-eyed, returning good for malice, she had proffered unguents designed to take years, she said, off a lady's face.

Laying aside her veils, Binah washed her hands and busied herself crushing herbs. Anna watched impatiently as Binah added wine to the herbs she had crushed, poured the mixture into a cup, tasted it, and brought it to her. Cradling her son with one hand, Anna took the cup and drained it.

Her women clustered, whispering dubiously. Binah shut her eyes as if veiling any anger she felt: she too was a woman under scrutiny.

"You are being ridiculous," Anna snapped at one of the hovering nurses. "If Helena wanted to poison me, she would have done so already and much more privately!"

Expertly, Binah eyed the infant. "Your young Caesar suffers from wind," she announced. "Here. Let me show you." She lifted the child out of Anna's arms, patted him on the back in the precise way that Anna had not quite yet gotten the knack of, then gave him back. "He needs more milk."

Always someone else's needs, Anna thought. Her father's, her brother's, her husband's, and now her son's. Was she no more than a purveyor to men's needs? She remembered what Irene had said before her marriage about the similarity of the roles of Empress and hetaira. That applied to a Caesarissa, too; hetairai, Anna was sure, were under no need to produce heirs.

"Calmly, Caesarissa," Binah told Anna. "The babe can detect your mood through the milk."

Anna sighed, then again, more deeply, as the herbs took effect. Gradually, the pull of Alexius's lips at her breast subsided along with the ache. Finally, the baby slept again, and she could hand him off to be bathed for at least the third time today.

The sun chose that moment to emerge from behind the clouds. Light flashed on a table against the wall, and Binah turned toward it. Lying there were a knife with a carved bone handle, a sword of fine steel, and a great ax, such as a guardsman would carry. Binah turned even more pale, if possible, than when she entered the room.

"Caesarissa, you see! I was right. The ax frightens even Helena!" a maid cried. The woman sounded triumphant: it was seldom that anything even startled Binah. Now she seemed visibly to sway.

Anna ran forward to steady her. Despite the heaviness in her breasts, she was lithe again. In the last days before her time, she had felt like one of those immense fish, laden with eggs, that sometimes profligates carried over land from the great inland sea of the Rus: swollen, gravid, tied down, easy prey. Little as anyone else valued the fact, Anna was herself again.

"You are studying weapons?" Binah asked, recovering herself. "So soon out of childbed? Where got you those weapons?"

"The guards brought them to me, seeing as the man who bore them had no further use for them," Anna replied, oddly defensive. What right had Binah to ask, let alone in such a tone?

Did she imagine that Binah sighed, or did she simply hope so?

Binah put out a hand to touch the knife. The blade sliced her finger, leaving a smear of blood on the blade. She looked at it, staining her white, white skin, and touched the blade again.

"May I keep this?" she asked. Assuming permission, she tucked the knife into some fold of her garments. The gesture taught Anna much. By what right did Binah refuse marriage when Anna had been compelled? How did she permit herself to take, as Anna suspected, a lover—or lovers—as she chose? What right had she to be so discreet and so adroit that Anna, for all her spies, could not be sure of the truth?

"The weapons belonged to one Thorvaldr," Anna probed further. "You knew him, I think."

Binah nodded gravely. "Indeed yes. He attended you. I think he was some sort of nephew, grandnephew, to—"

"Your father's guardsman."

"My father's friend Nordbriht, Caesarissa. My father is not an Emperor: how should Varangians serve him? Nordbriht has fought and worked at my father's side for twenty-five years. He carried me on his back when I was not much older than the young Caesar here." Her eyes turned gentle as she gazed at Alexius.

Binah picked up the ax. She hefted it experimentally, then, slowly, painfully, achieved a version of the guard's drill. Predictably, a woman squealed in horror. *I am surrounded by fools*, Anna sighed to herself. *All except Binah.*

Another reason, besides the excellence of the woman's teachings and medications and the need to keep one of Leo Ducas's closest kin as hostage should the man prove mad again, to retain Binah in attendance on her.

Binah laughed sharply and set the great ax down. "A foolish chunk of metal, that," she observed. "It would make a far better plowshare or pruning hook, don't you think?"

"It is for war," said Anna.

"War is no task for women," the nurse ventured to speak up.

"It is no job for women," Binah agreed. "Or for men."

"It must be glorious," Anna said. "The challenge of protecting one's entire empire, of matching one's strength and courage against—"

Binah shook her head. She leaned over the sleeping infant and touched his hand, despite the frowns of the nursemaid. "*This* is the true challenge," she declared. "You fought and bled like any guardsman; but, your travails over, you produced what will be, God willing, a man who will live to better success than dealing death to other women's sons."

Even in his sleep, baby Alexius curled his fingers around Binah's—*the one with the blood smear?* Anna wondered. The tall woman looked down at the child with tenderness and a kind of longing different from the avid, noisy baby worship of Anna's lesser women.

"Look at this grip!" Binah cried softly. "So strong, so sure. Fifteen years from now, he will not just grip our heartstrings but a sword. Or, were he a man of the North rather than New Rome, an ax like Thorvaldr's." For a moment, she looked haunted. "It is so very easy," she said, "for a man to kill. Or to die."

She withdrew her hand from the child's fingers. "Just. Like. That. So small a thing, but all that love, all that promise, all the labor that went into turning babe to man is gone. And everyone who cared about him is bereft."

Binah raked the roomful of women with her gaze. "I see no glory in that. Satisfaction, perhaps, if one must protect one's own."

"You do not agree that defending the faith and the Holy Places—"

Binah smiled. "God is all-wise and all-powerful, yes? Then, truly, He needs our love and obedience, not our defense, surely, or that of barbarians from the West?"

Anna coughed, just in time, then blessed herself.

Binah took a deep breath. "My mother doubled the quantities of the herbs," she whispered to Anna. "She says it looks like a long campaign. Does the Augusta accompany His Sacred Majesty this time?"

Anna grimaced. "The Augusta hates campaigning and will not go this time. And she has forbidden me."

Binah shook her head. "Such a fine child," she mused. "Why would you want to leave him?"

"Because, glorious or not, war is something I must understand if I am to learn all the arts of rule!"

"His Sacred Majesty is a living example," Binah murmured. "One who wishes to rule must first rule himself. Or herself."

As Binah herself did? She was practically a cloister in herself. Once again, she touched Thorvaldr's weapons, this time almost tenderly. Anna formed a sudden, breathtaking image of the two of them standing together, tall and taller, dark and fair, the fair head bending down to her . . .

The man who was dead would not have compelled or importuned a woman like Binah. He would have adored her, as all the guards seemed to. Granted, they served Anna eagerly, doing all, or almost all her will, speaking with her of battles by the hour, but Anna knew the difference between indulgence and adoration.

"How is your mother?" Anna asked Binah when the silence drew itself out embarrassingly.

"Packing." Binah made herself laugh. "She is heart-glad to be permitted to return home, but she fears for my father. He is too old to be riding around like a young man. She knows this is the price for her departure, and she says it is too dear."

"Nonsense," snapped the nurse. "Your father serves the Emperor and rides at his command."

"He is too old!" Binah's violet eyes flared, and again Anna intervened.

"Helena, *Kyrios* Leo is in better health than my father, yet my father rides to war every year. As does Isangeles. And Bohemond."

Again, that flare of fire in the deep, long eyes.

"Why do you hate him so?" Anna asked. The women pressed closer, scenting prey.

"Aside from the fact that he thought I could be backed into a corner and fondled without impunity? Had he pressed any closer, he might have joined the ranks of eunuchs." The women laughed, for once including Binah in their mirth. She was strange, but Bohemond was *barbaros*.

Anna gasped with shock.

"Caesarissa, you see only the valor, the audacity. This man is a wrecker, a taker."

"But a warrior, nonetheless." *What am I doing defending Bohemond? Anna asked herself. He is my land's enemy. I, not Binah, should proclaim my hatred of him.*

"Wonderful," said Binah. "Your Imperial Father is a warrior; he holds this Empire with his sword. Some are called to do so, and His Sacred Majesty was born to it. But are there no other things he might not rather do, do you think? Spend time with his children or his grandchild? Contemplate the nature of God?"

Anna blinked in surprise.

"Those are choices that my own father has made. And I do not want to see him deprived of the time he has earned to rest, to spend with my mother. Or any other way he wishes to spend it. He should be breeding horses, not riding them to death."

"The Emperor commands." Anna could be haughty too. "That is why Leo Ducas rides out."

Binah inclined her head. "And because it will enable Mother to go home."

They stared at each other, visibly resolving not to quarrel, especially not before the others: the tall woman and the tiny one, both of whom adored their fathers. Would anyone love them the way their fathers loved other women or other causes? The thought hurt Anna; Binah seemed not to care.

"Would you like to ride out too, perhaps assist my mother?" Anna asked. For the life of her, she could not keep the edge out of her voice.

Binah shook her head. "If I am commanded, why, of course, I ride. Like my father."

If what Anna suspected were true, Binah was already in mourning. Her clothes were dark, simple; yet that was how she always dressed: nunlike except for that awe-inspiring beauty. Something glittered against that darkness.

Binah followed Anna's gaze. She detached an ornament from her garments: a butterfly wrought in gold and jewels. It seemed too massive to be work of Persia or of Ch'in.

"They tell me this is part of my dowry." She laughed briefly. "Quite simply, when Mother and Father took me up, it was pinned to my swaddlings."

She took it off and held it out to Anna. The ornament felt strange; even the facets of the amethysts adorning it seemed to prick her fingers. She returned it to Binah.

Alexius woke again, wailing. This time, Anna rose and lifted him herself. His warmth did feel better than an ax. And, just perhaps, it would make a better weapon, too.

"He will never be Emperor," she mused.

"He is lovable in his own right," Binah insisted. "Is the Purple all that matters?"

Anna laid the child down again. Alexius might wail and kick, but there was no fire in him. Even as reluctant a mother as Anna could tell that.

"It is all that matters to me," Anna told her. "For so *I* was bred."

"They're coming!" screamed a lookout.

That won cheers from the camp. Those cheers subsided as the longed-for resupplies from St. Simeon came into sight with their escort. Even Tatikios's men mounted, preparing a sortie to protect the caravan.

"They must have lost three hundred men," the *strategos* muttered.

Theodoulos ran his eyes knowledgeably over the pack train the diminished force of knights escorted. There rode Rainault, his helm dented, the device on his shield almost obliterated, but fighting to sit straight in the saddle of his limping horse. Even the merchants rode like soldiers.

The Frank reined in his tired horse nearby, almost toppling from the saddle. Theodoulos eased him down.

"You should have seen them," Rainault's voice rasped. A long pause, while he drank from the goatskin Theo tossed him.

"I should have been there," Theodoulos reproached himself.

"You might not have made it out alive. It was a nasty bit of business . . . I tell you, if it weren't for the merchants themselves, there'd be fewer of us here to buy their wares.

"Merchants, we thought. Rich, fat merchants. The Turks surrounded us—doesn't matter how outnumbered they are, they always try to circle you—and the merchants threw off their cloaks and fought like . . ." Rainault fought for some term more polite than "a thousand devils." "They fought like paladins," he finished, then stumbled to his knees. "God, I'm tired. The Bishop will probably keep us up all night singing hosannahs."

"We could see if Adela has any food she's giving away," Theodoulos suggested.

Rainault grinned sardonically at him. "You're our expert on caravans, aren't you? Don't you want to see this one? Besides, they told me to summon you."

He needed Theodoulos's arm to raise him. Then, tired as he was, he led the way toward the head of the column, raising his voice to a hoarse shout.

"My lords, I brought the Greek!"

"Well done!" Count Bohemond unhelmed, his face grimy, streaked with sweat, with blood from a bitten lip caking his mouth. "You should have been with us!" he greeted Theodoulos, who bowed, oddly flattered.

To his surprise, Tatikios stood nearby.

The caravan's master dismounted and pulled off his helm.

"My God," Theodoulos whispered.

Leo Ducas stood watching him. He swayed with exhaustion, but he was smiling.

 20

Y**ou knew!" Theodoulos glared at Tatikios. Ignoring the grin-**ning Franks, he raced toward his foster father. "What do you think you're doing, risking your life?"

"Everything I can!" Leo snapped back, and caught him by the arms, half embracing him, half leaning on him.

He's too old for this, Theodoulos thought. *When did I become my father's keeper?* he asked himself. Then they were pounding each other's backs despite the mail that bruised their hands. Theodoulos's eyes stung.

Leo's arm about Theodoulos's shoulders, he greeted the Franks with the care he might have used in the presence of the Emperor. For once, Rainault's gossip had done its work well; his fellows crowded around to see Theodoulos's foster father.

The Bishop Adhémar came forward, and Leo knelt to him, drawing murmurs of approval. He greeted the lady Adela with the admiring courtesy Theodoulos had seen him use on Caesarissa Anna.

As Rainault had predicted, Adhémar drew out his thanksgivings and ceremonious inquiries until the men who had fought their way back to the camp outside Antioch were almost reeling. Finally, Tatikios imposed on his status as an outsider to bear Leo Ducas away to his own quarters.

That left Leo with only a regiment of servants to endure and to assent to their offers of wine, food, hot water, and bed.

"Help me out of this damned armor, will you?" he asked Theo. He unfastened his sword belt and laid it aside. Theo helped him pull off his mail. He remembered that armor from when, as a crippled lad, he rode from Peristrema into Hagios Prokopios to buy supplies for his master and meet the newcomer from Constantinople. Leo stretched, then began to ease his stained, padded tunic away from back and shoulders.

"There's salve in my packs," he told Theodoulos. "Would you mind getting it? I swear, I've rubbed sores in five places."

He stretched again. This time, he flinched. "Don't say it, son. I know I'm too old for this."

By the time Theo returned with the salve, his foster father had wrapped himself in a robe and was gazing in a direction he hoped would produce hot water.

"If Tatikios can produce a bath in this camp, he travels like an Emperor," he commented. "Holy Bearer of God, how do people here stay clean? Or don't they?"

Theodoulos shrugged. "They're not as bad as all that."

"I know, I know. You like them. Someone has to."

Theodoulos turned to pour both of them wine.

"Better water it," Leo commented. "We're both almost staggering. Speaking of which, I take it your leg doesn't trouble you?"

"It got me across the mountains," Theodoulos said.

"Better you than I. Fifteen days by sea. Rough seas. I think I'd almost rather fight Turks." He drank off the wine and set his cup down.

"Sir," Theodoulos began, meeting Leo's ironic, raised eyebrow, "you shouldn't be here. You shouldn't put yourself at risk. What would we do without you?"

Leo laughed. "Do you know how many people have asked me

that in the past several months? To answer your questions, I'm here because the Emperor commanded it. Because we struck a bargain: supplies that no one else was willing or able to provide in return for . . ." He let his face light up. "I'm taking Asherah home, Theo! Home to Hagios Prokopios. Ioannes hasn't done all that badly under Hasan, we've kept in touch; but Alexius promised me support and a monopoly for rugs, if we can start that business up again. Asherah, you can imagine, is overjoyed. She has had a bellyful of Byzantium."

"What about you?" The words came blurting out before Theodoulos could stop them. It was not that Theo did not love Asherah, but he had tended the sores rubbed on his foster father's back from living in armor and supported him in the exhaustion that Leo's latest bridge between merchants and Western knights had cost him.

Leo helped me to manhood and a future as if he, not some nameless wanderer in the caves, truly were my father. Why will he not let me help him?

Leo smiled that abstracted, charming smile at Theo that had won him so many hearts. "How can I be happy, seeing Asherah so desolate? The children—Manuel is doing well in Alexandria, and we're negotiating a marriage contract. Binah, as you know, has remained with the Caesarissa. What you don't know is that she had a son."

"Binah had a son?" If Theodoulos didn't sleep soon, he would probably collapse with his head on the table.

Leo laughed. "I wish she would marry. No, the Caesarissa. She named the child Alexius, predictably enough. She seems to like Binah, who says she's an apt pupil and very curious about you, God help you. The girls . . . Rachel and her husband stay in the East. Shoshonna, though . . ." Leo poured himself more wine and gulped it. "She's in Jerusalem, God protect her."

"So you came out here to see what the chances were of . . ."

Leo shook his head. "I came here to see you, too. They trust you, Theodoulos. And your mother and I rely on you to protect Shoshonna and the rest of the family if you reach Jerusalem. Don't worry about the property; it can be replaced. But . . ." His voice broke. "Whatever you have to do for your sister . . . Theo, we are going to have to count on you."

Theodoulos rested a hand on the older man's shoulder. "On my soul."

Leo shook his head. "Anything you need, you shall have. The letters have gone out."

"For Shoshonna."

"And for you!" Leo snapped. "You are a son of my house." He rose, then flinched again. Theo stood to support him as a servant came in with hot water.

"God, Theo, let's not fight," his foster father said. "I did enough of that today. I've earned my reward. I just want to live to get home and enjoy it in peace."

But his eyes were dubious as if they looked into a future where no peace could ever exist again.

"Sir?" Theodoulos asked. "Father?"

Ah, that won a smile from him!

"When you see my daughter Xenia . . ."

The smile grew wider and warmer. "You should come home and see her," Leo said. "You'll never get these years back, you know, and she is almost ready to marry."

"Kiss her for me, will you?"

"Son, with all my heart."

Which was, of course, how Leo pursued anything he cared about.

In January of 1098, pursuing a phantom holiness, Adhémar expelled the women from the camp.

"Foolishness," ran the whisper through the younger knights. "We are too hungry to whore."

Theodoulos assumed that Adela would be exempt from the general ban, which meant a risky journey to the ports or into the mountains, under threat of Turkish attack.

"There are not two rules," she told Theodoulos, as she finished packing, "one for me as my Lord Uncle's niece and one for camp followers."

"I shall miss you." The words slipped out. A thought struck him. "May I ask leave to ride to the port with you?"

He could visit the merchants, ask them to give Adela credit or at least good prices.

Adela managed a smile. "Does your general not require you?" she asked.

Theodoulos looked down.

"I do not think he will remain here much longer. He has fought with Count Raymond about compensating the knights who lose horses. He wants us to besiege the city, but from a distance, perhaps cut it off by sea. And he does not trust"—Theodoulos dropped his voice—"Count Bohemond."

"All you Greeks have a problem with that," Adela pointed out tartly.

"Ah, lady," Theodoulos blurted, "if we could but have you *speak* with the enemy, you would win us Jerusalem with a single word."

Fool, he thought. *Fool. Men tell women how sweet their words are. You . . . you praise Adela for a sharp tongue.*

Adela was a Norman, a descendant of the doughty women of the north. It pleased her.

"What . . . what will you do now?" he ventured to ask.

I will never see her again, something wailed at the back of Theo's mind. *She belongs to neither of my peoples. And what have I to offer her?*

"What women do," Adela said. "I shall wait at the port. There is nothing for me at home." She laughed bleakly. "If you can even call it home. My husband's brothers prefer me to be a pilgrim widow who might never return rather than a chatelaine and a drain on them. Besides, I count on reaching Jerusalem. I *plan* on it and pray for it night and day. Surely, my uncle will bring me with him."

Her eyes lit and filled. Greatly daring, Theodoulos reached out to touch her hand. "And if he does not, Rainault and I will come and fetch you. We need you with us, you and your shield of faith."

She flushed as if he had offered her flowers or a poem of his own making. A lesser woman might have been silenced; Adela won her fight to get out the words she wanted. "On that day, I shall be delighted to see you, sir."

"Lady, lady! The horses are waiting!"

Even as Adela whirled to reply to the summons, Theodoulos lifted the hand he still held to his lips and kissed it.

Theodoulos handed Tatikios fair-copied notes from the last, acrimonious meeting of the princes. "I wish you weren't leaving, sir. Antioch is too rich a prize to toss to the Franks."

"Tell that to their lord Bohemond," Tatikios snapped. "I know he wants it for himself. But you'll know more of that than I. I gather you'll move into his camp."

Theodoulos nodded, trying not to feel wretched. Rainault had offered him a place in the camp; the Count had only grinned and welcomed him to a *man's* service.

"My usefulness here is about finished," said Tatikios. "I don't trust my lord Bohemond, and I can't work with Isangeles." He used the name for Saint-Gilles current in Byzantium. "So I'm off to Cyprus and strategy in exile before some accident finds me."

The *strategos* flattened his palms against the table that had not yet been packed. "You're sure you won't reconsider and come along with me? You've done good work for me, Ducas, I'd say that in the presence of the Emperor himself. What do you face here?"

"I don't know, sir," Theodoulos said.

"In the name of God, man, then why stay?" Tatikios demanded. "These barbarians won't thank you for it. They'll use you up and toss you away."

"Did my father put you up to this, sir?" Theodoulos cut into the argument.

Tatikios had the grace to look away. "He is a persuasive man. Frankly, I agree with him." The general raised his chin as if listening for noises outside his quarters. "Well, what is written is written."

"I thought we had free will," Theodoulos pointed out.

"We do. But we are not in the City and don't have all day, more's the pity, to argue it. Just tell me one thing. What do you hope to gain from these people?"

"My father asked the same question. I don't know, sir. I only know that some of them have become *my* people. Now they're terribly far from home, truly strangers in a strange land. I can help them. They want Jerusalem? I am not a prince, not a knight, even. But I understand this land, and I can give them a chance to survive in it. Leo talks about building bridges between the nations. You're one such bridge—and so am I. It's not much, sir. But it's why I can't go with you. Please don't order me to accompany you."

"And if I did?"

Theodoulos grinned at him. "I grew up in the south, by the cave cities. I am very good at disappearing."

Tatikios shouted with laughter. At least he would ride out of Antioch grinning. It turned retreat into a form of victory.

"Theodoulos Ducas, you are welcome to a place on my staff anytime you care to claim it. God bless you."

Theodoulos bowed, and Tatikios strode out.

And then he was gone.

 21

The long shadow fell across the last of the fragile spring light that Rainault was using for his chronicle.

"Write it down, lad, write it down that if this siege isn't broken soon, I'm going to have to return to Italy."

A blotch spread across the page, as Rainault leapt up.

"My lord count! This is an honor." Rainault gestured him to a seat formed of saddles, rugs, and cushions, a refinement of the caravans that Theodoulos had showed some of the knights.

Theodoulos rose more decorously.

"Sit, Greek." Bohemond gestured him to sit back down. "You're practically family by now."

"You honor me." Theodoulos smiled, shocked at his own satisfaction. He rummaged in his stores for the wine Tatikios had bequeathed him. Bohemond gulped the good wine as if it were grape squeezings from anybody's vineyards.

"Ah, that's better! Rainault, why such clouds in your face? You'd think I had told you that the True Cross was a mere block of wood."

"But, sir . . ." Rainault brought the word out as if he spoke of a lost love. "Jerusalem. What of freeing Jerusalem? Or liberating Antioch from the Turks?"

"As we did Nicaea?" Bohemond shot back. "Italy needs me. Besides, sometimes a warleader learns to retreat, to live and fight another day."

Rainault gestured at several men who hovered outside to come in and listen.

Bohemond stretched out long, long legs, and beckoned too. "Come on in, lads. I thought I'd tell you before I told the 'princes.' "

For a big man, his sarcasm was almost elegant. Theodoulos nodded respect and framed his question with great delicacy.

"If you were a magnate of the Empire—and His Sacred Majesty gave you a title of nobility—I should ask what reward might keep you here," Theodoulos said, observing the man from beneath lowered eyelids. Knights affected to despise merchants, but bargained even more ruthlessly.

Bohemond's blue eyes flared like a knot of wood when the fire has struck a pocket of sap, then swiftly narrowed. "As you know, I am not a wealthy man, and I've been put to the further shame of seeing the Count of Toulouse recompense my nephew Tancred when I cannot. This cannot go on."

The knights muttered that he was a great warleader, he was *their* warleader, and, by Christ, he deserved reward, any reward, he cared to name. Theodoulos only smiled.

"Ah, Greek, you are a clever man. You sit and wait for us to betray ourselves. What would keep me here? The very prize that has drawn me here." He gestured in the direction of the city's walls.

"Who has a better right to claim Antioch?" Rainault demanded.

The other knights jumped to their feet, cheering. They reminded Theo of colts in the spring, excitable, easily aroused by mares or word of battle—and ample word had come. Kerbogha *was* on the march from Mosul. If Bohemond left the host right now, they might as well all turn Turk.

"My lord, may I ask?" Theodoulos ventured again.

"You will anyhow," Bohemond said. He poured for himself, then—high favor—filled Theodoulos's cup. "I like you, Greek. You're twisty, but you're close enough to my age that when you put your mind to it, you think like a sensible man."

Theo almost spilled his wine.

"So, ask!" Bohemond commanded.

"I think," Theodoulos told him, "that the princes were unimpressed when you said you needed to leave the army. If it were fitting to bet on a Bishop's words, I would wager that Bishop Adhémar asked you if you came to Syria to make your fortune or make your soul."

Bohemond snorted like a warhorse. "Adhémar! He is more saint than warrior, for all the airs he gives himself." That was going too far, he could see from the shocked eyes of his knights. He signed himself, the others following suit.

"I give you my word. I *will* return to Italy if my terms are not met."

"When, lord?" one of the knights asked.

Bohemond smiled. "Not yet. Not quite yet. Kerbogha is on the march. Perhaps as his army nears Antioch, our masters may reconsider."

To his own astonishment, Theodoulos found himself ready to cheer with the younger men. Then his eyes met Bohemond's again. He was grinning, well enough: Bohemond had never been one to let his own men down. But his eyes were afire with more than pride at their praise.

He has a plan too good to share.

At some point, though, they would learn it. And then they would ride the whirlwind. Or—how long it had been since Theodoulos had remembered his old studies—upon the back of that dragon called the tli.

Spring brought armies—as well as fresh green—to the fields. The Emperor Alexius campaigned in Asia Minor, and the princes had appealed to him. If Alexius relieved the city, Bohemond could whistle for it.

"What about Kerbogha?" asked Rainault, butchering the name.

Bohemond laughed. "Let Baldwin worry about him! He's camped outside Edessa. But when he comes here—and he will—Jesu, we shall have battle enough for an army ten times our size!"

How cheerful he was. And why not? In the end, Bohemond had had his way, as he so often did. Raymond de St. Gilles had joined forces with Bishop Adhémar to decide that only the church could award fiefdoms in this land—but, so great was their need for Bohemond, that if his troops entered the city first, it would be his. Theo had seen full-fed tigers that showed less satisfaction at the kill.

The dust kicked up by Stephen of Blois's departure had settled on the road. He would not be missed. The Franks he led, however, would.

"And so departs our valiant leader," Rainault commented.

"Let him cry on the Emperor's . . . shoulder," remarked a younger knight. "Wasn't he always praising—"

Someone glared him into silence and pointed at Theodoulos. For a wonder, the Frank subsided. Amazing: so he had won that much respect from the Franks, whether for an open purse, a willingness to fight, or—and he thought this was more than likely—remaining behind when his general departed for Cyprus.

"Charity, charity," rebuked Raymond of Aguilers, coming, as Rainault remarked, to sniff out what news he could.

"Fulcher says Stephen complained of illness," Theodoulos said. "In the liver, perhaps, or the heart." The Franks laughed. "Well, it is for his wife to put the courage back into him."

That drew a ribald howl from the younger men. Theo smiled inwardly. His own friend Adela was named for Stephen's wife, although all it had brought her was a longing for Jerusalem.

My sweet friend. There. He had admitted it. He had had letters from her that he read in secret and stored away. Why, he was turning positively Turkish about her, wasn't he? A lady was a secret. A beloved secret.

Wasn't that how Leo regarded Lady Asherah?

Surreptitiously, Theo crossed himself. What had he to offer a lady of the West? Some used parchments, perhaps, or a contract with traders in Aleppo? Their faiths were different—*aye, but so are Leo's and Asherah's; their ages were somewhat different—but we both are widowed. She has no children. She would be a good mother for my child.*

He had entrusted a letter to one of the departing Franks to convey to Adela, gold to insure the man's secrecy, and hints of an intrigue to keep him interested.

"Sir Greek," asked Raymond, "you keep your wits about you. What have you seen upon the road?"

"Dust," said Theo. "Dust and the usual back-and-forth of traders, mostly Armenians."

Rainault laughed. "Name of God, don't bring that news to our lord Count, or he'll call out his cooks again."

Theodoulos signed himself. Raymond grimaced—*you still do it backward*—but Theo was a tried companion now, *their* Greek, not the Emperor's.

"Sirs?" One of Count Bohemond's footsoldiers stood, waiting to draw their attention. "Sir, Count Bohemond sends me as a herald to the army: be ready at sunset for a raid into the enemy's lands."

Rainault jerked his chin at Theodoulos. *The hunt is up.*

"Well, then, there's trouble afoot," said Raymond. "I had best return to my master, who may need a scribe. Do you, Sir Theodoulos . . ."

Theodoulos shook his head. Knowing what emphasis the Franks put on knighthood, he would rather not claim an accolade he had not earned.

The armsman turned to him. "My lord the Count bids you also hold yourselves in readiness."

At sunset, Bohemond led his army eastward out of the camp, as if he planned to mount an attack on Kerbogha.

"Damn Turks will have a quiet night," Rainault observed.

Already, the dew had begun to gather. The birds had ceased singing, whether because the sun had set or out of fear of the army as it passed. From Adhémar's forces came the familiar marching hymn:

> *"Lignum crucis*
> *Signum ducis*
> > *Sequitur exercitus;*
> *Quod non cessit*
> *Sed processit*
> > *In vi Sancti Spiritus."*

Bohemond's knights took up the tune, verse following verse, the sacred shifting gradually into the scandalous, then dying out as someone put an end to the viler rhymes.

They marched silently now. The night was broken by the clatter of horse hooves, the ringing of mail, the faint grumbles of "how long are we going to march," and the whispered rumors that accompanied any sortie from the camp.

Then, the command came to halt. In the middle of Syria. With no enemy in sight. The army paused, puzzled.

"Now, what do they think they're doing?" Theodoulos heard someone grumble. He heard the word passed toward the rear of the column. Rainault leaned over to speak to him.

"Won't *they* be surprised?" he asked. "As shocked as Count Raymond and the bishop, and far less jealous."

Theodoulos shook his head. "Don't you hate to owe Antioch to an apostate? Look you, he betrays his city because his master fines him and because—"

"His wife betrayed him with a *Turk!*" Rainault hissed back. "No wonder this Captain Firouz turns to us. When we take the city, he can be Christian again and put her away."

"*If* we take it," Theodoulos replied. "If. What if he did send his son as hostage? How do we know he's telling the truth?"

Rainault laughed under his breath. "I would rather fear the wrath of every Emir in the East than cross my lord."

Ponderously, the army turned and marched back toward Antioch. Men rode along the column, ordering silence.

Someone in the ranks chuckled. "I'll warrant the count has a trick planned," he said, and was hissed to silence.

"It is a rich jest," said Rainault. "I wish we could share it, but our oaths . . . our immortal souls would answer . . ."

Theodoulos nodded. His horse's hoofbeats lulled him. The night drew on, enforcing a kind of peacefulness despite the need to keep constantly alert, despite the fear that clawed at his guts, seeking to escape through his lips in a cry or in flight out of danger.

Bohemond, he could well believe, had no such fears, neither on a battlefield nor in the secret battlefield that had been his meeting with the lords of the Franks.

He had stalked about his quarters, past the seated princes. His head was held high and a light owing nothing to the sunset seemed to shine about him. Standing slightly behind him, where the princes could see him, was a man about the age of the youngest knights, with the strong-marked features of an Armenian.

"Tonight," Bohemond told them, "if God favors us, Antioch will be given into our hands."

Even now, Theodoulos had to smile at the shock and doubt that had marked their faces, followed by shock. *What has the fox got planned now?*

Raymond of St. Gilles studied the young man. "This is your spy?" he asked, a world of contempt in his voice. Theo, scribbling frantically to take down an account of the meeting, nodded to himself. The Count was one who would use a spy, but detest him. Bohemond detested only the spies he had not bought.

"This is the son," Bohemond told him, "of one Firouz, a captain of Antioch, in command of the Tower of the Two Sisters and the wall beside it. My hostage. His father has given Antioch into our hands."

He paused, then smiled a leopard's smile. "Into *my* hands."

He whirled to stare at his peers. He blotted his brow with a square of fine silk. Even as the light faded, Theo saw that it had been dyed imperial purple, a color carried only by members of the Emperor's family.

"If we are to take the city," Adhémar of Le Puy cut into Bohemond's exultation, "we must know what you plan."

"Some weeks ago," Bohemond said, "I met Firouz. He is a convert to Islam who would return to Christ if he could, and who has not cut his ties to the Armenians of Antioch. He is high in the Turks' government, but he hates his master, who caught him hoarding and fined him."

"How did you find this man?" Godfrey's voice was chill with disdain.

"From a spy, who did not wish to be served up on one of my cooks' spits," Bohemond laughed. He paced again around the darkening room. "Only today, Firouz sent his son—the youth you see—to me to say he was ready to put Antioch into my hands."

"But *why?*" asked the Bishop.

"Firouz learned that his wife had proved . . . unfaithful to him, with a Turk."

The youth from Antioch muffled a cry of outrage.

"Firouz may be a traitor, but he is no fool. He commands the Tower of the Two Sisters, right across from Tancred's fortress that my lord of St. Gilles has been so good as to maintain."

An ironic bow to Count Raymond.

"We have but to lead our army out eastward, as if we go to fight Kerbogha, then, after dark, turn around, creep back to the western wall, bringing our ladders with us. Firouz will admit a small party of knights and then, if our courage holds and God is with us, Antioch is ours!"

Even Raymond's eyes lit at that, despite his envy.

We are going, by the grace of God, to take Antioch tonight.

The rumor winged across the army. Hope and desire glowed in the eyes of knights and infantry alike. It seemed even to glitter in the stars. *Hush,* Theodoulos wished them. *You will betray us.*

He sent his awareness down into the land. So many armies had ridden over it, to and from the fortress they now attacked. Let the land shake as they mounted to the walls, and they could forget their hopes of Antioch today or ever.

Watchfulness. Quiescence . . . deep within the earth . . .

A jab in the armored ribs . . .

"I can't believe you were actually sleeping as you rode," Rainault whispered across the space dividing their two horses.

Theodoulos shrugged. His chain mail rustled slightly. "I've had plenty of practice," he said. "Even if most of it was on camels."

"Quiet!"

The sky was paling as they returned to the city, heading for the west and northwest walls. Banners began to fly at the eastern horizon as Bohemond arrived before the Tower of the Two Sisters and signaled his army to halt. The knights dismounted.

"They probably saw us go, decided it was a holy day or something, and are sleeping it off," Rainault commented, then fell guiltily silent.

Bohemond strode among his men, choosing sixty among them.

"The Greek too," said Count Bohemond, beckoning Theo forward. "I need him for languages. This wretched tongue's his birth speech, and he has the Arabic besides. Haven't you, Theodoulos?"

He nodded and went to stand with the chosen knights. Bohemond's *other* men.

How high the wall was! A faint light, overshadowed by the rising sun, still shone in a window in the tower. Theodoulos fixed his eyes on it, refusing to look down. Don't think of the men climbing up, rung upon rung, below you. Don't think of an arrow punching through your armor and into your spine, the gout of blood from mouth and nose, choking off the death shriek. Don't think of skilled hands, toppling the ladder backward through the air, or the long fall to the

CROSS AND CRESCENT   175

bone-breaking ground. Or your loosening bowels, which you should
have tended earlier. Climb. Mount into the sky.

22

W**hat's that?"**
Theodoulos froze at the question.

Down from the ladder, into the earth, delving for the strength
that he knew lay in the land for him, Theodoulos sent his awareness.
You do not see us. We are not here.

Power surged upward, seeming to heat his armor.

Theodoulos shut his eyes and forced himself to climb. *Think of it
as a cat far, far below, or rocks falling,* he wished at the guard. The
power quivered within him, and he knew he could make of it a
weapon, say, a ball of fire, to kill the too-alert guard.

He will die soon enough.

He heard a tired man's footsteps away from the wall.

The light grew closer. A shadow crossed and recrossed it—Firouz
pacing up and down. His brows were furrowed, and sweat rolled down
his face so that his padded silk clung to him.

"We have so few Franks," he blurted out in Greek as Theodoulos
stepped through the window. "Where is Bohemond?"

Theodoulos translated swiftly. "Tell the traitor," Fulk, who led
Bohemond's force, ordered him, "we have Franks enough." He
counted off man after man, dispatching each out along the walls to
take the other towers that were in Firouz's faithless guard and the
keeping of his brother.

Then they leaned out and gestured: set out the other ladders.
More men began the climb. A silent, vicious battle for control of the
walls spread from the three towers now in the Franks' hands.

"Tell my Lord Bohemond it's time," Fulk ordered an infantry-
man.

He started down the ladder, but it broke beneath him. He fell
without a scream. Fulk swore under his breath. "You and you . . ." He
pointed with his chin and his dripping sword. "Along the walls. Kill
as many of the garrison as you can. The rest of you, down into the city.
Wake the Christians. Bid them join us. You too." He gestured at
Theodoulos.

Rainault ran out across the wall. Theodoulos descended, shouting for all Christians to come aid him, as they valued their souls. He and the other men pounded on the doors, raced beneath the shuttered windows of great houses, and dashed shouting into churches where worshipers knelt even now.

Shouts met and crossed his own. A priest in one of the churches began to pound the wooden semantrons. Horns began to blow in the streets and high up above in the embattled walls. Other horns echoed from outside.

The Christians of Antioch boiled half-dressed out of their homes, some armed, some carrying only kitchen knives. Killing any Turks in their path, they flung open the Gate of St. George, then swept to the huge Gate of the Bridge, opening it. The army outside rushed through the gate like a great wave after an earthquake has stirred the deepest seabed.

Over the shrieks of the dying came the cry, "God wills it! *God wills it!*"

Did God will that that Armenian would slit a woman's throat, or three Greeks would practically tear one Turk asunder?

Over here.

The silent command drove Theodoulos into a narrow, twisting street, still empty of Greeks, Turks, or Armenians. How dark it was here: how peaceful. He leaned panting against a wall.

Too old and, like his foster father, far too civilized.

Here. Come to me.

He signed himself.

This way.

With a sigh of "God wills it," Theodoulos obeyed the compulsion of that voice. Past that house, into an ancient building that might once have been a church. Down a flight of stairs into a way so dark that Theo's hands went out. It was like a cave. He traced the wall and ran beside it just as he had been taught by the old priest who had raised him. His fingertips, wise in the way of old stone, told him that this had been cut in blocks older by far than Justinian's works. He traced ancient symbols, sacred signs: perhaps Peter himself had walked this way. Or perhaps a figure older by far, one for whom the cup was a more natural symbol than cross, crescent, or sword.

In here.

He gave the door a push, and it yielded. The room before him was dimly lit, but he could not mistake the painting of a somber-eyed Christ in majesty that loomed above him. Much of the paint had flaked off the plastered stone, but he could still see the eyes.

A window from far above captured the fine golden light of first dawn and cast it down to shine upon the altar. On it stood a silver cup. The light picked out the craftsmanship that had gone into the cup—some Christian Pheidias or Polycleites, certainly, had sculpted those tiny figures, twelve of them, and in their midst . . . he had never seen that face before; and yet he knew it. Heart and soul, he had always known it. Compared to it, the painting on the apse's curved wall behind the altar was a caricature, daubed by a nasty boy. The eyes of the Figure on the chalice studied him with even more care than the painting overhead. At the end of time, those eyes would regard him again, and he could only pray they would be merciful.

"Did you call me?" he asked.

Silence. For now, judgment was suspended.

He averted his gaze from the Figure to the robed woman painted on a panel to the right hand of the apse itself.

"Did *you* call me?" he whispered.

Oh God, he was hearing things. Perhaps it was the rotten food, the long march, or the lack of sleep. Perhaps it was pure cowardice. And perhaps he was going mad.

The leg that had been crippled since his mangled birth collapsed, toppling Theodoulos to one knee. He bowed his head.

He signed himself in apology and laid aside his sword. The woman's face seemed to soften, almost to smile. The cup on the altar glowed.

No, he could not leave this to be snatched up as spoil, to be used, perhaps for the red vinegar that passed for wine among the poorest knights, perhaps to be tossed from hand to hand, stamped into the mud by accident, or handed over to a bloodstained priest who mumbled his Creed and garbled his doctrine.

A reddish light seemed to glow within it, spilling over like wine poured by a generous hand.

Take up the cup.

Theodoulos went to both knees. "Did you summon me?" he whispered. "I will keep it safe. I pledge you my soul on it."

Rising, he walked forward toward the altar.

Thank you, Mother, he breathed.

What was he thanking her for? As he neared the cup, he expected every moment that the light from the window would catch him in its beam, burning him where he stood and leaving only ash and shards of white, calcined bones behind on the ancient paving stones.

He stripped his mailed mittens from his hands and tucked them into his belt. Even so, blood stained his hands, the blood that had stained evey man's hands since the Fall.

Blood falls at birth, too. My son. My beloved son.

Theodoulos's eyes filled with tears.

He signed himself again, then reached out to raise the cup as, so often, he had watched Father Meletios in Peristrema Valley. It was, he saw, *two* cups, the one so splendidly carved, the other plain, its lip crudely turned, yet embedded in the outer cup as an uncut ruby might be set in finest gold of Ophir. He gazed down into it. Shadows seemed to pool within it, as if he gazed at the end of a long day into a wine so deeply red it was almost the Purple of Empire—or of the light from a goddess's womb—and contemplated his own dreams. His child. His home. A woman whose face he could not see. The voices of people he loved. His foster mother; his sister Binah, smiling in satisfaction. Oh God, only grant that he lived to return home!

Shouts broke in upon his thoughts. The soldiers should not find this place, he vowed! Perhaps, he could lure them away, like a wild bird protecting her chicks. They would not desecrate this chapel any more than they would desecrate the shrines of his home. Their approaches were buried now, but he knew that those silent, sacred spaces, like bubbles of air breathed into the stone at its formation at the beginning of time, still lay beneath the earth.

He thrust the cup within his mail shirt and padded undergarment, bowed respect at the altar, backed halfway out, then ran for the door. Behind him, the light went out. As he escaped out the door, it shut behind him as firmly as the gates of Eden.

Theodoulos ran from Eden into Hell. The streets were piled with bodies—Armenians, Turks, Greeks, Franks—with more dropping every minute. Women and children crouched against the walls, some already dead, others huddled moaning with fear.

"Into the church!" he screamed at them. "It's sanctuary!"

They stared at him, their eyes almost as dull as pebbles.

He brandished his sword. "Go on! Get in there! I'll guard you."

He rushed a knot of children clutching a woman's skirts. They screamed and ran the way he pointed with his sword.

He flattened himself against the wall in time to escape being trampled by a troop of horsemen, richly clad: Yaghi-Siyan and his guards, fleeing toward the gorge leading to the Iron Gate and out onto the hills.

"To me, to me!" another voice, deeply accented, screamed.

Shams-ad-Dawla, the ruler's son, kept his wits about him as he raced to hold the citadel.

"Here!" Theodoulos screamed in Arabic, then in Greek. Would he respond to an enemy first or an ally? He ran forward toward the Turk, brandishing his sword. Shieldless, he might be, but better than a shield lay against his heart.

What seemed like an entire troop of armsmen rushed between him and the Turk. "What, you there, Sir Greek?" a great voice shouted.

"My lord Bohemond!" Theo's voice cracked.

"You're too old for your voice to break, Greek! Come on! Let's show these lads how we *old* men fight!"

The morning light seemed to leap about Bohemond's helm like a crown of fire.

Up the streets of Antioch they raced, faster and faster until the heavier and older of the knights dropped back panting, and one of the armsmen collapsed onto his knees. Older than they, wearing heavy mail, Bohemond outran them.

The Citadel was barred against them.

"Well," said Bohemond, "best not to achieve all your heart's desire in one blow. That way lies the sin of pride."

"Do you think, sir, we might find reinforcements and then attempt to take it?" Theodoulos asked.

"You're a cautious devil, Greek," said the Frank. "I'll blame this idea on you when I tell the princes."

He sent two knights to fetch reinforcements. Then his face brightened. "If my banner cannot fly from the citadel itself, I'll raise it as high as I can," he declared.

His banner bearer ran toward the tower overlooking the citadel as Bohemond waited. Incongruously, in the heart of a battling city, they rested.

"Ah!" Bohemond laughed his great laugh as his banner waved from the tower above the citadel. It was purple, like the kerchief he bore. The dawn winds let it flare out to its full size, and the morning light shone upon it.

Far beneath, the invading army saw the banner and cheered like madmen. Bohemond hurled them—and himself—against the citadel. Too few, by far. Even he fell back, wounded. Theodoulos ran forward to support him. The man's vitality under his hands as Theo caught him by the shoulders came like a palpable shock.

"An old man needs a crutch," Theodoulos told him. "Let me get you out of here."

"I've taken worse and fought the day out," Bohemond told him, starting to push away. Theodoulos released him and watched as he fought not to collapse as his injured leg gave out.

"Come on, lord," he said. "Show yourself to the army. And then let me bandage this leg of yours. Do you want it to rot?"

Bohemond grinned at him. "At least I'd die as Prince of Antioch."

Edging his shoulder beneath Bohemond's armpit and shouting for his guards, he led the Count back down into the city, where the streets seethed and he practically had to walk on a pavement of corpses.

A cheer went up as the fighters saw Bohemond, who scarcely leaned on Theodoulos at all. Theodoulos slowed to let him walk, rather than limp along. The wound had bled through his bandage. Again, Bohemond pushed him away.

"I'll make it on my own back to camp or die trying," he told Theodoulos. "I owe it to them. Do you understand?"

"Then *walk*," he said. "I'll catch you if you fall."

"No man has served me better," said Bohemond. "I will remember this."

Somehow, Theodoulos got Bohemond back to camp and seated, his wounded leg stretched out before him. He laid out fresh water, wine, and clean cloths. The wound continued to ooze blood.

"What's all this?" demanded Bohemond. "Wrap it up and forget about it."

"Do you want it to rot?" asked Theodoulos again. He gestured at the servant, wishing for the busy women Adela had drawn about her and protected. Oh God, Adela. If only it were evening and his tasks were done, so he was free to write to her. "You, find me spiderwebs. And build a fire. I am going to have to burn that wound," he told the count. "How many men do you think it will take to hold you down?"

"None," said Bohemond. He grasped his chair.

"All Franks boast," Theodoulos told him.

"I know my limits," said Bohemond. "But you, do you know what in hell you're doing?"

"My brother is a physician," Theodoulos said.

"All I can say is you have a damned strange family," the Count observed.

You don't know the half of it.

"I've heard of stranger," Theodoulos retorted. "Someone even told me about one family of princes in which the lady armored herself and rode to war with her lord, who bequeathed an empire to the son strong enough to seize it."

For a mercy, Bohemond laughed at that description of his own family. "Bring on your irons, Greek. But I don't need anyone to hold me. I'm even strong enough not to knock you head over ass."

Theodoulos studied the tall Frank. He had been drinking steadily since he had gotten back to camp, and that would have to do. In Alexandria, there would be poppy or mandragora, even rare opium from Ch'in. Here in Antioch was only the lord Bohemond's will.

Wrapping his hand in cloth, Theodoulos plunged a spare knife into the fire, withdrawing it from time to time, then spitting on it to see if it was hot enough. When his spittle danced on the glowing metal, he withdrew the knife from the flames and turned to the Count.

"That's a fine blade ruined, you know."

"Brace yourself, my lord," Theodoulos said. "And forgive me."

"Make it quick," ordered Bohemond. He tightened his hold on his chair.

Theodoulos laid the red-hot blade on the open wound and began counting. Too short a time was as good as not at all: too long was unnecessary torture. When Leo's Emperor had been blinded, the iron had not been hot enough and the job had been botched. Thank God Leo was not here.

Bohemond stiffened. His hands tightened and went white beneath the blood and grime as they grasped the chair. The wood splintered. His flesh sizzled and cooked as if he were an Armenian spy.

Theodoulos remembered his friend, throat slit, turning on a spit. *Are you avenged?* he asked. A revolted noise gurgled in his throat.

"If you're going to puke your guts up," Bohemond forced the words through gritted teeth, "don't do it on my feet."

Theodoulos took the knife away and jammed it into the dirt. He made himself draw long, deep breaths.

"You'll live," he said.

The first servant had returned with cobwebs and stood watching in sickened fascination. "Give me those and go away," Theo told him. He smeared salve on a cloth and laid cobwebs on the salve.

Bohemond leaned forward. "What does *that* do?" he asked.

"Prevents rot," Theodoulos told him. "Hold still now."

"Hurry up," the Count ordered. "I want to get back to my city."

Theodoulos wrapped the bandages about Bohemond's leg. He'd feel different about returning to the captured city the instant he tried to put his full weight on it. Carefully, Theo raised the leg and set it on a box.

"Why don't you sit and catch your breath, my lord?" he suggested, smooth as any courtier. Bohemond was sweating heavily. Theodoulos wiped his brow for him, then laid a cloak about his shoulders, ignoring a diatribe about fool goddamned nursemaid Greeks. He eyed the wine, poured more into a pitcher, and watered it well.

"The city . . ." Bohemond repeated.

"My lord . . ."

Bohemond groaned, more from the crowd of men waiting to see him than from the pain, Theodoulos thought. He glared at Theodoulos. "You told them to come to make sure I couldn't move," he accused.

Theodoulos grinned, wolflike, at the Count. "A good idea. I wish I *had* thought of it. Why not hear them out and then, if you still feel like moving, we'll *carry* you into your city?"

"Like an old man," Bohemond muttered.

"No," said Theo, choosing his words deliberately. "Like an Emperor."

"Look here, my lord Count!" one of the knights interrupted. He pushed forward an Armenian peasant, who stumbled to his knees before the Count. In his hands was a stained bag that he presented to Bohemond.

"Open it." The Count gestured. After all, who knew? It might contain serpents.

The peasant opened the bag and tipped out its contents—the head of Yaghi-Siyan. Ah, that brought a cheer from the assembled men. God, the camp stank. Theodoulos would never get the stink out of his nostrils.

"Two brothers found the emir," explained the peasants' escort. "He was riding along one of the mountain paths and his horse threw him. They found him lying there and killed him. The other man took his belt and the sheath of his sword. Sold them for sixty bezants apiece!"

Bohemond laughed, more faintly than usual. "Well, I suppose my new princedom can pay that much for Yaghi-Siyan's head. See to it, will you?"

Theodoulos almost choked at Bohemond's effrontery. No doubt,

Count Raymond would have to pay for Yaghi-Siyan's head, unless Bohemond acquired the city treasury soon.

"I'll be back fighting tomorrow," Bohemond promised. "You tell my men, why would they want to sleep when they can kill Turks! If you find any of the sleepy, swiving bastards asleep in my city, burn down their houses! My Greek and I will show them the way, won't we, Theo?"

My Greek.

"You should rest first," he told the Count. Was the man indestructible? The horrible thought of a Bohemond who never slept, whom he must attend so he could never send word of this victory to Byzantium, hit him like a sword swing to the head.

"Oh, all right, if you will cease your whining," Bohemond agreed. "When Adhémar threw the women out of the camps, I thought we'd rid ourselves of the nags. Still, I've just one more thing to do."

"What's that, lord?" asked one of his knights.

"You all, I want you to witness this. And you, Theodoulos, kneel. That's right. In front of me. You think I want to march across the square with this leg on me?"

Theodoulos. Not "Greek" nor the other names he had for him. Was this revenge for the cautery? Theodoulos knelt.

"Rainault, over there. Fetch me my sword."

Rainault's face, hastily wiped somewhat clean, shone with the force of his grin as he obeyed.

Bohemond's first blow to Theodoulos's shoulder almost sent him flying. He braced himself for the second.

"Sir Theodoulos," said Bohemond with immense, if tired, satisfaction. "Rise."

The knights—the other knights—cheered. Theodoulos's vision blurred. He had not known himself to be so well liked. He turned hastily away and gazed out toward Antioch, pretending to study the walls. Bohemond's purple banner flew just below the citadel, but he saw it only as a shadow. Damn it, of all times to choose to weep, why must he choose now?

Adela, the thought flitted through his mind, *would be delighted*. It was better to think of her than of what the Emperor would probably say. Or what the first thing Theodoulos had ever won for himself might cost his family.

23

A cloth soaked with vinegar tied around his face, Theodoulos gestured at the bodies that lay near the sanctuary of the desecrated Cathedral of St. Peter, even tumbled before the episcopal throne. The June heat had speeded the bloating, and the reek of blood, of bowels released days ago in death, of rot that would breed plague before long. They might have only days before Kerbogha arrived, and these bodies must be buried before then or this second siege would be short.

"Haul them out, and make it fast. The Legate Adhémar wants to give the Patriarch back his throne as soon as he can."

Assuming the Patriarch survived the prison fever.

Men came at Theodoulos's orders, for was he not now a knight? Not men, he thought. Tafurs. No doubt, the price of their obedience would be added to whatever price he would have to pay for his knighthood. As a knight, he was responsible for them. Their leader, he recalled with a shudder, had been a knight once, too.

As the Tafurs dragged off the stinking corpses, Theodoulos saw why Bohemond valued them—they willingly accepted tasks that made other men blench.

"*They* won't starve, no matter. Theo, you're just helping them scavenge supper." No one had laughed at Sir Rainault's jest over a very scanty dinner last night. Long under siege, Antioch had devoured most of its own stores. Rations would be shorter still when Kerbogha's army reached the city and besieged *them*. Only the spices found in Antioch's storehouses rendered the worst of the meat almost palatable. Enticing fragrances of cinnamon and cumin overlaid rot in the cook pots of the army. A pity; they might have used those spices in trade with the merchants whom Theodoulos had been rubbing their hands together: one bezant for a shriveled loaf; two, golden as the yolk within, for an egg; fifteen for a chicken.

Theodoulos nodded thanks at the ravaged altar that Adela was not here. My lord Bishop of Le Puy had told him that he sent letters to his niece. Theodoulos had written briefly that he was made knight and wished her well. He had sent her no gift—not by her uncle's messengers and not from the plunder of the city. He had an aversion, he discovered, to plunder. Except for the cup he had found—that he had *rescued*, hidden now beneath his gear. Perhaps he should send it to her to keep it safe. No one could have stopped Adela from trying to aid the helpless. Women and children had died when the city fell; the sight of them might be as mortal to her as the pestilence that would surely follow if those brutes of Tafurs did not shovel these rotten corpses into the earth by sunset!

Oh God, now he sounded like Bohemond. Limping on his injured leg, the man who had become a kind of lord to him was up and fighting at all hours, roaring with laughter as he fired a house he knew held sleeping Frankish soldiers, shouting as they raced out of it for them to come and fight Turks! A merchant could turn away. A logothete would be expected to demand rest. A knight had to follow his lord.

Theo knew Turks: they would make Bohemond's very name a monster that mothers would use to terrify their children. If any children lived through this war.

A shadow fell across his shoulders. The land trembled, and Theodoulos shuddered. The land had danced at Nicaea, too: was this an aftershock of that victory just as, years later, a warrior might wake up from a dream of havoc?

He made himself turn slowly, as if surveying the cleansing of the cathedral. The shadow grew longer. When Theodoulos would no longer appear startled if he turned, he looked to the source of the shadow. King Tafur stood, leaning on his scythe, in the door of the church. Pale eyes flicked over Theo's cloth mask with disdain. Even wearing it, Theo fought not to gag as the madman's feral reek hit his nose: Death, but without his pale horse. He had probably already devoured it.

Theodoulos swallowed and made himself speak to the madman. "Kerbogha's come, then?"

"Nearer now." The words rustled like a shroud from the Tafurs' lord. "Good fighting. Knight."

He bowed slightly, disdainfully, and faded out of the great door, lured by new deaths.

Theodoulos stood guard on Antioch's embattled walls, as much to keep the Christians in as to keep the Turks out.

Still, the Franks kept sally points secure. Men could take the road from Antioch to the port of St. Symeon. If their courage held.

"Why does the count shout now?" Theodoulos asked.

"Man, where were you born?" Rainault inquired. "In a cave?"

Theodoulos raised an eyebrow. "Actually—"

Sir Rainault cut across his words. "Don't you know? William of Grant-Mesnil is married to our lord count's sister Mabilla."

Theodoulos whistled under his breath. The Franks among whom he lived now had webs of connections as treacherous as those of Byzantium. So, this William had gone missing. So that was why the Count had stalked through the city, whipping up the forces, shouting all night for volunteers to man the walls. The ropewalking—sliding down from the walls—had begun. Ropedancing, Bohemond had shouted, was more like it.

Would he truly hang men of rank, men who were even kin to him?

It all fell on Bohemond now, didn't it? The Count of Toulouse was sick again. Even Adhémar the Bishop, Legate of Pope Urban, had fallen ill. Had the Franks truly expected his holiness to protect him? These days, the odor of sanctity, like much else about Antioch, held a charnel reek.

Theodoulos gazed out past Kerbogha's camp, longingly over the walls.

Letters could come and go from the city. Theodoulos, whose hands were likelier to be stained with ink than blood, had more than his share. Letters from Leo Ducas had been smuggled in. Alexius the Emperor had paused at Philomelium with his army, campaigning in the south. Philomelium lay on the road from Nicaea to Iconium. From Iconium, one could reach home—the caves and cities of Cappadocia. If he could take Adela there . . .

> The Caesar John Ducas opened the road to Attalia, down which His Sacred Majesty sees fit to ride. He has no need to ask where he can command, but he has asked for my company as far as we ride together: he, I should assume, to reinforce your walls at Antioch; I to my home.
>
> I am forced to consider safety over personal inclination. Your foster mother and our household travel with me, and I have His Sacred Majesty's word that no affront will come to them.

So Lady Asherah, who had refused to appear at the palace in Constantinople, traveled with the Emperor's armies? Theodoulos suppressed a grin that would have drawn questions from his fellows: she would be safe, but she would hate every moment of it. No doubt, Leo was thanking God he had found a way so safe to convey those who were nearest and dearest to him. God only knew what sort of devil's bargain Alexius and Leo had driven.

> *Binah remains with the Caesarissa Anna: I can by no means prevail upon the Emperor to release her from her service—especially when she finds its yoke so light. And I must confess that I* (ah, here it came) *rejoice to know I can be of service to my Emperor and to my family: they shall have the protection of all Byzantium as far as our roads lie together. Thereafter, it is my kinsman who has assured me, as I told you when we last saw each other, we shall have proper escort home.*
>
> *Reports of your well-being and your success gladden my heart, and I have endeavored to put them in proper frame so that they are understood.*

Theodoulos could only imagine Asherah's reaction, let alone the Emperor's. He had no need to imagine his sister's; her thoughts touched his mind whenever he composed his mind in meditation.

Keep me informed, she begged, her thoughts stirring the leaves of the Tree of Life so that they glistened like the emeralds of Hind. *My young Caesarissa wishes to know. Especially, she wishes to know about the Red Count. I do not like this.*

Beyond the unhappiness that Theodoulos sensed, but would not press Binah to reveal if she chose not to, he realized that she did not like Bohemond, and it troubled her that Theodoulos did. Name of God, sometimes it troubled Theo, too. Ah, that drew a reluctant mental smile from her!

There had been some talk about an embassy to Philomelium, to beg the Emperor to intercede. It might have been intriguing, Theodoulos tricked out like a Norman knight, entering the Emperor's presence, saluting like his brothers in arms, not going belly-down in the dust of the Byzantine camp. It would have been no shame in him to beg, although he knew a man of knightly family would rather have died. *No need to travel,* he thought: *we can all wait for death to take us here at Antioch if the Emperor betrays us.*

He knew his anger at Alexius was shared by the knights. The other knights.

Bohemond had quickly broken off dreams of an embassy to Alexius. He had even suppressed the knights' murmurs—for now.

"Either he is true to his word or he is false. In any event, by the time he arrives at our gates," said Bohemond, "we shall either be victorious or we shall be dead."

Alexius Comnenus, Emperor of the Romans, sat in his camp at Philomelium, an icon not so much of war, though he wore armor, but of rule.

Leo Ducas could not imagine Alexius spurring to a hopeless charge now, or storming a citadel as Theodoulos's letters out of Antioch described Bohemond. The man could be a grandfather! What was that Theo had said? Bohemond had taken a wound that would not cease to bleed, so Theo had had to burn his leg? Leo swallowed hard. The memory of Leo's own Emperor Romanus's blinding was decades in the past, but he would take to his grave the maimed man's screams, old Menachem's pleas, the stinks of burning and vomit—and Asherah's light grasp on his arm.

Time had made Leo a different man as well. He had ridden in an Emperor's suite before and after Manzikert, trailing a setting sun, not one that shone in majesty at zenith. Now, Leo stood alongside kin he once spurned.

How strangely it had all turned out! If he could not imagine Alexius scaling walls and firing houses, he also could not imagine Theodoulos knighted by Bohemond himself. Nordbriht had roared approval and gone off among Alexius's Varangians to brag about the success of one of his cubs among their distant cousins. Alexius had narrowed his eyes, and Leo felt his belly chill.

Nordbriht dared not exult anywhere near the women of Leo's household, and neither did Leo. Asherah, whose anguish for kinfolk slain in the Rhinelands had turned her against all Franks, had been horrified past hope of pride: only her knowledge that Leo was relieved to have achieved this much protection for his family had reconciled her to traveling with the army. She lived among them, but apart, more secluded than the Basilissa had ever been when she journeyed with the hosts: whispers among the regiment were that Leo, the strange Ducas, the one whom no one really knew, lived like the Great King of Persia. Contests had begun in the army—see who could catch a glimpse of the madman's exotic wife!—until Alexius himself had ordered them to cease.

Leo glanced at the light slanting through the door of the tent. Not long until sundown.

Now, Leo stood in attendance, his armor glistening, the silk sheathing it rich with color. The "princes" had been sadly shabby in Antioch, which had once been so splendid, the time he had ridden in at the head of that embattled caravan. They would be in worse case now, having achieved their desire, only to find themselves besieged.

You could not say that of the Franks' kinsmen in attendance here, could you? Leo eyed them. Stephen of Blois, handsome and plausible as ever, stood in a position of honor. He had vowed early to Alexius; he was husband to a princess; and he had fled a city he believed doomed, bringing word of its impending destruction to the man he had sworn to serve. Let him lounge about, writing honeyed letters to his wife in the hope that she would not be bitterly ashamed. He would find a cold bed and a colder reputation in the cold lands of his home than Alexius—or the men who had fled after him from Antioch— accorded him.

A few nights' sleep and a number of huge meals had caused William of Grant-Mesnil, brother-in-law to Bohemond, to lose that starved-wolf look that always made Leo think of Nordbriht as he had first met him, just before the full moon rose. He too had made sub-mission to Alexius, pronouncing city and brother-in-law lost.

"And I alone escaped to tell you?" Leo had asked, his eyebrow raised, a deadly tactic in Alexius's court. Alexius had shaken his head almost imperceptibly, and Leo had subsided.

"We have a choice," Asherah had whispered to Leo only that night. She lay close to him, as much for protection as solace, flinch-ing at each watchman's call or the sound of Christian hymns. If Leo had known what his bargain would cost her . . . *"If Antioch is lost, Theo lives in mortal peril—if he lives at all. But if Antioch is not lost, they will march upon Jerusalem. And Shoshanna, her husband, all our people there—their lives may wither as if the tli turned on its wings and breathed its fire upon them."*

Leo would never equal his wife's scholarship, but he knew enough to fear the darkest aspects of the tli.

"They are your own vassals!" Guy exploded from the ranks of Alexius's officers. He had been in service almost all his life to the Em-pire, not warring against it.

He flung himself at the Emperor's feet. "Most Sacred Majesty, you accounted his lordship of Toulouse a friend. My own half-brother Bo-hemond you named sebastocrator, with rich gifts and strong promises. I beg you, do not abandon your servants and break your oaths now!"

Immensely tall, lean like a hunting dog, he toppled, dropping in the full prostration of the court, his proud head brushing the rugs of the Emperor's tent.

"Our cousin Stephen says he saw Kerbogha's army camped outside the City," Alexius said. "Rise, sir. I break no oaths. We came here to reinforce the army, but if the army be already lost . . ."

"At least, let us *see!*" implored the Norman.

Tatikios moved from his position near Alexius. "They would not listen to me before," he said. "What makes you think that they would listen now—or welcome our help? That is, if any live."

"Will no one else plead with me?" Guy cried. He laid his face down upon the carpets.

His kinsmen from the Western lands looked down at him. William, he who had married Bohemond's sister, turned away. Disgusted, no doubt, by the sight of a Norman officer in the Emperor's service who lowered himself to beg.

They had been almost subdued, those lean, ill men Leo had seen at Antioch and who had treated his foster son as their brother in arms. Theodoulos had clung to him as he had not done since his wife died. *Why, this has made a man of him as my own battles made one of me*, Leo had reluctantly thought. *He has become the man I prayed he would be*—only so much thinner and worn! He was a knight now, however, and he clung to the men of his new loyalty.

"How would it profit us," asked Alexius, "if, in gaining Antioch, we jeopardized the Queen of Cities herself?"

Alexius's eyes kindled, no doubt marking those who took his gold and waited for a chance to take all else.

"Sire, Raymond de St. Gilles waits only to give the city into your hand," Guy persevered.

"*Kyrios* Stephen here says the Count of Toulouse is ill and Bohemond"—Alexius's mouth handled the name with fastidious disdain—"rules all, with the title of 'prince.' That being the case, from where should our reward come?"

"The '*kyrios*' Stephen?" Guy raised his head and snarled. "I would tell him to his teeth—"

"*Silence!*" ordered the Emperor.

Leo stirred, drawing Alexius's attention. *You dare to disagree?* his sharp gaze asked.

Leo opened his mouth, then closed it. His family lay encompassed by the army, vulnerable to Alexius's lightest word. Those men were dying, would all die in Antioch, and Theo—his son Sir Theodou-los—with them. He hated himself.

Yet, Leo was of Byzantium, soul-deep. He had refused the chance to strive toward the diadem for himself and must serve the man who held it: his august kinsman knew his disquiet and would, in due course, inquire about it—if he saw fit. And if not, well, he was the Emperor.

"We shall pray for our brothers in Antioch," Alexius said. He signed himself and rose. That left the others no choice but to sign themselves and depart. Leo made his own prostration, then made as if to leave. Alexius's eyes flickered: *stay.*

He stayed. The tent emptied.

"Of all the men near me," Alexius began, "I should think you would have less reason to love the Franks than any. Oh, certainly, your son dwells among them, has even won his spurs"—his eyes sparkled with malice at Leo—"that is, if he still lives."

"He lives." Leo's voice was low. "I have letters from him."

"I consider Theodoulos's new service highly suspect, Leo. So I will see those letters. And son or no son of yours, I will not risk my army and my faith with my city."

"What of your faith to these men?" The words burst from Leo. "You even called Isangeles—Raymond de St. Gilles—friend."

Again, Alexius grinned. "These 'princes' mean so much to you?" he asked.

"Not *they!*" Leo cried. "The sanctity of your word!"

Like Guy, he fell to his knees and lowered his head abjectly. "We promised our aid. Guy may still be your servant. I repeat: *may.* But if we turn toward home now, do you think Bohemond will ever forgive us? Do you think that, if he lives, there will not be consequences? 'The Greeks turned their backs upon us,' they will say down the generations. And we will bear the burden of their anger."

"Since when did you learn to prophesy?" Alexius asked ironically.

Leo's heart sank: there was no gaining any advantage of the Emperor when he was in such a mood. "Since Manzikert," Leo retorted. "When I lay wounded beneath the stars after that dreadful day, praying for death, and watching the sky spin on its axis."

"Guy is Bohemond's brother, Leo, but you? I will know to whom your loyalty is due!"

Leo lowered his head, face to the carpet. "Where it has always been. You are the Emperor. You hold my oath." *My son, my son. Alex-*

ius, you protect your boy from your own daughter, that brilliant, deadly little princess . . . but you forbid me to protect mine.

"I will obey you," Leo said. "That was never in doubt."

"To you, perhaps," whispered Alexius.

God help me, with every day he changes further from the boy and man I thought I knew, Leo realized.

"Most Sacred Majesty, like the centurion, if you say come, I approach; if you say go, I depart. But you have engendered today a hatred that will last for generations. These Celts are not the passionate children of your daughter's histories."

Alexius laughed, totally unconcerned. *The more fool he,* Leo thought, *since he often campaigns accompanied by wife or daughter. His nurses, he calls them; but he keeps them under his eye.*

"My daughter plays with her fantasies."

"The Celts are good haters," Leo argued. "This land breeds good haters."

"Dear cousin Leo, if you are, by any remote chance, threatening me . . ."

Leo tensed. Now Alexius would call his guards. *And Asherah will be left defenseless in the middle of the armies of Rome. Her knives are sharp: will she follow the Jews of the Rhineland into death? Oh God, protect my love. A quarter century was not long enough. Eternity would not be long enough.*

Eternity dragged out. Leo hadn't realized an Emperor could slow time too.

"Listen to me, kinsman," Alexius said softly. "For I will say this only to you, I shall say it only the once, and I shall permit such an outbreak from you only the once. I am for *Empire.* It is *mine,* granted me by God and won by my sword. You say you retreat to Cappadocia. But many live there who call you master.

"If you even dream of extending this mastery of yours toward the diadem . . . if you think of it even once, I shall know . . ."

"God forbid!" That old threat! Leo had refused the chance years ago, before Alexius won the throne. Had he forgotten? Leo dared to raise his face to study his cousin. No, he had never forgotten. Would never forget any man who might threaten his crown.

No wonder he had not allowed Binah to leave his daughter's service. She was hostage for Leo's good behavior in the south. Still, just let him reach home safely, and it might even be that Binah's power had grown enough to free her. Once Leo had her home, he doubted Alexius could spare men to punish him.

How odd to see the Emperor's forethought fail. The past few years, he had seemed inhumanly composed, almost omniscient. But now . . . now, he seemed to have dwindled. *I have seen a brother become an icon.*

It was cause for grief as well as fear.

It is not the diadem, Leo thought. He struggled to *push* the words he had heard from his father-in-law and his wife, sojourners in the Empire, at Alexius. Magi might speak mind to mind, and Leo was no magus; but he seized at the thought as a man slipping off the crumbling lip of a rockfall grabs even at twigs.

I strive not even for God, but for the living land, which abides as wave after wave of people pour over it, as they have done in all the years since the Flood, and which will survive them.

Compared with the land itself and what underlay it, even the might of Byzantium was but the creature of a moment.

He bowed his head. Alexius would return to Byzantium and the great place in history he had won with fire, wit, and sword; Leo, if the Emperor let him leave this tent alive, would gather to himself in Cappadocia the shards left after battle raged back and forth across the outraged earth.

Tears stung his eyes. He had a daughter in jeopardy and a son: let God bless him sufficiently to gather them in, too, and he would never ask for another thing.

Truly, Leo? Oh, you liar. You will ask; patrician though you are, you will *beg,* just as Guy, Bohemond's half-brother, begged and remained a man and a noble for all his humility.

Well done, you good and faithful servant. The voice resonating in his skull was female—but not Asherah's, or Binah's, or even that of his mother, who, in any event, had rarely praised him.

The voice rose from beneath the earth, and Leo remembered it. *Do you claim this man?* it had once asked Asherah. His life had hung upon her answer. Now, Leo shook from the force of its approval, which was almost as hard to bear as its threat.

"Leo?" The Emperor's voice, more subdued now, sounded over his head. "Are you ill?"

"Majesty?" Leo rose, but kept his eyes lowered.

The Emperor approached, laying a hand on Leo's shoulder. Remarkable how much he looked like a man who had once been his friend.

"I shall pray for your foster son among the *barbaroi* and for your daughter in Jerusalem. Tell your wife, assuming she values a Christian's prayers."

"She will value yours, Majesty," Leo said, blinking away tears. He backed outside. If he hurried, he could return to his camp before dusk.

He had begged and been refused, but he felt no humiliation. He could still even love the man who had refused him. He hurried toward his own camp, sheltered within the army and guarded by men of his own, who eyed the soldiers of Rome as if they were enemies generations old.

Thou preparest a table before me in the presence of mine enemies . . . Alexius had been kinsman, not enemy.

"Leo!" The figure calling to him wore silken veils and leaned out of the tent they shared.

She would have run to him, heedless of all eyes, heedless of her own abhorrence of exposing herself in the midst of an army camp, if Leo had not hurried to her.

"Sunset is almost here," she said. "Come in, come in and wash."

She tried to pull him after her, but Leo's knees almost buckled, and she reached out to support him. He raised her veils with trembling hands. He could smell the dinner her women had cooked. The fragrances of chicken and pomegranates and heaven only knew what else made him dizzier.

"Leo, are you ill?" Asherah demanded. She gestured sharply, and the people crowded into the main room of their tent vanished.

"What's wrong?" she whispered. "You're shaking."

He had her in his arms now: she was real; she was his; and he was safe as long as he could hold her warmth against him.

"You are so strong," he whispered. "Do you draw your strength from the earth itself like our daughter?"

He buried his face in her hair. Who would seek Empire if he had this?

"Alexius," she whispered. "Did he . . ."

"We do not go to Philomelium. The Emperor returns north, back to the City. God preserve Theo, because I cannot."

"And we ourselves?"

Oh, she was too acute altogether. It was part of why he adored her.

"I think," he forced the words out, "that it is time and past time that we begin our own preparations to leave the army and move south. Home. Oh God, Asherah, it will be good to see home again."

Asherah nodded. "That must wait until after sundown tomorrow. Do you see the first stars in the sky? The Sabbath is here. You shall have that much peace, my love."

She smiled at him, then freed one hand and beckoned. Servants hurried forward, relieving Leo of his armor and easing him into a bro-caded robe, bringing him herbed warm water that eased the chill in his hands and the stinging in his eyes. As he reached their dining table, the chanting—hushed on account of the army—began. Leo watched the lamplight on his wife's now-serene face. A presence seemed to hover over her, a woman formed all of light and wisdom, a manifestation, he knew, of the divine that Jews called the *Shekhinah*. So, Asherah had progressed in her studies even farther than he had dreamed. How long would it be until she had left him totally behind?

Never.

Leo glanced up at the bright creature that held hands of fire out over his wife's head as if in benediction. He was an outsider, would always be an outsider, but out of love, it spoke to him. In that regard, it was very like Asherah. And it was another riddle to trouble his soul.

His eyes dazzled from the presence, even reflected in his wine cup. He bowed his head, listening to the Hebrew rituals he had learned over the past twenty years, trying desperately to draw their peace into his very soul.

No *wine filled the chalice that Theodoulos rescued the night Bo-*hemond seized Antioch. Any wine the army had was preserved for the sick. Some of the knights had taken to bleeding their horses for nourishment, a trick Theo had seen on the steppes, but which surprised him in the Franks: he certainly would not profane the cup! He gazed into it as if it held wine and as if he, like Asherah or Binah, could divine the future or other places on the trembling surface of the wine.

His quarters, a room in a decent house nowhere near the sites that Bohemond had marked for burning, were shadowy, and he thought he saw shadows stir. Or perhaps it was only that he had so hoped for relief from the Emperor—and from his foster father. A letter from Leo had reached him.

"*Forgive me*," was practically its entire burden. *The Emperor decrees, but my father suffers for it*, Theodoulos thought, with a resentment that was no longer borrowed solely from the Franks he lived among.

"*He* fights alongside us," Sir Rainault had said. "My lord Count made him a knight. He may be a Greek, but he's ours."

It was good that he was somebody's—as long as he was alive. He was a man and a fighter now. It was right that Leo protect his household; Theodoulos, as a man and now a knight, would protect himself and the men of his new fellowship.

The question remained: what should he do with this chalice?

Footsteps pounded into the hallway, and Theodoulos thrust the chalice into his clothing.

"If my lord Count finds you sulking, he'll burn this tent down too, you know?" Rainault greeted him.

"I'm not due on the walls," Theodoulos replied. "In fact, my lord sent me away. Ever since I helped clean out the Cathedral, he's been surprisingly easy on me."

Rainault grimaced. "Well, don't go turning priest on us. We need your wits."

Theodoulos made himself smile half guiltily. "I thought I might hunt up the Legate," he said.

"Aha! And see if His Eminence of Le Puy has received letters, perhaps from a pretty niece, is that it, brother?" Rainault clapped him on the shoulder.

Do you really think Adela's pretty? lurked at the tip of Theodoulos's tongue. He had never considered Adela's beauty as a quality apart from Adela herself. She was a lady—his lady, as Rainault thought—and therefore above common gossip. Theo would no more have spoken about Asherah or his sisters.

"Won't that be a noble contest? Who shall wed you and Adela, Adhémar by the true rite, or the Patriarch with your Greekish ritual?"

Theodoulos shook his head. The June sun had burned him dark, but he knew he flushed. "Weddings? We'll be lucky to live past sundown," he said. "And I am a landless man."

"Not for long," Sir Rainault laughed. "The Count will fill your pouch. To Adhémar, then, Sir Bridegroom!"

To his surprise, Theodoulos found himself laughing.

The work of war and healing, building up and casting off, went on throughout the city. Armed men on all the streets watched for fires or traitors, took their watches on the city walls and gates, or hurled themselves, still vainly, at the citadel that Shams-ad-Daula had yielded under protest to Kerbogha's deputy, Ahmed ibn Merwan.

"What knights those men would make if they weren't pagan!" Rainault said, gesturing at the heights.

"Better than some who were baptized," Theodoulos agreed. Better than he himself, with his divided loyalties.

The usual crowd of people demanding, praying, hoping for something surrounded the Legate's household in the camp. Theodoulos and Rainault, presuming on their rank, shouldered through the petitioners and begged admission.

"I couldn't get in here unless I was with my lord the Count," Rainault remarked slyly to Theo. "They must know you."

Theodoulos rolled his eyes. It was true that the Legate had always greeted him courteously, that he had never seemed to wave aside anything that Theo might say as if far more important business awaited him (as indeed it did). Theodoulos had ascribed it to the bishop's fundamental decency. Now, he wondered: had he been so kind for his niece's sake?

What do I have to offer? With the Emperor in retreat, I may not even keep my life.

"Does it seem to you that even more people than usual buzz about the Legate, Theo?" Rainault asked, ever the gadfly.

"Quiet!" Theodoulos hissed. Astonishing how a house captured by Franks in Antioch could remind him of his long-dead master Meletios's cave, adorned only by a few pottery shards and ancient figures that everyone else considered blasphemous.

"Ho, look at the revered Raymond," Rainault said, laying a hand on Theo's shoulder. He flinched, afraid that the chalice he carried in his clothing might be dislodged.

Raymond of Aguilers, the Count of Toulouse's Chaplain, emerged from an inner room.

"Look who's here!" murmured Rainault. "And in such a state!" The chaplain's face was tear-streaked but radiant, as if Christ in Majesty had looked down from the mosaics of the cathedral's apse and told him, "Well done, thou good and faithful servant."

Ordinarily sparing of words, even sardonic, now he dashed across the room, almost embracing the two young knights. "Come see!" he cried. "My lord St. Gilles has brought us a miracle!"

Theodoulos and Rainault edged into the Bishop's study after the chaplain. It teemed with princes. Count Bohemond leaned against the walls, arms folded over his massive chest, and winked greetings in response to his knights' respectful bows. Count Raymond of St. Gilles sat at a table across from the Bishop, so excited that health and a younger man's vigor seemed renewed in him for the first time in months. The chaplain sank to his knees, his hands clasped.

"Look at my lord Bishop," whispered Rainault.

Unlike Raymond of Aguilers, Adhémar kept his face impassive.

The hidden chalice seemed to burn through Theodoulos's undertunic. This would not be a suitable time to present it.

"Go on, man," Raymond de St. Gilles encouraged a kneeling man. He was short, as if he had not had enough to eat early in life, and paunchy, as if, even during a time of famine, he had spent years making up for his earlier death.

"I've seen him," whispered Rainault. "Mostly, I've seen him— and heard him—drunk. *Now* what's he done?"

"That is Peter Bartholomew," Raymond told him. "The stone that the builders rejected . . . he has had a most holy vision."

"Go on," the Count of Toulouse urged again. He was a prince; he was used to instant obedience; but his voice as he encouraged Peter Bartholomew was gentle, reverent.

The man joined his hands as if in prayer and held them up to the Bishop. "It was the time of the earthquake—you remember, mighty lords?"

December 30: there had been fires to fight and hell to pay.

"I fell to my knees, weeping and praying in terror."

"Probably drunk," Rainault repeated.

"I prayed as I never prayed before. Then, suddenly . . ." Peter Bartholomew raised his face with its sun-scored seams and spreading veins, and it was transformed. "Suddenly, an old man appeared to me, accompanied by a tall and wonderfully beautiful youth."

"Ah!" Theo was not the only man to gasp. Raymond of Aguilers buried his face in his hands, and his shoulders shook.

"This man," the Count of St. Gilles asked wistfully, "this . . . this *young* man—what did he look like?"

The chalice resting against Theo's heart seemed to warm.

"Great lord, he was wondrous handsome. I am a poor man, barely know my letters, but I would swear on my immortal soul that I have known his face my whole life."

The Count blessed himself. "Did he speak?"

In the entire crowded room, only Peter Bartholomew dared to draw a breath. "It was the old man who spoke, my lord. He claimed to be . . . he was St. Andrew. 'Go to the Bishop of Le Puy and Count

Raymond,' he said. 'Tell the Bishop he is much to blame for not speaking to the people . . .' "

"And to me, lad," the Count asked. "What was the good saint's message to me?"

"I was supposed to show you the hiding place of the Holy Lance, the one that pierced Christ's side."

Rainault fell to his knees beside the chaplain. Tears ran down his cheeks. "Christ has not turned from us but sent us a sign, as warriors of God!"

What *did* that young man look like? Theodoulos wondered. What if he pulled out the cup he bore right now and asked Peter Bartholomew to identify the Face upon it?

Too many miracles, Theo, lad. Look at Adhémar.

The Legate chewed on the peasant's words, one eyebrow raised. Always lean, he was gaunt now, and his face wore an unhealthy pallor. Had he been giving away food he needed to grow strong again? When Adela had been here, she had put a stop to that. Now, the Legate's eyes, wonderfully intelligent and filled with thought, were the most alive part of him; and they were skeptical.

"And then what?" the Bishop interposed dryly.

"Saint Andrew said he would show me the Lance right then. He lifted me up into the air, dressed only in my shirt, and bore me to inside the city—we had not yet taken it. I found myself standing outside the Cathedral of St. Peter, which the Turks polluted with their filthy rites."

The light shining in the windows seemed to tremble, picking out the scars on Peter Bartholomew's face, transformed now by tears and rapture.

"He led me in to the south chapel and vanished into the ground! Almost instantly, he reappeared, carrying the Lance."

"Why did he not give it to you?" asked the Bishop.

"He told me to come back after the city was taken with twelve companions and search it out. Then he snatched me up and carried me back to the camp."

The Count of St. Gilles slipped from his chair onto one knee. "Man, why did you not come to me the instant the saint returned you to us?"

Peter Bartholomew's face was on a level with Count Raymond's. "I am but a poor man, lord," he replied. "Who would listen to the likes of me?"

The Count buried his face in his hands.

"Besides, my master William-Peter ordered me off on a foraging expedition to Edessa. Even there, St. Andrew and . . . *he*—his companion—appeared to me. They punished me . . . oh God, my eyes! Struck like St. Paul because I disobeyed them. St. Andrew told me that God will protect us, that all the saints long for resurrection so they can fight alongside us."

Even Bohemond signed himself.

"So, when your eyes healed, you returned to Antioch," the Bishop took up the questions, "but you still had not the courage to speak. Is that so?"

Peter Bartholomew bent his head. "I dared not. In March, William-Peter said come with me, we shall go to Cyprus and buy food. I am only a servant, lords. I must follow my master's orders!"

"Indeed you must," Raymond of Aguilers interrupted, "and finally, finally, you are about your master's business!"

"It was Palm Sunday eve, we lay at St. Symeon, and St. Andrew appeared again. Oh God, I was so frightened! But the saint told me not to be afraid, he had instructions for my lord Count to follow once he came to the River Jordan."

"For God's love, let me hear!" The Count of Toulouse grabbed Peter Bartholomew and shook him.

"My lord, my lord," Bishop Adhémar reproved him. "Let the poor man answer our questions. Now, you lay in the same tent as your master? And while all this talk was going on, he saw and said nothing?"

"He heard, my lord," said Peter Bartholomew. "But truly, he saw nothing."

"And then?"

"We turned around and rode back to Antioch. I tried to see the Count, but I was turned away. So I went to Mamistra, on my way to Cyprus."

"Disobeying a holy saint's command?" asked Adhémar.

Peter Bartholomew burst into tears. "I tried! I did try, but my master forced me onto the boat. It was driven back three times. Finally, we went aground on an island, and I was sick for a long time. When I came back, Antioch had fallen. I almost fell too, crushed by horses. Then again, St. Andrew told me I must speak to the Count and to you, My Lord Bishop. I told my friends, who laughed, but I came anyway. The chaplain was kind to me"—Raymond of Aguilers sobbed audibly—"and brought me before my lord Count. I told all to him. And now . . ." He spread out his hands to show them, grimly and empty.

"In five days' time," Raymond of Toulouse cried. "Five days! I swear, there shall be a search for the Holy Lance in the south chapel. You—"

To Theodoulos's horror, he realized the Count was speaking to him.

"You had the task of purifying the Cathedral, did you not?"

"Yes, my lord." Theodoulos kept his voice level.

"And did you see or feel anything at all?"

Only the foul presence of the Tafurs. Theo closed his lips before those words could slip out.

"Nothing, my lord."

"You shall come with us. Perhaps you will be granted better fortune. Pray for it, young man."

Theodoulos sank tactfully to his knees and bent his head as if in prayer.

"Meanwhile, my good friend—my *brother,*" cried the Count, flinging his arms about the peasant, "you shall rest in the care of my own chaplain. Take him, Father, and treat him as if he were my own son."

"Amen," said Raymond of Aguilers. Reverently, he rose from his knees and approached Peter Bartholomew, helping him to rise as if he were a bishop. "Let me find you some worthy housing, some food. Come with me . . ."

Chaplain and visionary disappeared. The tension in the room decreased.

Theodoulos met Adhémar's gaze. The Bishop was not impressed, not at all! Surely, it was not just the rebuke to him. He was an aristocrat, a prince of the church, and Peter seemed like a madman. And . . . Theo recalled. Surely, Byzantium housed a Holy Lance.

At least one.

He rose from his knees, giving a hand to Rainault, who practically wobbled from the force of his emotion.

"Five days," Sir Rainault breathed. "And you shall make one of the Twelve to seek the Lance! If envy were not deadly sin, how I should envy you!"

A worker's shovel clashed against another piece of rock. He started to swear, remembered the place, then scraped painstakingly away as if he dug at a city's wall, not within the south chapel of the Cathedral of St. Peter. Theodoulos sighed, considering the growing trench in the chapel's floor and the mess of rock and earth surrounding it. All his labor, all his sweat and dread supervising the Tafurs as they purified the cathedral had been wasted.

And now it looked as if they had wasted their time here as well. The day had begun with such hopes! Only last night, a meteor had fallen on Kerbogha's camp.

"Let him *burn*," Sir Rainault had whispered.

"God wills it!" had rung through the camp and the embattled city. Spirits had not been higher since the city's gates had opened to the army. Even the smells of smoke and blood, remainders of an assault that almost took a tower on the southwest wall, could not daunt them. Only failure could; and now it looked as if failure might be the crown to Peter Bartholomew's visions.

Theodoulos shook his head. Here he was, one of twelve witnesses, and he was dozing off in the chapel, lulled by the steady grind of the workmen and the heat of the day. He dared not fall asleep; he too might dream dreams or see visions. And Antioch had enough of that already.

Peter Bartholomew's visions had been followed by the testimony—the rival testimony, Theo reminded himself—of Stephen of Valence. The night the tower almost fell, he and some brother clerics had gone to the Church of Our Lady for a service of intercession. The others had fallen asleep. Stephen, however, had beheld a figure of marvelous beauty who had spoken to him and been glad he spoke to a good Christian. A cruciform halo had crowned his head, and when Stephen had asked, the figure had admitted he was Christ. He had left Stephen with admonitions to Adhémar and exhortations that the army return to a Christian way of life. If they did, he vowed, he would send them protection in five days' time. A lady with a shining face and St. Peter himself had also appeared. Adhémar, who did not believe Peter Bartholomew, believed Stephen of Valence.

In the exultation that followed, Adhémar had even succeeded in getting the princes to swear—from Raymond and Bohemond on down—that none of them would leave Antioch without the consent of all the others.

One team of workers tired and was replaced by another, the honor of service hotly contested. Finally, Raymond of St. Gilles stirred.

"I suppose it was too much to hope for," he said. "I am still not well. If you find anything, send me a messenger. Perhaps I shall return." Signing himself before the altar, he walked unsteadily, slowly from the Cathedral, as disappointed and ill as he had earlier been exalted.

The day dragged on. His chaplain remained, encouraging the workers, speaking in a low voice to the Bishop of Orange, who also lingered.

"Wait!" Peter Bartholomew's voice rose to the height of the Cathedral's roof. He tore off the fine clothes that Raymond of Aguilers had forced him into. Wearing only his shirt, he leapt into the trench carved by the workers in the chapel floor.

"Pray!" he ordered. "Pray!"

Theodoulos sank again to his knees. *Don't let the army be too disappointed* was his prayer.

He could hear Peter scrabbling in the trench, an enormous, hopeful rat. A cry of joy followed.

"Let me see!" shouted Raymond of Aguilers, as the usually self-contained chaplain hurled himself into the trench. "There it is!" he cried. "There! Oh, God bless you, Peter, God bless you!"

He pulled himself from the narrow pit. "I saw it," he told the Bishop of Orange, tears streaming down his face. "I saw the Lance and embraced it. Brother, bring it out!" he called.

Peter Bartholomew emerged from the trench. In his hands he clutched what he clearly believed to be the Holy Lance—or the spearpoint that had been fastened atop a shaft, long perished in the earth now. It was scarcely the size of a man's hand. But it shimmered in the sight of every man in the Cathedral, unless it was their tears that caused it to glow.

"Quick!" Raymond turned, and his eyes fell upon Theodoulos. "Someone run—you, sir—to the Count and tell him. Tell him the Lance has been found. It's been found!"

Raymond sank to his knees, raising his hands over his head in exaltation.

Theodoulos rose from his knees and, as he was ordered, ran.

25

I don't understand it," Rainault commented as he and Theodoulos followed Peter the Hermit out of Kerbogha's camp. "The Turks make our ropewalkers look positively loyal. None of them trust one another, and they're deserting as fast as they can. Yet Kerbogha demanded unconditional surrender."

"Wouldn't you?" Theodoulos asked. "When your back is to the wall, you bluff. You yourself admire their courage. Now, all we can do is prepare for all-out battle."

"They are mad," Rainault replied. "Mad. They have to have spies in our camp. Even if my lord Count roasts another lot of them, they've got to have spies. They must know of the divine visitations granted us."

"Detailed instructions," Theodoulos agreed. "Down to orders not to pillage the enemy camp. Which makes good tactical sense, when you come to think of it."

"And," said Rainault, "we have the Lance."

"The Turks think it's a fraud," Theodoulos said.

Rainault shrugged. "It's breathed new heart into men I expected to disappear."

Meanwhile, the city was becoming a whole lot hungrier.

So the embassy riding to Kerbogha to propose withdrawal had made sense. Peter the Hermit, foremost of the civilians who rode with the army, led it. With him rode Herluin, his translator, who was a Frank, but one who knew Arabic and Persian.

Theo's own fluency had earned him a place on this venture and some very shrewd stares from Herluin, who contrived to edge his horse in beside Theodoulos.

"May I speak with you, master . . . I mean, Sir Theodoulos?"

Theodoulos inclined his head. Herluin knew entirely too much more than the languages of the East: now was hardly the time to parry about Asherah's family, but Theo would be damned if he lied. Knights were not supposed to lie; of course, most of them did.

Herluin smiled slyly, then asked, "What did you overhear in Kerbogha's camp?"

"I think we might have gotten them to agree to trial by battle if Peter the Hermit hadn't demanded they all convert," Theodoulos said rashly. "I take it the idea was to defy them, not to reach terms."

Rainault had approved, of course; Theodoulos found the ideas either of outrageous terms or trial by combat rather foolish. Rainault would say that knights were born, not made—even if his own lord had made this one.

"Everyone's angry at Kerbogha to the point of blood feud," Theodoulos said. "Let us win this battle and we can simply ride up the coast toward Joppa, with Emirs competing to sell us oranges and horses. If we only had another month or so . . ."

"We haven't got it. Our horses are almost gone, and so is our food. If we don't fight tomorrow, our honor's gone too."

Theodoulos shrugged. In this talk of honor, Herluin was more a knight than he. Honor for Theodoulos lay in remaining alive and protecting the people he felt called upon to stand by. Like the Emperor himself, he must play both sides: honor lay in playing well. The current battle by prophecy did not seem to be helping.

Herluin was right about one thing. With Count Raymond bedridden and Adhémar ill, Bohemond assumed command. By sundown, he would have Antioch—or nothing at all.

Ill as he was, in the early morning, Adhémar armored himself and was helped into the saddle. He at least had a horse. Some of the knights rode asses or oxen, while others would march into battle beside common armsmen. Each prince raised his banner. The shabby knights and infantry lined up in six armies. Men vied to stand close to Raymond of Aguilers, whose honor it was to carry the Holy Lance into battle.

The gate opened. At Bohemond's signals, the men of the West marched out, past heralds who had come, far too late, from Kerbogha. The Turks withdrew, further and further, luring the Franks out where the entire army might be exposed.

Bohemond signaled, and Herluin laughed. "My lord fox!" he cried. "Look, he sends Rainald of Toul to protect our flanks."

"We'll have all we can handle here," Theodoulos said. He spurred his horse, and the battle separated them.

He heard a scream and rode on, huddled small beneath his shield for fear of arrows, past what had once been the Bishop's standard-bearer. Around him like a grey, deadly wave poured men carrying clubs or scythes. Some wore sackcloth, while others went into battle bare of skin and armed only with their nails and fighting rage. Bohemond hurled the Tafurs against the Turks again, and again. Up ahead, King Tafur brandished his scythe. Appalled yet thrilled, Theodoulos saluted him with his sword.

"They're breaking!" someone screamed. "They're falling back!"

White light exploded on a hill. Theodoulos cried out in anguish at its strength and splendor. The light had not blinded him, but it might have struck him with madness.

"Look!" he screamed. "Over there! On that hillside!"

"There they are! All in white, on white steeds!" someone else shrieked. "Saint George! Saint Mercury! Saint Demetrius! Pray for us! Fight with us!"

God help us, thought Theodoulos. He screamed a battlecry and charged, following the shining figures.

The Turks fell back before him. More of Kerbogha's allies must be pulling out. *Don't get yourself killed, lad, just before you win,* Nordbriht had always warned him. *Careful.*

I promise, old wolf, he thought at his old teacher.

"Saint Andrew! Saint Andrew!" men chanted.

What! Had *he* appeared, too? It must be too many blows to his helm, Theo concluded. The army pressed onward toward the Iron Bridge.

"What's that?" cried Rainault, pointing with his bloody sword.

"They fired the grass," a footman said. "My God, it'll go up like tinder. If the wind's wrong . . ."

Theodoulos glanced around him. Adhémar looked as if he needed a shroud, not a new banner bearer.

"Look! Over there!"

Theo turned in his saddle. *What, more saints?* That flicker of light at the corner of his eyes, teasing it upward . . .

Did the sun glint on giant metallic wings, swooping and dipping, gliding from one thermal above Antioch to another? Did the tli now stoop upon its prey, opening its unimaginable maw to spew fire out onto the withered grass before Kerbogha's army?

"That madman set the fire himself to keep his army together. God, what a crazy bastard. What a knight he'd make!"

It isn't Kerbogha, Theo wanted to explain. *It's the tli.* And knew he dared not so much as open his mouth. The wind was rising now. If the wind blew harshly upon them, the fire could turn, could leap any barricade they built.

You can stop this, my son. The woman's voice, rising from his heart, made him shudder.

"I can?" Theodoulos blurted.

In the mountains, he had curved the light itself, letting him and his friends pass by unnoticed. What was fire but a form of light, of power? It was the dragon's breath; but even the tli could turn on new enemies.

Turn, he wished the fire. *Turn aside.*

Make it real, my son. You can. You can.

Sweat trickled down his ribs as if he stood in the midst of the fire, engulfed, yet not consumed.

He extended his arm and slashed down with it as if he were Count Bohemond himself. Moses had divided the Red Sea: surely, Theodoulos might be vouchsafed power over some sparks and embers?

And the fire wavered, then burned back the other way. Theodoulos sagged against his saddle's high cantle.

"You all right, man?" Rainault asked, riding up and patting Theodoulos for wounds.

"I will be," he whispered. "Look at the Count!"

Bohemond, his sword dripping blood, his shield hacked almost into kindling, rode across the field.

"There he goes!" Bohemond shouted. "Kerbogha, you buggering coward! Come back and fight!"

Not even the army's cheers could drown out *that* voice for long.

Antioch, his men proclaimed, belonged to Bohemond. He had won it; he had protected it; and now, backed by the three saints they had seen shining on a hilltop, he had driven away Kerbogha.

Raymond de St. Gilles insisted that the city belonged to the Emperor, that Alexius should be told. Bohemond shrugged and ejected everyone's armed men but his own from the towers he controlled, then from the Citadel itself.

"So *now* the high and mighty Alexius would come?" Bohemond demanded. "When would it please His Mightiness to hold out his hand for the city we bled to take? By God's wounds, if I live until the Second Coming I shall never forget that he abandoned us. Antioch is *mine*."

Kerbogha's deputy, Ahmed ibn Merwan, had watched his master driven off and promptly announced his willingness to surrender the Citadel. Raymond had sent his banner, the banner of the senior prince of the host, but Ahmed had refused it. To Raymond's poorly concealed rage, Ahmed preferred to surrender to Bohemond. Waiting until Bohemond arrived, Ahmed had marched his garrison out, safe under Bohemond's protection, denying Raymond even the relief of a massacre. That would have been galling enough. Not much to Theo's surprise, it turned out that Ahmed had had a prior arrangement with Bohemond. Worst of all, however, came when Ahmed, and many of his men, converted to Christianity and joined Bohemond's army. Bohemond, fisher of souls in a city sacred to St. Peter:

Bohemond's younger knights were betting Raymond of Toulouse might not survive the humiliation.

26

Did that Turk really *ask you to stand godfather for him?*"

"Ahmed ibn Merwan?" Theodoulos supplied the name for Rainault, knowing that the chronicler-knight would spell it however he chose. He laughed. "Only because my lord Count was not there. But he arrived in time for the baptism after all."

"I would like to know what you had to do with the surrender of the Citadel," Rainault muttered.

Theodoulos managed not to smile. "Look there!" To distract him, Theodoulos pointed at an armed party that the Count of Toulouse's men admitted over the bridge. "From St. Symeon, do you think?" he asked.

"Who cares?" Rainault asked. "Now, if they were traders with loads and loads of fresh food and perhaps a flock or two, they would be worth watching."

Foraging parties were nothing unusual. Some of the minor lords were always riding out in search of food or plunder.

The smells of burning, rot, and ordure, both human and animal, clung to their scanty meals. So many bodies had fallen into the rivers and wells that the water was poisoned. Food spoiled quickly in this heat, and was eaten anyway.

At first, it was the old, the young, the wounded, and the desperately poor who died of a fever that seemed to wither them overnight, as if a dragon's breath melted the vitality and the flesh from their bones.

Theodoulos's foster brother Manuel, he who thrived so in his Alexandrian medical studies, had spoken of this fever. It was the same one that had taken Alexander the Great's companion—and later, probably, Alexander himself.

Some of the greater lords had already left Antioch, keeping themselves safe under the guise of forage or plunder. Count Bohemond had talked of raids that sounded at least as enticing as the promise of cooler, sweeter air.

One of the riders who dismounted hastily was unusually slight, unusually quick, unusually hesitant. Theodoulos blinked, then groaned.

"Brother." Theodoulos pointed again. "Look there. At that rider."

The blood rose to his temples and started to boil there. Despite the heat of the day, his hands turned cold, not in fever but in sheer rage.

"Oh no," he muttered. "What a fool. What a perfect idiot. Go back!" he shouted. "Go back where you have a chance of being safe!"

"Where else should I be? They said in Cyprus that my uncle was ill, so I came back as was my duty."

The rider's voice rose higher than any man's. Small, capable hands in chain-mail mittens tugged off the close-fitting helm with its uncomfortable nasal. A matted braid of long, pale brown hair tumbled down the boiled leather harness Adela had found God-knew-where and wore as if born to it.

Rainault started to laugh.

"Are you mad?" Theodoulos demanded. "In this heat, you can die of the weight of that armor."

"You can die from an arrow without it," Adela retorted. "At least I was glad to hear my lord Count knighted you."

"This is no place for a woman."

Adela glared. "It looks like no place for man, beast, or madman, let alone ladies of good sense. Sir knight, you overreach yourself. I came to tend my lord and uncle the Bishop Adhémar. What better place for a dutiful niece and daughter of the Church?"

"The Bishop's been ill for months. Why, all of a sudden, do you become so concerned?"

"I had not *heard* before," Adela snapped. "St. Symeon was burned, remember? We wandered over half of creation, then found a ship that would take us to Cyprus, and we are mortally tired."

"Coming here to rest could prove mortally tiring," Theodoulos told her. "Why don't you go home?"

"Home?" Adela's eyes flared up. "Home? Home *is* where my uncle is until we can reach Jerusalem. If he lives that long. Dear God, Theodoulos, this is not how I left him."

Theodoulos reached out to shake her and could not let go. The touch of her warmed his hands, eased the chill in his heart. There was heart's ease even when she shouted back at him.

No, his friend Adela had no particular beauty beyond a freshness of complexion, browned now by wind and the summer sun, and that incredible Norman vitality. Her hands were chapped, callused from needle and, these days, ladle and probably sword, rather than smoothed with the lotions of the East. Her hair was draggled from the

helm she wore, not glossy with henna and covered with the most ex-
quisitely gold-threaded of filmy veils. If she could manage a keep,
speak one language well, manage not to starve in another, and understand enough Latin to follow the Mass, she had more education
than many ladies of her station.

Theodoulos had grown up among fragrant, exotic, learned
women, had been married young to a girl as shy as she was short-
lived. Adela now—she was a field flower rather than a Damascus
rose. Such blossoms, Theodoulos recalled, were strong of stem, hardy
of bloom, and came back each spring, year after year after year.

"You don't need me, do you, brother?" asked Rainault.

"Oh yes I do," said Theo.

Rainault laughed. "For what? To stand beside you before my lord
Bishop when you—"

"Someone needs to escort the lady to the Legate," Theodoulos
said. "Someone else. Because if I stay here any longer . . ."

"You might learn some sense!" Adela retorted. Rainault grinned.

Theodoulos gave her shoulders what would have been a firm
shake with anyone but a Norman woman, then released them and
strode off, in the grips of a colossal, warming rage and something that
bubbled underneath it and seemed far too much like incredulous joy
for his comfort.

Adela's laughter behind his back sounded high-pitched and angry.
He had insulted her, and God grant he would not have hell to pay for
it—from her or from the Bishop, assuming he had strength enough.

On second thought, let the good old man live, and he could scold
and inflict penances all he chose.

"I will talk sense into the Greek. I promise, lady, he will speak you
fair," Rainault threatened in a voice intended to be overheard.

"He must do so of his own will or it is worthless, sir." *Ohé, Rainault, take that! And serve you right for a meddlesome bastard.*

"Here now, what is this?"

"My lord Count!" Theodoulos stammered, which made him even
more furious. Bohemond had a genius, it seemed, for catching Greeks
at a disadvantage.

"Come on back, Sir Theodoulos." Bohemond gestured. The older,
taller man's blue eyes sparkled with a laughter that was going to erupt
soon and probably make him die of humiliation.

Adela had flushed beneath the color the sun had given her. Lacking what composure her usual skirts might have given her, she ducked
her head in an awkward bow. *A little late now to be ashamed, isn't it?*

Theodoulos raised an eyebrow at her with a wicked delight that he knew would annoy her.

"Stand up straight, lady! Wear your harness with pride!" Bohemond ordered her, grinning and showing those white teeth. "My mother always did. Always thought she had courage enough for an army."

Adela tried to tidy her braid and stand soldier-straight.

"And you, my bashful friend, do you disdain this lady because she shows herself willing to fight?"

"God forbid," Theodoulos whispered. He felt his face burn, but not with the beginnings of fever. If he were ill, would Adela tend him, too?

"Now, you speak like a sensible man, well able to prize a lady of courage. Take this lady by the hand and welcome her," Bohemond ordered. "Then, conduct her to her uncle."

He started to turn away with a magnificent swing of his shoulders. Then he turned back. "First, though, I think, you should find her a place where she can change to robes more suitable for tending a Papal Legate. Her current guise might distress him, and he is not at all well," Bohemond added in a more subdued voice. "Not well at all."

Theodoulos, dreaming, found himself standing in the cool shadows of a rough-cut flight of steps, descending into the earth. The opposite wall, rearing up over his head, was of golden stone. Tiny glints of light where the sun touched danced along the joints of the ancient wall.

He was going home. He pressed his head against the rock. Water ran alongside him, in some secret course buried beneath the stone. He had only to speak to the rock—for how should he of all men strike it?—and sweet water would gush forth to satisfy his thirst.

There was comfort in the rock, in the growing darkness as he descended the stairway until, finally, he looked up and saw the sky as if from the bottom of a dry, clean shaft. Who was that woman up ahead, beckoning him forward? Binah? Asherah? His mother herself? She had passed on ahead long ago, but surely she sent a daughter to show him the way. This was their place, after all. They had come to the end of the stairs. The sun was gone, and stars had come out.

They turned down a quiet corridor. Light sprang up along the walls as they passed. In an enclave on the right, Theodoulos saw an altar and could have wept for its familiarity. Carved, it was, of the living stone, and on it stood a figure he remembered from his boyhood: a woman infinitely strong.

"Remember this," the voice murmured, as sweet and tempting as the

hint of water running beside him within the stone. "Remember. Your life *will depend on your memories.*"

"God's my life, Theodoulos, wake up! Wake up now!"

Theo's hand, halfway to the knife he kept with him, paused. He knew that voice. What fever madness had stormed Rainault's brain, waking him like this? A few moments, a few steps more, and he might have seen the home from which he had been divided all his life.

Because it was expected, he cursed his friend's eyes and protested.

"I'm not due on guard," he told Rainault. He rolled over on his back, refusing to move. Maybe if the man went away, he could sleep again and return to that dream of sunlight and water and the golden stone on which Jerusalem was built.

"Adhémar wants you."

"Adhémar can't want me. The Legate from the Pope in Rome doesn't wake up in the middle of the night and ask for a jumped-up Greek secretary."

"He's dying, Theo." Rainault's voice was husky. "And there isn't a man in the camp who wouldn't envy you the chance to do anything at all for him. Now, move!"

"Sweet Jesus," Theodoulos exclaimed and rolled off his pallet before Rainault could give him a shove. Adela! What would become of her? They would have to get her away from the pesthouse that Antioch had become. Would she go?

An image of Adela standing before the carved tufa of his home, Adela holding his daughter (a thought too precious to be entertained for long), fleeted through his mind. How would he get her home? And what would they think of her there?

It vanished, engulfed in the larger concern.

Adhémar was dying. *Now* what would they do? His hand had been over them like a father's for so long. Would they quarrel over his inheritance and struggle, each for a different course, until his entire house was rent asunder?

Theodoulos rummaged in his chest for a tunic he knew he had, less faded than the others and clean, unless someone had been in here before him. There it was!

Wrapped about the cool silver of the cup he had found. With Rainault urging him to haste, Theo pulled the tunic on over the garments he had slept in, then fought his way into his shabby footgear. He snatched up a bag—as a scholar, he could be expected to have some strange medicines about him—and thrust the Cup into it.

A crowd had gathered outside, but it parted to let him through. Many men already knelt in the darkness, broken only by a single torch. They had all lived in his shadow, like that of a green tree, blighted now and dying. They hurried toward Adhémar's deathbed.

"Took you long enough," a voice muttered. Theodoulos nodded respect at a man he recognized as one of Count Raymond's.

"I shall pray for him," Rainault was saying of Adhémar.

"You, man, and everyone in this camp. Except maybe Peter Bartholomew. Mind you, my lord and I believe that God sent the Lance he found to us in our hour of need, but this talk that God has struck down the good bishop . . ."

Whispers of power brought Binah out of a sleep in which she wandered a road far beneath the surface of the earth. She had never seen it except in her foster parents' stories, which always ended with "but all that is gone now."

She lay motionless in the narrow bed that the Augusta had decreed for such as she, who served the Court, and allowed memories of places she had never walked to scroll out once more in her mind.

The queen road joining the underground cities was rubble now, its walls collapsed beneath the weight of the earth. The chamber of her mother's enthronement and her own birth had caved in when the earth shook. Nevertheless, in her dreams, Binah saw those places and knew that somehow, when the time was right, she would find some way of mending what was broken, righting what had been set awry, rebuilding what had been cast down.

The whispers of power intensified, calling her, calling anyone—calling any*thing*—that might be capable of response. (She sensed, far away, Theodoulos stirring in troubled sleep, Asherah opening her eyes, instantly wary and alert.) *You are in no danger*, she whispered into the stillness within her mind, giving what comfort she dared.

She sniffed: was something burning? The kitchens were too far away for her to smell spoiled food or garbage and, in any case, the Caesarissa kept her house as meticulously clean as Asherah herself.

Binah rose in a sudden, supple move and dressed quickly. Dark was like daylight to her; no need to kindle any light that was certain to be observed. Strange as she was, no other woman would share quarters with her even here in the Caesarissa's house, where rooms were in shorter supply than at the palace.

The Caesarissa had a home; why not she herself?

She had been told how much it was that she had even a room to herself. Who knew what she might do with so much privacy? The Augusta had arched her brow as if imagining excesses from some Babylon of her fevered orthodox imagination, and Binah had been hard-pressed not to laugh.

She opened a window and took a deep breath of the night air. Here, the reek of the lower city was dispelled by gardens. Something moved in the shadows, and Binah's heart twinged. Narrow as her bed was, on nights like this—she shook her head. She had been rash, and she had paid.

It was not as if she planned now to entertain lovers or perform sorcery in what was almost a nun's cell, although the Augusta made it sound as if Binah had the best room in the palace.

She must admit it: the solitude had made her years as a hostage almost endurable. But she was weary of observation now, weary almost past control. While Thorvaldr lived, some escape, some respite had been possible. But he had died, and the little Caesarissa had *looked* at her so knowingly.

Binah had been careful; how could Anna have known what she knew?

Have I taught her too well?

Soon, it would not matter. Theodoulos was well beyond the reaches of the Emperor's army and more than a match for the Franks, and Leo had reached home, where he had defenses that Binah knew in her soul could protect him. There was no reason any longer to remain—*except faith broken*, she reminded herself.

It was the sort of thing that would trouble her father, she knew. For him, even a pledge given under coercion was a pledge to be honored.

Mother and I can bring him around, Binah assured herself uneasily. Persuading Leo that his honor was not broken, however, was not as easy as wheedling coin or silk from a stern father, which, in any case, he had never been.

The siren song that waked her made her shut her eyes. *I want!* She told herself. If not Thorvaldr, then something of her own, starting with her home.

Might it be worthwhile, she wondered, to cloud minds other than those of the little Caesarissa? Make them think that they had *allowed* her to return home?

Starting where, fool? With the Emperor? And he warded by his God and his priests and that glorious termagant of an Augusta who hates you?

She thought that if she could avoid the Augusta, she could cajole the Emperor. Somehow. Her violet eyes narrowed appraisingly. He had looked at her before and turned away, as if some vision of his boyhood friend's disapproval stood between him and a woman he admired. Nevertheless, when faced with the choice between his goals and loyalty to that boyhood friend, he had never hesitated to put Leo Ducas second. Binah need feel no compunctions on that grounds at all. And to progress from arousing a man's desire to changing his mind . . .

She shook her head. Had she her full powers, she might try. But Alexius was, after all, away on campaign. And the Augusta was here, watching, criticizing, hoping that one day the woman who called herself "Helena" would place a foot wrong.

For herself, Irene was welcome to banish her. But Binah could not bear disgrace to touch her family. So, she would simply leave.

She caught up a veil and slipped out the door. She sensed minds, wary, but fogged with sleep, nearby. Guards. Guards even here in the Caesarissa's own house. It was the matter of an instant to intensify that longing for sleep, then glide past them. They dared think they could restrain her? For a follis or some other base coin, she would show them the folly of treating her as an ordinary woman, to be reprimanded and confined and, worst of all, prayed over.

It was time and past time to go.

If she could slip from the palace to the Ducas family house on that shabby side street near the palace, she could cast wards and send herself home in spirit, she thought. She might even dare to translocate herself. That bore its risks, but it might be safer than commanding a place on one of the caravans that still dared travel to the south.

The house first, she determined. Out of this noxious atmosphere, she would be able to think more clearly.

What was the matter with her thoughts? That idea made her pause. Power had whispered her awake, and she thought it had been her dreams. She closed her eyes and listened with her inner senses. Music wrapped around her senses, music and incense and the tones of some incantation that rose, then faltered, as if whoever chanted were not quite certain of what she did.

What *she* did. Binah tested the strength of that incantation and allowed it to draw her as if she followed a scent. The power intensified, luring her closer. Bitter, potent, a spell she might easily master, if she wanted to coerce what lay upon the earth and wrest it out of frame.

Only one person in this house would have such a desire. When had Anna learned such spells and where?

Caesarissa, I did not teach you this!

Tears filled Binah's eyes and spilled onto her cheeks. "Why, you're sorceresses!" Anna had accused Asherah and Binah, so innocent, angry, and fearless had she been. And such a fool. Binah could have broken her mind right there and then.

It would not, she suspected, be well to try now.

It was those books, those books of her old tutor Psellus. Binah's father had said he was not to be trusted, but Leo was practically the only man in the empire who would have dared say that, and not even Alexius would have believed him. The old intriguer had not been just a scholar; he had been a thaumaturge.

Now, his last student, working alone, had decided she was frustrated at being offered only morsels of power instead of the feast she sought. Being gifted, she taught herself. Being angry, she went sadly awry.

Binah's heart chilled. *Has she the child with her?* she thought in horror. Rather than risk an innocent's contamination, she would interrupt the Caesarissa right now; she supposed she could scream and manufacture some wild story of an intruder or three. She tiptoed to the Caesarissa's door and pressed herself against it, trying to listen with all her senses. She cast her sight throughout the house and sighed with relief.

The child slept with his nurse; after all, it was not as if Anna were that devoted a parent. Nicephorus Bryennius rode with the army. Anna harmed no one but herself.

For now. Binah suspected that just as she herself grew in power, Anna would learn.

What is it to me? she asked herself. Her father might serve this woman's father, but that did not bind her, did it?

Oh, Anna, Anna. Again, the tears came. That child who had accused her, with the crumbs of honeycakes still smearing her fingers and mouth. Who had risen with a fine lady's manners when the news from the Rhineland had arrived and excused herself. Who had won her father's heart and—she might as well admit it—a piece of her own with an earnestness that had enchanted them past the promises and threats that she thought she ought to be making.

This is not what I wanted for you, Binah thought.

What had happened to that lovable little girl, whom Leo had smiled at, certain that, as a girl-child, she had wanted only affection and kind words?

Even then, she had been angry, self-pitying, ambitious. She had attempted to regain a position she had lost almost half her life ago by the means permitted women and she had failed. Because she was not one who could easily submit, she had turned to other means: just perhaps, the presence of someone like Binah in her household, the touch of Binah's mind on hers, had twisted her. Binah had done nothing right, but whatever she had done, she had done to protect her family.

At least I have not failed in that.

If she escaped now, she left the princess in jeopardy from power that Binah herself would have hated to invoke. Even now, the traces of it made her almost ill from revulsion. That was where it started: with the people sensitive to power badly used sickening and weakening.

But thereafter, Anna exposed the people close to her to deadly risk. Who knew how far the contamination might spread? Her father would expect her to take what steps she could to safeguard what he still, inexplicably, valued.

If I remain, perhaps I can destroy those books, Binah thought. That would not suffice: Anna's memory was almost as keen as her own. *If I cannot teach her reason, perhaps I can teach her caution. Or terrify her myself.*

The one thing she could not do was abandon her. It would be like setting her infant son down between fires and expecting him not to burn himself.

Binah sighed and crept back to her tiny room. For fear Anna would detect it, she dared not even ward it against the song that insinuated itself into the very fiber of her being. When morning came, she vowed to herself, she would fight. For Anna's soul, which her father would want Binah to protect, as well as for Binah's own freedom.

Why, I am bound to them as if I loved them like my own, she thought. She sent her outrage out into the night air and sensed, more than heard, the chanting break off. Did the Caesarissa think thaumaturgy was easy? The more fool she.

She smiled thinly and cast herself into a sleep, as if a general ordered his troops to retreat, regroup, and plan their next attack.

27

Adela stood near her uncle's bed, her face composed. *Traces of tears* streaked it in the flickering light, but her eyes were dry, lest they miss a single task that she might find to do to ease the dying man. Anything, even the smallest, might save him, her watchfulness clearly indicated. Her delusion struck Theodoulos to the heart.

Adhémar had passed beyond the time when he struggled against his fever. He did not even seem to sweat, and fever still cast a deceptive flush of health over his face. His hands, empty now, lay against covers, from time to time plucking at them. The great ring of his office almost slipped off his finger.

Adela dropped to her knees and captured her uncle's hands, brought them to her lips, then rested with her face against them.

"Holy lord?" Theodoulos too dropped to his knees.

Adhémar's face kindled, as if light grew in a noble lantern, his soul shining through the bones of temples and arched eye sockets.

Adela straightened, releasing her uncle's hands. The Bishop gestured weakly. Theodoulos took up one hand and, heedless of infection, kissed it. The wasted fingers pressed his faintly, and the weary face almost smiled.

"Niece . . ." The merest breath of a word, another laborious gesture. Adela touched Adhémar's other hand. To Theodoulos's astonishment, the dying man brought their hands together.

Father Meletios had known when he collapsed in Hagios Prokopios that his time was running out. He had joined Leo's and Asherah's hands, wedding them when no one else had dared.

Adhémar's lips moved, mumbling words Theo could scarcely hear, except with his heart. Latin words. Jumbled words. Holy and welcome ones to him. Ioannes should be here to stand beside him. Not to mention Leo and Asherah. They had raised him; they had witnessed that short-lived marriage to a girl whose face Theo scarcely remembered, overshadowed now by Adela's.

Theodoulos signed himself with his free hand. "I promise," he whispered. *"Volo."*

Adela whispered something that Adhémar took as assent. Her voice trembled, along with her fingers. He squeezed her hand, offering comfort. Offering himself now and for the rest of his life.

Adhémar sighed and released their hands. His fingers went slack, and Adela caught her breath.

"Is he . . . ?"

Theodoulos leaned forward and laid his fingers against Adhémar's throat.

He shook his head. "Not yet," he mouthed. The blood pounded in Theo's temples—or was he simply hearing the rustle of wings, an honor guard of archangels, come to bear the Bishop home? His own eyes were tear-blurred, but when he looked, when he listened with those other senses that he knew quickened within him (but that he feared), the Bishop's death chamber seemed filled with rainbows. They solidified under Theo's gaze, drawing close, their great wings furled. Their colors deepened.

Ah, I know you. Theodoulos looked up at them. Raphael, at the bed's head; Gabriel at its foot; Michael and Uriel to either side. *I beg you, let him go gently.*

In his own time. The words seemed to quiver in the crowded space.

A pitcher stood beside an altar, hastily set up for the last rites of Adhémar's church. To Theodoulos's shock, the Lance lay upon it, sent from Count Raymond's private chapel for what healing it might work.

"Swear." The voice rustled up from the bed. "Protect . . . She is stranger in a strange . . . land."

Theodoulos laid his hand on the holy thing. He felt a rough edge nick one finger and the warmth of a drop of blood.

"I swear, sir," he said.

Reassure the sick, he had always been told. Adhémar knew that he was dying. The best reassurance Theo could give him was obedience—and his pledge of safety for his niece.

He turned from the Lance back toward the pitcher. At least Adhémar need not die thirsty. The water here had gone foul; this was what—vinegar and water? The drink of the legions, the drink soldiers had handed up to Christ in a moistened sponge on the tip of that very Lance he had just laid hands on?

Theodoulos drew the silver goblet he had rescued from the sack of Antioch from his bag and filled it. A drop of blood from the cut the Lance had dealt him trickled down the crudely turned rim of the cup contained in its elaborate framework of apostles: the water shimmered as if even the archangels bent over the cup to ask: *Do you see that?*

Bless it, he implored them.

He knelt again by the dying man.

As the rim of the cup touched Adhémar's lips, his eyes opened. "What . . . ?"

Theodoulos made sure he sipped, then held the Cup for him to see. The silver seemed to brighten where his cut finger had touched it. Where Adhémar's lips had rested, it shone gem-bright. The Bishop's eyes fixed on one face, out of all the faces framing the Cup.

"There . . . there *he* is . . ." Adhémar whispered. "Come for me . . . ?"

Theo's heart pounded.

"There . . . then I have not failed . . ." Adhémar breathed. "I feared . . . so much . . . Thank you." Again, his hand came up to touch Theo's, then the Face that shone out from the superlative workmanship of the Cup. *"For now we see through a glass, darkly, but then, face to face: now I know in part; but then shall I know even as also I am known . . ."* Adhémar murmured. His face flushed again, with joy this time.

Then he yawned. Theodoulos did not need to touch him to know that the pulse in his throat would be feeble and erratic.

"Maybe he can sleep now." Adela's voice was unnaturally taut so it would not break. She flinched, hating her own lie.

"Jerusalem," Adhémar whispered.

It did not matter. A priest hurried toward his master with oils and prayers, and Theodoulos and Adela withdrew.

"I suppose the Bishops of Orange or Albara will take up his yoke." Theodoulos kept his face masklike as he passed them. Already, they were dividing the spoil? Could they not wait until the good old man was dead?

To Theodoulos's surprise, Raymond of Aguilers knelt among the people waiting outside. So the Count had sent his chaplain along with his holiest relic, had he?

"We are losing our Moses," he whispered. "I heard Count Bohemond say he should be buried in Jerusalem."

Theodoulos bowed his head. His eyes stung. He knelt, hoping the chaplain would leave him alone while they waited for the announcement that they all dreaded.

But the man was shrewd, mercilessly shrewd. "He sent for you, Sir Greek. Why, I wonder, did he send for you?"

So, let the battle come down upon his head now, Theodoulos thought. "He made me promise on the Lance that I would care for the lady Adela. He joined our hands . . ."

"Did he wed you?"

"No!" Adela cried, low-voiced.

"I think he tried," Theodoulos admitted. He looked at Adela, who glared at him, then turned away, tense with anger.

"I will marry the two of you. Or the Bishop of Orange, should you prefer."

"No," Adela said. "No."

Raymond's eyebrows rose: what? Her uncle had made a marriage for her, and she refused?

"No, my daughter?" he asked. For a wonder, his voice was gentle.

"I do not choose to wed," she declared.

Theodoulos drew breath raggedly, testing the wound she dealt him. True, he had shouted at her when she rode back to Antioch, but only because he hated to see her throw away her life. He could have sworn that along the line of march, there had been moments when her heart reached out to his. As his to hers.

You will just have to heal, he told it.

Now Adela did look at him. Her eyes filled, but she blinked the tears away.

"No," she said again.

He turned away but could not leave. Was that the only word she had for him, this stubborn Norman? Her kinsmen could not take a city without laying it waste: why would any of the breed serve his heart any differently?

"Lady, your uncle wished it. You are alone in the world; he is a knight, well favored by his lord, and . . ." Raymond's eyes studied Theodoulos as if he would melt him down into coin.

"Enough, I beg you," Theodoulos told Raymond of Aguilers. "The lady has truly had enough to bear." *And so have I.*

He would have bowed and left them there, but Adela's hand on his arm restrained him.

"You were not always so blind, Theo!" she cried. "Why is it that all of you, all of you brave knights, can swear to march into the Holy Land, and not I? Do you alone have faith?"

"Then . . . then . . . it is not that I . . . not that you do not wish . . ." The bleeding in his heart had stopped. A moment more, and he would be warm again. He might even be happy.

Adela stepped forward to take both his hands and rest her head against Theodoulos's shoulder. Oh God, how right that felt.

"Oh Theo, you have never been such a fool. My very dear, loyal fool. What honor remains to me 'if I prefer not Jerusalem above my chief joy'?" Adela asked.

Theo pulled his hands free, then clasped her against him as he had longed to do for months. Adela was tall for a woman, and her arms around him, despite the presence of the chaplain, were strong. He did not know whether his embrace gave comfort or sought it. He did not care if it were improper.

"We could go together," he offered. "I would not forbid you."

Adela laughed sadly. "Would you not? And if I were with child, Theo my dearest? What then?"

It struck him like a lance in the heart. Adela's refusal did not just cost him a wife: it cost his little girl a mother.

Wrong, Theo. It cost her a mother *now*. Still, Adela had not rejected the idea out of hand. She had allowed Adhémar to join her hand with his. She did not hate the idea of his child, or—his breath came faster—flinch from the thought of how they would conceive it. That was hope of sorts.

Hope? It was wealth unparalleled.

"I have a daughter," he stammered. "And lands, such as they are . . . if you agree . . ."

Adela shook her head as it rested on his shoulder. His arms tightened about her. She felt so good. He could never let her go. Adhémar had ordered it; no one would think him wrong if he insisted—no one except Adela. She might submit because she had been raised in a stern mode that treated man and woman, husband and wife, as figures on a chessboard, to be moved back and forth at the behest of the lords that played them. It was not submission that he wanted, but Adela herself. Insist on his rights under her own laws, and she would never forgive him.

Not to mention what his foster mother and sister would say!

If I were with child. He imagined nights with her beside him, not just their bodies joining, but their minds meeting, talking and watching the stars until, reluctantly, they knew that they must sleep. It would take time, but if she consented, if they had the time, he knew they could create more than children between them; they could build something like the love and trust that nourished Leo and Asherah—and that he longed for.

"Remember Hagar, Theo?" The woman who had given birth in the mountains, abandoned the child, then hope and life itself?

Theodoulos bowed his head against Adela's hair. It smelled like new-mown hay. How had she found time to wash it?

"You are right again," he admitted. "I could never let you risk yourself. Or our child."

"You see?" she asked, stepping out of his embrace with a sigh. "Let it be thus, then: we remain brother and sister in Christ until Jerusalem."

A garden shut up, my sister, my bride . . .

Adela put up a hand to touch his face. He moved so that his lips brushed her palm. "Don't look at me like that, Theo, or my resolve will break. In Jerusalem, we will wed. If it is God's will. And if you still want me . . ."

"If I want you!" He stepped forward, to have her in his arms again, to kiss her for the first time until her knees buckled and he could press her against the length of his body.

Oh God, what a time to burn with desire, with my lord the Count's chaplain standing right there.

Raymond edged between them.

"That is a noble resolve, daughter. And you, sir knight, are you content?"

Not content. Never that, until she is truly my wife. But satisfied, for now. He made himself smile. *"Volo,"* he whispered as he had before Adhémar.

For the first time, Adela looked down. She even flushed.

Leaving Adela to keep vigil over her uncle's body, Theodoulos headed back to his quarters.

To his surprise, Rainault fell in at his side.

"We're going to miss the Bishop," he said.

Theodoulos nodded.

"I heard he wants—wanted—you to marry the niece. And she refused."

"She wants to wait until Jerusalem."

Rainault shrugged. "And you *listened* to her? You agreed?"

"She has as much right to see the City as we do," Theo told his friend. "God knows, it's cost her too."

Home, friends, uncle, youth—she had scarcely a garment that had not been mended again and again. If they were spared, Theodoulos would see her richly clad. For now, however . . .

"Seeing as you're to wed her, do you know what provisions the bishop made for her maintenance?" Rainault asked, practical as any merchant.

"I don't care," said Theodoulos. Let the Frank be shocked, if he cared. God, he was tired. After kneeling in prayer all night, his leg ached. He would have to remember not to favor it. And to get his weight off it as soon as he could.

"I suppose the Bishop thought Count Bohemond would do something for you."

Theodoulos shrugged.

To his surprise, the Frank laid an arm over Theodoulos's shoulders. "You really care about her, don't you? I'm sorry you can't have her now."

"Adela *is* my wife. Or will be," Theodoulos told him. "You can stand up for us at the Church of the Holy Sepulchre."

"God willing." Rainault crossed himself.

Theodoulos dropped his bag of medicines—*and* the Cup—then turned to his friend. "Rainault, I need some cloth. Decent, dark cloth. For Adela."

"This is the man who wouldn't take anything when Antioch fell? But now he wants cloth. Not silk that any man in his right mind would want. No: our Greek knight, who's grown up with the riches of the Orient, wants—what, Theo? Wool? Decent English wool? The trouble is, he wants it right now."

"I mean to pay for it," Theodoulos said. He had wanted to stand before Asherah and vow that he had taken no plunder from the sack of Antioch. Except for the Cup, which she would have rescued, as a holy thing even if it were Christian.

"I'm sure the Count will take your coin." Rainault's sarcasm was palpable.

"I'm sure he will."

"Let's see what we can find." Rainault led the way.

Theodoulos's blood might race at how sheer cotton or clinging silk of Hind, perhaps picked out with gold, might drape over Adela's body, but he passed them by. Damask, perhaps, or brocade? Adela would refuse to wear anything so fine. He ran his fingers over a light, sober wool: evaluating, appreciating—it was better to stroke fine fabric than nothing, he supposed. It was too dark for her coloring, but it was better than anything she had.

"Take it as a gift, man," the Count growled when he offered to pay for the fabric. "Not as spoil, if you're so queasy. I shall be the first to give your lady a wedding gift!"

Once again, Theodoulos stood before Adela. Then he knelt, holding out his choice to her, displaying it as skillfully as a merchant in the bazaars. She took it, laid her head upon the good fabric, and wept as she could not weep before.

28

Adela had mastered the art of weeping with rage. She had shed the shabby pilgrim, the poor knight, and now wore decent robes stitched from the fabric Theodoulos had given her. To his mind, she bore herself like the great lady she was. An enraged great lady, which he found no unfamiliar sight. Or one that he was fool enough to treat lightly.

"I'll kill him!" Adela declared.

Theodoulos set his hands on her shoulders, to comfort where he knew he dared not restrain.

"I will!" she vowed. "I'll cut his throat myself! That blaspheming liar!"

"Adela, Adela."

She pulled free of his soothing hands. "My uncle—if ever a saint walked the earth, it was he. Who did more for the poor among us? Even His Holiness honored him and called him friend. And this . . . this upstart madman of a Peter Bartholomew has another of these lies he calls a vision and proclaims that *my uncle* burns in hell for doubting the truth of the Holy Lance!"

"You surely do not deny that the Lance is holy, do you, lady?" That was Rainault, sounding shocked. Oh God, let him keep a still tongue in his head even if Adela lashed out at his patron.

"Did you not say, Theo, that the Emperor already has a Lance in Byzantium?" Adela watched the consternation in Theo's face, the confusion in Rainault's. "Hah!"

"But you do not, truly, trust the *Emperor's* word, do you?" Rainault interrupted.

Adela waved a hand, dismissing his question. "To make matters worse, to make them truly worse, this Peter inflicts another vision on the army, then tells us, it's all right now, my lord Bishop has been prayed out of hell by none other than your own Count Bohemond, who once threw a filthy cheat some coins! Thirty pieces of silver, if he was feeling generous, which I doubt."

"Oh my God," muttered Theodoulos. Miraculously, Rainault seemed to be taking no offense.

"No offense to the great counts," Adela went on, "but in Peter Bartholomew, they have an evil counselor."

"The walls are thin," Theodoulos commented. "Anyone might overhear you, Adela. And then what? You lose the element of surprise. Come, my lady. My very dear lady. You have been kept inside too long. Let us walk, and you shall tell us what lies in your heart."

"What *else* lies in the lady's heart," Rainault gibed. "You are a good niece, a pious widow, a dutiful lady, and I respect your grief. So I will not write your words in my account of this pilgrimage."

Adela glared at him.

In Constantinople, she must have gone decently veiled. Here, although the presence of two armed men showed her rank (and she would have scoffed at that), she might walk as she chose. Seeing Adela's eyes soften, Theodoulos would have been just as happy to be alone with her. Still, Rainault's presence kept them decent by Theo's standards, if not by the laxer morals of the Franks.

Watching Leo with his wife had taught Theodoulos well. You dared not dismiss a lady with such fire in her soul. Not when she was in a rage; not anytime at all. But you could not allow her to work herself a mischief. Adela was grieving, angry, restless. It was much that she allowed Theodoulos to distract her.

The walls of Antioch loomed ahead of them.

"Are we going to stay here forever?" Adela demanded.

"You know we aren't fit to march yet, lady," Sir Rainault told her. "You have spent yourself nobly tending people stricken by the fever . . ."

"Meanwhile the great lords—your own Count included—ride out and carve out fiefs in the countryside," Adela snapped.

"What do you say, Theodoulos? Do we send more men to Byzantium telling Alexius, 'Here is your city of Antioch; please come and claim it when you choose'?"

Theodoulos shifted, uneasy. "One thing I learned in Byzantium is to avoid such talk where it can be overheard."

Adela snorted. "If you think Alexius should have the city, you should serve the Count of Toulouse, not Bohemond."

"This one bites, Theo!" Rainault laughed. "When you wed her, do you think you can gentle her?"

Adela glared impartially at both men.

Theodoulos shrugged. "My lady is what she is, and God forbid she change. But, brother, in all humility, my mother and sisters have taught me that a lady's qualities are not to be discussed as one might discuss a warhorse's strength or endurance."

He allowed himself a faint smile at Rainault, who flung up a hand to acknowledge temporary defeat.

"Where I do agree," Theodoulos went on, "the only place, my dear lady, where I agree with Master Peter, is that, if we do not speedily make a decision to set out, we may wander in the wilderness for ten years before we reach Jerusalem. Jacob served seven years for Leah and seven more for Rachel: Adela, are you minded to wait that long for our wedding?"

She put out a hand to cover his where it still rested on her arm and pressed it. Theodoulos's world brightened. "What does Count Raymond say about this latest vision?" she asked, much subdued.

"Now there, we are all of one mind, lady." Theodoulos chuckled. "I met Count Raymond's chaplain, who is much concerned. He says the count is convinced the Lance is genuine—'he blessed himself, and the others followed suit'—but this latest vision about who should wield Antioch . . . Raymond of Aguilers is not certain that it can be trusted."

"Oh, they have all spent too much time in Byzantium!" Rainault exclaimed. "Much too much, especially the Count of Toulouse. Watch him dodge and squirm now. He believes Peter Bartholomew's words. But when he has a saint appearing to him in a vision, saying, 'Give the city to the man who took it, if he is a good man,' he complains that Peter Bartholomew speaks for Bohemond! Back and forth; back and forth. It all makes a brave, brave show."

Bohemond may have wept and prayed sincerely for Adhémar's soul, but there was no denying he enjoyed the stalemate into which Adhémar's death had cast them.

"Don't you *want* to reach Jerusalem?" Adela asked.

"I ache to see Jerusalem. It's like a wound," Rainault admitted. "But I am my lord's man."

"Ten years," Theodoulos murmured. "Ten years."

"It took the original Children of Israel forty," Rainault pointed out. "Of course, they were fed on manna and did not have to worry about provisions."

Adela shook her head. Then, as knights came up to her to offer condolences upon her uncle's death, she composed herself quickly. Many of the men who spoke to her with such gentleness were of Count Raymond's army. Angry she might be; she received their words with downcast eyes and proper words. The pressure of her hand on Theodoulos's arm told him what price she paid for her self-control.

Let him get her alone, and he would dare to take her in his arms, hold her until the tenderness flowed from his heart into his touch, gentling her as he had seen Leo gentle Asherah countless times. And then . . . he flushed . . . and then . . . Adela was a widow; she knew of men, or one man, in any case; as her anger cooled, that passion might turn itself elsewhere. And he would be there.

Theodoulos's letter from home contained as much of fear as of relief. Still, the relief was so great, Theodoulos shut his eyes to savor the comfort Leo's letter gave him.

> *It appears that St. Andrew certainly wills that you and your companions march upon Jerusalem. I mourn with you the death of the most holy episcopus Adhémar.* (Leo was being sly, Theodoulos thought, in using the Greek, correct term.) *It may be that if His Holiness Pope Urban makes pilgrimage to Antioch, one of the sites consecrated by St. Peter himself, he would choose a worthy replacement for the Legate.*

Safe—or relatively safe—in Cappadocia, Leo could have no idea how rash his words might be.

> *Your mother charges me to give you her love and her thanksgiving that your heart has healed. In her own words, "Leo, I would tie myself into knots to welcome any woman Theo chooses after so long. If she is a woman of kindness and character, we shall suit very well—if she pleases." She sends these earrings as a gift for her. Your Adela seemed like a sensible woman when we met. I leave it to your judgment how much to tell her of us and when. May you reach Jerusalem in health. Embrace your sister and her family for us. God keep you all in His protection.*

So, Asherah would accept a Norman into her home. It was not, after all, as if she were unused to Christians. Where Asherah led, Binah would follow. Probably. Binah remained in Constantinople, no doubt weaving threads from the palace to Pera and south, where Leo oversaw the rebuilding of the family's home. Adela had met Leo: it remained only to be seen whether she would accept Asherah. Jerusalem would be the test. In Jerusalem, she could meet Shoshonna and her husband, the rest of what was still Theodoulos's family. Please God, Adela proved able to open her mind and heart.

Please God they all survived until then.

Theodoulos was not at all happy that Adela had exhausted herself caring for the sick. At least, though, it had silenced her calls for someone, anyone, but preferably herself, to murder Peter Bartholomew for slandering her uncle. If her fight to save lives had left her so strained that Theo daily feared that she too would sicken and die—*Holy Bearer of God, spare this woman I love!* Theo prayed daily—her care of the ill, the wounded, and the dying had given her an awareness of the shifting currents of opinion in city and camp that was . . . well, it was Byzantine to a degree that Theo personally found astonishing for a Frank.

In the end, Adela's shrewd judgment had been echoed by the army. "Let them who wish to have the Emperor's gold have it, and those who wish to have the revenues of Antioch likewise. Let us, however, take up our march with Christ as leader, for whom we have come."

Noble words. The army's threat to tear down the walls of Antioch that it had scaled months before with such great thanksgiving seemed to have accomplished rather more.

In November, those who had a mind to departed Antioch. They were singing hymns. The singing stopped when they reached Ma'arra, which lay under siege.

"I begged my lord," Rainault, who had taken an arrow through the arm, told Adela as she knelt at his side, sponging his shoulders and throat. The wound was clean; the surgeons had been able to withdraw the arrow, shaft and head, without leaving barbs or splinters to fester in his flesh. But hunger, exhaustion, and weariness of soul had let the fever in, and now Rainault struggled for life.

"I begged my lord to come with us," he muttered again, raising his head until the cords of his throat glistened with sweat and effort. "I went down upon my knees. I would have squirmed, belly down, upon the tiles like a twisty Greek, but he pushed at me with one arm and told me to get up and 'no meant no.' "

"Does it surprise you?" Theodoulos asked. "He promised to make you rich. More to the point, he wants an empire. If not Byzantium it-self, then his own."

"He could have the kingdom of God!" Rainault cried.

"His fever spikes up at sundown," Adela told Theo. She gestured for a servant to hold the Frank down until she could pour hellebore

down his throat. She needed Theodoulos now, he thought content-
edly, if only to help her with her patients.

Finally, Rainault lay muttering in his sleep.

"I'll help you change the dressing on his arm," Theodoulos offered. His friend's body was hot and dry, the wound swollen. But
not—thank God—rotten yet.

"It should be drained," he said, "or the poisons in it will kill him.
When my lord Bohemond was wounded at Antioch, I held a red-hot
blade to his flesh, and he healed clean."

Adela shook her head. "It's too late for hot iron now," she said.
"His heart could not withstand the shock. But we should drain the
wound."

"Let the surgeons do it," Theo urged. "You will fall ill yourself."

Even Asherah could not have outdone Adela's glare at him. Had
he not been so afraid for his friend, it would have made him homesick.

"If I did not sicken and die in Antioch," Adela snapped, "I will
not die here. I tell you, I *will* see Jerusalem. And I am resolved upon
it: so will he."

"Jerusalem?" Rainault's voice was hoarse. "Are we in Jerusalem, or
are we in hell? I'm burning . . ."

"You must live to reach Jerusalem." She rested her hand on Rainault's sound shoulder, pressing him back on his pallet with an ease
that wrung Theodoulos's heart. Rainault had been—still was—a
knight; he should have more strength left. But the fighting, the rotten living on the march, and the drain of the long waits, the quarrels
among the great lords while Jerusalem lay in the hands of unbelievers, had exhausted the Frank: his weakness was as much of spirit as of
body.

They had all been exhorted to hope. Hope? It was a poor enough
thing compared to the gold that Raymond had offered every lord but
Bohemond for their support: still, hope was what they had.

And maybe it was the greatest thing of all.

"Live. You must fight this thing."

"Fighting. Always fighting. Pray . . ." Rainault's voice trailed off
into mumbles.

Adela looked into Theodoulos's eyes. "You think he is going to
die, don't you?" she whispered.

Theo shook his head. "I pray not. He could not have better care."
He reached out and tenderly brushed a strand of hair from her face.
The firelight glowed on it; its kindness made her look as if she were

well fed and rested, like a lady cherished and safe in her home.

"But this fever . . . food, if he could get it down and if we had it . . ." There was food of sorts to be had if one consorted with Tafurs. Frankly, he would rather die.

So that left the other remedy: faith. Let the great lords supply Rainault with a reason for living; let them show their need for him, and he would rise and ride. *My God, what an army,* Theo mused. The Emperor had seen only its greedy side: devout himself, if Alexius saw the faith in this army, a faith that rivaled his, he would leave his jeweled palaces and come fight at its side. Christendom would free the Holy Land, restoring it to Christ . . .

What happens to my kinfolk, Theo my son? Memories of Asherah's voice, as passionate as it was sarcastic, cut across his reverie. They could not win for losing. For some of them to live, the rest had to die.

He looked over at Adela and pressed her hand. Day after day, his love and respect for her increased. Now, he longed only to lead her away to some place where they could wash the stench of the tents, the army, the city under siege, this whole appalling army from their bodies and souls. *He leadeth me beside the still waters . . . He restoreth my soul . . .*

The need that he had been too tired and too scrupulous to act on clawed at him. Adela's fine robes had long been packed away. She was thin again, as she had been when they crossed the mountains; she had never been dirtier or more drawn—yet the strength in her shone like opal in its matrix. She met his eyes, not mistaking the hunger he knew they betrayed, avoiding it, or concealing her own.

Much passed unnoticed in war. In Jerusalem, she had sworn to wed him: possibly, no one would have much to say if they claimed each other now. Adela was widow, not maid, and she wanted him. The need simply to live for the moment flared up in him like fire that burns up a branch and encounters a pocket of sap. His hand upon hers tightened. He watched her fingers tremble, then her lips. He bent to kiss them.

"We need food," she said. "And faith."

"I need you," he whispered, kissing her parted lips again. Christ, they were like water in the wilderness to a man dying of thirst. "Oh God, I need you." Theodoulos's head spun. He pulled Adela closer, joyously aware when her strength turned to compliance.

Count Raymond's siege tower rumbled toward the walls of Ma'arra. Someone in the camp started singing a hymn, then broke off. Rainault muttered in his fevered dreams. Adela sighed and turned her face away, resting it against Theo's shoulder. Longingly, he touched her tangled hair, then freed her.

"Faith," Rainault whispered. "Faith. Sweet lord Jesu, let me visit the sites of Your Passion and I shall die in peace. Let me . . . only let me witness . . ." He gasped.

"His lips are cracked," Adela murmured. "Perhaps he'll let me give him some water. Hand me the cup, will you?"

She paused, hand out. "Theodoulos?"

"The cup," Theodoulos whispered. The Cup he had rescued in the hidden chapel the night Antioch fell. The Cup that had failed to restore Adhémar—or had it? He died with a vision of Christ before his eyes; he died in hope. That could not be called failure.

"Keep him alive until I return!" Theodoulos promised Adela. She stared after him, too tired for amazement or protest. Then he dashed for his quarters, hope aching like a wound.

The silver chalice glistened up at him, the deeply incised eyes in the tiny faces of its intricate frame seeming to comprehend his need.

Perhaps it was not life the Cup granted, but a man's heart's desire. At the very least, it would give a dying friend one last drink.

Cup in hand, Theodoulos returned to find Adela struggling to restrain Rainault.

"Got to get up . . ." he muttered. "Turn me loose, woman. Turn me loose! We're marching to Jerusalem . . . Oh God, will we never get there? Will they bargain it away for thirty pieces of silver? Talking . . . waiting . . . treachery everywhere . . . even my own dear lord . . ."

Theodoulos handed Adela the cup, then pushed the Frank back onto his pallet. "None of that," he urged. "We'll get you to Jerusalem. My oath on it. Knight's oath now, remember?"

Rainault's too-bright eyes focused on him. "Sir Greek," he said. "Saw you . . . saw you knighted m'self. Who would have thought . . . a bookish man could fight like ten devils? My book . . . if I die . . ."

"I'll take it with me to Jerusalem. I'll finish it for you, even. Are you satisfied?"

Rainault lay back, panting. "Jerusalem," he whispered.

"My word on that too. But you're not getting off this easily," Theodoulos told him. "You're too stubborn to die."

Adela came back with the filled cup. Theo smelled familiar herbs, dispelling the stink of fever poisons and old sweat.

"Here, try to get this down," he urged and raised the Frank. Rainault's shivers shook his own body.

Adela held the cup to Rainault's lips. He tried to twist away, death putting up a struggle to claim prey it had marked.

Not yet, Theodoulos dared tell it. *Go away.*

"Try, sir knight," she whispered. "Try. Try."

The silver rim of the cup pressed against Rainault's mouth, pinching until he drank. He licked his lips, blinked, then sipped, paused, and drank again. One hand came up to touch Adela's and he sighed.

"Better?" she asked.

"Ah, lady, your Greek is a lucky man. I should like to see you wed."

"Perhaps you will."

Theo felt Rainault's shivers subside, but kept his arms around his friend, willing strength into him.

"A little more?" Adela asked, her voice gentle. Gradually, urging and coaxing, she got Rainault to drain the cup.

"Sir Greek"—Rainault spoke through a prodigious yawn that frightened Theodoulos—"you have seen Jerusalem, have . . . have you not?"

"Yes, brother."

"Will we truly see it, you and I?" Rainault's hand came up to clasp his.

"We shall *all* see it." Theodoulos made his voice deep and strong.

"God grant . . ." Rainault's voice broke, and his eyes rolled upward.

"Theo?" Adela gasped.

Theodoulos laid a hand against the side of the Frank's neck. His flesh was soaked, but already cooler.

"Asleep." Theo's voice was husky. He bent his head, resting his cheek for a moment against Rainault's matted hair.

Abruptly, he wanted nothing himself as much as sleep. Light shone upon the Cup. He should ask Adela to put it away. He was aware when she disentangled him from Rainault, easing him to a pallet by the fire, then of nothing more.

January—July 1099

1099

The Final Assault on Jerusalem

29

*E*arly in the new year, Count Raymond left yet another town in flames and led his surviving forces on to Palestine. As befitted a pilgrim, he was bare of head and foot.

"Jerusalem," muttered Rainault. After the fever that had almost killed him, he was Tafur-thin. His eyes blazed with longing, rivaling the city's burning walls.

They had tied him onto Theo's one surviving horse. Theodoulos led it, while Adela, scorning the chance to ride pillion, walked beside him. The smoke from the dying city made their eyes water and their lungs ache. By the time the army finally stopped coughing, someone began to sing again.

"It's not going to work," Rainault muttered.

"You're still here, aren't you?" another knight asked him. "I'd have thought you would leave when your master turned back. Hell, even his nephew Lord Tancred has gone over to Count Godfrey and dwells in his camp now, not Count Raymond's."

"I am not my lord Tancred," Rainault said, keeping his voice down. "I best serve his uncle Count Bohemond's interests by going on to Jerusalem. And"—he produced his best argument—"when I was wounded and like to die, I took a vow to go on to Jerusalem. I will finish my book there. Ask the Greek, whom my lord Count knighted, or the Lady Adela."

"The Greek? You'd trust him? And his lady would say anything he told her to."

Theodoulos started to bristle.

Rainault held up a hand.

"The dogs are barking. Let's move on, brother," he said.

At Antioch, Rainault would have challenged the man. Here, he saved his strength. It might be the beginnings of wisdom; Theodoulos suspected it came as much from a weariness of spirit, disappointment, even, that he could not follow at his lord's back in a forest of bright banners up into Jerusalem.

Paien unt tort e chrestiens unt dreit. The pagans are wrong and the Christians are right.

Here, however, deciding that pagans were wrong and Christians were right was not as easy as it had been for Count Roland, his Emperors, and the twelve peers. Arab conquerors had thrown the Turks out of Jerusalem. Al-Afdal of Egypt entertained Frankish ambassadors in Cairo. And Alexius Comnenus sent messengers impartially to all.

Some of the Franks had even begun to learn Arabic.

And just when they heard that Antioch was in danger, other letters from Alexius declared him ready to set out for Syria and urged—ordered?—the army in the East to wait for him until the end of June. It wasn't as if anyone believed, after Philomelium, that Alexius would appear; but Raymond's willingness to believe the Emperor had all but caused an insurrection.

Alexius had been Leo's friend since boyhood. He had saved Leo's life. He had even tried to spare the life of Leo's own Emperor's sons. What had happened to him?

He became emperor.

Dear God, even the thought of that power was enough to twist a man. Theodoulos put a protective hand to his pouch. In it lay the last letter he had received.

> To my beloved son Theodoulos: Guard yourself as I pray God
> to keep you in His Hand. The news I bring is bad. This letter is
> written to you from Byzantium and goes out in the train of the
> emir's ambassadors. His Sacred Majesty has received them and
> declared his intention to be strictly neutral in the coming battles.
> Furthermore, he has disavowed the men of the West and
> prefers the dynasty of the Fatimids to the Franks for the protection
> of Orthodoxy. While, after what we saw in Antioch, I can under-
> stand that—the Franks are no respecters of the Patriarchs—I fear
> that this repudiation of pledges he made will cost him and the em-
> pire dearly, if not now, then in years to come. God keep us and our
> sons from harm then.
> As for now, God keep you from peril, though I fear a more

useful prayer is that your faith and your courage shield you from harm. The messenger should have brought you gold. Use it as you see fit to ensure your safety and that of your promised wife, your sister, and our family in Jerusalem. Destroy this.

With a pang, Theodoulos threw this letter too into the fire.

Like a great dragon, the army left a trail of fire along the coast. They would burn their way to Jerusalem and leave it in flames too. This was to be accounted a great deed. What was worse, it was a deed in which he had acquiesced.

"My lord your foster father?" asked Rainault. It should have been beneath his dignity as a knight even to comment. The curiosity intrinsic to the Levant had infected him, and that was a fever from which no one ever recovered.

Theodoulos felt his eyes go secretive, remote—a hard sight for a man who was his friend. "He fears for us."

"So do I," said Sir Rainault. The effects of his fever at Ma'arra still marred him. "I fear that Count Raymond will not leave this place until it falls, or until we all are dead. And I will never see Jerusalem."

Theodoulos stared past the rising sparks into the night sky as if he expected to see the immense wings of the dragon that coiled around the world's axis shut out the stars. Long before, when the land itself had rebelled, he had helped to snatch brands from the burning.

He needed no prophet to know that was his task again.

They were hungry in the darkness before dawn that Good Friday, April 8, before the gates of embattled Arqa. Adela's hands were empty of bread.

"Peter Bartholomew has finally run mad," she told Theodoulos with immense satisfaction. "You heard that last dream of his, didn't you? Now he has Christ, Saint Peter, and Saint Andrew all telling him that Arqa *must* fall. More likely it's Count Raymond who says that. Or his chaplain."

Theodoulos shook his head. He brought what word he could to Adela—fearing what she might hear from other, less discreet informants. At least, it was not as bad as her reaction to Peter Desiderius's vision. "Another damned priest envisioning my uncle in hell!" Adela had exclaimed. Theodoulos had been hard-pressed to restrain her from storming into Raymond of Toulouse's presence to denounce the man.

Life had been easier for Adela when she had had her uncle's ear. Now she must glean her information where she could, usually through Theodoulos. He knew it galled her: not that she had only him to work with, but that she could not, like the men around her, act directly. And that too struck him as familiar. As he had learned from years of watching Leo with Asherah, attempting to shield or thwart such a woman would lead only to disaster.

Today, at least, she would watch. God knows, it was a sight from which he would have given much to spare her.

"Even Bertrand, your uncle's own standard-bearer—" Theodoulos began.

"My uncle trusted that man," Adela snapped. "It is hard, always waiting to be told what men think I should know."

"Come, is that any way to talk on Good Friday?" Theodoulos asked. "And when we hope to see a miracle?"

Adela sighed. It sounded suspiciously like a snort.

They all hungered; but Peter Bartholomew had been fasting for four days, ever since, his last vision assailed, he had turned, inevitably, to thoughts of fire.

"I not only desire it, but I beg you to light a fire," he had said. "And I shall submit to the ordeal by fire with the Lance in my hand. If it is truly the Lord's Lance, then I shall emerge unburned, but if it is a false Lance, I shall be consumed by the fire."

Why did it always have to be fire? Theodoulos asked himself.

The answer came in a fit of blackest sarcasm. *God wills it.*

The last of the Tafurs stood away from the dry olive branches they had been heaping up since dawn, forming them into rows four feet high, thirteen feet long, and a foot apart. They would burn with a transparent, deadly heat. The crowd too had been gathering since dawn, lured by a spectacle such as this land had probably not seen for thousands of years. How many clustered here? Tens of thousands, Theo calculated, the size of a city—with more watching from the walls.

Adela at his side, Theodoulos exploited his standing as a knight to press forward until they had a good vantage point for what he wished he did not have to see.

Around noon, the fires were kindled. The dry wood caught with a roar as if a dragon breathed upon it; great flames shot from the dry wood into the clear air. The people nearest to the fire thrust back into the crowd, unable to withstand the heat that shimmered in the spring air. How would Peter be able even to approach those deadly rows of fire, let alone pass through them?

The crowd pressed forward, dry-mouthed, hungry. Was this how the Romans had watched in their Coliseum when, in Nero's or Diocletian's day, lions were unleashed upon helpless Christians?

This time we do it to one of our own.

"There he is." Rainault appeared at Adela's side.

Of course Rainault would be here to witness and to write.

Wearing only a tunic, Peter Bartholomew stood barefoot before the fires. His long fast and the hardships of sustaining his visions left him curiously wasted. The flames seemed to be reflected in the burning eyes that were the most alive part of him. Beside him stood the Bishop of Albara. He held the Lance, wrapped in an embroidered cloth.

Like a huge wave, the crowd sank to its knees and prayed. Peter's coming ordeal was like single combat: man against fire. Could the exaltation of his faith save him? Might another miracle occur?

The Bishop of Albara handed Peter the wrapped Lance. His eyes blazed brighter than the pyres before him. Clutching the Lance, he leapt into the narrow passage between them.

"Oh God, how can I look upon this?" Rainault moaned and bent his face over his hands.

"He's stopped!" someone gasped, while other babbled rumors had the man collapsed, crisped already within the burning wood.

"Do you see?" a woman screamed. "It is Our Blessed Lord, standing unconsumed just as He harrowed hell! Look, he takes Peter by the hands . . ."

The logs were stacked only four feet high; the flames rose higher. For an instant they parted, and Theodoulos saw Peter Bartholomew's face. The halo that surrounded it was the visionary's burning hair, but his eyes bore a look of rapture.

Shadrach, Meshach, and Abednego had stood in the fiery furnace as if in a bath, and angels of the Lord had walked among them. *Let the man live,* Theodoulos prayed. *Whether the Lance was truth or fraud, let him live.*

Adela pressed against Theodoulos's shoulder. "Make an end, man!" she urged. He flung an arm around her, and devil take anyone who commented.

"He's coming out!" the crowd gasped.

Peter stumbled as he emerged; Raymond Pilet caught hold of him and fell back, his hands scorched.

Peter Bartholomew brandished the Lance over his head at the crowd. "God help us!" The scream ripped from his lungs.

"My God, did you see? His tunic, untouched; the embroideries that hold the Lance, not even singed . . ."

Screaming in awe, the crowd pressed forward.

"If the fire doesn't kill him, the mob will." Rainault rose from his knees and looked about sardonically. "Get her out of here," he ordered Theodoulos.

It was past his power; inexorably, the crowd pressed them forward until they could not help but see how the crowd assailed the mystic, snatching at his tunic, trying to touch him anywhere they could. Peter screamed as rough hands fell upon his burns and urgent bodies jostled him. He toppled, his back twisting in a way that made even Adela flinch.

"Let the man breathe!" Raymond of Aguilers ordered, helping bear Peter away to life or death.

"Did you hear, do you know what happened?" a spearsman shouted at Rainault, heedless of the gulf of rank between them. "Jesus appeared to the Blessed Peter in the flames and told him, 'You shall not cross without wounds, but you shall not see hell.'"

"He fell into the flames," Adela said.

"Lady, he was pushed by the crowd, eager to touch him."

"I saw what I saw," Adela said, low-voiced. "The vision failed. No man can live with the burns he took. And even if, through some miracle, he lives, the crowd may well have crushed him to death. Surely, if his visions were true, Christ would have spared him."

She kicked at the ash that lay underfoot. "He should have not said he saw my uncle in hell." She shuddered and signed herself. "He should not . . . but I would not see anyone cast into the fires. Not even my worst enemy."

Abruptly, tears ran down her face. She turned, her hands going out to Theodoulos. "Theo . . . I still have the cup, remember? From when Rainault almost died. If we brought it to Raymond of Aguilers, perhaps . . ."

Heedless of the crowd that screamed and pushed about them, Theodoulos drew Adela's hands, so capable and work-worn, to his lips and let tears of thankfulness fall upon them.

"Surely," he forced the words out, "Adhémar looks down from heaven and blesses you."

Raymond of Aguilers doubted but admitted them. Twelve days later, Raymond proved right when the visionary closed his extraordinary eyes upon the world he had spurned. "Your talisman failed," he told Theodoulos and gave back the cup.

Fearing that the Count of Toulouse would seek to claim cup as well as spear, Theodoulos received it with some relief. Even through its wrappings, the silver tingled against his hands. The Count kept the Lance with all reverence in his private chapel; Theodoulos returned the cup to Adela.

"Peter Bartholomew had his miracle," she insisted. "He saw Jesus, not through a glass darkly, but face to face. God rest his soul." She bit the words off. Then, she added, "But he should not have said what he did about my uncle."

30

The lady whom the Emperor's court called Helena Ducaina and whom her foster parents called Binah paused, waiting for two men to leave the narrow street. It would have been a simple thing to force them away, simpler still to blot them from the face of the earth; but they might have family who would raise an outcry.

And above all else, Binah did not want an outcry. She had escaped the Bucoleon, drawing light about her like a cloak until the fabric of reality shimmered and she disappeared within it, able to elude spies, guards, and even the Caesarissa who had a lawful claim upon her services. She had "looked in" upon Anna before she completed her escape; the young mother slept after nursing her baby, a sight that filled Binah with envy and a kind of mild unease lest in seeking power, the Caesarissa lose what else she had. She had seen Alexius's daughter eye the Westerners with as much fascination as repulsion: it was a look she did not trust.

It was hard to be a demigoddess in this age. It had been one thing in Cappadocia, with sympathetic foster parents conniving to give her as much freedom as they could. In the Emperor's court, the laws were strict, and the rules of conduct stricter still. Even Caesarissa Anna's life was hedged about with rules: a woman such as Binah, whose father lived under imperial sufferance and whose foster mother was, at best, one of a subject people, had perforce to observe all the customs while reaping none of the benefits.

Were there any benefits?

The memories that had come upon her when her courses began reminded her that she had once enjoyed not just freedom but power. More, even, than her beloved foster mother and teacher: Asherah claimed she went her own way, but it was a way often channeled into side eddies of obligations, desires, duties, and, above all, the need to ensure her family's safety. And when those duties were all met, Asherah could be distracted above all by love.

Asherah held Binah's foster father Leo's heart in her capable, gentle hands. As far as Asherah was concerned, that made it all worthwhile. But there was only one Leo in the world.

The two men left the street. Well and good. And about time.

Drawing darkness over her like a second veil, Binah slipped past the blank walls of houses that had seen more aristocratic years and that loomed up on either side. She opened the weathered door to the house in which Leo Ducas had grown up. No one had disturbed the wards she had set the last time she was here: servants there were, but few, and those few dismissed during the evenings to their own homes. She was finally alone and unobserved. If all went well, Caesarissa Anna would not need her until the next day. And if all went ill, she could blur the Caesarissa's memory again.

Here (at least now that she had removed the icons from the rooms she had selected as her own) she could breathe freely, if not act with the autonomy her heart was beginning to demand. That made it infinitely safer than the palace or Pera, where she could claim kin, but where any step from decorum might jeopardize an entire community. She had no desire to set Asherah's people at risk. They had had a hard enough time with Asherah, who was merely, as she herself would have phrased it, "witchy."

Not bothering to kindle the polycandela, Binah glided through the cool, shadowed rooms that held secrets of their own. She would have liked to know her father when he was a boy. She would have liked to have known her grandparents . . . very well, her foster grandparents. She had met them a time or two, aged, strained, clever faces that studied hers, asking: *Who are you? What are you?*

Even then, she knew better than to reply.

With Leo and Asherah rebuilding in Cappadocia, Theodoulos away in the East, and the younger children about their lives, safe with families of their own, this house belonged solely to her. She might have a workshop here, a library, a lover: indeed, she had the first two. The third? As "Helena Ducaina," in the court so strictly overseen by the chaste Irene, she had created the character of a woman as scholarly as the Caesarissa Anna, therefore a fit companion for her. It had taken some effort: "Helena" was a name the Emperor himself had bestowed upon her. She sought to downplay a beauty that she knew could thwart her goals: she was more than human, so it stood to reason that she was . . . what was the old phrase from her mother's faith? Terrible as an army with banners.

Like Asherah before her, she was more admired than loved, more feared than desired. Had the Emperor been younger, less wrapped up in his wars and his family, he might have drawn her eye: but he was like a brother to her father, and that would not have been wise. The Count of Toulouse had been ancient by the standards of a human girl like Anna, but he was Christ-obsessed.

He had had a rival, a companion whom he envied and despised, tall, distantly akin to the guardsmen who eyed her and sometimes did more than that, although they thought it was a dream. *They* wanted no more but that: *this* man, this Bohemond, wanted all. He had stared at her in open court and tried to edge her out from the crowds into some hall or garden where, as he thought, his greater height and strength would put her at his mercy. There had been a strength to him, an intensity in his gaze, even to the flare of his nostrils, that she appreciated. But she had met his eyes and knew: this man *wanted*. Land, women, honor—what there was to want, he wanted all of it. He attempted to take the high road, but something had grown up twisted within him—a love of stratagems for their own sake, a passion to snatch, to have, to keep, and to take what belonged to others. Perhaps, she had speculated, just as a diversion . . . so she had let him come almost within range just once, long enough to know herself repelled by him.

Nevertheless, he fascinated the little Caesarissa, whose husband, a perfectly decent man, watched her as a dog would watch a master it adored but imperfectly understood. Binah kept a distance that was prudent for a mortal and fastidious for a woman in her apparent position. Had Anna's husband been more perceptive, he might have sensed how angry his wife had grown in her discontent. That remained Binah's concern and her very private battle.

The courtyard here, with its overgrown gardens, its still pool, was pleasant in the late spring and early summer. It would have been good to walk beside the water again with a man's arm about her waist, seeing their united reflections, perceiving herself as small and fragile against his strength.

It was, she thought, an illusion she was not to have.

A flicker of power drew her attention. Yes, the shrine to the Christians' goddess still held power on which she could draw. They were sisters, that goddess and her own mother: the power was hers by rights, and its presence eased her mind.

She knelt beside the pool. Here, no one would interrupt her, demand her presence, her service, her attention. Here, she could gaze into the water until the visions emerged.

She stared at her own reflection in the pool: the grave pale face with its archaic smile—a *cruel* smile, men said at court, not knowing how right they were—violet eyes, the Gorgon coils of hair. Her father had told her of the Medusa mortared into the cistern. She was none such: but she would always be drawn to water, caves, and the hardness of stone.

She stared into her reflection's eyes until she saw past it to the earth itself. The land stretched out before her like wrinkled silk, carelessly flung down. She flinched from the sights of burning, of sieges, of dying men. Did these barbarians know no more than to damage what they could not understand, to destroy what they might be permitted to possess only for a time?

Show me what I seek! she commanded the visions. The Sight had been hers since her earliest years. Coming on more strongly since she had gone from girl to woman, her vision had become stronger still in the years since she had truly known her woman's power.

Ah, now she saw Theodoulos, her brother in that ancient stone womb: older than she as this world knew age, but far younger in the mortal world where he chose to live. His powers limped as badly as he himself would have limped if their mother had not cured him with her touch the day of Binah's birth.

He was not alone, she saw. A woman walked at his side, the daughter of one of these younger, brasher peoples. Theodoulos loved *that?* She was worn past even pleasantness. But she touched Theodoulos's arm, and he brightened. *That stick mated with my brother? Look again, Binah,* her instincts told her. Well enough. The woman—the lady—had a strength that compelled Binah's respect, even for the merely human. The man they called friend had madness in his eyes. A passion burned in him and a wild sardonic humor she found oddly attractive. Briefly, he lured her, but the lust in him was not for a woman, never for one woman, but for a queen among cities.

She looked farther still, for the children born of Leo's and Asherah's own bodies. They were grown, one a learned doctor, the others mothers of children of their own, but they would always be the infants, treasuries of possibility, whom Binah had cherished when she was little more than a child herself and before the fullness of her own powers awoke. Rachel was safe, or reasonably so, in Persia. But Shoshonna in Jerusalem . . . she had a husband, children, a household, and merchants dependent upon her. Besides which, Shoshonna was *hers* and must be safeguarded.

They all would have been far stronger had their rearing been entrusted to her—as of course it was not. Theodoulos now: she would have had much to teach him too, but he had been a man grown when Binah's powers had come upon her. She would simply have to wait, Asherah told her, for decades, even centuries, if need be, until she had daughters of her own to teach them her own way.

And just how was she supposed to arrange *that?*

She smiled, her lips as cruel as those of an ancient Korë. If she chose, when she chose to have her children, perhaps even her daughter-heir, she would have to choose their father. Perhaps, if the obsession came upon her, the Caesarissa's husband . . . he was cleanly, decent, even moderately intelligent.

No, there was no one that she wanted now.

The starlight flickered in the pool. Abruptly, the sky went dark, as if the wings of the great dragon, the tli, hid the stars from sight.

She bent lower over the water. Darkness moved upon its face, and it rippled into the shape of land she remembered from her journeys in the East: the road to Jerusalem. Theodoulos, God help him, his strangely compelling friend, and that lady of his.

Still, Leo had approved of the lady, and what Leo approved of Binah would defend. She looked deeper, hoping to find Theodoulos out, clambering with his usual awkwardness along the lower branches of the Tree of Life, as he had when, in the mountains, he had called for her help.

But Theodoulos was asleep. Asleep alone, more was the pity. Would he know to call on her? She wondered.

Deftly, her consciousness reached out to touch his.

Now, he would. And when danger came, as it inevitably would, he would reach out to her. She would be waiting.

For now, other things remained to be done.

She drew a deep breath and summoned the strength for them. Incarnation under the sun was hard, she thought. When her mother had dwelt beneath the earth, even diminished by this age of the world, which fought not to believe in the likes of her, she could set the land rumbling as if in rejection of invaders she despised. Embodied, fully human, as she thought, Binah had much to learn. Study had helped: Asherah had given her the secrets of the tli, and she might even be strong enough now to will herself gone from this place. Medea, the stories ran, traveled in a chariot drawn by dragons. Binah had no such chariot, but she knew now that the tli could bear her, or at least her consciousness, from place to place. If she cared to will it, she could be in Jerusalem tonight.

It might be safer to go home. Asherah would care for her if she arrived sapped of all her strength. Longing for the land of her birth swept over her. The water rippled, and she saw the familiar caves, and those that had collapsed, the churches dug into the cliff faces, and the stippled, colored dunes and chimneys, frozen in time, of Cappadocia, the new caves now being excavated. But the Queen's road and the Queen City where her mother had given birth to her lay forever buried. Gently, Binah touched it with her mind, then turned her thoughts toward Hagios Prokopios.

The house, burnt during the last crises, had been rebuilt. Once again, its walls gleamed white against the tufa and the tender grass of late spring. Home. Leo still hoped she would return. He should know better: Alexius treated her kindly, but "hostage" was a word familiar in the courts. Even his own son, the Caesar Ioannes, who had supplanted Binah's Caesarissa Anna as heir, had been a hostage once.

Smiling, she let herself step forward, out of her body and into the vision in the pool. The water glowed silver at the touch of that which bound her to her body and to the spirit plane on which she traveled now. Into the great house, into the courtyard, past the lower rooms where the guards slept. Old Nordbriht woke and sat up, his sheepskins slipping from his scarred shoulders, as if he sensed her passage.

Peace, dear old wolf, she thought. He had carried her on his back when she was a child.

He sighed, laid aside his ax, and composed himself for sleep again. The sign he made was not the upstart Christian gesture.

Up the outer stairs and into the corridor off which Leo and Asherah had their rooms. It did not do, her mother's sacred writings said, to look upon one's parents' nakedness, but the night was cold: surely, they would be covered by sheepskins and blankets of their own.

Their door, solid in appearance, but evanescent as smoke to her in this guise, rose before her, and she passed through it. She stood in spirit at the foot of her foster parents' bed, watching them both sleep. Leo, his own God bless him, lay serene, the austerity of his features in repose softened by contentment: Asherah lay beside him, her head upon his shoulder. As she watched, Asherah opened her eyes and focused upon the wraith standing before her. Somewhat to Binah's surprise, she flushed. Refusing to speak, for that might disturb Leo, Asherah sent her thoughts to Binah.

Your father rests. Withdraw: I shall come out to you.

Obedient, courteous, and most tactful, Binah drifted back through the carved door. An instant later, Asherah joined her, her own projection glinting silver.

Wraith and wraith clasped hands, or tried to. A breath of substance flowed across Binah's astral "fingers." Both women smiled.

Is there danger? Asherah asked. Her great eyes flared.

Those we love are beset by dangers, Binah replied. No time to tell her mother now of the dangers that Binah saw about *her;* they were unimportant compared with what she saw ahead. *We must be ready to rescue them if we can.*

But how? The Emperor will not succor them. Asherah looked profoundly unhappy: she and Leo differed only in their opinion of the Emperor Alexius.

Come out with me. Perhaps the land will yield us secrets, Binah suggested.

They drifted down the stairs, through the courtyard, out the gates onto the land. A whicker drew Binah's attention to the stables, where she perceived life: a colt, not many weeks born, stood on slender legs nearby. If he lived, he would be one of the splendid black horses for which Cappadocia was famous. She watched the colt, a miracle of newness, for what was a long, long time for one soaring free of her body. Time was different; space was different. If only she had no need to return to the imprisoning envelope of flesh on which she still must depend.

Later, she had been assured. Later.

She let herself soak energy up from the land that had nurtured her and her mother before her, all the way back into the deeps of time. In the caves below the surface of the earth: if she cared to, she could even trace the roads to the chamber of her birth, wrought of a huge bubble breathed into the stone when it was molten at the founding of the world. Her mother must have known what she was about to give birth to her, even if she had erred before when Theodoulos had been cast out among strangers. He still had not the strength or the awareness that he should have had. Well, he would learn. He was learning. But he had chosen and his choice was mortal life.

Other such caves there were, other ancient ways—and there were many such in Jerusalem, which drew its sweet water from deep within the living stone. There would be a pathway down and through the bowels of the earth and out to safety if Binah had to go to Jerusalem and carve it out herself.

Asherah was shaking her head, the eyes of her spirit form wide with awe. *Child, you have gone far beyond me. I can see your need; I understand what you show me—but I am only mortal. I cannot see what you look at.*

No? But Theodoulos—could he see?

Asherah paused, considering.

He might, she said slowly in Binah's mind. *He might.*

If he does not come to me, he will come to you. Tell him to find his own escape—his and his sister's.

Asherah leaned forward in spirit and brushed her cheek against Binah's. *I wish we could embrace,* she said, her thought-voice wistful. Followed by *I wish Leo could see you.*

There was no time. Already, the faintest pallor lit the sky, and the horizon lightened to the point where Binah, at least, could discern the difference between a black thread and a white.

I must return, Asherah said. Involuntarily, she turned toward the room where Leo slept beside her body. *If Leo cannot rouse me . . .* Her own face paled at the thought of his terror.

With a final phantom touch of lips to face, Binah withdrew in a cloud of silver. With a rush, the winds between the worlds snatched her up and carried her back to her body as if she rode on dragon's wings.

With her soul firmly housed in flesh once more, the silver nimbus that kindled about her subsided once more. She caught up her cloak with some regret: it would be pleasant to spend the night alone in this house without concern of demands upon her time (limited), her faith (skewed), and her orthodoxy (nonexistent). The Caesarissa would wake soon and, no doubt, call for her. She hastened back to the palace. The lion did not roar, nor the bull bellow. Wraithlike, she drifted through the silent halls, leaving no reflection in the polished stone.

31

H o!" *a man cried.* "*Let her fly!*"
　　A hawk darted from an outflung arm like a missile from a catapult into the air. With a terrible velocity, it stooped and struck a pigeon, which plummeted through the air onto the ground.

The knights cheered.

"God grant it is an omen," Rainault said hoarsely. He had not written at all in April, as if the fire that had killed Peter Bartholomew had killed some spirit within him. But this past month, he had scribbled furiously.

Telling lies for Bohemond, Adela called it when his back was turned. *Bohemond* and *Jerusalem* were pillars of Rainault's faith. *Bohemond* had long ago shown himself made of ordinary clay. Jerusalem, however . . . it might bring him healing, Theodoulos hoped.

The rumors eddied through the army like a strange tide. The pigeon was not an omen; it was a warning in truth. It had been a messenger bird, carrying news of them to their enemies.

All through May, the army marched up the coast. At Arsuf, it turned inland. Toward Jerusalem.

"Not long now," Theodoulos promised his friends. His heart ached to see them brighten. The months with plenty of food and rest had restored some of the flesh they had lost; but they might never lose those fine networks of faint wrinkles around the eyes, from staring too long into the hot distance or facing their own fears. This was no land for moderation: you desired it with all your might, or you broke.

Those who had remained with the army were not the sort to break. If they had been starving to death and someone said, "At sunset you will see Jerusalem," they would have crawled till darkness fell.

They reached Ramleh at the start of June. The city, they were told, lay three days away, through the ancient, rounded hills of Judaea and places whose names echoed in their earliest childhood memories: familiar as their faith and as much beloved. So now they rode, even those on guard, as if through the sort of dream from which one woke, weeping and longing to dream again.

Theodoulos came upon the Count of Toulouse kneeling beside the road, his horse cropping the grass at the verge. Fearing that the Count had been taken ill, perhaps that he had even fallen, Theodoulos flung himself out of his saddle and rushed toward the older man, then paused.

The Count bent forward and kissed the earth. Taking up a blade of grass, he made the Sign over it, then raised it to his lips as if it were a Host. Tears poured down his face.

"My lord," Theodoulos breathed, shocked. "Let me help you mount."

Raymond of Toulouse shook his head. "Put off thy shoes from off thy feet," he husked. "For the place whereon thou standest is holy ground."

It was not the bush that burned, however, but the dream in his eyes.

"It is all holy, lord," Theodoulos said. "The land grows holier still as we draw closer to the city. You shall see . . ."

"Tancred thinks to fly his banner in Bethlehem," murmured the Count. "Bethlehem! How can any one man think to possess Our Lord's birthplace as a fief?"

Theodoulos shook his head. "These thoughts are too high for me," he said. "Come, let me help you to your horse." Inspiration struck him. "You but delay the first sight of Jerusalem to your people."

At Emmaus, envoys from Bethlehem met them. A procession marched out from the Church of the Nativity. Rainault's face shone now like Count Raymond's, transfigured as he neared the fulfillment of his greatest hope.

In the cool of the evening, Theodoulos walked out along the edge of the camp, Adela with him. The wind blew down from the hills, stirring the olive groves.

"Olive trees?" Adela asked. "It seems past belief that soon, I shall see the Mount of Olives!" She leaned against Theodoulos's shoulder, looking up into the sky.

Theodoulos kissed Adela's forehead, and she pressed in against the warmth of his body.

Small matters like Jerusalem's mighty walls and a garrison of Arabs lay between her and that desire, Theodoulos thought. And between his desire and its fulfillment.

He too was dreaming dreams and seeing visions. Or hearing voices. He could hear Asherah's voice murmuring ancient words: *Blessed art Thou, O Lord our God, King of the Universe, who kept us in life, sustained us, and permitted us to reach this joyous occasion.*

Christ Himself might have spoken those very words in that most ancient tongue. He translated the words for Adela, who thought them beautiful, some poetry of his own.

My God, how would he explain to her about Asherah? And yet he must . . . He would wed Adela with a clean conscience or not at all.

She smiled at him and took his hand. "Not long now, please God," she said. His heart caught fire.

A shadow moved at the edge of his field of vision.

"Adela, behind me!" He reinforced that order by pushing between her and whatever it was that he saw. His sword rasped from its sheath: blasphemous, it seemed, to draw it where Christ had walked, but for Adela to die so close to Jerusalem, never seeing it . . . surely God would not be that cruel.

"My brother?"

The word was a whisper. Theodoulos whirled to see a woman staring at him. Her skin was darkened by the sun, her hair and face only partially concealed by the fine veil she wore. The woman was richly jeweled, much of it wrought from heavy golden coins, and her lips were a thread of scarlet.

She looked like Asherah . . . no, Binah . . . she looked only like herself.

Theodoulos bowed in the Eastern fashion to her. "We are all brothers and sisters here," he said.

She shook her head, but lifted her veil. "No, you are not the one," she sighed. "I watched when they led my people into captivity, watched and wept. I heard your horses, the wind in your banners, and I thought, surely they come now, surely they come swiftly, and I came to greet you . . ."

The woman wept. "But you are not my lost children, not quite. Not even you, for all you have a look of them."

Theodoulos darted a glance over his shoulder at his friends.

"Lady," he dared to ask, dared to keep from dropping to his knees, "may I know your name?"

She smiled. "Why, everyone knows that!" she said. "It is Rachel."

Beside him, Adela blessed herself.

"I am far from home," Rachel said, "or I would take you there, bake you fresh cakes, and order a kid killed for you."

"Thank you," Theodoulos said.

"Promise me you come in peace," Rachel said.

Theodoulos bowed his head.

"You cannot?" she asked. Her voice rose in pain. Her eyes filled.

She was so like Binah, so like his foster mother: the wealth of dark hair, the flashing eyes, the grave face. She was like those very-long-ago maids who had once bedecked the stone image of his mother.

"Perhaps," Theodoulos offered, "one day we shall not weep. Next year, perhaps, in Jerusalem?"

"I shall pray for my people to return," she whispered. "I pray you, give them welcome."

Not daring to speak, Theodoulos bowed his head.

When he raised it, Rachel was gone. The sound of weeping lingered.

The Hebrew of the Psalms of Ascent Theodoulos had heard sung the last time he reached this spot echoed in his memory. He saw now, not with his eyes, but with his heart.

"Not long now," he said again. It had become almost a chant in default of the Hebrew that, Greek that he was, knight that he was, Christian that he was, he dare not sing.

As one person, the riders about him dismounted and bared their heads. Adela kicked off her shoes, picked them out of the road, and tucked them away in a saddlebag.

Up ahead rose the never-to-be-forgotten hill. Crowning it towered the massive, venerable walls of Jerusalem. The Tower of David loomed halfway down the western wall, overlooking the road. Within the walls, like a gem surmounting a crown, rose the great golden Dome of the city's heart.

Adela dropped to her knees.

"Jerusalem," Theodoulos said with immense pride. *If I prefer not Jerusalem above my chief joy . . .* How Leo had wept when he first saw the Holy City. Asherah had stood at his side, her hand on his shoulder, her face white with emotion, her eyes drinking in the sight.

Rainault fell upon his knees. He buried his face in his hands and wept passionately, as if he were a child who had been beaten, then forgiven and offered his heart's desire.

On Tuesday, June 7, in the year of the Lord 1099, as the Franks reckoned time, the army of the West camped outside the City of David. If these had been the days of Joshua, the sound of rams' horns would have made the great gates of the city crumble and open to them. This was Jerusalem, not Jericho; her gates were shut. The scarred walls showed hasty traces of repairs. Jerusalem the Golden was locked and garrisoned against them by Iftikhar ad-Dawla, who was no feeble general.

The city had been taken before. It could be taken again. But every time Jerusalem fell, mankind bled for it. Even now, they could see fields empty of flocks, but filled with refugees . . .

"Those are Christians!" Theodoulos blurted out. "He's driven them out!"

He looked for men and women dressed in the garb of Jews and found none. Iftikhar must still find the city's Jews to be of use. In which case, Leo's daughter and her family must still be alive. God only grant it. His eyes scanned the roads, the fields, for any sign. Let him see Shoshonna and her people and, so help him, he would bring them into camp and protect them with his knighthood, his cunning, and his last drop of blood.

In the distance, he saw the sweeps of wells, but never the sight that was old when Rebecca went to the wells to water a stranger's flocks. The bodies of a few animals lay scattered near the water.

"Poisoned," he muttered.

"What?" Rainault demanded.

"So we can't use them," Theodoulos explained. "It isn't hard: throw a carcass or two into the water. In this heat . . ." He shrugged. Muslim physicians had worse poisons, too, would they lower themselves to use them: no point going into that. The army's situation had just worsened. Only Siloam lay open to them, and the pool was vulnerable to missiles hurled from the city itself. The next water source was miles away.

Theodoulos stared up at the blazing sky. He pulled his helmet off, then his mail hood. Wind tugged at his sweaty hair. It was said that the wind in this place could actually drive people mad.

"Lord God of Battles," complained Rainault, "I am sick to death of sieges."

"Not another vision," Theodoulos groaned.

Sir Rainault hefted a shrunken skin of what might have been watered wine, but was probably watered vinegar, decided to wait, and set it down.

"It's got to be this damned wind," he said, then blessed himself. It was ill done to speak of damnation outside the walls of Jerusalem, especially when the siege was going so badly.

He set his head down on the splintered wood box that served as a table when they had any food to put on it and stayed motionless until Theodoulos thought that he had fallen asleep. Between fighting and foraging, the Frank had every right to. Rainault wasn't sleeping well either. More or less casual in his approach to writing in the earliest days of the campaign, he had grown more remote—especially since his recovery from his wound.

The sirocco blew until pack animals and herd beasts died, and the diminished army camped outside the walls of Jerusalem thought they would run mad.

Perhaps, Theodoulos thought, they already had.

On the advice of a hermit who seemed more than three-quarters mad himself, they had stormed the walls in the heat and dust of high summer, short of food and water, and lacking all siege machines. Sane men would not have attempted it, much less been surprised when they were driven back. Conclusion: these were not sane men.

Rainault raised his head and swollen eyelids. His eyes were reddened from dust and exhaustion. "You may as well go ahead and drink," he urged Theodoulos. "Don't think I don't know you were waiting for me to wake up. I wasn't sleeping."

God forbid Rainault know how worried Theo was for him. Obediently, he drank and controlled his grimace. Perhaps he would have to break down and buy some moderately decent wine, or they would all die of thirst—*as children are doing as I sit here*, he thought with a spasm of pain. Back in Cappadocia, Asherah probably crooned over her foster grandchild right now. Theodoulos wanted nothing more than to provide her with others.

"You may as well tell me about this latest vision," Theodoulos retorted.

"You mean Adela hasn't told you?" the Frank jeered, grinning.

"She's been trying to set up a kitchen to feed the women and children. Someplace, she says, where the last shall be first, at least to eat."

"Bless her," said Rainault.

Theodoulos signed himself, then held the poor, diminished wineskin out to his friend in silent command. *Drink, then talk.*

"Adela must know," Rainault began. "You know she's attached herself to the party of William Hugh of Monteil, her other uncle."

"Adhémar's brother." Theodoulos nodded.

"In any case, Peter Desiderius gained admittance . . ."

"Another of those prophets?" Theodoulos moaned. "Heaven give me strength."

"Heaven give us all strength. This holy Peter claims to have seen a vision of Bishop Adhémar, who orders us to give up selfish plans . . ."

"That's one in the eye for Tancred, isn't it?"

Rainault laughed, then went on. "We're supposed to walk in procession around the walls of Jerusalem in true repentance. If we do all this, God will give it into our hands in nine days."

"Iftikhar ad-Dawla will probably split himself laughing, while that garrison of his will fall off the walls seeing who can stick his ass out furthest," Theodoulos commented, then looked over his shoulder.

Rainault laughed. "Well, that's one way of taking the city. Admittedly, I'd prefer to gain it as a reward for piety and good fighting, but . . . To make matters worse," he added, "we're supposed to start with a three-day fast."

"Now that really sounds like Adhémar, rest his soul."

"Doesn't it just? Raymond of Aguilers and some of the bishops are to preach, and we're all supposed to swear unity. Especially Tancred and Count Raymond."

Theodoulos simply swore.

As a very hungry July dragged on, the army dwindled further. Siege towers defaced the ancient golden stone of the Holy City. Jerusalem held all his hopes. Here, he would save his foster sister and her family. Here, he might set down the burden of the silver cup he had rescued from the sack of Antioch. And here, he would be wed. Or it might be that here, he would leave his bones.

32

The darkness beneath the earth, the caverns that had sheltered Asherah long ago, now offered no refuge. She whimpered, then bit her hands against making another sound. As the Mother had given birth, the entire great bore of the tunnel leading from her chamber had shuddered and heaved. "The Lord is One," Asherah snatched a second to think. That *should* be her last thought.

She tried to grasp the rock of the Mother's birthing stool. Surely it would not move though all else was swept away. There was blood in her mouth, blood on her hands, and, somewhere nearby, a child wailing.

A child. Asherah reached out to grasp it and clutch it to her breast. Then a second of dust, rock, enemies, and wind swept her up. The Mother's great feline guards had nudged at her, and she had found herself, clad in ancient treasure, standing in the safety of the upper air, clutching the child and looking desperately about for Leo, who had always protected her and vowed he always would.

She had always known how Leo felt when he woke screaming. She too dreamt and woke gibbering of horrors, but that had mostly ceased upon her marriage. Now, Asherah remembered the turmoil beneath the earth, where Leo fought one battle against men, and Asherah fought for life itself. As she midwifed the child, she had had the Mother's presence to comfort her. But the earth had trembled and that presence had disappeared. Once again, she had been alone.

Asherah wrung her hands and moaned. She had known such portents before: the brooding *arslans* of Anatolia and the man bearing a lion's name, along with his companion, who was a wolf; even the tiny, deadly, glittering creatures that clustered around her as she was led from the underground up into the light and what safety remained on earth.

Then, she was back, the earth was heaving once again, and she was alone and without protection. Not even God replied. Sobbing and shivering, she staggered upward—she would be her own protection and that of the child!—dust and blood and ashes in her mouth.

Upward into the light! But overhead flashed the brazen wings of the tli in its most dire manifestations. The butterflies that the Mother had given her as a guard and fee flew upward to contend with it, flared into sparks, and then were gone.

Then, her arms were emptied: no child of her midwifery or of her own body's labors. She was no longer Asherah; she was Rachel weeping for her children, all her children, all gone; and the city cast down, ah woe!

She would have to go to ground again, hide, cowering into a space as small as she could squeeze herself until the terror went away and she could emerge and scrape together whatever shards remained and use them to rebuild her life.

Perhaps it would be easier to die. So very easy . . . simply stand in the way of the tli, scream, draw its attention . . . see, already it had scented human blood, it was turning, it flew toward her . . .

Its claws clasped her, to draw her up into the air toward its unthinkable lair, and she screamed.

"Asherah, Asherah!" Leo's voice, heavy with sleep, called her back from that terrible journey. Fear trembled beneath the reassurance she knew he was trying to put into his voice.

"Asherah!"

She struggled from nightmare toward the light of day. An instant more, and she would be able to look up at him, feel herself safe once more. There was no safety anywhere, was there, for her and hers? Never was; never would be.

She whimpered, and the punishing grip on her shoulders slackened. Leo could never bear to hurt her. She sometimes thought he even hated himself for her labor pains.

His face twisted with a reflection of her own anguish.

With a gasp, Asherah returned fully to the world. The trembling of the earth had subsided. But somewhere a wild wind blew, feeding great fires in a world that was more threatening than even she had feared. Job's comforter that she was, she had been sent to bring back word.

She gasped with relief. The roaring was gone for now, and she no longer saw the flames that had waked her, screaming.

First, though, she must reassure Leo. "My husband, my heart's dearest," she whispered.

His hands drew her close against his warmth.

"My love, do you know who I am?" Leo asked. He had not heard her. She wrapped her arms around him as if surrendering herself to his embrace, giving and demanding joy from him. She rested her face against his heart. Of all the refuges left her in the world, Leo's love had always proved the strongest. And he dared to ask if she recognized him! She would recognize him in Gehenna, if it came to that, and trade her soul to ransom his, thanking God for the privilege. She freed one hand and dashed it across her face. Not blood or sweat, but her tears wet it.

"Leo Ducas," she replied, somewhat indignantly. "I know you perfectly."

"Thank God." He drew her close. Just for a moment, she allowed herself to rest in the sanctuary he had always created for the two of them. She would even forbear to ask which God they should thank. Just a moment longer, she wanted to beg, but she dared not. There was danger, death by fire and sword for others whom she loved.

Leo took her face in his hands and gazed deeply into her eyes. From the first moment she had seen him amid his enemies and hers, she had loved that steadfast look of his.

"What did you dream, beloved?" he asked. He had never thought her mad. "What trouble do you see this time?"

She knew he had hoped that returning her to Cappadocia, which her heart and hard work had made into her home, would take away dreams. *Can you take away the horrors of which they are warning?* As much as she loved Leo, she knew he could not do that.

But since their marriage, she had waked screaming only a few times. Once, she had run to her father's rooms to find him collapsed over an ancient scroll. His death had been so swift it was painless, she had been assured. The last time she had waked in such mortal terror had been several years ago. Then she had lived in fear for several weeks until surviving traders brought news of the slaughters in the Rhinelands by men of the army that had marched on Byzantium.

"It's Theodoulos, isn't it? Or Shoshonna?" Leo asked.

"It's all of them," she whispered. "All my children. My city." She pulled her hair over her shoulders, then tightened her grasp on it as if it were a mourning garment she must rend.

Leo caught her hands and held them with one of his. "This was worse than your last dream," he said. "Asherah, you must tell me. Perhaps this time there is something we can do. Perhaps we do not have to wait until word of disaster reaches us and we can only mourn."

With his free hand, he reached for her robe and spread it awkwardly over her shoulders. She gestured and he released her hands. She straightened the soft fabric of her robe and huddled into it even though the July night was warm. He made no move to embrace her again.

"Jerusalem," she told Leo. "The Franks have broken through the walls. So angry they are, so terrible. Oh God, Leo, your Emperor should not have disowned and abandoned them." Her voice broke and angry tears poured down her cheeks. "He should have destroyed them, root and branch, like the cursed Amalekites they are!"

Leo's face paled. He stared down at his hands, those immensely gentle, capable hands she loved. For thirty years, almost, he had used them in the service of their life together: to sit idle while others died was not his way—and yet . . .

"I heard you call out for Binah," he said. "Did she come to you in your dreams?"

Asherah shook her head. "Not this time. Binah can do *nothing* now," she said hollowly. "She is still very young . . . in this incarnation."

"She is a woman grown."

Leo's laughter contained the usual shock even though he too had listened to adepts of Hind and Ch'in explain about the transmigration of souls.

"Leo, she is still a very young goddess." Asherah looked down, uncomfortable with the familiar blasphemy. "She appealed to us be-cause she is still so very young that"—she smiled at Leo—"she thinks her father can do anything in the world."

Leo's eyes turned tender, then dropped. Asherah followed their gaze. She drew her robe closed across the deep cleft between her breasts, then captured his hand.

Her husband sighed. "Let us assume Binah will have greater power than you when she is grown." He rehearsed the familiar argument. "For now, yours is the greater knowledge. Is there a thing that can be done? I cannot believe that your dreams torment you thus only to bring us news of catastrophe. If we have to wait to hear that the Franks have sacked Jerusalem, I think I shall go mad myself."

Asherah huddled in on herself. Leo tried to draw her comfortingly close, but she shook her head violently.

"There is," she said, "a way. I could . . . I think I could go there . . ."

"No!"

She raised her eyes challengingly at him.

"The tli?" he asked in horror.

"God no!" she cried. "I would be flung off even if the tli were feeling benevolent. And it isn't, right now; my dream proved that."

"One solitary Jewish woman in an army that's run mad," he asked more rationally. "What could you do there for Shoshonna and the children?"

The tears gushed out.

"You'd only die with them!" Leo's hands shook as he tried to strike a light and kindle a lamp.

"I would not go alone," Asherah added. "Binah. I would need her strength added to my own to make the crossing."

"I forbid it!"

At least, her anger kept her from weeping any more.

"I mean," Leo retreated, "you and Binah are women. You are not warriors."

"Self-evident, Leo. Although I suspect what powers we might summon would surprise you."

"But with what consequences to women who have been peaceful all their lives? You're damned right I listened to the sages out of Hind. I fear those consequences. You—you're protected by your faith, but Binah? If she turns violent . . . like her mother . . ." Leo shook his head. He took a deep breath and rose hastily. "Sending Binah is a bad idea. You shall send *me*. Just let me dress and get my weapons."

Asherah had to laugh or she would weep again. Binah was not the one Leo should be worrying about, but then, he had a blind spot about the little flawed princess, his old friend's daughter. If it came to that, he had much the same blind spot about Alexius the Emperor. Leo, she told herself furiously, thought everyone was as faithful as he. It was one of the things she loved most about him, but at this moment she wanted to shake him into enough skepticism to help them all survive.

"Leo Ducas! As if I could simply send you, just like that! It won't work, my love. I can translocate. I can even draw on a companion's strength to take him with me. We could go together."

"I will not risk you," Leo said.

"But you are willing to risk yourself. How is that any different?"

"They're my children too," Leo said. "You risked yourself giving birth to them. This is an ordeal I have a chance of surviving. Come, Asherah, think of a way I can reach them," he tried to order her, but his voice broke. "In the name of God, Asherah, think!"

"There is another way." Asherah was dressing as hastily as Leo. *And years ago, in this very room, they had waked, dressed, and then parted: he to Peristrema to lead armies, she to the cave cities that underlay her world. They had clung to each other as if the world would end when they parted. She had never seen any reason to change her mind about that.*

Leo whirled. "What is it?"

"It requires," she said sadly, "a sacrifice."

Take thy son, thine only son, Isaac, whom thou lovest . . .

"You gave birth in peril of your life. My dearest, it is my turn to offer to give the gift back."

Asherah shook her head, smiling a little at Leo's fervor. The young man who had pledged his life to a doomed Emperor, the upright young officer who had stood as her protector, the wily bargainer for her people's lives—in this older, wearier man's readiness to sacrifice himself, she saw all of them and loved them all once more.

"If that were the price, I would *never* let you go alone," she told him. "In this sacrifice, the blood falls upon my hands. I must spend the life of a young and innocent creature."

She wiped at her eyes, then spoke before her husband could jump to some appalled conclusion that would do neither of them any good. "The black colt, Leo. The one with the white blaze on the brow. We need him."

Leo narrowed his eyes. "Nordbriht says that his people used to offer white horses to the barbarian gods that he is *supposed* to have renounced. Asherah, wouldn't a lamb be more suitable for a sacrifice? Especially since this isn't time yet to send the goat out into the wilderness for Azazel?"

Fully dressed, Asherah collected herbs and small boxes in a cloth bag, then went to the door. Automatically courteous, Leo opened it, and they descended into the courtyard. Its walls were freshly whitewashed and they shone in the moonlight. Through the courtyard. Past the spot beneath the walls where a much younger Asherah, newly married, had watched out the night beside Nordbriht. Past the ground-level quarters of their manservants who doubled as guards. They were forbidden weapons, but Leo and Nordbriht had trained them anyhow. At least, Nordbriht did not wake and insist on coming with them. He would ask too many questions, and the terror with which Asherah had waked told her how short a time they had if they were to act at all.

Out to the stables.

"You should not be outside the walls at this hour," Leo told her and reached for the sword that he had automatically belted on.

Oh Leo, Leo. So pathetically eager to risk himself for her and for their children. If it were simply for herself, she would never risk him, never let him go.

She was not certain that what she planned was at all permitted to a child of Israel, even though the book in which she had found the means contained other texts that she knew held no danger or blame. *Let the sin be on my head,* she prayed.

Inside the stables, they found the black colt upright on spindly legs, leaning against the mare in a pause from nursing. He turned his head at their approach, and the white blaze on his forehead gleamed like a diadem. The colt should have had years to run free before they even began to train him, years as a beast of burden, perhaps, or, if he grew fleet and skilled, as a warhorse, years of siring colts and fillies that carried on his bloodlines before he spent his final years out in a green pasture.

Asherah stepped into the stall. "So," she whispered. "So." The mare, recognizing her, whickered and nudged at her hand in case she had brought any sweets. She trusted Asherah, traitress that she was.

"Surely, you cannot do it here before the mother," Leo protested. "You do not even seethe a kid in its mother's milk!"

A tear rolled down Asherah's cheek. Oh, Leo. Even after all these years, his ability to imagine new, horrible rituals and to forgive her for them still saddened and astonished her.

"It's not like that, Leo," she assured him. "I do not kill the colt. At least, not now. Bring him outside, behind the stables."

Quickly, she haltered the mare and held her lest she turn on Leo as he picked up the colt. He was still so small! Asherah could have carried him herself, taking all of the responsibility for her acts upon herself. But since the colt was to be Leo's mount, he must bond with him, the sooner the better. She let her hand rest on the white blaze crowning the colt's head. He was wonderfully warm and soft, and his brown eyes seemed to stare into hers as if he were well aware of what she planned.

Asherah sighed, bent, and kissed the colt on that white star. A hot tear spilled over onto it. *Forgive me,* she thought at him and at the mare. *I have children of my own and I must save them.*

She gestured for Leo to carry the colt to the small ring behind the stables. Only a few lamps shone in the sleeping house; only a few stars gleamed high above. It was just as well: the last thing she needed was curious friends, servants, cousins, and guards—for all of her life, usually the same people.

Leo set the colt down and stood watching her. She did not want him watching her now.

"My Leo," she said, "go and prepare for a journey. Arms and armor, all that you will need."

"Where will I go, my heart?" he asked. The trust in his eyes made her want to weep again.

"Jerusalem."

He raised an eyebrow.

"I told you, we cannot tame the tli to bear us. But if my studies have been of any use, tonight this colt shall carry you there."

And God help us all.

Leo looked down at the colt, clearly measuring it against his own height.

"Have we any armor from the West in our stores?" Asherah asked. Alone with Leo, she could safely discuss the secret cache of arms he had collected. Being Ducas, he might be said to have a right to them—although if the Emperor heard, he might also be deemed to be too great a risk to live.

"I shall take a shield. But I prefer my own armor," he said. "It suits me after all these years. In any case, I doubt that any of the Franks would mistake me for one of their own." Incongruously, he bowed to her before he left.

Asherah crouched, taking the colt's muzzle between both hands.

"You shall do what few beasts have done," she told it. "You shall grow overnight to a creature strong enough and worthy enough to bear my love to Jerusalem overnight and back again."

Leo had always taken justified pride in the horses he raised, as fine as any in Cappadocia, a region famed for them. In fact, their breeding had been one of his tasks. Asherah had been content to admire them, ride as she needed, feed them sweets, and supervise their sale on the rare occasion that Leo could be persuaded to part with any. Bless the man, he usually preferred to give them to cherished friends as their sons grew to manhood.

The horses of Cappadocia were renowned for their speed. How swift they could truly be, however, few knew—Asherah and Binah among them.

If only the colt before her were lifeless ebony like the magic horse in the Persian tales, which could fly across Asia in a single night, carrying a young prince and his stolen bride! Asherah had no such good fortune. Instead, she must use one of the most dubious rites in the arts she had so painstakingly learned all her life to cause the colt to grow overnight to his full strength.

If her magics worked, the horse could race to Jerusalem in time to let Leo try to save Shoshonna, Theodoulos, the babies, and anyone else he could. *Assuming that they* can *be saved*, Asherah conceded to the watchful stars and the large-eyed colt. She shivered a little in the night wind. The colt shivered too, and she laid her heaviest veil over his back.

There was a price for the rapid growth, the speed, the power she would bestow upon the poor little thing. He would grow up overnight into such a horse that poems were written about. But he would live no more than two years or three. So her own children might live, she would sacrifice the years that the colt might otherwise have had of play, of useful work, of honorable retirement.

You could lose both.

You could even lose Leo.

Any rite carried with it the need for courage. So, for that matter, did life.

If she did not try, she might lose them all in any case.

"Forgive me," she whispered to the colt. "Survive the next few days and what life you have will be an honored, easy one."

She hugged her victim, which snuggled against her and lipped her hair. Hungry again, was he?

Sighing, Asherah knelt and inscribed a Solomon's seal in the night air. Lines of flame sizzled and crackled, bounding her and the colt, her matrix and her prey, into a space that was not quite of this world, but quite safe from it.

The starlight fractured, shedding opalescent rainbows on her face and hands, surrounding the colt with glory as if he were a creation in one of those mosaics with the shimmering golden tesserae that the great churches lavished on idols.

Asherah began the chant. Her voice, resonant in the sealed area, made the colt jump. She stroked him, then draped the veil resting on his back so it covered his eyes. The lights might frighten him, and she did not know what would happen if he tried to bolt. The power in the ancient words made her sway. Sighing with relief as she achieved the last of them, she crouched before the colt.

The creature shuddered, but stood fast on all four tiny hooves. Asherah began the second chant, then bent to touch the colt's hooves. On the left forehoof, she inscribed the sign of Leo's victorious faith: *Chi* and *Rho*. After all, those letters had helped win the Empire that had produced Leo. They might well aid him in gaining his heart's desire. When she took away her hand, the letters gleamed silver on the colt's hoof.

The colt would grow. The horse would be strong, running and fighting for Leo at need.

Then, she laid her hand upon the right forehoof and inscribed the Hebrew letters that meant "life." What an irony, she thought. But this did mean life of a sort, if not long life for the colt. She breathed upon this hoof, and the characters she had inscribed also gleamed silver.

Last of all, she leaned forward, laid her trembling hands on the colt's cheeks, and blessed him. She whispered into soft ears words she could scarcely pronounce, much less translate—compulsion, exhortation, praise, encouragement—all of Xenophon, she thought, compressed into a few moments' ritual.

The colt dipped his head onto her shoulder. Her trembling shook them both. The ground seemed to rock as if a giant troop of horses thundered by. Overhead, the light splintered into more and more brilliant shards. Asherah cast her arms about the doomed, beautiful creature.

"Begin," she commanded.

The word was far too like the words with which Scripture and the world itself began for her to say it without remorse for what she did. She took the burden for her act upon herself. The colt shuddered violently, and she absorbed its trembling just as, years ago, she had absorbed the birth pangs of a goddess.

The light exploded overhead. *Asherah? Mother?*

She should have known a rite of this importance would attract Binah's attention in faraway Byzantium. Her foster child perceived in the twinkling of an eye what Asherah attempted.

Was there no other way? Binah asked.

None, she whispered across time and space to Binah.

Then the colt screamed, as if anticipating the trumpeting of an enraged stallion. Asherah unlocked her arms from about the damp neck.

And the colt grew. Already now, he teetered on legs that might have belonged to a six-month-old—a well-grown one—then to a yearling. Beneath the veil, the colt's form shuddered and shifted; and he screamed again, racked by growth pains. Tears poured down Asherah's face.

Courage, Mother.

She never faltered in the ancient words that the ritual required of her.

With every word, the colt grew still taller, heavier, finer. Now, his back elongated, his tail lashed, and his neck arched. Magnificent.

Asherah smiled inwardly. Words from Job thrust themselves into her memory, stubborn pedant that she was, and brought her comfort.

> Hast thou given the horse strength? Hast thou clothed his neck with thunder?
>
> Canst thou make him afraid as a grasshopper? the glory of his nostrils is terrible.
>
> He paweth in the valley, and rejoiceth in his strength; he goeth on to meet the armed men.
>
> He mocketh at fear, and is not affrighted; neither turneth he back from the sword.
>
> The quiver rattleth against him, the glittering spear and the shield.
>
> He swalloweth the ground with fierceness and rage; neither believeth he that it is the sound of the trumpet.
>
> He saith among the trumpets, Ha, Ha; and he smelleth the battle afar off, the thunder of the captain and the shouting.

The symbols of her faith and Leo's gleamed now on the stallion's forehooves.

Asherah sighed, leaning forward until her head rested against the full-grown horse, stronger now than she, and so beautifully young. The stallion lipped her hair as the colt had done.

You should not love me, she told him. Yet, if she were his destroyer, she was in some senses as much his dam as the mare from whom she had stolen him.

Leo shall have the naming of you, she promised. The horse would love him, must love him.

She took down the wards she had created and stood trembling in the starlight. Hearing footsteps, she turned, her hand going to her knife.

She almost cried out. What seemed like a ghost stood before her: Leo as she had first seen him, solemn and erect, his eyes lighting at the sight of her.

He wore the armor he had used since his parents had sent him out on Romanus's disastrous campaign eastward. The years had fitted it to him and him to it; even if Frankish armor might let him pass unnoticed, he would fight better in familiar gear. He carried a saddle and what else Asherah had told him to bring as well as a shield taken from a mercenary. That, at least, might give him some measure of disguise—but not enough that any Franks could say in truth that he was there to spy. (What they might lie about was beyond Asherah's understanding.) His helmet might hide most of his face, but she knew her Leo and she always would.

With a low cry, Asherah hurled herself forward. He kissed her softly, as if he feared that his chain mail would bruise her. He should have overcome that fear years ago! she wanted to say.

His eyes went to the horse nudging against her, and his lips parted in wonder. If his hands had not been full, she knew he would have signed himself.

"You took such a deed upon yourself with no help or absolution," he mourned. "My poor love. You must be exhausted as well as heartsick."

Now he did set down his burdens and open his arms to her. How good they felt; she could rest this way for the rest of her life. But the horse had little time, and her children might have less.

"Nordbriht woke," Leo warned. "You are going to have some explaining to do about why he cannot accompany me."

"I will not do this twice," Asherah declared, knowing that "could not" was more truthful. Besides, what horse would grow overnight to a size that could bear *him*? "Take this horse, Leo. Ride. He will bear you to Jerusalem tonight in safety. Use him with love, for he has only a few years to live."

"What is his name?" Leo asked.

"You must give him one yourself."

Leo turned to the horse. When he saddled him, the beast stood as if trained to do so. Asherah's veil still lay over his head. Leo seized it and bound it around his arm as if he were a Frank himself.

"Sweet love," he said.

"You look like the boy I loved at first sight," she told him. Beneath his helmet, Leo smiled.

Then he turned the horse toward the east. The stallion reared, gleaming hoofs striking sparks from the stone. The ground trembled as the horse trumpeted and spurned the earth.

A moment later, the horse had borne Leo away. Asherah flung out a hand, then sank to her knees, wrapping her arms about herself to keep warm.

After a long few minutes, she forced herself to her feet. It would be dawn in a couple of hours, and the household must not go untended.

33

Overhead, the stars spurted fire, and a great comet stretched across the sky, trailing glory behind it. Beneath him, the black horse, a miracle of newness, ran so swiftly that he scarcely seemed to touch the earth; but where his hooves struck, sparks flew upward until Leo felt as if he rode through a globe of flame that burned but did not consume him.

Leo settled himself more comfortably in the saddle. For years, it had been the tasks of younger men to ride hard, to fight hard: like Joachim before him, Leo now fought primarily with his wits. He remembered, though, he remembered how he had ridden hard across the land he had made his own. It was more than Empire to him: driven out by Turks, he had returned to his home by grace of his kinsman and adversary Alexius, sealed to it by gold and tears and blood.

The land unrolled before him as if the Cappadocian stallion he bestrode raced forward upon a carpet woven of the finest silk. The earth seemed to turn as they raced toward Jerusalem. The familiar tang of horse, of leather, and of iron fired Leo's blood.

Leaning forward, Leo touched his mount's neck, which arched in response. How marvelous the creature was, mane blowing in the wind created by his swift passage. So very young and swift and doomed, created only to bear him to Jerusalem and back again. Asherah had taken the blame, she said, upon herself. She took too much upon herself, Leo decided.

When he reached Jerusalem, then what? God send that he find a way within and deliver his children. Each hoofbeat seemed a separate word, merging into a prayer: let him live; let him live long enough to spare his children; let him live long enough to spare his children and bring them home. Every one of those pleas might be enough— *Dayenu*, as Asherah would pray: but alone, none of them were enough for Leo. He wanted them all.

Perhaps. He would trade his own life if that would guarantee even a chance of the children's safety. To his astonishment, he realized he was afraid.

The horse, however, was secure in his rider. The stallion had no fear, thank God. A beast, a magnificent beast without the wit to know what Asherah had stolen. Now, Leo could smell the attar of roses that had scented her veil before she had used it as a horse blanket. He shut his eyes to savor it, blended as it was of his earliest memories of her. Her trust in the dark moment of his Emperor's blinding had been her first gift to him; like all of her gifts, it came with risks and tears and blood attached. Their land. Their children. This horse. And, of course and always, Asherah his love.

In some ways, he thought, she *was* her Law. He remembered one passage he had translated laboriously as a gift for her and how she had wept as she read it:

> For the Torah resembles a beautiful and stately damsel, who is hidden in a secluded chamber of her palace and who has a secret lover, unknown to all others. For love of her, he keeps passing the gate of her house, looking this way and that in search of her. She knows that her lover haunts the gate of her house. What does she do? She opens the doors of her hidden chamber ever so little, for a moment reveals her face to her lover, but hides it again forthwith. Were anyone with her lover, he would see nothing and perceive nothing. He alone sees it, and he is drawn to her with his heart and soul and his whole being, and he knows that for love of her she declared herself to him.

They had had so much, so many years, and none of it was enough.

Leo stared east at the horizon. No, that was not the rising sun he saw, but flames on the horizon, flames rising from within the walls of the Holy City of Jerusalem. Fear seemed to kindle deep in his guts, like a ball of sea fire. He called to his mount, urging it to greater speed. The stallion reared, screaming and striking out. The letters inscribed upon his hooves—*Life* and *In this sign, you shall conquer*—shot out tongues of flame.

"I shall call you," Leo decided, "Aster." The name meant "star." It might be unoriginal because of the starlike blaze on the horse's head, but Asherah had, in a sense, created this mount for him; and the names were well matched.

Aster reared and screamed as if thanking Leo for his name. Poor beast: never had Leo owned as fine a horse.

He wondered where they actually were. He almost thought he could smell the sea. Had the creature bespelled from colthood into supernal speed already reached the Holy Land? Even now, did he race up the coast before turning inland to Jerusalem? Anything was possible. They seemed to fly like a comet.

Now it was time, and past time, Leo gave thought to how he would enter Jerusalem. Was he, did he truly think, a Frank to risk himself in a mad enterprise? Would he truly set his horse at the high walls at the world's navel and leap over them into the city? A Frank might very easily kill Leo for possession of Aster: it would be best to hide him, and, God knew, there were places enough outside the city. Some even belonged to Asherah's family.

He would do better to enter the city on foot as befitted a Christian, a penitent, and a father who wanted to survive long enough to find his children. He would have to do so by purely human means, he feared. He was no creature of the earth, like his foster children. What sense of the land he had was restricted to the caves beneath the place that had chosen itself as his home. Perhaps that might wake here in the Mother of Cities to serve him, but he had best not count upon it. There were caves and tunnels beneath the city. If he could slip into them, he was certain he could find the marks that would lead him up into his daughter's house. It was strongly built and might hold out long enough for her to lead her people underground already—assuming she realized the need before her guards were overwhelmed.

To Leo's astonishment, he found himself praying for Iftikhar ad-Dawla, that his defenses could hold out long enough for Leo to save his family.

And if you fail, Leo, what will you do then? Die with the children to show Asherah that your defense of her people has never been a sham? She knows that, fool. What good is your death if it leaves her alone? It is not enough to save your children; you too must live.

Up ahead, the horizon darkened—was that smoke? Sweat rolled down his face beneath the helm as if he neared a great fire. Leo pressed his legs against Aster's sides, urging him to greater speed. The black stallion raced eastward, scenting battle.

Aster thundered into dawn and toward Jerusalem. He might scent the battle from afar and not fear, but Leo remembered too much to share his horse's exultation. He had survived the disaster at Manzikert, the slaughter of Peristrema, and the madness of battles beneath the earth. He had faced down the wild hunt and hacked his way down the road to Antioch. Each time, he had more to lose—and more to fear. But the horse, especially one as young as Aster, deserved not to be distracted. At least, this time, Leo told himself, he risked no one under his command.

Leo laid a hand on Aster's neck. It was wet, but not lathered, and the horse's breathing was unimpaired. Where there was battle, there were robbers as well as fighters; and Aster was a horse men would kill for. He would have to find him a hiding place, somewhere close to water, then walk the rest of the way to Jerusalem unless he could somehow find a lesser horse. The sparks that had flown from Aster's hooves subsided as the speed of his passage slowed to slightly more than the full gallop of a normal horse.

Leo recognized this road, recognized the place where the caravan had stopped. Here, he had his first sight of the Holy City, and here he wept with thankfulness. Now, it was crowded with families, some pushing crude carts, some carrying nothing at all, who fled as he thundered by.

And he wept once more.

If a city were under siege, expelling those unable to fight made sense, didn't it? Andronicus would have done it in a heartbeat, assuming the ancient traitor had a heart. Curious: the people fleeing the city seemed all to be Christian. Some dropped in their tracks, and very few others possessed the strength to carry their bodies to where they might be buried. At best, they dragged them over to the side of the road and arranged them as decently as they could. The wind had blown the coverings off their faces, which turned up to the sky in mute reproach.

My God, why hast thou forsaken me?

So . . . Iftikhar had retained the Jews of the city? It was not necessarily an advantage, especially if Jerusalem was falling. Leo could not even spare a hand to bless himself, but he prayed as he rode, and one of the things he prayed was that Asherah would never know.

The sun beat down on his helm. Aster had carried him through night and morning within sight of his goal, and the day was hot.

"I'll get you settled, boy," Leo muttered to the horse. Children might die on the road. One of his own fought to break down the ancient walls that loomed before him, smoke rising from within them, while others clutched infants and struggled about whether to fight or flee. But the horse that had brought Leo here would be lovingly, if quickly, tended before he moved on.

From letters, Leo knew that water during the siege had been in short supply. He thought of stopping by a collection of huts to ask where water could be found, but even the eldest men there recoiled from him.

If this were Cappadocia, the land sense that had been Leo's gift from Father Meletios would have told him where water could be found. Well, Leo would have to try. *This is the home of my faith and my wife's,* he thought. *I do not ask for Galilee. I do not ask for the Jordan. But a tiny pool, too small to be noticed . . .*

Please. Sweat rolled down his face, stinging where helmet and razor had scraped his face. You'd have thought, after all these years, that his skin would be hardened to it. Another reason not to weep: pain.

Aster's head came up at the same time Leo sniffed water. The horse slowed to the walk of a normal beast, and Leo turned him off the road. Dismounting, he led Aster away, past a stand of trees, into brush that preserved some tinges of green even in the high summer of Palestine. His horse moved with surprising quiet. Aster had to be tired; even the Greek and Hebrew characters Asherah had inscribed on his hooves seemed dimmed.

Leo almost had to step in the tiny pool before he realized he had found the water he had prayed for. Swiftly, he backed Aster: the horse had so few years allotted that letting him drink too soon and founder himself would be an even greater crime than usual. Pulling off his helmet, Leo unsaddled Aster, hid the saddle in the underbrush, rubbed him down quickly but thoroughly, then covered him with his blanket.

Aster should be walked until he was cool, then allowed to drink.

It would make sense, too, for Leo to wait until dusk to attempt entry into the city; but love and fear did not contribute to good sense right now. How wonderful if he could assume that the magic that had grown Aster into a warhorse overnight would have taught him not to drink too fast. Asherah had not shadowed her soul and exhausted herself for him to abuse her creation.

What else can you do, Leo? He had used the land sense to find water and such safety as might exist in beleaguered Judaea. Could he cast the wards he had often watched Asherah raise? He had practiced them, but she was so much more skilled. Wards would mean no one would come this way and find Aster. No one would steal the means of his journey home or wait here, by the horse, to ambush the rider. He shed his mail and settled himself to wait. God, he was too old for this. He ought to be home, spoiling his grandchildren—*assuming he reached them in time.*

Aster nudged at him, as if trying to assuage his master's inexplicable human terror. Leo flung an arm about him in return. Already, Aster had grown from young stallion to mature horse. It might even be, if Leo's mission lasted too long, he would return to find a horse too old to bear him home. Leo glanced up at the sky. The sunlight was slanting toward the west now, and the sky was dark with smoke that made his heart chill.

Leo stretched out his arms in invocation. He knew his Hebrew was accented. Perhaps God would understand, all the same. He traced the first sigil, chanting. Light blossomed and grew beneath his hands, and he thanked God not just for the additional measure of safety, but for another weapon given into his hands.

Pulling his mail back on over his aching shoulders, Leo gave Aster one last hug, patted his glossy neck, then started toward Jerusalem.

 **34**

The hymns of priests, bringing siege ladders up to the walls, had long been replaced by the screams of the dying. Theodoulos shuddered. He glanced about beneath the Norman helmet that had replaced his own two or three battles ago. Its nasal had scraped his face raw, or perhaps he had bitten his lip long ago; but the blood, salt, and smoke rasping his throat made him gag.

Perhaps now, he could escape to the house in the old Jewish quar-

ter near the New Gate without being cut down for desertion. Or perhaps, they would simply think he had finally decided to claim a share
of the loot for himself. Godfrey of Bouillon might declare he would
never loot, but Tancred was his man; Tancred had tried to claim
Bethlehem and had sworn to loot the Dome of the Rock. Worst—if
there *was* a worst in this disaster of a victory—Tancred's camp
fronted the New Gate. If anyone entered the quarter, it would be he.

You are out of time, Theodoulos, his usual voices exhorted him.
Move!

He dodged behind the wreckage of what had been a house before
a boulder from a siege engine turned the rubble into rocks and dust.

The tli seemed to hover over Jerusalem, breathing fire and slaughter down upon the city. From within the Zion Gate, Iftikhar ad-Dawla
had hurled flame—fat, resin, and pitch mixed with hair and flax—
into Count Raymond's camp. Godfrey had used crossbows to fire the
padding that protected the battered walls. The Franks had recoiled,
then struck back. The battle was over. Now the massacre began.

Theo's race toward the houses between the New Gate and the
Holy Sepulchre was nothing less than a descent into the kind of hell
mouth carved upon the doorways of the great churches in the West.
He stumbled over bodies, their arms flung out, their glazed eyes still
wide with their last agony, so often that he no longer recoiled. His
feet were wet. When he looked down, he saw them reddened to the
ankles with blood.

How would they ever scrub it from the golden stones?

Already, shields and banners rose outside the greater buildings
proclaiming, *I hold this by right of my sword!*

Well enough. Theo was a knight; he had a shield of his own that
he would raise outside his home if he got there in time. If not . . . He
shrugged beneath his mail, instantly regretted it, and plunged on.
He almost measured his length in the bloody street. Looking down,
he saw he had stumbled over a knot of three children, too wasted
by the siege to be useful even as slaves. A sane man would have wept.
Theodoulos pushed by and ran on.

Christe eleison, he began, then broke off his prayer. He did not
want God to see this.

"*Theo!*" It wasn't just the terror in that high, shrill scream that
stopped him in his flight, but the voice itself. God have mercy where
there was none, but what in the name of God did Adela think she was
doing here?

Throwing away her life, Theodoulos. Just like you.

Theodoulos whirled, sword in hand. Adela had backed against a blackened wall, her arms spread as if she fought to cover an entire family. A broken sword dangled from its cord along one wrist, dripping blood. She had no helm, no shield, but her jaw was set and she faced down the man who tried to pry her away from the family she had clearly decided to defend with her life.

"Move, you foolish slut." The voice of her attacker gurgled with a throaty satisfaction, as if the man had sated himself on blood.

"Rainault, no!" Adela screamed. As Rainault swung, she brought up that pathetic fragment of sword, astonishingly enough, in time to parry the blow of a Frankish knight in full training and drunk on battle rage. Barely, she turned the blade aside, then staggered away. The blade rebounded against her broken sword and crashed against the wall, drawing sparks from the wounded stone.

Now what was he supposed to do—rescue Adela, or find Shoshonna? Adela shook her long hair, matted now with blood, back from her grimy face and screamed his name again.

"Adela!" he cried. "Rainault, what do you think you're doing?"

Rainault pounced, dragging Adela away from the people she protected and hurling her to the ground. He flung the children aside from a woman who had sheltered behind Adela, then flung himself upon her, growling.

Had the man who had called him "Sir Greek" and leaned on his shoulder turned, like Nordbriht, into a man-wolf? Had his fever returned? Theo rushed forward, joining Adela as she leapt onto Rainault's back, clawing and pounding at his face and shoulders.

"Damn you, get back, Adela," Theo gasped. "You madwoman, what are you doing here?"

"My uncle's business," she panted. "When I heard—stop it, Rainault, damn you!—I heard they were killing . . . I came out to see . . ."

"Get away from him!" he cried at Adela, who had never obeyed him yet and never would. That was fine, as long as she lived.

He *knew* about the man-wolf. Its strength was greater than mortal, fearsome. If Rainault had transformed, he had become stronger than human, and less than an innocent beast. And all in the service of Christ. *Kyrie eleison.*

He had been a peer, a brother once. *Christe eleison.*

Theodoulos jerked Rainault's head around. No, that was not a wolf's muzzle beneath the helm, but a man's face, twisted by a kind of bestiality exalted into sheer violence. *The face of war, Theo. You wanted to be a knight.*

Here *is a knight.*

Wrapping his hand around the hilt of his sword, Theodoulos brought the pommel up against Rainault's chin with enough force to daze him.

Rainault laughed. "Don't you understand, brother? They must die. They all must die. An army's coming up from Egypt, and the enemies of the faith must *die!*"

"And you plan to rape them all before you kill them?" Amazing that the contempt in Theodoulos's voice didn't sear his throat worse than the fire and smoke. "All by yourself? You really think you can? That's a great deed, a man's deed, isn't it?"

Rainault tensed to break free. He was younger than Theodoulos, better trained, and stronger. *One last try, Theo, and then you had better cut his throat and be done with it.*

He had to spit anyhow, so he spat in Rainault's face. "Attacking the helpless. Attacking Adela, who saved your rotten life. Call me brother, will you? Then, by Christ, you had better call me Cain because you're not going to live through this night's work."

"You think you can kill me, Greek?"

The bubbling, violent rapture was fading from Rainault's voice. Maybe that was even a glimmer of sense Theodoulos saw in his eyes.

"I'm probably not good enough. But when I was made knight, I knew it was to stop bastards like you. I don't *know* you, Rainault. I don't *know* you!"

Rainault's head jerked from side to side in rhythm with Theodoulos's blows. Astonishingly, he made no attempt to defend himself. The woman beneath him pushed herself free and ran to her children, who huddled in Adela's bloody, tattered skirts. Then Rainault went motionless, as if gathering strength.

Last throw of the dice, Sir Greek.

"Tell me, Rainault, tell me, *brother*. Is this what you wanted Jerusalem for? Is this the thanks you offer?"

No, Theo hadn't been mistaken. That was consciousness, the light of human reason, that he saw dawning in Rainault's reddened eyes. And with human reason came human shame.

"Look," Theodoulos said. "You damn near killed Adela. The Papal Legate's own niece, for God's sake. Would you have raped her too?"

Judging from the reek of him, the woman Theo had saved hadn't been Rainault's first prey. He fought not to vomit.

"By God, it's a knightly deed, isn't it—to gain Jerusalem and damn your soul."

"Oh my God," Rainault whispered. "Oh my God . . ." He choked on the words of contrition. Theodoulos eased the pressure of his knees on the man's body. Rainault pulled off his helmet and flung it away. Tears rolled down his face. He struggled up to his knees, hands against the hacked paving, then brought them up, bloody, to smear over his face.

"Oh my God!" he cried. "Look where hellmouth gapes open for me! No mercy, no repentance anywhere!"

He pointed toward a new outbreak of fire.

"Jesus!" screamed Theodoulos. "That's the synagogue! They've fired the synagogue!"

He had spent his entire adult life among Jews. He knew them, knew that they would gather in a refuge they believed sacred in a sea of madness, seeking comfort from God and their own community.

They would *burn* together, as they had in the Rhinelands and countless other places in all the long thousands of years of their history.

Even now, did Shoshonna beat at the flames with her hands while her children screamed?

Theo's eyes seemed to blank out as if blinded by a gust of madness.

When they cleared, Adela was kneeling over him, her eyes full of terror, while Rainault supported him. The family Adela rescued crouched nearby, watching her as if she were a defending angel.

Theodoulos struggled to his feet. "I've got to get home, got to know . . ." he murmured through sobs.

"Got to know *what?*" Adela grabbed his shoulders and tried to turn him to face her.

"My sister. Her children. Her household." Theodoulos started up the street. Of course. They were merchants. They had resources that the emir needed for the siege, so, when he expelled the Christians, he kept "his" Jews. And now . . . there was a chance, a dim, outside chance, that Shoshonna had chosen to shut herself up within the house and retreat deep within the caves over which it stood.

Screams rose in the streets, blotted out by death.

"May their bones be ground on wheels of iron!" Theodoulos screamed. He broke into a run, almost immediately stumbling over the headless body of a man who had had no protector like Adela to stand between him and the Frankish madmen.

Adela was at his side, bearing him up. Her arm around his shoulders, supporting him, made him feel as if he could run forever.

"Why, Theodoulos, why?"

He had a debt to her, to get her out of the city and into the dubious safety of the camp. But she was safe for now, and his sister . . .

The time had come for the whole truth to be known between him and the woman he had sworn to marry in Jerusalem. Adela's eyes might never glow with welcome for him again, but what was that against Shoshonna's life—or the truth itself?

"My sister's in there!" Theodoulos told her.

"What are you talking about?" Behind him, Rainault swore.

"Your sister?" Adela gasped.

"Your father is a Ducas, a prince of your city." Rainault again, still half dazed as if he recovered from a night of drinking. "I thought your only sister was the Lady Helena, at court."

"Her real name is Binah. Leo Ducas is only our foster father," Theo said. "He's married to a Jewish lady, didn't you know that? Her name is Asherah. Their daughter and her family, God help them, are in Jerusalem—if they're still alive."

The floodgates opened, and now the truth could pour out—a blessed relief in a world that seemed to hold only anguish.

"Why do you think I know so many languages? Why do you think I know the trade routes? Leo's Christian, I'm Christian, brought up by the monks, even, but my brother, my sisters, and my foster mother are some of those Jews you're so busy killing, and I like them a damn sight better than I like this slaughterhouse."

A gentle pressure to his other side; the woman he had helped save, greatly daring, picked up his hand and kissed it. Theodoulos shook it free. Her thanks were well enough; her understanding was a blessing; but she was not Shoshonna.

"Leo told me to help them, save them. I've got to try or die with them!"

He stood waiting for Adela's eyes to fill with contempt, for Rainault to raise his fist—or his bloody sword. Overhead, clouds seemed to hide the moon; or were they the wings of the tli he feared?

"Not alone," Sir Rainault said. "Not alone. That is, if you will allow me to serve. Maybe, to atone just a little." He paused, visibly gathering courage. "Brother?"

Theodoulos drew a deep, trembling breath. Never, not even after crossing through the highest mountain passes, had he been this exhausted, this terrified—or this thankful.

"We're wasting time," Adela reminded him.

"Let's go," he whispered.

"God forgive me," begged Rainault.

Praise God, beyond some scarring to its walls and some crumbled plaster, his family's house was undamaged. Theodoulos spared an agonized glance toward where the flames of the burning synagogue had subsided into a bloody glow. Anyone in there must be long dead.

The shutters were up. Perhaps the people he sought had remained within.

A knight's shield quivered above the door, a conqueror's claim to the house.

Theodoulos swore hideously in at least four languages, brought his shield forward, and adjusted his grip on his sword.

"You're not trained for this," Rainault rasped at him. "Let me take him."

"You'd challenge to save the lives of *Jews?*" Theodoulos challenged him.

Rainault's eyes filled. He looked down. "Then I'll avenge you when you fall," he said. "And try to get them out after. The least I can do."

"It's a start," Adela encouraged him.

"Better think again," Rainault said. "Someone else seems to have the same idea of fighting for this. Sure you don't want help, two against two?"

Theodoulos gestured uncertainly at Sir Rainault and started forward.

A tall man stood, his back to the battered door, his long sword held in both hands to warn and ward off the Norman who studied every move he made.

"He's old," Rainault hissed. "Hasn't got a chance."

Beneath supple mail that fitted him almost as well as silk, the man who guarded the door was thin, almost gaunt. His face was concealed by a helmet of unfamiliar design. He wore no mail upon his hands, which were suspiciously long and fine: the hands of a patrician forced to battle in the street.

Theodoulos blinked.

"Hold," the man wearing the too-fine, old armor of an aristocrat of Byzantium commanded.

That was Leo's voice, but with a chill in it that Theodoulos had never heard before. It was horror. It was repudiation of what lay about them: the rape of children, the blinding of sick men, the looting of holy places, the devastation of a city—especially *this* city. It was rejection of the tli, which overflew what remained of the Second Temple.

And it was a father, resolved past terror, to fight for his children.

Calling to Leo would only break his concentration.

The Norman's blade came up, and Leo's rang against it. He blocked the swing, forcing the younger fighter's blade back.

"Run, daughter!" Leo Ducas shouted. "Run!"

Theodoulos heard cries from within the house. Leo set his back more firmly against the door, barring not only his enemy's way in, but Shoshonna's attempts to break out to help her father.

"You can take him," Adela muttered. "Stab him in the back."

"It's not knightly," Rainault hissed.

"Knighthood be damned," she spat. "Will you strike first, or must I?"

Theodoulos started forward. His foster father's helmet had come off and Theo saw how, at his approach, Leo's face had paled in despair. He must think he was facing a mob.

"Leo," he cried. "Father!"

"Shoshonna, for the love of God, leave me!" Leo Ducas screamed, his voice breaking. The Norman hurled himself forward.

The young knight and the older man grappled. Leo tried to hurl him away, to bring up his sword and reach for the small, final weapon he always carried, but the Norman beat down his guard. Another blow. Leo staggered, then fell. Theo heard him sob once.

"Ho!" Theodoulos challenged, raising sword and shield.

The Norman just looked at Theodoulos and laughed. "Wait your turn," he said. He bent forward. "Do you yield?" the knight asked Leo.

"Never," he gasped.

The Norman raised his sword over his head, preparing to drive it down through the mail into Leo's body.

Theodoulos hurled himself forward onto the intruder's back, bringing them all down in a heap.

Smoke, fire, blood, and repeated blows that felt like hammer on anvil dazed Theodoulos. When he came to himself, remarkably battered, he found himself sprawled protectively over Leo while Sir Rainault and the stranger circled, parried, and struck viciously.

Rainault was good, Theodoulos had long known that. But this man was younger, fitter, perhaps better trained to start with.

"Take my knife," Leo whispered so painfully that it brought tears to Theodoulos's eyes. "He can't . . ."

The blade, its handle slippery with his father's blood, fitted into Theodoulos's palm. Adela steadied him, and he wavered to his feet. Maybe he had enough strength left in him for one rush, just enough to use that knife to punch through the bastard's mail and into his guts before he skewered Rainault.

Adela would have to take over, he thought. Assuming she survived. The Norman slashed, and Rainault screamed and fell.

How long are you going to wait, fool?

Theodoulos staggered forward, gathered speed, then, just as he planned, brought up his knife and fell with it against the Norman's back.

The Norman bellowed in agony and outrage—knights simply did not stab other knights in the back—and fell. He did not move again.

"By God, Sir Greek, shrewdly stabbed!" Rainault fought for his old mocking tone as if it were part of his battle for atonement. *Let things be as they were, when I was still innocent.*

"Are you all right, brother?" Theodoulos asked.

"Not dead," said Rainault. "Not dead yet. Help your father. He put up a good fight for a man his age. Should have been born a . . . oh God . . . it *hurts* . . . a Frank."

Somehow, the two of them, leaning on each other, staggered back to where Adela and—my God, this was his little Shoshonna? she was a grown woman and so beautiful even now!—knelt, tenderly removing Leo's helmet, chafing his hands. He coughed and brought up blood.

"Tell your mother," he whispered. "Asherah . . ." Even now, his voice grew stronger as he breathed the beloved name.

"You tell her," Theo said. He fumbled at his belt for his pouch.

"So you've still got that fancy cup," Rainault said, his voice faint. Incongruously, he chuckled. "I know, you thought I was out of my head with fever when you made me drink from it a while back. I didn't say anything, thought you wouldn't want it known that you'd broken your own rules about looting. A holy thing, isn't it? You rescued it?"

Theodoulos nodded. "Shoshonna, is there any wine left?" he asked. His sister darted inside the house. He supposed it was too much to ask for her to stay there, so she might as well make herself useful.

She returned with a pitcher. The wine in it was of such surpassing quality that Rainault, even injured, raised eyebrows at its scent.

Theodoulos filled the cup he had borne since Antioch. He had meant to use it in Jerusalem to celebrate his marriage, then leave it here on the altar of the Church of the Holy Sepulchre. He had meant to do a lot of things.

He knelt by his foster father. Leo gestured him toward Rainault, who shook his head.

"Only one miracle," he gasped, "to a man. Lord, I am not worthy, I am not worthy. See to your father."

The women raised Leo as gently as they could. Shoshonna bent forward to kiss his cheek. Theodoulos held the chalice to his lips. Leo drank, then gasped as if the draught sent fire racing through his body. He brought up a bloody hand to catch the cup so he could look at it. Light erupted from the vessel, making his hand glow too, the bones shining within the fragile flesh. With his other hand, Leo blessed himself.

"See to your friend." Leo gestured again, this time for Theodoulos to tend Rainault. "And quickly!"

"I'm not fit, sir. Got to make it to the Holy Sepulchre and be absolved." Rainault coughed and brought up blood. "One drink from that cup should be enough for a lifetime."

"And now I've had mine, you mean?" Leo asked softly. "My son, I thank you. Take the cup to your mother, who will know what best to do with it. Shoshonna, daughter, perhaps *now* you'll be willing to go home?"

Theo's sister had much of her mother's beauty—the long, dark skeins of hair, the great, thoughtful eyes, and a fire that Theodoulos remembered in Asherah. "This *is* my home."

Leo shook his head. "Not anymore, child. This is a Christian city now." Tears filled his eyes. "It is no safe place for you, dear heart. Not for now."

Shoshonna's eyes blazed. "Not for now," she agreed. "But we'll be back one day. On my people's souls, by all our dead, we shall come back!"

Leo nodded. "God will hear that promise."

"I'll get ready," she promised and disappeared within the house, followed by the nameless woman and her children.

"Finally," Leo said. He turned to Theodoulos. "My son," he asked, "do you think you can get everyone out through the tunnels?"

Theodoulos managed even to laugh. "Tunnels are my element," he reminded Leo. "A legacy from my mother, remember?"

Leo let his eyes close, restoring his wits as the Cup had restored his health.

He roused himself to look at Adela. She flushed and pulled at her hair: the only time she had seen Leo she had been dressed as befitted a lady, and he had bowed to her like the prince he was. Now, only the golden earrings that had been Asherah's gift to Theodoulos's intended bride remained of their encounter.

"Lady Adela," Leo said. "I remember you. Will you go with my son? He has a certain amount of wisdom, tied as he is to the land. But he is capable . . ." Leo paused. ". . . of certain mad enthusiasms. I would hope you can settle him . . . well, perhaps not."

"I have nothing," Adela told him. "No great kin, no dowry now, nothing. They will think I am dead."

"You are a dowry in yourself," Leo said. "And in your word. I believe you pledged it to wed Theodoulos in Jerusalem? Well, here we are. I call on you to honor your pledge now, as the good bishop, may his soul be blessed, bade."

"Remember, Adela?" Theodoulos asked. "I swore by Cup and Lance. Adhémar joined our hands," he reminded her. "That is, if you are still willing."

Adela's hands fluttered. Theodoulos watched in unholy appreciation. Shocked, by God, for the first time in all the years he had known her.

"Just like this?" she asked. "There should be witnesses . . ."

Christian witnesses, she meant.

"Witnesses?" Leo asked. "*There* are your witnesses." He pointed at Rainault, then at the Cup and the figures glinting upon it. "Say it to them. Say it to *Him*."

"But I am nothing!" Adela protested once more.

"Be nothing, then," Leo said. "Be lost. Stay lost to your old people. We have found you and we shall never let you go. You will like our home, daughter. Here. A talisman. In place of a ring, just for now."

He reached within his pouch and produced his "talisman," a butterfly wrought of red gold. "This is the medium of exchange. One butterfly—for one ring. And one life." His face lit. "By the grace of God, we shall pick yet another shard from out of the ruins and cherish it!"

Adela looked down, flushing. "This is very old," she murmured.

"So are my wife's people," Leo said. "Theodoulos has told you?"

Adela nodded. Leo smiled encouragingly at her. "Even now, you wear the earrings she sent you. She will be happy to hear that. Happier still to meet you."

He took her hand and pressed the butterfly into it, closing fingers about it, then raising her filthy hand to kiss it. "Let me tell you, child. I approve of this match. Didn't Theo tell you? I wrote it in my letters when my wife sent you the earrings. You are not a dreamer, are you? I thought not. Theo is dreamer enough for two. If you have a hard head and a good heart, no one can ask for more.

"Theodoulos!" Leo commanded. "Come here and take this hand from me. And you, sir, of your kindness, hold up that Cup in witness."

Transfixed by Leo's gaze, Rainault crawled over and held up the Cup in bleeding hands, turning it so that he and Adela could look into the Face framed by tiny vines. Leo placed Adela's hand in Theodoulos's clasp. Their eyes met, and the fire he felt had no kinship with the flames that gutted the Holy City.

Together, they renewed the vows that Adhémar had first made them say.

"There," Leo said. "There. Shoshonna, this is your sister. Treat her kindly on the trip home. And you, Adela, do not let my wife's ladies bully you. Or Asherah herself."

Ah, *that* brought up her head! Thank God Theo had chosen a woman of strength.

"You'd like to see them try?" Leo asked her. "They won't *try*. But if you don't defend yourself, it will simply happen. Shoshonna will tell you. Daughter, I trust you to help your new sister find her way."

Shoshonna nodded. She had seen her father rise after taking a mortal wound. No doubt, she would promise him anything. And, being her mother's child as well as his own, she would keep her word.

Leo kissed her, then turned to this strange new daughter-in-law of his. "They will look after you. Now, I plan to be home before you in time to welcome you. But, in case I miss the feast, will you accept my blessing, child?"

Adela knelt. Leo laid his hand on her head, smoothed her hair as best he could, then kissed her forehead. To his surprise, she clung to him, weeping.

"Is this how you welcome your husband, daughter?" he asked tenderly. "I beg you, be good to my son, Adela. We all know what it is to be desolate."

Gently, he released himself and joined her hand with Theo's.

"Your wife, Theodoulos. I approve." He smiled with the peculiar sweetness that had won Theo's heart since the first time a crippled boy living on the charity of Father Meletios had seen the stranger from Byzantium. "Now, my son, you had better go. You have a long trip back."

Leo was healed. Theodoulos had witnessed the miracle. Nevertheless, he embraced Leo carefully. How could he let his foster father go off alone, unguarded?

Adela stood at Theodoulos's shoulder. Let her stand there always. There would be time, he thought. Years, if God were kind, starting with this trip. Time enough to know each other's minds as they knew each other's hearts. To learn—his breath caught—each other's bodies, perhaps conceive a child. Leo was right as he so often was: another shard saved from destruction; Theo's own heart mended; his pattern set. Thank God.

"Will you take this man with you?" Leo asked, gesturing toward Rainault. "Sir, you have been a brother to my son. A son's place is due you in my home."

Rainault staggered over to him, falling, rather than kneeling, at Leo's feet. "Thank you, my lord. But I swore to die in Jerusalem," he said. "I have betrayed my sword. Get me to the Church of the Holy Sepulchre, Lord, and I will not trouble you further."

Leo stood, then raised Rainault to his feet, supporting him easily with one arm.

"You had better go," Leo told his family.

Adela picked up one of Shoshonna's children. Theodoulos laid an arm over her shoulder, guiding her into the house, to the hidden stairs leading to the tunnels carved ages ago into the living rock of the city. He gazed back once. Leo stood there like the angel at the gates of Eden, protecting them, yet barring the way.

Jerusalem, as he said, no longer was their home.

 35

Leo tried not to weep. In the midst of the wrack of Jerusalem, Theodoulos was healed, his life's pattern set once more in pleasant lines. What joy awaited him at home, watching how Adela and Asherah dealt together. It was a new bridge to be built with the younger races of the West. What a joy if the tall, Frankish Adela could heal his wife of her anger.

Still, he had grounds for sorrow. Jerusalem lay wasted. His children were leaving him, all but Sir Rainault, the most recent and surely the most tormented of the people whom his life had wished on him and demanded that he heal.

"If you will not accept a son's place from me," Leo asked, "what may I offer you?"

"I've reached Jerusalem," Sir Rainault said. "Nothing else is left me except to atone for what I did and finish my book. You know what I have done?"

"Apart from befriending my son and helping save my life?"

Leo drew the younger man closer in against his shoulder. He could feel the death in him. Was that why Rainault had refused a second draught from the cup? A pity Theodoulos had taken it with him: perhaps with new life in his veins, Leo could force Rainault into valuing it. But the cup was gone. Wits and faith would have to do.

"Worse," sighed Rainault. "I didn't just betray my sword, you know. I betrayed my faith."

"Rainault, leave your sins for the priests. Let's get you to them, so you can start doing what else you have to do. You have a book, you say?"

Balancing Rainault against him, Leo edged away from the house. The shield might as well stay up. With his family safe, the place held nothing more that he valued.

"I was writing a history . . ." Rainault gasped a little, then bit his lip. ". . . for my lord Bohemond. A tale of . . . the glorious battle for God . . . Jerusalem . . . I've been trying to finish. Have to finish it, but my head's spinning so . . ."

Leo chuckled, feeling Rainault's shock. "So you are a man of the book? Among the Jews and Muslims, that alone is enough to protect you. As I should know. Come, son, we'll get you to the Holy Sepulchre, and if your head's spinning, why, you can speak your tale to me and I'll write it down."

Rainault managed a smile. "Theo did that once. You won't like what I have to say either."

"That's all right. Write it the way you want it."

"Theo said no one would absolve me." Rainault's voice sounded high and frightened, much younger.

"Theo said that? He must have been angry and frightened," Leo reassured the knight. "He was raised by a monk—the man who joined my hand with my wife's, as a matter of fact—and I know Holy Meletios taught him forgiveness is infinite where there is true repentance. Do you truly repent?"

"Oh God!" Rainault turned his face away so Leo would not see him weep. His shoulders heaved.

Anger began to heat Leo's veins, and he fought it, lest Rainault sense it and think it aimed at him.

God, let this poor knight die more easily than he lived.

So Rainault thought he could conceal the loss of blood, the dizziness, the ebbing strength? Without a miracle, he was lost; and, as Rainault said, there seemed to be only one miracle to a customer. Unless, of course, the Holy Sepulchre had other things in mind, or a peaceful death counted as a miracle too.

"Don't despise me," Rainault said after a long time.

"Despise you? Never," Leo reassured him.

"I am afraid to confess."

"Then you shall write your confession or dictate it to me to write. God will hear you, here of all places. And God will listen. He is not nearly as strict as Theodoulos."

Rainault laid his brow against Leo's shoulder. This time, he did not conceal his weeping.

Slowly, they made their way toward the Church of the Holy Sepulchre. The streets still reeked of blood, although they no longer ran with it. The screaming had stopped. Leo heard a few anguished moans, the buzz of flies, the tramp of hooves and booted feet. Dawn would cast light on a foretaste of hell.

Except for Franks, priests, and castaways like himself, was there a soul left alive in the entire city?

Bells sounded from the church.

"They'll be praying, sir," Rainault said. "Help me get to them. Help me pray."

Leo steered him into the stone pile that brothers already had begun to scrub clean. Rainault staggered, and Leo edged him toward a weathered bench against the cool wall.

"Do you want me to get your book out for you?" he asked.

Rainault gestured, and Leo searched the man's pouch. So, this was his book? Stained, battered sheepskin, much scraped, much crossed-out. A wretched hand: Leo could scarcely tell abbreviations from separate words.

Ah, finally, some decent writing . . . Leo recognized Theodoulos's elegant, monkish letters. A few blank sheets remained in the last quire.

"Now, what is it you need me to write?" he asked. Quickly, he delved further, seeking pen and ink cake. He spat on the ink and prepared to serve as secretary to a dying knight.

Rainault drew a shallow breath. He was shivering now, and Leo wished he had a cloak to wrap around him. If there were a Brother Infirmarer present, he would have blessed him. But Rainault was speaking, and Leo bent to his dictation.

"And so, by God's will, our enemy was overcome. This battle was fought the day before the Ides of August—"

"That's not right, is it?" Leo broke in.

"Poetic license," Rainault retorted, with an ember of his old, sardonic wit. "I beg you, sir, let me finish."

Leo bowed his head and took more ink.

". . . before the Ides of August, our Lord Jesus Christ granting it to us. May the honor and the glory be to Him for all the ages of the ages. Let all souls say, Amen!"

"Amen," Leo agreed. "Is there anything else?"

Rainault's shivering grew stronger. Leo could hear his teeth chatter. "One . . . one thing more . . . of your charity."

The words tore out of him with a deep sob.

"Oh God, my God, I am heartily sorry to have offended . . . offended . . . Thee . . . Write that! Listen, do you hear the bells? It's too late now . . . time for prayers, not books . . . get me there . . ."

Rainault gasped, his eyes blanking. Leo touched his face and hands. The man was freezing despite the heat of the day. The bench beneath him was soaked now with his blood.

Leo wrote a few words: Rainault's confession. He put the book safely away in his own pouch, then raised the knight from the bench. His back would ache for weeks, but never mind that.

"It's time to find the priests, son. Come on. A few more steps."

Leo half led, half carried Rainault toward the sanctuary. His knees loosened, and he fell in a patch of sunlight, just as the chanting rose.

Omnipotens sempiterne Deus . . .

Rainault sighed. "Oh God, the sound . . . I'm no scholar, Lord. Not like Theo. Please, tell me what the words say."

Leo shut his eyes and laid his cheek against the man's head. Joachim's words that last Passover: *"and to the son who lacks understanding . . ."*

"I'll translate for you, my son," he said. "Never fear." He listened for a moment, recalling his Latin. Most of it was more suited to trade than theology, but the mysteries were close enough to the ones he had been brought up in that he thought he could comfort Rainault without violating the letter of the Law as he fulfilled its spirit.

" 'Oh God, who has vouchsafed to redeem mankind by the Passion of His Only Begotten Son"—some words went missing there—"we beseech Thee that we may be made worthy to be partakers of His resurrection . . .' "

Rainault sighed. Leo pressed his hand. " 'Receive, we beseech thee, Almighty God, this sacrifice which we present unto Thee, in remembrance of Him who graciously embraced the Cross and grave to blot out the sins of the world . . .' "

"Mine too?" Rainault asked. "Mine?"

Not long now, Leo thought. He grasped the man's hand more strongly.

"I am certain of it."

He went back to his translation. His Latin *was* rusty, but, thank God, it would serve. " 'O eternal God, who hast willed to declare to us by the mouth of the prophets that in the glorious sepulchre of Thine Only Begotten Son, His flesh should not see corruption . . . We beseech Thee, O Almighty God, that the pledges of our redemption, which we have redeemed by faith, may both deliver us from the tomb of our sins and bring us to the glory of a blessed resurrection, through Christ Our Lord . . .' " He could feel Rainault's hand rising as if to bless himself and did it for him, Roman fashion.

The chant swelled, then subsided.

Rainault turned to Leo as if to thank him. His eyes filled with joy and with the blue sky, only slightly tainted now by smoke, that shone overhead. His eyes shone so with joy that when they glazed over, the sun itself seemed to dim.

"This is my beloved son," Leo whispered. He shut his eyes until the tears ceased.

When he could again control himself, he looked up. He hated to call out in a sacred place. Perhaps a priest would come. Instead, a shadow fell over him, and Leo tensed.

It was Count Raymond of St. Gilles.

"My lord Isangeles," Leo greeted him, bowing over his dead.

The Count inclined, a brief courtesy. "You are Leo Ducas, are you not? Cousin to my liege . . ."

Leo chilled. Oh God, after all this, to be taken up as a spy. *You have your wits, Leo. Use them.*

"As you see," he said, "I am unable to rise at the moment. I pray you forgive me. My son's friend Sir Rainault"—God forgive Leo indeed that he knew no more of the man's name than that—"seems to have passed from the trials of earth to the joys of heaven. At least, I managed to bring him here . . ."

To his astonishment, the Count's eyes filled with tears and he knelt beside Leo, taking part of the weight of the dead man on his own shoulders.

"Your son served us well," the Count said. "As you did when you brought supplies to Antioch."

"My son has always spoken well of you, my lord," Leo said. "And you have kept faith with His Most Sacred Majesty."

"No more than my oath," said Raymond of St. Gilles.

He helped Leo stretch Sir Rainault out on the ground.

"Did your son's example so inspire you, then, so that you followed him humbly and alone?"

God forgive me for a hypocrite.

"One wishes to appear well in one's son's eyes. I understand that Count Bohemond knighted him after the way of the princes of the West. I but acknowledge the magnitude of the honor."

"It's a rare man among the Greeks who possesses such understanding of our ways," the Count approved him.

Leo allowed himself to look away. God grant it him for modesty. The Count stooped to draw a cross on the dead man's brow and close his eyes. They were dulling rapidly; the day would be hot.

Leo nodded. "I sent my son away on errands of my own. So it becomes my duty to see that this vassal of Bohemond receives Christian burial. He left this . . ." Leo fumbled for Rainault's book.

The Count of St. Gilles took it. "Probably full of lies," he said, "seeing that he was always Bohemond's loyal man. More loyal than the Count deserved. Still, the story of a man's life always has *some* worth, and this man, who fought for the Faith, will be a good example. Besides, 'what is truth?' asked Pilate. Even Pilate has his place in the Gospels, and, at the end, his soul will be weighed with the rest of us."

"Rainault was a good friend to my son, my lord. I wish I could say so to Count Bohemond. And I should like to do something in his memory."

"The priests will be glad of an offering, if you have a mind to make one."

Leo inclined his head. The Count beckoned. Two men approached.

"Take this knight and see that he receives proper burial. Here is

Sir Theodoulos's father, Leo Ducas. He is a patrician of Constantinople, and he speaks with my voice. He will supply you with what is needful . . ."

Taking the hint, Leo reached for the small pouch of gold, the one he carried outside his garments. One of the men took it with a deep bow.

"*Count* Leo"—Leo forbore to raise an ironic brow at the sudden promotion—"shall require an accounting of you, and if he does not, I will. Come to the tower, my lord. I shall present you to Count Godfrey. Come and listen as we decide the rule of the Holy City we have finally won back from the pagan."

"I am not worthy of such high company," Leo began, but the Count would hear nothing of it. Still, Leo held his ground as the conquerors from the West left services and headed toward the tower.

"Do you know, they offered to make me king," St. Gilles hissed to Leo, "but I would wear no temporal crown here, of all places, where Our Lord wore a crown of thorns."

Leo murmured approval of such humility, and St. Gilles flushed, the reluctant thanks of a profoundly proud and private man.

"So now, they plan to name Godfrey over there the Advocate or some such title."

Godfrey of Bouillon walked by. Leo had seen him in Byzantium. Sweet God, now, he looked like an exalted skeleton, for all that he was a good fifteen years younger than Leo and more than twenty years younger than St. Gilles.

"Do you ever regret?" Leo dared ask the Count of St. Gilles.

"When my Lord Jesus demands account of me, I can tell him I have kept every oath I ever swore. I am his faithful vassal, and after his, the Emperor's. Count Godfrey will serve well enough. Besides, the time has come for younger men to take over . . . our sons, my lord. Just as your son has already served."

"I am very proud," said Leo, "of all of my children."

"I like you, Ducas," said the Count. "So I will tell you to your face that I pray daily that the bitterness that your kinsman, my lord the Emperor sowed, in abandoning us at Antioch may not one day cause him to reap a bitter harvest."

Again, Leo inclined his head. "So I already told His Sacred Majesty." *I almost lost everything I love for my truthfulness.* "I, in turn, pray that your victory in Jerusalem does not result in a harvest of pain for all our peoples. Those who dwell—who dwelt—here have long memories and aching hearts."

This land breeds good haters, Leo thought. *And don't I just know it.*

"Will you not stay with us?" the Count asked again. "At least eat, drink, rest for a time . . ."

"No," said Leo. "I have fulfilled my vow. Like you, I must be about my father's business."

And you are not the only proud man who has refused a crown.

Leo bowed deeply in the manner of the Franks, then turned quietly to go. Jerusalem lay in Christian hands. He supposed he should rejoice. But it came at far too great a price, tainting what fire and sword had bought.

Leaving the Tower, Leo returned to what had been his family's house. His shield was still up, though defaced with a clod of horse dung. No one had torched the area yet: probably thought it might prove useful. Well, he would set his house in such order as he saw fit.

From a storeroom, he found cotton, straw, pitch, and naphtha that Shoshonna, clever girl that she was, had managed to hide from the defeated emir. It was not as good as sea fire, but it would ensure that no Frankish lord would have the use of this place.

Leaving his family's home in flames above him, Leo set out, torch in hand, into the tunnels that led out of Jerusalem, a secret of Asherah's family passed down from generation to generation since the last time Jerusalem was destroyed. He had never walked these ways before, but Asherah had taught him well, and his footsteps were assured. In the torchlight, the stone shone the gold that had helped give Jerusalem its name.

He smiled tenderly, thinking of how, when they were young in Cappadocia, Asherah and he had explored the caves as well as each other's hearts. When he was young, the stone had not burdened him thus, or could he not remember? All he knew now was that he felt as if the entire weight of the city, the devastated city, lay on his shoulders.

Light glinted to one side. Leo paused once again to explore. He was far enough underground that fresh air came in through the old shafts—or else he might have been smothered as his house burned and sucked out the air from the ancient ways.

Holding aloft his torch, Leo entered a side cave. He let the smoke stain it: a *Lambda* and a *Delta*, for Leo Ducas, so he would know his way back. The side cave opened into a tiny dome. Against one curved wall stood a rough altar over which presided an image of Mary, Bearer of God—or was it she?

The statue looked older by far than his faith. Her immense breasts and thighs were bared, reminding him . . .

Theodoulos, his eldest, his obedient son, had indeed taken the Cup to his mother.

Well, it was probably better than having to explain to Asherah why safeguarding a Christian chalice should be any task of hers.

Leo nodded respect at the battered altar. He reached out and touched the cup, then left it where it rested. This was one cup that could pass, one burden he would not have to bear.

How doth the city sit solitary, that was full of people! How is she become as a widow! she that was great among the nations and princess among the provinces, how is she become tributary!

He did not know when he would be able to rest. Even when—if—he reached home, he would have Asherah to console and the entire work of mourning to see through.

He gazed at the old figure above the altar. It had but the rudiments of eyes and lips, yet they seemed to smile at him. The city had been laid waste before. At least, his children would survive.

He would be home before them, and their arrival would comfort Asherah. It would be interesting to see what Adela made of her new husband's family. Leo rather thought that she and Shoshonna would eye each other warily yet, at the end, make common cause. And Adela would have a defender and handmaid in that woman she rescued.

Leo sighed. It was not that he feared the underground—quite the contrary—but these were not *his* lands, and the stone pressed so upon him. Another burden, like that poor young knight's death.

By the time he emerged beyond the captured walls of the high city, he found himself almost alone. So far, only a few of the Christians who had been expelled had ventured back, not that Leo could blame them. Leaving the road as quickly as he could, he doubled back, concealing his path as he made his way toward the warded pool beside which he had left Aster.

The horse trumpeted at the sight of him, arching his glossy neck. Leo's eyes filled again at how his need had simply usurped years that Aster should have had. And yet, how many horses died in battle without accomplishing half so much? For that matter, how many men died thus?

He tried to put his arms about Aster's neck, but the horse recoiled from the blood reek. Leo could hardly blame him for that. Magnificent as he was, he had not been trained for battle.

Leo peeled off his chain mail and hurled it into the brush. He grimaced then, and made himself retrieve it. Dramatic as it might be to renounce arms forever, it was a foolish gesture. More slowly, painfully even, he removed the rest of his clothing. The cup might have renewed his life, but it could not restore to him the energy of a twenty-five-year-old man. Or even a forty-five-year-old.

He could measure out his life in the scars his flesh, as well as his spirit, bore: most recently the wounds to body and soul that he had suffered in Jerusalem.

Might as well take a priest to you now, old man, he thought.

He sank into the water, which lapped about his shoulders until he sighed with relief. If only he could lie there and never move until his body and spirit healed. As thoroughly as he could, he washed, then dried himself with the clean tunic he had packed so he need not return to Asherah stinking like a Frank. He had seen their courage as well as their squalor: still, he was glad to be clean.

He wanted his home. He wanted a proper bath and Asherah's skilled hands rubbing nard into the bruises where the rings of his armor had been driven into his flesh. He wanted simply to hold her and be reassured that peace remained in the world. Before all else, however, he knelt and thanked God.

Leo Ducas knew he was a lucky man. Had learned it all over again. He could only pray that God would know he was a grateful one.

Dressing hastily, he packed his helm. He was tempted to find the caravan he knew Shoshonna would join and ride with it. There would be comfort in having his children about him, joy in watching Theo reclaim his life. And there would be great entertainment in watching tall, grave, and above all *Western* Adela change from widow to wife once more, not to mention the comments that would no doubt be passed. Leo remembered the early days of his own marriage and chuckled.

But Asherah was waiting for him. She would fear for him, and he could not bear that she hear the news of Jerusalem's fall from any other lips.

He saddled Aster, who pawed the ground, eager to fulfill the great purpose of his life, which was to *run*. The letters on his hooves glowed brightly once more.

Leo took down the wards he had set and mounted. A word of praise made Aster prick up his ears and hasten home, spurning the land. His hooves drew silver sparks from the earth and stone. The stars came out overhead, and Leo felt as if his horse flew like the magic creature in the Persian tale. The wind whistled through his hair until, finally, he felt clean. Leaning out over Aster's neck, Leo looked down, drawn by the glitter of tiny lights, each one of them a soul dear to him. So, Theodoulos had led his sister, his wife, and their people out through the tunnels of the Holy City now laid waste, and they had found their caravan.

Leo smiled to himself. Exodus from the Holy Land or not, Shoshonna would soon insist Adela wash her hair and put on clean clothes. Theodoulos would grin and start counting the hours until the caravan made camp and, finally, he could claim the woman he had loved for so long. *God bless, son*. Theodoulos and Adela would have long days and nights to begin to build the type of bond that Leo had forged with Asherah. The fear, the shock, even the shyness would pass, and then they could turn to each other in the night for comfort and more than that. He remembered. Oh, how he remembered. He wished them joy. He wished them peace.

His thoughts touched them in blessing before he signed to Aster and turned his back upon Jerusalem.

1104–1111
Constantinople—Dyrrachium

 # 36

he Emperor of the Romans suppressed a hiss of pain. Anna eased his foot upward onto a cushion. Vicegerent of God upon Earth and Isapostoles, peer of the Apostles Alexius Comnenus might still be; but the Emperor suffered from gout and was subject to the orders of his physician and the ministrations of his loving daughter Anna. Loving she was; learned she might be. But she was not his heir.

"How did you find your stay on the Island?" Emperor Alexius asked his kinsman Leo Ducas.

Imprisonment had made the older man even leaner and more silvered of hair. He raised an eyebrow at the verbal barb.

"Boring," Leo replied.

He reached out a long arm for the wine pitcher, to pour for his Emperor and himself, but Anna forestalled him. Even well-watered wine was no good for a man with gout.

Ruefully, her father laughed. "I remember," he admitted.

"At least you were a boy when *you* were exiled there, Majesty. You would not have believed the insolence—and the monotony—with which the monks tried to command me to convert my wife. Or set her aside." He shook his head, incredulous and still resentful. "You, at least, have not attempted that."

"I also do not command the tide to turn back," Alexius Comnenus said. "In fact, that might be easier than speaking against the wife of a man who is still besotted after thirty years. That lady of yours! While you were . . . away, she stirred up the folk of Pera. My physician dinned your case in my ears; your daughter, my own child's good friend, went about the palace ashen-faced—"

"Ah, that's my girl!" Leo said, holding out a hand to Binah.

She knelt at her father's side, cradling his long hand against her cheek.

"Even my lord the Count Isangeles spoke in your behalf. What *were* you doing in Jerusalem, Leo? How did you get there—or don't I want to know?"

Leo looked away.

"You have no idea how comfortable that makes me," the Emperor said.

"Your Sacred Majesty is in error," Leo said. "I had months in prison to learn precisely how comfortable it makes you."

"And then, there were the people in Cappadocia, Romanus's old home."

Anna turned sharply at the name of the Emperor whom Leo had served even after her grandfather had turned against him. Was her father's old friend turning traitor at last?

"I am, in a manner of speaking, your voice in the south," Ducas reminded the Emperor. "They too paid well to enlarge me."

"They paid so well and so promptly—unlike poor Bohemond"— her father selected another elegant barb and drove it precisely home—"that I wonder I ever consented to let you go. You are a dangerous man, cousin."

"Only to my Emperor's enemies," Leo laughed. "Romanus is long dead, may God grant him peace." He signed himself, but did so alone. "The gold of my ransom allowed you to make that bid for my lord Bohemond's head, did it not? Take the gold, Majesty, and be thankful. No one begrudges it."

It was a fine thing to know oneself valued that much, Anna thought. Ioannes Caesar, her brother, had served as a hostage. But Anna had only been a wife. If she were to vanish, would her father even care? He had other daughters. For that matter, he had other sons. But only one heir.

Riding in the East near Kastelmuni, which was, generations ago, a holding of the Comnenus family, Bohemond had been captured by the Danishmend Emir. Alexius had offered twice his ransom to keep Bohemond where he was or get possession of the man himself. So Leo actually had on his head the price of *two* counts.

How Anna had screamed with laughter. "He's taken!" she had cried to Binah after hearing the news. She had longed for the threat posed by the tall Frank's pranks and rebellions to be neutralized, prayed for it. Nevertheless, a certain zest seemed to have vanished, like the air after a thunderstorm.

Binah had raised an eyebrow in an elegant gesture that Anna suspected she had been born with, rather than copied from the aristocrats at court. "Who?" she had asked, aggravating creature that she was.

"The Count," Anna had exulted. "That Bohemond!"

"Him." Binah had shrugged disdainfully. "Everyone in this city gives him far too much thought."

"Did you learn that from the Varangians?" Anna gibed. That was unfair, and she knew it: many times Binah had dutifully attended her when Anna summoned officers in their crimson silks or listened as Tatikios, who, God knows, was no Varangian, but as senior an officer as ever rode with the Franks, spoke of battles. They were courtly, indulgent, deferential to their Caesarissa. But their eyes brightened in Binah's presence and followed her every movement.

Sometimes, Anna wondered . . . but always reproached herself, then, for a lack of charity: Binah was upright, so devoted to her studies—*as Anna had wished she might have been allowed!*—that she had refused all offers of marriage. Surely, she was as chaste as she was studious. Like mistress, after all, like maid. When she finally won the diadem, perhaps she would not allow Nicephorus to share it. Perhaps he should enter a monastery: fit punishment after years of a marital bed she had not sought.

"The gold is useful," Alexius agreed. "Gold is always useful. Once again, your Jews helped me."

Binah's father raised his chin almost angrily at Anna's father. How dare he defy the Emperor?

"They are not 'my' Jews," Leo said. "They are Asherah's people." He paused. "And, to some extent, after thirty years, as you say, they have become mine. They are your obedient subjects. And *they*"—how delicately he emphasized the word—"have never let me lack support. Nor has my wife."

Thank God almost a decade of marriage and several children had rendered Anna immune from blushes, despite the brightness of the room. Leo Ducas was older than her father and thinner, far thinner, almost ascetic despite his Persian silks. How hard it was to watch what almost looked like a soldier-saint, while listening to the voice of a man passionately in love with his wife. The lapse in control was embarrassing. Anna was certain it was a breach of court ceremonial.

Sunlight poured in from the gardens. It cast a golden halo about her father as if he sat enthroned in a mosaic, not upon a chair, suffering from gout. But it also shone upon his most trusted—and most aggravating—cousin Leo, who had no right to such splendor. Any other man would have preened at the implied comparison. Leo simply squinted his eyes against the light.

Binah, attendant to Anna and even more skilled than she in medicine, gestured imperceptibly. *Shall I withdraw?*

Anna shook her head faintly. Binah would probably only eavesdrop.

"Stay, stay, my daughter, if you have leave. Caesarissa, I beg you grant it," Leo appealed to Anna herself with a smile that she had to admit was utterly persuasive. "I see her so seldom, you must admit. Stay by me. It has been so long since . . ."

Anna gestured. Binah filled a cup for her, then sat again at her father's feet.

His face lit as Binah turned a face so purely contented at the sight of her father that Anna's own heart twinged. Only attendant to a princess Binah might be, but her father loved her without constraint. *He* would not deny her anything she had proved herself fit to hold. He was delighted with everything his daughter did. Anna had children, and already they were disappointments; two were daughters; and the boys would *never* succeed to the Purple. Not unless she herself preceded them.

The loss of the diadem that had been promised her as a baby grieved her so sorely that it cast a cloud between her and her children. No such cloud overshadowed this old man, scarcely cleansed of the stink of his imprisonment for treason.

The thought was disloyal. Had she been younger, she *would* have flushed with shame and guilt.

"None of us get the chance to see much of you, Leo," said Alexius. He was man, not Emperor, in that moment.

"And you won't, either, if you keep sending me to ecclesiastical prisons."

"You failed me." It was a whisper.

Leo released his daughter's hand and sank to his knees, beginning the full prostration. He moved with far less ease than the last time Anna had seen him so contrite. Binah bit her lip on a murmur of pain.

"I did my best," he said.

Binah had been one of the first to greet him upon his return. All her usual control gone, she had run weeping to him and washed the dirt off his face with her own veils—a gesture that made Leo weep and release one arm from around his wife to embrace her too.

"You failed," the Emperor repeated.

"I do not always fail," Leo said. He rose from his belly and returned to his seat, shrugging almost insolently. "And I am not the only man of Byzantium who has failed against Bohemond. The trick is not to fail at the last. And remember, I beg you, Majesty, whose friend the Armenian was that the so-worthy Count stopped to succor."

Alexius laughed and gestured at his cousin to fill his cup and drink. "Leo, you have too damned many friends. Too many damned friends, too," he added meditatively.

Leo looked into his cup as if dreaming dreams and seeing visions. "They tell me that Kastelmuni's lands are in good heart. They will be even better once you can reclaim them. But anger will not help your gout."

"Cousin, you sound like a seasoned courtier!"

Leo shook his head. "*That* is the last thing I would have thought anyone could call me!"

"No? When you knew that Bohemond's kin had wrought his ransom, you rode straight here and confessed your knowledge."

"What else should I have done? Would you have trusted me otherwise?"

"I am not sure," said the Emperor, "that I dare trust you now."

"You threw me into prison," Leo repeated. "You put my innocent wife under observation. Let me beg you, kinsman, by the love that was once between us. Next time you distrust me, kill me out of hand. My people have no more gold to give."

Anna's father stiffened. *No one speaks to the Emperor that way!* She might be furious at him; she might scheme to force from him what he would never give her. But he was still the Emperor and her father!

Binah tightened her grasp upon her father's hand. He patted her cheek with his free hand and sat waiting. "You see," he said, "I have outworn my fear. My daughter, however, has not. You are frightening her."

Anna restrained herself from raising an eyebrow. It was hard to imagine that Binah feared anything.

Alexius leaned back and laughed. "You get all the gossip from the trade routes," he accused. "Just as my daughter hears every last rumor from my guards. If she were not such a good child, I would not countenance the time she spends with them. But this hobby of hers for the military—she is an intelligent girl, and it is a harmless pastime."

Anna stiffened. Once again—and before this man—her father rebuked her. He knew she studied the armies because a ruler needed to understand them. But instead, he treated her interest as a pastime. The armies, like the crown, he reserved for his precious heir.

Leo relaxed. "This story . . . my lord the Count is right out of a tale of the border lords."

"Is it true," Alexius asked, "that even from prison, Bohemond ruled Antioch?"

"And advised Kilij Arslan, the Red Lion himself. Did you hear what he said?" Leo chuckled.

The Emperor looked about as if he wanted to spit. "After all, David, exiled from his home, became a great captain for the Philistines! That's perilously close to blasphemy, is it not?"

"Your Majesty Himself has said thus," Leo agreed.

"Damn Baldwin anyhow, taking the Holy City after his brother Count Godfrey's death. I wish Isangeles had taken the crown of Jerusalem when he had the chance. He would have brought me a princely gift."

"You know Isangeles was prouder than a rebel angel. He would not wear a crown of gold," Leo half apologized, "where Our Lord wore one of thorns. He told me. And now they are all legends," he sighed. "Maimun, Sendjhil, Darkat—Bohemond, St. Gilles, Tancred. They in the Holy Land have memories as long as Persians' for tales."

"I heard a story of one Lady Melaz . . ."

Leo raised an eyebrow. Living among men and women who were more Persian than not, he seemed reluctant to mention a lady's name. Yet, had not this Melaz made herself, Anna wondered, a byword?

"The lady, I am told, is a poet," Leo said. "Perhaps she will write her own songs."

"Are you in those tales too, Leo?" asked the Emperor.

"Good God, I hope not!" Both old men laughed.

How dared Binah's father sit here, sparring with her all-powerful father about a throne whose right to contest Alexius granted with every joke? Oh, it was not *fair!*

"So long as Your Sacred Majesty remembers; I am not the only man of our kin to have failed with Bohemond," Leo remarked.

The Emperor flung up a hand, in extraordinary defeat. "And so, after I offered two hundred sixty thousand in gold, this Gumushtekin compounds with Baldwin of Edessa to pay Bohemond's ransom, and off he goes with this lady poet. An unlikely Ariadne, I should call her, although Bohemond, like Theseus, contrived to betray her quickly enough."

Anna shook her head, uneasy. It should surely be nothing to her whether Bohemond rode off with Turks, ladies, or sheep. What she felt was too close to envy for her soul to be at ease. Her husband Nicephorus Bryennius was loyal, attentive, even, after his deferential way, capable of the sporadic and, more often than not, bothersome burst of passion. He was water to Bohemond's red wine.

Binah stirred, drawing the light in the room around her like a gemmed cloak. "I heard that for love of Bohemond, the lady converted; and that the Count married this valiant lady off to one of his own vassals. Frankly," she went on, "that makes me think less of the lady."

"For converting to the Light?" the Emperor reprimanded her. "Surely you have learned greater Orthodoxy in the years you have served my daughter. God shield you if the Basilissa overhears your words."

Alexius knew as well as anyone that between Irene and Anna's attendant there was great courtesy and no warmth at all. Her mother's hostility to Leo Ducas and his works probably would extend unto the seventh generation.

Binah bowed in apology. "I do not fault the lady for becoming Christian," she said. "If the tale we hear is true, her actions have made it impossible for her to live in the Dar al Islam—the house of Islam," she translated hastily. "They would slay her for their honor. Where I do fault her is for consenting to be passively married off, not to a friend of the Count's—for he has no friends, not even his wild nephew—but to his vassal."

"You see marriage in another guise, do you, my dear?" Leo smiled.

Binah laughed. "The man who wants *me* would want no other," she declared. She tossed her head, her dark hair glinting in the afternoon light, which picked out highlights richer than the Purple. Her eyes flashed violet, with a splendor almost frightening in one who really was little more than a girl, the adopted daughter of a man under a cloud and his disgraceful consort.

You like *Asherah*, Anna reminded herself. The lady had treated her kindly as a girl, had sent her books and medications, had given her a sapphire bracelet of such superb stones that only now she was coming to appreciate. But she was still an outsider.

"Lady, God grant you such a marriage," said the Emperor. He stared at her—*my father is entranced!* Anna thought in horror.

How *could* he? Anna's mother was the most beautiful woman she had ever seen, and her father had always been a faithful, devoted husband—hadn't he? Her cheeks heated as she remembered rumors some twenty years gone about her father and the former Empress who should have been her mother-in-law. Had Maria's son Constantine wed Anna . . . she sighed, her eyes filling.

No one had ever wanted Anna like that, not even Nicephorus, for all his stroking and prodding and sad-eyed glances. Men smiled at her and bowed and called her Caesarissa, but look on her as they looked on Binah? Even if they wished to, they would not dare. In a little while, no one would dare anything that she did not will.

Leo Ducas cleared his throat. "Cousin," he began.

My God, he's rash enough to chastise his Emperor! Anna thought. Despite Leo's professed horror of ballads, Anna had heard the songs about him, latest Ducas in a series of border stories that turned the entire family into a legend.

"Ah, brother, why do you let your child run wild? I swear, if we had not begun negotiations with the *kral* of Dacia for my heir's bride, I should speak to you about a match for her."

Binah froze. Her father simply stroked her hand.

So, Alexius would take the reward that all Anna's care, all her studies, all her labor had earned and toss it, like a bracelet of fine sapphires, to her maid. That was no better than tossing her brother's hand to a barbarian, which, revolting as the idea was, served Caesar Ioannes right.

"What is your heir's bride's name?" Leo asked politely.

"Something like Priscilla—no, Priska, that's it. It makes no difference: we shall give her a suitable name to use when they succeed me. 'Irene'—now that is a fine name for a Basilissa."

"I am certain," Leo said, "that your advisors and the Basilissa would consider a princess of Dacia a far more suitable bride for Caesar Ioannes than my girl here."

"But you must secure your daughter's future!" the Emperor scolded his cousin. "Gossip has a thousand idle tongues, especially when the lady is beautiful. God grant she wed, and that soon, and give you grandchildren. How many do you have now?"

"Theodoulos has written me that he and Adela have had another boy! I admit I have lost count," Leo Ducas laughed.

Alexius drank, breaking the spell. "Bohemond always does *some-*

thing," he said. "It is one of the few things I can count upon in this fickle world."

"He is not altogether evil. My foster son loved him after a fashion, you know," Leo admitted.

"I must confess your son Theodoulos worries me," the Emperor told him. "Bohemond actually knighted"—he used the proper term—"him, and he fought at Jerusalem. To make the puzzle worse, he even wed the daughter of Adhémar."

"Niece," Leo said flatly. "You know the bishop was a man of genuine sanctity. I would walk through fire to swear that Adela is niece, not daughter." He took a measured sip of wine. "They are very happy together. Adela has proved almost as quick as a Venetian in learning the accounts of our house. Asherah is well pleased."

Alexius laughed, laying aside his dignity in Leo's company.

"Well," said the Emperor, blessing himself, "it hardly matters. The Bishop is dead, and so is the Patriarch of the West who appointed him. Franks are not immortal."

"No," said Leo. "They are not. They can die, and they can be defeated. As at Harran. Now Baldwin, not Bohemond, is a prisoner, and Jerusalem is without its king. Its earthly king, that is."

"Shall I arrest you again to have money to buy him from the Muslims?" Alexius asked lightly.

Leo looked away.

"You don't approve."

"No more than I approved the strategies at Manzikert. Nor does it matter what I approve. You will do as you must for the good of the empire—and because you can. So why ask me?"

"Because," said the Emperor, "you tell me the truth."

Leo flushed and bowed, sincerely, for a change.

"Most Sacred Majesty," he said, "you must take counsel of yourself. Bohemond will head West, and you had best prepare—"

"There is no *time,*" protested Alexius. "Look at me. Look at this preposterous rotting foot of mine. I have turned my daughter into a nurse when she should be nursing my grandchildren. When I go on campaign, my wife travels with me . . . Does your lady," the Emperor persisted, low-voiced, "travel with you because she wishes to, or because you want to keep your eye on her?"

Leo held up a hand. "I am under too deep a cloud to dare receive such confidences," he said, strapping the burden more firmly upon Anna's father's back.

Any other courtier would have listened avidly and sympathized with his Emperor against his wife. In that moment of renunciation, Leo Ducas seemed more royal than her father, which should not be possible: tall, thin from prison, austere like St. Demetrios or St. Michael. Take away that polite smile, heritage of a lifetime of imperial skirmishes, and he did indeed look like a warrior saint, as the Count of St. Gilles had said.

The old war dog was gone now, dead after a burning section of wall had toppled upon him.

Alexius smiled and held out a hand, touching Leo's arm. "Are you ever sorry you didn't make the running for the diadem?"

Shock flickered in Leo's eyes along with the impulse to gasp out "Good God, no!" Anna was too well schooled to laugh—but it was a near thing.

"Had I desired to rule," Leo told his Emperor, "I would not be alive for you to frighten me thus with accusations. They are only words. Say, instead, words of absolution, I beg you. Or execute me now."

Alexius tossed back his head and laughed. "Ah, cousin, do you see your daughter's face? I must be silent, lest she tweak my foot for me. Ah lady, lady, you are too like your father and will *never* be a successful courtier."

It was Anna who was tempted now to give her father's foot a pinch or a push. He wanted ministers and servants he could trust as he trusted Leo, bound to him in love and obedience as well as fear. She was herself trusted thus and loved. She was allowed to know things, to perform small tasks connected with the crown. But the true responsibilities and rewards—those were reserved for his son.

Her father and this . . . this *man* could jest about ambition as if it were a privilege they could have but not she. Never she. Anna shut her eyes against angry tears. She would learn the lessons she had set herself. She would master Psellus's books, that last teaching that had been kept from her because of her sex, that even Binah begrudged her. She would show her father. She would show them all. Somehow. And then, after his death, this palace and all that lay within the empire would be hers.

"Seriously, cousin, had I wished to try, I would have tried earlier, when I was young and you were newly enthroned. I would not have brought my son up as a physician, and I *would* have brought him up Christian."

"Didn't you tell me once you were married by a Christian priest?"

"By a living saint. But religion follows the mother. After all, the mother is the one parent you can be sure of." Leo smiled. He, for one, was totally sure.

"Your son is Manuel, I recall. After my elder brother. Don't I owe him a wedding gift?" asked the Emperor.

"I just heard that he has a daughter." Leo smiled. "I hope she will study medicine like her grandmother."

"Would he like to come to the City?" Alexius asked. "As one of my personal physicians?"

Binah put out a hand to her father's shoulder or he would have been on his knees again. "If you wish to give my son a gift, Majesty, let him stay and study, safe and obscure, in Alexandria. We none of us have any desire for crowns."

"Sometimes I think you'd have done better at ruling than I."

Leo shook his head. "Your illness makes you sad. My wife and daughter shall see you have drugs that lift your heart. I would have done my best, you can be sure, but it would not have been good enough. Rome needed a man of arms, and you are by far the better *strategos*."

Which was why such good training was lavished on Anna's brother while she herself charmed a *strategos's* knowledge from her father's officers.

"Never mind that," said the Emperor. Visibly, he shrugged off his darker mood. "Wine, daughter," he commanded.

"Your foot will throb and burn," she told him.

"She is a good daughter, a loyal girl," Leo said. He had always liked her, even trusted her. "You should listen to her. Don't I listen to my children?" He patted Binah's hand again.

"My foot hurts *now*." Alexius held out his cup. "It can't get any worse." He cast Anna a glance she understood. And instantly obeyed.

"I saw a cup once that cured all bodily ills," Leo said. "I could—"

"In Jerusalem?" Alexius broke in. "I shall never make pilgrimage there now; that is certain." He sipped his hard-won wine and leaned back, staring into its depths. "Where do you suppose he is now?" he asked.

"Bohemond? Not in Antioch, if he is as shrewd as we know he is."

"He'll turn up," the Emperor prophesied. "When we least want him, that's when he'll turn up."

Leo drank thoughtfully. Binah stirred. Even the sunlight seemed subdued.

"I know that look," Alexius said. "Even on you, cousin. You want something, don't you?"

"I'd like Binah—Helena, if you will—to come home. Asherah is hardly welcome in the palace, but she would like to see her daughter."

"She's living in your father's old house, not Pera?"

"Asherah and I thought that was safer for her people, although I promise you, my wife is harmless."

Alexius almost choked on his wine. "Leo, no one who controls that many caravans or can raise that much gold is *harmless*. Your lady Asherah stays in the City. Your daughter can visit her anytime she wants, but she *will* return to the palace. But you, old man, you, I am sending to Cilicia."

Leo started. "As you say, I am an old man. I should be back home, counting the camels with my grandchildren or dozing in the sun."

"You break my heart. Cilicia. I need you there. This time, do not fail me against the Franks."

37

You've *kept this house up well,"* Asherah told Binah. *"I like the* rugs and cushions inside and the roses here. The place doesn't look so bleak. When I first came here, it was like I imagine a monastery must be . . ."

Binah glanced about the courtyard as if seeing it with her foster mother's eyes. *For the first time,* Asherah thought, *this place seems to welcome me. Even the idol—no, my Leo venerates the image of what he calls the Mother of God, and I would not hurt him for all the world by calling it what it truly is.*

Binah, of course, was comfortable with the image. Did it not represent *her* mother? She took care to protect Asherah from that thought. When she was a tiny thing, Asherah had seemed tall and strong. When had she become so tiny?

"You met Father's parents then?" Binah could never maintain for long the fiction that the long-dead, impoverished aristocrats were her grandparents; and, bless her parents, they never pressed her. Her true mother—the caves beneath the earth seemed to stretch out, an ancient, intricate track, within her mind. One might even say she *was* her mother, as she was all women. But Leo and Asherah had raised her; mortal though they were, she loved them dearly.

Asherah grimaced. "It was not the easiest of meetings. It could have gone worse, I suppose. Leo's father was glad enough to kiss me and escape to his books. His mother . . ."

She was relieved that Father had not gone mad. Although seeing him married to a Jew . . .

"You love this house because it is Leo's, don't you?" Asherah asked.

"Isn't that why you agree to live here when you know you'd feel safer in Pera?" Binah asked. Actually, she had come to terms with every stone in this house. It seemed to glow now with a warmth Leo had told her it had always lacked—a home, after all these years of holding secrets. Granted, it still held a few. Binah smiled deep within her thoughts where even a mortal as skilled as Asherah might not perceive it.

Beautiful doomed young men, her mother beneath the earth had pictured during her ordeal. Asherah had never forgotten the image. Binah, as she grew up toward the unimaginable maturity she had only now begun to perceive, remembered the men. The Caesarissa's ironic comments about how the guardsmen followed her with their eyes: they were tall and strong, with the beauty of superb animals. She could make them desire, she could make them forget, and she sometimes did. And if Asherah sensed anything, she forbore to comment.

Leo would have been distressed that his beloved child shared instincts from the ancient world; Asherah never forgot that her foundling had been goddess-born beneath the earth. Still, Binah had taken pains to hide the fabrics, the perfumes, and the incense that could stir a man's passion on nights when the moon was full. No sense distressing people whom she loved. Their lives were short enough already.

How long ago had Binah come to realize that the people she loved had lives as short to her as a dove's life seemed to them? When Theodoulos's first wife had died, perhaps? It was different from death in battle: far more intimate and frightening. She was not ready to be a goddess, all alone. From her mother, she had the gift of life immeasurably prolonged, if not immortality. If she chose it, as Theodoulos had not.

"Have you heard from Father?" Binah asked.

Asherah's eyes glowed, taking years off her age. "He is well. Scheming in Cilicia with the best of them. There was some sort of battle; Count Bohemond lost, but the details—there *are* no details; your father is being cautious. Now no one knows where the Count went. Leo tells me he made a quip about Bohemond and Heraclitus: *you never step in the same river of trade twice*. No one else appreciated it, of course. But he sounded sad. The black horse he named Aster died. He lived longer than your father expected. Probably because he loved the horse so."

"Is he taking it hard?"

"Your father takes everything hard. He has always cared far more than is good for him."

Binah looked away, almost angry with her foster parents in that moment. What right did they have to live, like Aster, for only such a short time while she went on and on? What right did they have to this serenity about age and death when Binah faced a choice that terrified her?

"Let's not raise swords against each other." Asherah broke a silence that had grown uncomfortable. "I know why you do not choose to live in Pera."

"Because the Caesarissa wishes me to live in the palace. Or to follow her to her home."

She and her foster mother exchanged a knowing smile—no, a grin that would have shocked the man they both loved best.

"And because you are hostage for Leo. Perhaps, even, to some extent, for me."

And for the other thing that my father loves. This devouring Empire he serves, even now. She guarded the thought from Asherah, who sensed a defense going up and raised an eyebrow.

"You have the power to translocate," Asherah remarked. "Do you not? You could escape at any time?"

Binah nodded.

"It is a great relief that you have become that strong. Somehow, if you must draw on that strength, your father will be relieved enough at your safety that he will not . . . notice anything else."

Leo had raised Binah, yet, after all these years, her power was the last thing he thought of. It was a pity he had not brought back that cup from Jerusalem. It was safe where it was, however, on an altar dedicated to her Mother and, by extension, to Herself. One day, perhaps, she would seek it out.

"Do you think there is cause for worry?" Now, that was not fencing, but a shrewd dagger blow.

"I still worry," Binah admitted, "about the Caesarissa." The admission came as a relief for which Binah blamed herself. She was coming into the fullness of her powers: why burden this creature of a moment with her fears, like a human girl running to her mother?

Because this wise woman raised me and is as much a mother as I have. Asherah pleated the veil that lay across her lap.

"What else has happened? Surely she is still good enough to you. I know you have reinforced the compulsion you laid upon her in your first meeting."

"When she saw more than she should and called us sorcerers?" Binah could feel her lips narrow into the smile that raised hackles on mortals other than her foster parents. "Oh, my protections hold, they hold. Trust me for that. But Anna has been *testing*. She grows stronger. She reads sometimes when I am not around and hides the books. Once, when I was so angry that I thought, 'Mother and Father are safe, and I no longer need be a hostage, I shall come home,' I prepared to leave, but I sensed some . . . some terrible working, and found my little Caesarissa setting up wards to practice such spells as I hated to think she even knew!"

"Daughter, if you are alarmed, you know you do not have to stay there," Asherah cut in. "Not to protect us."

"I am safe from her. Remember what I am!" She held out her arms, inviting Asherah to look at her. *I do not stay here even for you, but for this land, which Father loves. He would wish it.*

"Terrible as an army with banners," Asherah agreed. "I admit, I was worried when the Emperor demanded you be called Helena. Too much imperial favor is worse than too little for a woman."

Binah met Asherah's eyes. Of course her mother would have suspected that she had calculated the possibility of an intimate connection with Anna's father. *I do have* some *scruples,* she thought mildly at Asherah and was not surprised when the older woman raised an eyebrow as if she had read her thoughts.

Binah had dismissed the possibilities quickly. The Emperor was devoted to the Empress Irene, who watched Binah as a mother-in-law might scrutinize an eldest son's unworthy wife. Besides, the man was of her father's generation.

Asherah shrugged, visibly abandoning an unpleasant line of reasoning. "Do you *worry* about the Caesarissa?" she asked. "She was such a promising little girl. She has been happy enough in her marriage, hasn't she?"

"Let us say she has been adequately content. The Caesar Nicephorus is a well-meaning man, but Anna is . . . other than that."

"Other than well-meaning?"

"Ambitious. You knew that. Her father refuses to recognize her talent for rule, or her ambition, and her frustration grows, like a canker in her heart."

Asherah shook her head, her eyes thoughtful. "Leo and I had such hopes of her. Do you see any reason . . ."

"Left to my own thoughts, I would say she is flawed now past curing. But you always said she was important. And she belongs to my father, who cares about her."

"He sees her as another little girl to cherish and protect. As he sees you, if you were not . . ."

Asherah glanced away, clearly searching for a change of subject. The fruit trees, perhaps: some of the guardsmen Binah had chosen as her lovers had helped her plant them. Now, the trees were thriving, their leaves stirring thirstily, whispering secrets. It would have been a good evening to walk beneath the trees with a man whose fair hair would glint in the moonlight, whose arms and height would make her feel as frail as one of the ladies of Byzantium, and feel his passion kindle hers before he forgot all except in dreams. But Asherah was here: no chance of diversion tonight.

What was it her mother had said one of the few times they had spoken of such things? *You take what you need, more like a man . . .*

Father is not like that, Binah had protested. All her life, she had known him bound to Asherah with a tie as passionate as it was profound. It was a pity that Binah would probably never know love like that, and chastity was no part of the heritage of the goddesses beneath the earth.

Theodoulos was nothing like her. Cast out of the caves, he had been raised by monks who feared his mother. He had some power, but not all. In Binah, however, the strain bred true and so powerful that, as she matured, sometimes it frightened her.

"It is not just that the little princess belongs to Father's friend and through him to Father. Some fate attends her," Binah said. "I am certain of my instincts."

"But not your study? Your gifts will exceed mine . . ."

"When I am fully grown. But even you have said you do not know what 'fully grown' is for a creature such as I."

One of the things that Asherah understood and Binah did not was patience.

"So, the two of us, together, should be able to look more carefully than one alone, is that what you think? And you have made this place your own, warded it so we will be safe. Shall we use the pool here? It has been helpful before."

"I thought . . ." Binah hesitated. "I have a mirror, made of the black glass of home, like Father's little knife."

"You *are* worried, aren't you? More than that: afraid."

"Yes," Binah had to admit to her human mother. "I am afraid."

Binah's admission of fear won her a few hours of preparation: time enough to eat, to rest, and, for Asherah, to pray, drawn apart into the faith that had always been one of the few things that Binah had refused to learn from her. She hoped Asherah would take time to eat and rest as well; the silver in her mother's long, fine hair saddened Binah.

As the last blaze of sunset faded from the garden walls, Asherah raised her hands, casting the Solomon's seal that warded them with the ease of long practice. Power rose from beneath the earth. Asherah shivered, but Binah savored its flow: *this is my heritage*.

"Theodoulos said that you can climb the Tree," Asherah said. "Show me. We can use the strength it brings."

Binah smiled. Holding out her hands, palms upward, she began a low-voiced chant. The fruit tree before her seemed to shiver, then kindle into light. Its leaves took on the gleam of peridots and emeralds, and its fruit glowed red and gold. Patterns of light crossed and recrossed the tree's branches and trunk.

"It is a Tree of Life to them that hold fast to it," Asherah murmured.

Binah knew what followed. "Its ways are ways of pleasantness, and all its paths are peace." She could not speak those words, not to Asherah and certainly not within the temporary peace created by their wards.

For they were not always true.

From a fold in her garments, she drew out a silk-wrapped bundle no bigger than her two joined fists. Unwrapped, it glowed in the light from the Tree, reflecting it and even the starlight high overhead. It was a globe of obsidian, which, cut in half and polished, took on a luster and a sharpness that few metals could rival. Like a sword, it was forged in fire; but it had had its birth, like Binah herself, in the depths of the earth.

She held it so that she and Asherah could both look into it, then slowed and steadied her breathing, preparing to enter trance. Asherah, with her greater experience and discipline, outpaced her.

Her eyes already fixed upon the black surface of the mirror, she had plunged deep in trance.

"Oh no," she murmured. "No!"

What did she see? Binah sought to join her mind to her mother's vision, but Asherah pushed her away.

"She used to be such a lovely little girl. Ohhhhh, I cannot permit this," Asherah moaned . . .

. . . and, on the instant, she disappeared.

I had no idea she too could translocate! Binah reeled with the shock.

What had Asherah seen that had so frightened her that she had cast herself free of the bonds that held her here in this garden?

Binah's pulses throbbed. The blood rushed through her temples with such heat that she thought she heard the beating of a dragon's wings.

Leo would come home, and what would Binah say then? She was surety for her mother—whether with the Emperor or against Asherah's own rash impulses.

Learned as Asherah is, she is only human. How dare she make that passage without me to protect her?

And besides, what was it that Asherah had seen?

She forced control upon herself, bent over her ancient mirror, and began the series of controlled breaths with which she summoned trance.

38

Anna wadded the parchment of the letter smuggled in to her the day before and tossed it into a brazier. It took a long time to burn. Binah would have brought incense to cover the stinks of grease and dirt: Anna knew which scents to use, including a few to calm the spirit and the racing heart. Instead, she watched the letter twist and crumble into ash. It took a long time to burn.

She had contrived, finally, to be alone. Her contrivances were a triumph, in fact: she had been permitted to withdraw from the Bucoleon to the house given her upon her marriage, a pleasant dwelling, not nearly as rich nor as straitly guarded as the palaces that had imprisoned her almost lifelong. Here, Anna kept the books she showed no one else. Here, it was almost safe to think her own thoughts, make her own plans. As she did now, preparing for the future she wanted.

Binah had not accompanied her, going off instead to visit her preposterous mother. Nicephorus had ridden with the armies to Cilicia; servants tended the children. And Anna's own mother had retreated to the satisfactions of the austerities at her foundation of Kecharitomene. Her father, of course, was otherwise engaged yet again, no doubt passing secrets of Empire on to dear, dear brother Ioannes.

Anna bit her lips to darken them. She had never been a beauty like her mother or her attendant; she had never before wished to be. Her hands trembled upon the door as she unlocked it. Summoning every scrap of discipline she had learned in a life full of frustrations, Anna forced herself to sit and fold her hands in her lap. She had never been good at waiting.

The moon rose in the sky. She waited in a dim room.

After what seemed like hours, she heard scrabbling at the outer wall, swift footsteps outside, in the gardens. An immensely long shadow fell across the room. Anna paled, then flushed.

Count Bohemond stood in the long window. He wore not armor but dark silks and leathers that set off his height, the breadth of his shoulders tapering down to narrow hips, the preternatural alertness of a predator—or one of the foremost warriors of the age. The firelight glinted off the brightness of his hair, cropped above his strong neck so that his helm would fit.

Anna let him approach her. She was no longer the fourteen-year-old maid who had stared, aghast and fascinated, at a barbarian, tall past belief, simultaneously fascinating and repulsive, from the West. Now, she was a grown woman, a princess, and a full-fledged player in the game that the Count had enjoyed for longer than she had been alive.

Tonight, both of them expected to rewrite its rules.

He bowed courtesy to her, but no deference. From his tunic he drew a square of purple silk, much faded now, that Anna remembered.

"It saw victory at my city of Antioch," he told her. "I even brought it to Jerusalem. And now, I return it to you, my lady." He sank upon one knee, a parody of knightly courtesy.

"You might have sent it with your letter," Anna breathed. "There was no need for this meeting. It gives me a poor idea of your caution."

"Caution?" The Frank laughed. "I did not win Antioch by caution. My father willed me an Empire, but said I had to conquer it my-self. How should I be cautious, of all qualities but humility the most wretched?"

He showed white, unbroken teeth and laughed. Even when he knelt, he towered over her. He smelled of sweat and sandalwood. The room grew too warm. If she rose now, it would look like retreat.

She would rather die.

"Was it rashness that let you be captured in the East?" Anna asked.

"Ah!" Bohemond laughed softly, deep in his massive chest. "You have heard the stories, I see."

"How should a lady trust a man who would abuse another lady's trust?"

"Melaz? I seized advantage from a Muslim, an enemy. I made her no promises, but did my best by her, marrying her to a sturdy man, providing her with the sacrament of baptism. I am in a manner of speaking a godfather to the lady, whose virginity should be restored once she is anointed. By holy water, of course—what did my lady think I meant? And," he laughed again, "if it does not, it is no great matter once she is safely wed. Besides, my thoughts have long been occupied elsewhere."

He paused to assess her reaction. "By contrast, Princess, you are Christian and an . . . ally's daughter. You deserve consideration."

"And what have you considered?" Anna asked.

"An alliance, of course!" Bohemond smiled winningly at her. "You were once the Emperor's heir. Why not ally with me and make your bid for power? It is not as if ladies in your family have not cho-sen Emperors of their own after the old one died. And it is not as if I am not fit to rule."

He stepped forward, looming over her. She smelled him: sweat and leathers and the sandalwood he must have gotten into the habit of using in his three years' imprisonment.

"I know," he said softly, urgently, "what it is to have high gifts, yet be thwarted by a father's choice. My own father favored my brother, whose gifts were less than mine. As are your brother Ioannes's."

Anna looked down at her hand, which bore the fetter of her mar-riage to Nicephorus.

"What man can join, man can put asunder," Bohemond told her. "My father repudiated my mother."

"What man can join," she echoed him. "But God?"

"When I am Emperor, Pope Celestine will dance to my tune. To *our* tune. You cannot object, I think, to my being from the West. Your father's . . . friend St. Gilles . . . came from further West than I. And your father is marrying his precious son to a princess from Dacia."

Bohemond looked down, far down, into her eyes. "We understand each other's minds, do we not? And we have always done so, since the moment I first saw you. Ah, such a great-eyed, solemn child as you were. How you disapproved of me, but do not think I did not see you watching me . . ."

"To write about you," Anna protested. Even to her own ears, her voice was reedy, weak.

He drew closer. "You have healthy children and time enough for more." His great, scarred hands, lightly brushed with reddish hair, rested on her shoulders. "I have always known there is fire within you. Yet you are wed to that Nicephorus Bryennius, who is scarcely more than a sword-bearing monk. Tell me, Princess, what sort of sword does he have? Does he know how to wake your fires—or just dutifully beget heirs?"

She pulled away from him. This went too fast. And yet her knees were weakening. Beneath the heavy silks of her garments, her body heated despite the night breeze. Her legs weakened, a sweet ache beginning within her core. She had known that ache at times, when Nicephorus, his passion quickly spent, lay snoring beside her and she had had to bite her lip against sobs of bewildered disappointment.

"By Christ, you're a lively thing, Princess. I can see the fire in you. We're a good pair, don't you think? Even to the fact that we both have brothers we despise. Brothers who possess what we would sell our souls to have."

She summoned strength to shake her head. *No.*

"Ah, by God, we do. Else you'd have summoned guards by now. Those big fair men who look like me and whom, the gossip says, you like. Overmuch, perhaps. Do you like them because they remind you of me? Tell me! I promise you, give yourself into my keeping, and you shall have no need of them ever again."

"Do you really think"—Anna tried for a scornful voice and failed miserably—"that I would set aside my marriage? Or that my father would name you Caesar?"

"What would it matter?" Bohemond asked. "He's not as young as he was, and he's been ill. Death comes to high and low alike, and an Emperor must leave heirs. Why not leave the Empire to the strongest?"

Like Alexander, Anna thought, feebly attempting to distract herself with scholarship.

Alexander was not here. Bohemond was. He reached out and swept her into his arms, pinning her against his chest. As always, he was himself: audacious and almost fatally attractive. The heat of his body weakened her knees. She felt an appalling desire to yield.

Bohemond was right. It would be like loving one of her father's guards, a thought she had entertained and atoned for during weary nights in her husband's bed.

Bohemond lowered his cheek to hers, his breath hot against her ear. Anna shuddered. "It would almost be worth taking you without the diadem." His hands moved up and down her sides, presuming a license she had not granted him.

"You *have* thought of me," he whispered against her hair. "Say it. Say you want me as I want you."

This was appalling. He coaxed her not just to adultery, but to treason. And he was winning.

"And when you turn on me as you did Lady Melaz?" From where had Anna summoned that last resistance? "Will you say 'she is a Greek Christian' and give that as your reason for abandoning me?"

He chuckled, and she felt the vibration of his laughter in her own body as well as his eagerness to possess her. Skillfully, he maneuvered her from the windows toward a door. How had he known it led toward her bedchamber?

Because, she rebuked herself, *this is not the palace, but a place more easily spied upon. Bohemond may desire you, but do you think he trusts you either?*

"Ah, Princess, you have come too far now to draw back," Bohemond murmured. His mouth came down on hers, his tongue probing insistently within, one hand squeezing her breast. She heard herself gasp. "And I do not think you truly wish to retreat. Does the fire burn now? Tell me!"

Desperately, Anna pushed free. This was a gamble she dared not make.

Bohemond laughed. "I know you enjoy playing with fire. I like that in you. But two can play that game too, better than one. The purple silk you gave me that I carried so faithfully—all these years with no hope of reward! Unkind of you, my princess. Unkind. How if I had a change of heart"—his voice turned from honey into a hiss—"and told your father?"

His hands were hard on her, insisting now more on her submission than her excitement. Nicephorus might be hesitant, occasionally clumsy; but he always had been considerate.

Again, Anna pushed Bohemond off. "No," she whispered. "No." It was the hardest word she had ever spoken.

Bohemond advanced upon her, the ardor on his face replaced by fury. "By God, I'll teach you to play fast and loose with me. And then you *will* do precisely as I tell you if you do not wish to lose all you still have!"

She was backing away, placing a table between her and the tall Count. Her body was betraying her just as she had thought to betray the Empire. If she could control her desire and her fear, she might summon breath enough for the scream that would protect her virtue, but cost her her place in her family and her Empire. The polycandela in her chamber flared into a noontime brilliance.

Bohemond cursed at her. *So,* Anna thought. His letter had been a lie, a ruse to fascinate her. He had not truly wanted her, save as a means to power and, perhaps, a female trophy snatched up on his road to power. He was shrewd past men's understanding: as he said, he had perceived that she was half repulsed, half fascinated by him.

Anna took another step back. To her own surprise, she laughed. The light was cruel to him. Now, Anna saw him as he was: a man not all that much younger than her father attempting to play the part of a young lover.

"What do you laugh at?" Bohemond demanded.

"Two fools," Anna Comnena said.

"Then be foolish with me!" he ordered and lunged at her. "Whom will you tell? Whom will you *dare* tell that I have enjoyed you? For I *will* enjoy you, Princess. Yes, that's right. Fight against me. I like it more when my women squirm and cry out . . ."

Anna tried to scream, but only a faint croak came out of her treacherous mouth. Once in his arms, she simply would not have the strength to fight him off again. And, even revolted as now she was, he still had power over her desires: she might not have the will. If he overlaid her, his great weight might crush her. Perhaps that, she thought with a spasm of terror that helped cool her blood, that was what he intended all along.

Again, the lights flared in the room. A shred of burning purple silk rose toward the ceiling. Its reek filled the air.

The Lady Asherah, Binah's mother, stood there, holding the incriminating, faded scarf to a polycandelon and watching the flame consume it.

"You will not touch the Caesarissa again," Asherah told Bohemond. She was not much taller than Anna herself, yet she spoke as if they were equals facing off for battle. "You will leave now, Count. Now. You have failed."

"What can the likes of you do to me?" asked Bohemond. "You are a Jew, a woman—how can you withstand me?"

Asherah laughed. "I shall not need to fight at all," she said. "You will doubtless wish to return to the West and raise an army. Armies run on gold. Not even you can expect the Emperor to give you gold to overthrow him. So, that means the bankers in Lombardy and the North. My kinsmen. How if I beg them to refuse? How if I make a refusal profitable?"

"By God, refusing me my gold will be the last thing that they do!" Bohemond blustered. "As this may be the last thing that you do, too."

He advanced upon her. Asherah raised her hand, drawing it down between them, then across at the level of her breast as if she were a Christian woman blessing herself. Light erupted where her hand had been.

"Go!" she whispered. "Go, or I promise you, you shall never take meat nor drink without worrying that it be safe."

Incongruously, Bohemond laughed. "You use . . . this . . . poisonous thing as your watchdog, Princess? I wish you better companionship."

"Yourself, no doubt?" Anna's voice came out poison-sweet and more assured. She trembled again, this time with rage and shame.

"I am at least a Christian."

"I owe the Emperor my people's lives," said Asherah.

Again, she raised her hand. It filled with light. "I have never used this on a living being," she remarked. "I wonder how long it will take you to burn."

Bohemond roared with laughter. "The kitten has a claw! But kittens can be drowned."

He advanced upon Asherah. She gestured sharply downward as if hurling something onto the floor. A column of flame leapt up.

"Leave," she said.

"Really?" asked Bohemond. "Do you think you can keep that up all night?"

"Of course not," said Asherah. "But what if it were seen from the gardens? And what if, next time, the fire is not a demonstration? You've seen men and women burn, haven't you?"

"I'll send you to the flames. Unless you like how the Greeks kill witches better. I hear they tie them in a sack and dump them in the Bosphorus."

"You've already burnt family of mine and butchered friends," Asherah retorted. "Never again. Now, do you leave, or do you find out how long it takes your lungs to sear?"

Asherah took a step forward. Light armored her, and her eyes glittered. Anna picked up a dagger from a nearby table.

"Stay out of range, Caesarissa," Asherah warned. "Count, I fear you have turned your accomplice against you."

Anna flinched. Unaccountably, Bohemond roared laughter.

"Well, it was worth trying," he said. He bowed mockingly at Anna. "If not trying very hard. Princess, think of this in your cold, cold bed. It would have been a pleasure to turn you from one of your icons into a woman. No, don't summon the guards. Some of them might be men I own, after all, and your watchcat here would lose all her trouble. I shall see myself out—the way I came."

"How will you get out?" Anna asked, curious even on the brink of disaster.

"Who knows?" asked Bohemond. "Maybe I'll play dead. In any case, I am not through with you yet—or with your family!"

He turned and strode out into the garden. They heard his footsteps crunch upon the paths.

And then he was gone.

 39

*A*sherah let her hands fall. The light that surrounded her died. She dwindled from improbable avenging angel to a small woman who would never be young again, a tired woman who had to lean against a table for support.

"How did you get in?" Anna blurted. "I should call the guard."

"*Now* you talk about calling the guard," Asherah sighed.

Asherah pushed away from the table with an effort. Her face was ghastly, strained, and her eyes glittered. Years ago, this woman had drawn steel—Anna remembered now—to defend her. Now, once again, Leo Ducas's strange wife stood as her protector. And this time, Anna might never forgive her.

"Pull your gown closed," she snapped at Anna, who pulled the crumpled silk up about her bare shoulder. Bohemond, damn him, had been right; part of her had not wanted him to stop. And what made it even more infuriating was that he had not even tried all that hard to seduce her nor cared that much when Asherah, not Anna, thwarted him. *If he had possessed her, would she finally have understood . . .*

"I swear, I will kill him," Anna whispered.

"Will you?" asked Asherah. "It's clear to me that you don't know how you feel about him. You should have called the guard before ever you let him come near you. You should have told your father—or someone—the instant he communicated with you."

Anna opened her hands, showing them empty. Just let Asherah try to prove the existence of any letter! And she herself had burnt the silk Anna had so rashly bestowed on Bohemond.

"Don't be *ridiculous*," Asherah snapped. "Look at the ceiling. There's grease in parchment. Your ceiling is smudged."

"But you, you are an intruder," Anna began.

"And you, you are not just a traitor, but an incompetent," Asherah told her. "I am out of patience with you. For years, we have been waiting for you to act like a responsible woman, not a spiteful girl. My husband had such hopes of you. So did I when I first saw you, so brave and gifted as you were . . . Do you not think Binah has told me of you? When she came to me and told me of your ambitions and your moods, I said, 'Wait, she is my husband's kin, and he is fond of her.' But now, you have jeopardized not just yourself but your father the Basileus. How can he defend what he holds when his own daughter betrays him?"

She drew a shuddering breath. "I might say that the affairs of great ones—of *Christian* great ones—have nothing to do with us, but your father has been kind, for a Christian ruler, to my people. And now, your folly puts my kin in danger. I will know what you plan to do about it."

The blood in Anna's temples pounded as if the flame Asherah had conjured had struck her in truth. She was furious, and she was ashamed. And, to some extent, she had to admit she was disappointed. *I will have him killed,* she thought. *Slowly. And I shall watch.*

"This time, I shall not fail to call the guards, lady," she whispered. "My father imprisoned your husband, and you are a Jew. Who will believe you?"

"What will you tell your father or your mother when they ask, for ask they surely will?" Asherah retorted. "All these years, when it's known that you dealt in herbs from Leo Ducas's wife and even wear"—Asherah gestured—"a bracelet that she gave you. You will look like a fool. A bigger fool than you are."

Anna cast the bracelet down upon the floor. Alexius might not execute her, Anna thought, but she would be cast out of the palace into a convent with as strict a rule as possible; and she was young! She had years left to prepare herself to rule.

But she saw her own near-treachery in the older woman's eyes. She had to blot it out.

"What right do you have to speak for His Sacred Majesty?" Anna demanded. "You hate my father. You hate all of us—because we are Christians. Because your people killed Christ. You're afraid even that the Emperor will order your precious husband to put you aside." Ah, she went white at that, now didn't she? "And now you seek to use the Empire to strike at the Franks, who killed your people."

Asherah shook her head. She was shaking, all her vitality drained. *Why, she's exhausted*, Anna thought. *And terrified*.

But not silenced.

"Hate is a sin," Asherah stated, her voice stronger than the rest of her, "but your logic is a disgrace. Either I have power enough to work my will, in which case what do I need your father for, or I am such a feeble, helpless thing that you should have no fear of me."

Her eyes on Anna, she reached for a silver wine pitcher and poured for both of them. "Forgive me. Fighting your battle against your erstwhile . . . suitor wearied me. If you pick up the bracelet you threw across the room, you can test for poison."

Asherah murmured over the wine and drank. Color returned to her face. Anna almost screamed with laughter: the woman simply appeared in here, summoned powers of the dark, then apologized for drinking wine first in the presence of a porphyrogenita?

"I do not *hate* the Franks, you know," Asherah said. "I dread them, and, especially I dread this Bohemond. Not for his ambition—that is more your flaw than his, although he is surely the hungriest prince of this age—but because he, like all his breed, is a wrecker. He destroys, and calls it building. Sometimes he calls it sport. Men like that over-set the balance of power in the land. I have lived through that before. We fought it in Cappadocia, Leo and I. And I tell you, I will not willingly endure it again."

Asherah gulped the rest of the wine in her cup. *I shall have that cup thrown out*, Anna promised herself. But something in her mind was weeping, remembering an unwed girl whom a loving woman fed watered wine and honeycakes. When had all that affection turned to gall?

"Just look what this wrecker has done to you, child!" Asherah's voice was gentler. "Of all the people in the world, you cherish your father most. I saw that the moment I first met you. But look at you now! One embrace, a few kisses, perhaps, and Bohemond has all but convinced you to revolt. Is an empire worth the betrayal of so much love?"

"Your husband is a traitor too," Anna whispered.

"No," Asherah snapped. "That is your own guilt speaking." The wine flush faded from her face, leaving it even paler than before, this time with anger. "Leave my Leo alone. You have just shown you cannot tell a good servant from a bad. Or a good man from a wrecker."

Anna drew breath to cry for help. One determined scream, and the guards would come and deal with this torment of a woman. Didn't she know that, in defending her husband, her family, her people, she put her life into Anna's hands? And she had already called Anna a traitor.

Anna's eyes filled. No one had ever defended *her* this way. No one cared enough. Bohemond claimed to have desired her, but he had tried to seduce her only as a shortcut to a throne. Her father used her as a kind of expert nurse and sounding board, but never, never gave her any real authority; and her mother spoke to her kindly only when she was perfectly compliant in her schemes to retain power after Alexius's death.

"Call the guards now, do," Asherah encouraged. "I am guarded against *any* power you can summon." Anna's eyes flashed sheer fury at the implied countercharge that she too practiced sorcery, and Asherah nodded. "And I am prepared to face judgment in Glorification of God's Name. Leo will understand."

Please God he understands flashed into Anna's awareness as clearly as if Asherah had spoken the words.

The lights in the room flared into a blinding glory. *I am going to get awfully tired of this*, Anna thought.

"My father will not understand," said Binah. "And neither will I. Don't call, Caesarissa. Don't even move."

Binah had always been taller and far more imposing than her mistress. Now, she towered over her, and her violet eyes sparkled. Wind blew through the garden, and the night sky darkened.

"Helena!" Anna cried. "What are you doing here?" Her knees

sagged. In a moment, her companion would take charge of her raving mother, and all would be as it had been.

"You know my name is really Binah," said the taller woman, moving to stand between Anna and Asherah. "It's one of the few things that you *do* know. But, like much else, you've managed to forget it. Lady"—she turned to Asherah—"you terrified me when you disappeared."

Anna took an involuntary step back. Had Asherah lied to her and put something in the wine after all? Her head swirled, and her breath came fast as if she had been running—or just been released from Count Bohemond's arms.

"I remember," she whispered. "I remember. When we first met. You *appear* here; you gesture; you mutter spells—you're sorcerers. Like mother, like daughter. And—oh God!—I trusted you. My father trusted you!"

Her hand went to the icon she wore on her breast. A wonder that it had not guarded her when Bohemond had fondled her.

"We trusted you, too, Anna," said Binah. "Anyone who hides Michael Psellus's library of forbidden books the way you do should be careful in her accusations." Her eyes flashed.

Anna laughed harshly. "And we were all betrayed, were we not? How very Roman of us all—plot on counterplot! No wonder the Franks think we are all corrupt!"

"You will not move, Caesarissa. You cannot move. Not until you swear—on that icon that you wear—that you will not harm us," said Asherah.

"And if I do not?" Anna had a surprise for Binah—Helena—whatever the woman called herself. She raised her hands uncertainly and drew breath to speak words that she had practiced only under her breath.

"Silence!" Binah commanded, and Anna lost the power of speech.

"You were very right. Her mind *is* poisoned," Asherah commented. "The books I sent her were philosophy, but for all the good they've done her . . ."

"Our Anna has always been a fine student. She has learned a great deal from Psellus's library. Let us hope that it hasn't extended to calling up Psellus and learning from his spirit!"

You accuse me of commerce with the dead? Deprived of speech, Anna thrust that thought at the other women.

"No more of that," Binah commanded almost offhandedly. "You

accused us, and you have done worse." She laughed. "Great Mother, you have gotten stronger, haven't you?"

"So your binding spell won't work on her this time?" Asherah asked.

"She broke it before."

"Can you eradicate what we see here in her mind?"

Binah shook her head. "Not unless I break her mind. I would not take that guilt on me."

The power that silenced Anna held her upright, or she would have fallen in a rush of pure relief. She stared at Binah, at the height and strength of her, the mouth taut in the cruel, archaic smile of an ancient statue, the voluptuous curves, so unlike icons, but like . . . like the most ancient statues that turned up sometimes in the south.

Binah had been born in Cappadocia and adopted by Leo, Anna recalled. Power shimmered about her. Asherah—she was a Jew and a scholar: blessedly familiar things. But Binah—was she even human?

"You led me a merry chase through the spheres. You could have been lost! You could have died." Now that Binah thought she had Anna safely disposed of, she turned to reprove Asherah.

"Binah, sometimes we take mortal risks because we have to, child," Asherah said. Oddly enough, she sounded apologetic. "You must get used to that—and to the fact that you cannot stop us. I saw the Count with her, and she was weakening. Don't ask me why, but Leo loves this woman as practically another daughter."

"And anything of Father's . . ." Binah shook her head. "It must be your mortal birth. I, however . . ."

So Binah was *not* human, not mortal. Had Anna, all these years, harbored a goddess as a servant in her house? It was insane, she thought—but it was possible. And now, she looked at the subject with sharp, terrified eyes. Yes. When she had first met Binah, the taller woman seemed to be a decade older than she. In the years that passed, Anna had matured until now, they seemed much of an age. Lacking as she did the lines of bitterness that bracketed Anna's mouth, Binah even appeared younger than Anna. Beautiful. Powerful. And deathless. The books spoke of such, and here one was, serving her. Yes, and withholding the powers that Anna needed to win what should be hers.

"You will have years enough to figure it out," said Binah. "But did I not once warn you I would not permit you to harm my family?"

Again, she raised her hands.

Asherah gasped out a few words. The polycandela flamed, and a few snuffed out as the oil within them was consumed. Thunder pealed overhead.

"It is enough, Mother. You may scrape and bow and accommodate, but I have had a bellyful. It is time for me to be what I am."

"You may have the strength, but it is too soon yet. Be what you are, but, strong as you are, you are very young as the world sees it, regardless of the gifts you inherit from your mother."

A flight of butterflies erupted from the garden and into the room, circling around Binah.

Anna wanted to hide her eyes. The lore in Psellus's books served only to terrify her further.

"You were such a promising child," Asherah mourned. "I know what has embittered you. If only the faith of which you make such a parade had been strong enough for you to offer up your disappointment, you could have learned to rule without reigning, to advise without commanding. But . . ." Asherah sighed.

Anna fought free of the compulsion placed upon her. "I want . . ." she gasped. "I want what you know. Teach me—or use it in my service to gain the diadem, and I shall be a better friend to your people than ever my father was!"

Asherah opened her mouth. *It may even work!* Anna thought, exulting despite her terror of Binah, whose face was as expressionless as stone.

Binah was shaking her head. To Anna's astonishment, however, she turned to Asherah, deferring to her judgment.

"Mother, what do you wish me to do with her? Do you claim her?"

Asherah laughed. "Ah, daughter, before you were born, your mother, deep in the caves, asked me if I claimed your father. Of course I did—just as I claim the Caesarissa. Your father cares for her."

"Then let her live, for all I care."

"With her mind unbroken," said Asherah, as if she pursued an important point.

"What are these people to you?" Binah demanded. "What's one set of Christians more or less?"

"For that matter, child, what are my people to *you?*"

"You took me in."

"Just so. And beyond that, you will do this"—Asherah was breathing rapidly—"because I ask."

Woman and goddess faced each other down. Binah looked away first. Then she shrugged, a hunting cat cheated of her prey.

"She may live with her mind unclouded. She may even dabble in these sordid magics with what I leave her; they will gain her nothing. But for her life's sake, her soul's sake, I want her oath never to speak of what she has seen, perhaps not even to *think* of it."

She walked over to Anna and laid her hands on her temples. How strong she was. Her hands were as cold as stone.

"I shall tell you what you may say. The Emperor gave me leave to go. We quarreled because I wished to spend some time with my mother. I left your service. And that is *all*. No treason; no sorcery; and the Count is merely another Frankish enemy of your father. Is that clear?"

Anna struggled to free herself, mind and body, from Binah's thrall. "What of the bargain I offered?" she asked Asherah.

Asherah came forward and put her hands on Anna's. "I am sorry, child. *Mene mene tekel upharsin.*"

It was no incantation, unless Scripture itself was a book of magic. *You have been weighed in the balance and found wanting.*

Refusal. Rejection. Failure.

"I will have your word," Binah told her. "Swear now."

The strong, long-fingered hands pressed inward at her temples. A little harder and . . . the room began to spin about her.

"You don't have to crush my skull," Anna said. If she were to lose her hopes and her allies—what was worse, by her own folly—she would at least not lose her courage.

Binah smiled thinly. Now the room did spin in good earnest. Anna felt Binah guide her to a chair and ease her into it. A gurgle meant that wine was being poured.

"Drink," said Binah. "No, there is no poison in it. See? Your own bracelet tests it. Such a fool as you are. You've worn that bracelet for years with no ill effects; shall you fear it now? You quarreled with a companion. The room is close. You almost swooned. That is what you will remember. Mother, are you content now?"

"Well content, Binah, so long as you can get me home."

"I will not even try to translocate, you have my word." Binah slipped an arm around her foster mother, sustaining her. "Don't try it again, not alone, I beg you, Mother. We could have lost you."

Asherah signed and leaned her forehead against her tall daughter's shoulder.

"Let's go."

"Wait," Asherah said, and turned to Anna. "For the last, Caesarissa. I am warning you. Ask nothing of me ever again. And if you do not want my curse, leave my family alone."

Binah drew out a cloak that she herself had stored away. Asherah, like Anna, was small: the cloak would fit and serve to disguise her as they slipped out of the palace—just two ladies, veiled and going home.

Anna began to weep. The sight of the two women's backs, decorously swaying toward the door, catapulted her mood from tears to laughter, which rose until it reached a pitch that even she knew was unhealthy.

She gulped and tried to get herself under control. And failed. So, moments later, did her maids. A messenger brought Anna's mother to her house. Irene tried to soothe her, pray over her, then slapped her. Finally, Anna fell silent, nursing her anger along with her hurt cheek.

The messengers she sent to Pera and to the old house so near the palace returned. There was no trace of the ladies that the Caesarissa sought. It was as if they had vanished off the face of the earth or retreated deep within it. They would keep her secrets. They would keep silent, and so would she; for she could not betray them without betraying herself. But they would, she knew, be watchful—wherever they were.

Anna allowed herself to be put to bed. She had always been scholarly, and now, in a matter of only hours, she had learned so much she wondered how her mind could absorb it without consuming itself with its own fury. She would allow herself, she promised, to go mad. She had, instead, vengeance and a crown to pursue.

Bohemond had never truly desired her: his words and his actions were all lies. Still, he had read her—a barbarian who understood a porphyrogenita better than she understood herself. She was useful: no more. She had been useful as well to Binah, whom she had trusted; and Binah had not only deceived her, but turned on her. Even—and preeminently—her parents saw her only in terms of her use to them.

She needed to find a use for herself. And allies who were of use to her, rather than the other way round. Strangely enough, she wished Nicephorus Bryennius were with her. Now, if he insisted, she could even close her eyes and imagine—*who will you pretend embraces you, Anna? What a fool you are!* There might even be another child—though she knew now that neither of her sons were likely to become Emperor. They were, like her, a disappointment. Still, if her father lived even a decade longer, her children could contract strong marital alliances.

She thought now that she could be "my dear" up until the moment she seized the diadem. And then? Well, if Nicephorus did not want it, she would rule by herself. It was not as if she had ever *not* been alone, at least in her own thoughts and ambitions.

She submitted obediently to swallow the composers her remaining servants held to her lips.

She would not always, she pledged herself, come out on the losing side. She was her father's daughter, and the thing her father knew to do in a war was win it. She wiped her eyes. A moment more, and she was reading and making notes.

As he had boasted, Bohemond did indeed escape safely from the City. Anna found that a source of bitter mirth. In fact, no one knew at all except his spies and Asherah and Binah, and hell only knew where they were. She trusted them to keep their word: she kept hers in all but her studies, which deepened and darkened.

She laughed, too, when Bohemond actually *did* feign death, turning his precious Antioch over to Tancred, and fleeing from Cantacuzenus, who had conquered him (at least temporarily). The halls rang with her laughter, not least at the thought of him lying in a coffin, a stinking cock providing the true charnel reek, while his knights tore their hair, mourned ostentatiously, and, under cover of night, helped their master out and shared food with him. How he must have hated to enter the coffin each dawn—except, Anna knew, he must have laughed, not just at his escape, but his ruse.

One of the Varangians actually suggested that anyone who wished to make sure Bohemond was dead should drive a stake into the coffin. She laughed at that too. She would have been glad to wield the mallet herself.

"Why do you care?" Nicephorus Bryennius asked her. His arms about her were a comfort of sorts. It was not his fault that he really was not strong enough for her—even if he did write an impeccably literary Greek. He loved her more than she loved him. Did she love anyone at all? Sometimes she wondered.

"Bohemond is our enemy," Anna said. Bryennius muttered something about women's hatreds—such as her own for her brother Ioannes, whom fickle city folk now called Kaloioannes. Ioannes the Handsome? He had been such an *ugly* child.

She laughed again when Bohemond, in a hellish resurrection, marched West. Mantled in the heroism of a returning conqueror, he preached his Eastern wars, giving receptions in the vast pavilions of the Emir Kerbogha, part of the spoil of "my princedom of Antioch." He presented one church with two thorns allegedly plucked from Christ's crown and donated silver shackles in token of his delivery from captivity to yet another church. This time, however, the wars to the East had another goal. Jerusalem had fallen. Antioch had fallen. Byzantium remained. To take it, he needed church sanction and an army, which he found in France, where Adela, wife of Stephen, daughter of a conqueror, proved eager to pour gold into his lap. And more than gold: it was she who gave the wedding feast when Bohemond wed Constance of France while Tancred wed her sister at the great church (at least, great to Franks, at Chartres).

Once again Bohemond had gold and royal favor. Once again, he preached holy war: this time, against Alexius, for was he not served by pagans and heretics? A fine fleet lay a-building on the shores of the Adriatic. Word came soon that Bohemond's lady was fertile—or else Bohemond had procured a child from some beggar brat. Anna could almost pity the Princess Constance. Almost.

The word came from Dyrrachium, where Bohemond and Alexius had warred a generation ago, that the Franks had landed. A worn-out rider, steppe-born, falling from his dying horse into a prostration within the palace confines. Alexius, coming in from a hunt and easing his boots from swollen feet, heard it. *Bohemond has landed.*

"Let us eat first," said the Emperor, "and see about Bohemond thereafter."

40

Did you see Bohemond's camp?" Two of Alexius's noble officers brushed by Anna where she stood, richly dressed despite the autumn's warmth and arranging medicines like a humble nurse and good daughter. Anna, not Irene, had accompanied her father on this campaign.

I rise in the world, Anna thought. *My father now trusts me less than my mother.*

Ill Alexius might be; formidable he still was. During the winter of Bohemond's siege of Dyrrachium, he had mounted the most audacious campaign yet—by doing nothing. That is, if "nothing" included allowing Bohemond to hurl himself and his armies against the Empire's western gate until all his treasury was devoured; if "nothing" meant hiring armies from Kilij Arslan and threatening the Venetians into blockading his city.

She glanced over her medications. Some there were, there had to be, that beclouded the mind, sapped the will. But if she used them on Alexius, what befell the Empire?

Her father had judged her, like Bohemond, to a hair.

The Franks who served her father—Bohemond's half-brother still among them—had not ridden out to speak to Bohemond. Alexius might trust them, but the sight of that camp . . .

Even here, Anna imagined she could sense the reek of the impoverished camp: sickness and blood and a winter's filth overlaid by the wet ash of a burnt fleet and the peculiar tang of Greek fire. Had Bohemond read his Homer that he would burn his ships, a desperate signal: *here I am and here I remain!* Anna doubted it. The gesture was like him—showy and desperate.

The empire had troops in the mountains, barring the passes, and the Emperor himself camped at Diabolis, checking deserters and advising his armies: use as many arrows as you need, but shoot at the horses, not at Bohemond's armored men.

"Give them wings," Alexius had said. Anna had seen the Franks in their ring mail, proof against arrows fired by anyone—Scythian, Persian, or giant. Mounted, they were irresistible, able to bore their way through the walls of Babylon. But if you shot down their horses, they became playthings even for recruits.

Bohemond could not escape. And, as summer yielded to autumn, letters from Bohemond came not to the Emperor but to another Alexius, the Duke of Dyrrachium. And when one of Bohemond's vassals deserted with fifty horse, he confirmed the rumors: plague stalked Bohemond's camp.

Anna had been present when Alexius signed the final version of his letter to the Duke of Dyrrachium, reproaching Bohemond for oath-breaking:

> You know perfectly well how many times I have been deceived through trusting your oaths and promises. And if the Holy Gospel did not command Christians in all things to forgive one another, I would not have opened my ears to your propositions. But it is better to be deceived than to offend God and transgress His holy laws. I do not therefore reject your plea. If you do truth desire peace, if you do indeed abominate the absurd and impossible thing that you have attempted, and if you no longer take pleasure in shedding the

blood of Christians, then come in person with as many companions
as you like. The distance between us is not great.

Oh, but it was, it was. At the very least, Bohemond would have
safe conduct back to his own camp: which was more than she would
have seen fit to give him. But Alexius was a rasher, or perhaps more
thoughtful, strategist than she. Not only did he send a letter that was
far more generous than Bohemond deserved, he sent four hostages of
high rank—Marinus the admiral and Roger the Frank, both of whom
understood what passed among Bohemond's people for customs; and
Constantine Euphorbenus and Adralestos, the man who could actually speak the outlandish Western tongues that produced names so
outlandish that Anna always had trouble pronouncing them.

Now, it remained only for Bohemond to knock over his king and
admit defeat—the hard part of any fight against him. He would not
permit the hostages within his camp, but met them outside. Chosen
for familiarity with the Franks they might have been, but instantly,
they fell to reproaching Bohemond. You see how badly your broken
oaths have turned out for you, they told him.

All of Alexius's armies knew Bohemond's answer. The tall count
had interrupted: "Enough of that. If the Emperor has anything else to
tell me, I should like to hear it."

So they told him. Cleverly, Anna thought, so that even Bohemond knew them for Alexius's men. He had spent his own time in
the East well; he was almost as skilled a debater as the envoys. He bargained to be met by the Emperor's closest blood relations outside his
camp, for the Emperor himself to rise and greet him when he entered
the tent, an absence of reproaches, and even excusal from bending his
knee or bowing his head to Alexius.

Why not simply hand over the throne? Anna asked herself when
she heard the account of this meeting.

"Peace, daughter," her father had ordered. The negotiations
dragged on: distant kin were substituted for close blood kin. Alexius
would not rise, but would greet Bohemond and seat him in a place of
honor, and on and on. After all that Bohemond took a sudden whim
to change the location of his camp, which reeked of plague. Wasn't
that just like him and all his race—no steadiness of purpose.

Besides, Alexius spent his mornings in council, his afternoons
having his swollen feet and legs tended by his adoring child. Anna
curled her lip. She knew how it was viewed: the loyal daughter, like
her mother, laying aside her natural reluctance to view battles to fol-

low her husband and serve her father. And if the daughter had a fondness for accounts of military prowess, so much the better: the patricians would have a suitable audience for discreet boasts. One day, Anna promised herself . . . She wondered if Bohemond had sought gold of the Jews of Italy and been denied.

The lion might have mange, but he could still roar at bay, and he had a heavy paw.

Bohemond wished to move his camp? "They should have destroyed it," she muttered.

She was overheard. Sighing, she resigned herself to yet another long lecture on the Emperor's strategy of mercy and how women could not forgive and forget. That might be true: but she had listened as Alexius had worked out his strategy of inaction on the battlefield, while campaigning on every other front.

Best they set it down to innocence. A woman scorned was a hissing and a laughingstock.

Today, however, ah, today, Bohemond would come to the Emperor and make his final submission. Anna had dressed as carefully as for a lover's meeting. Splendor made a splendid weapon, she had always known. She glittered like a living icon: Our Lady of the Medicine Chest.

Would Bohemond think she looked . . . he could not find her beautiful. No one ever had: being Bohemond, no doubt, he might assess the worth of her jewelry. Regardless of his lies, he had not done so before; and now it no longer mattered. She was porphyrogenita, victorious, and soon he would be nothing.

A *lie*, she told herself. Bohemond was Bohemond. It was still unpardonable the way her hands chilled and sweat and her lips trembled. Bohemond had not taken her. He had not even intimidated her. But he had shamed her in the citadel of her self-respect and cost her the service of two women who might have unlocked a treasury of knowledge that could, before now, have made her, not Caesar John, her father's heir. She would never forgive him.

"He wants *what?*"

Again, the officers paced by. A woman no longer young, a woman serving as a powerful man's attendant, even if she were a porphyrogenita, is invisible, of course. Anna had used that invisibility in the past to gain valuable knowledge. Perhaps, if she were visible, she would be heir.

"The man's presumption is beyond belief! He wants the Emperor to rise and take him by the hand."

"Someone should remind the Count: *he* is not Emperor."

"Only the Emperor is a match for him."

"His Sacred Majesty will not rise," Anna spoke up. To her satisfaction, both men jumped, which looked rather absurd because they had changed from their armor, which would have looked foolish enough, into heavily brocaded and gemmed court wear. What? Does a wine pitcher, a camp chair speak? The furniture does not: the Caesarissa Anna, thank you very much, *does*.

"I should think not, Caesarissa. But you must understand that some concessions are necessary, even with a defeated man, a proud man . . ."

Anna suppressed a hiss. Let her say one word to the contrary, and out came the homilies, the corrections. She would give her husband this much credit: he did not presume to lecture her.

Alexius would not remain on his couch for reasons of state. Alexius would not rise because his gout caused him unbelievable pain and because he would be dead and damned before he showed physical weakness before a man who, for all his failings, for all his failures, was younger, taller, and fitter than he.

As for taking Bohemond by the hand, if even Alexius's enigmatic cousin Leo Ducas prostrated himself as a matter of course in private, what right did a Frank have to privileged public treatment?

Being Bohemond, probably far more than he deserved. Even in the failure of all his hopes, he preserved some vestiges of splendor. Perhaps it was sheer audacity or unwillingness to give up—traits he shared with Anna.

"His Sacred Majesty told me," Anna spoke again, enjoying the men's discomfiture and affront, "that he will not rise. Bohemond will have a place of honor. My father will even hold out his hand to him. If that is not sufficient . . ." Anna achieved an elegant shrug, a shimmer of silk and gems.

"Caesarissa, he will die of the humiliation," one man warned her.

"He should have died before this." Anna let ice edge her voice. "He makes peace, he says, out of concern for his men. He used that lie when he offered to leave the siege of Antioch, if you recall."

The two nobles' eyes widened with surprised respect, as if she had suddenly emerged from beneath the carpets, dancing and shouting theological proofs of the existence of God. She would remember their faces and mark them down for punishment if she ever had any power.

Meanwhile, scribes, logothetes, and ministers had huddled, grimaced, and scrawled over the most recent drafts of the chrysobull, the treaty under which Bohemond would declare himself the Emperor's true man. No doubt Anna had a better hand and finer Greek than most of those so-busy ambassadors—but as well ask the sun to turn back in its course. She was not Joshua fighting in Canaan, but only Anna, who must tend her father. At least, her duties enabled her to be present. The parchment lay ready, waiting, and near it the Holy Word on which Bohemond was to swear, its pages weighted down by a gift to Alexius from St. Gilles, God grant him peace—the rusting Lance he had borne out of Antioch.

There would be some satisfaction in watching Bohemond as the treaty was read out to him: "This agreement with divinely crowned Majesty . . . I, Bohemond, son of Robert Guiscard, to be thy true man . . . moreover, I will make war on Tancred my nephew if he does not deliver the aforementioned towns . . ."

The problem with "some satisfaction" was that it predicated satisfaction *for* something.

Her father came to take his place. How painfully he walked, leaning hard upon her arm, his shoulders hunched, his eyes flashing as if daring any of the logothetes, officers, church officials, and ambassadors to notice. *He is* still *a better man than you all!* she thought with defiance.

Nicephorus Bryennius stepped forward. At least, he was dressed properly, no longer reeking of horses and the road. He had been making himself useful and more than useful in the negotiations with the Franks. An accommodating man, her Nicephorus, able to speak to Bohemond and Alexius both. A pity he was not more ambitious. Now he murmured brief requests for pardon and permission, and helped her settle his father-in-law.

Alexius's look of gratitude to Anna's husband stabbed at her heart. Her father was developing an old man's careful walk. Why had she not noticed?

Stay alive, Father. You must stay alive until I learn enough to inherit from you.

There, across from her, were the ministers of the *kral* of Hungary, father of her brother's intended wife. Perhaps, if Anna succeeded, she would simply ship back their barbarian princess.

Tumult erupted outside. Bohemond never did things quietly. Anna stiffened, consciously freezing her face into a mask of imperial dignity. Even now, she supposed, he might attack if he did not mind dying to take the Emperor with him.

Standing behind her father, hand possessively touching the back of his chair, Anna watched Bohemond. How dare this man, only a few years younger, preserve his vigor? How dare he press his points, long after he had admitted he was in the Emperor's hands? Worse yet, how dare he rise and ask to be returned to his camp?

"Are you going to let him?" Anna hissed at her father.

Alexius nodded once, almost imperceptibly. Bohemond withdrew. Moments later, the word came: the Count asked to see Caesar Bryennius.

Anna's husband might be persuasive, but Bohemond knew things that could silence him—and Anna—forever.

Anna glowed with triumph. For once, a night spent with her husband had been almost . . . almost pleasurable. How exultant Nicephorus had been at his success in persuading the Count to agree to almost all of her father's terms. His face had glowed as he led the taller man back into the Emperor's tent. His eyes had sought Anna's: *be pleased*, he wished her, as he had done all the years of their marriage.

Really, he is a handsome man, Anna told herself. She managed a discreet, because public, smile, and let secrets surface in her eyes. Nicephorus flushed deeply.

Thank God. He didn't tell. If Bohemond does not tell, and the witches do not speak, I am safe. For now.

The document lay on the table, to be read in Bohemond's presence, long pages of mellifluous Greek, declaring himself the loyal man of His Majesty and of his much-loved son, the Basileus Lord Ioannes, the Porphyrogenitus.

Anna bit her lip. Not even her satisfaction at the sight of Bohemond defeated, Bohemond swearing fealty, could change the fact that Ioannes remained heir.

Bohemond was a notorious liar—none knew that better than Anna—but surely, she thought, surely even he must shudder at the horrific risks his soul ran if he violated the first term of the great oath to which he assented:

> "I swear by the Passion of Christ Our Savior, who suffers no longer, and by His invincible Cross, which for the salvation of all men He endured, and by the All-Holy Gospels here before us, which have converted the whole world; with my hand on these Gospels I swear; in my mind I associate with them the much hon-

*ored Cross of Christ, the Crown of Thorns, the Nails, the Spear
that pierced Our Lord's side, giver of life; by these I swear to
you, our Lord and Emperor Alexius Comnenus, most powerful
and revered, and to your coemperor, the thrice-beloved Lord
Ioannes . . ."*

There her brother was again. She would not consider that. She
would consider the sight of Bohemond, hand upon the Gospels, gazing down upon the forgery of the Holy Lance that had been brought
from Antioch by another noble vassal from the West, acknowledging
himself defeated, and his oath witnessed, this month September of the
second indiction, year of our Lord 6617, or, as the Franks called it,
1108 after the birth of Christ.

Signing the oath in impressive procession were its witnesses. As
fee for this mighty oath, her father had signed in purple ink the
chrysobull that, he fervently hoped, deeded Bohemond the gifts that
should finally hold him.

At least for now.

That should very much be that, but, knowing Bohemond, Anna
doubted it. As the hieratic decorum of the court, transplanted here to
the imperial camp, eased, Anna found herself standing beside her
husband. A shadow fell across her. When she looked up, she saw Bohemond standing nearby.

Like a lamp that had taken years of battering, but was still bronze,
still richly chased, Bohemond nursed what dignities remained to him
despite his public humiliation. Nicephorus, of course, beamed, innocent as his wife and a man he had not even the wit to know had tried
to betray him gazed at each other. Worse yet, he turned away to speak
to the ambassadors of Hungary. How dare he be on such terms with
Anna's brother that his wife's kin were people he felt he ought to
greet!

"So, Caesarissa," said the Count, "here you are, a dutiful daughter. Do you regret?"

"I am where I belong, at my father's right hand." *Give him his own
back,* some evil genius prompted her. "Do you regret?" she asked.

"Only that I did not win this throw in the game." His pale blue
eyes deepened with amusement. "God grant I have a few years left. If
I am spared, I shall try again. I think, as I said before"—so he had, and
he was a madman to admit it here—"we are alike in that."

"What of your oaths?" Anna gasped, honestly appalled. How long
could he live? Two years? Three?

"If I do not try again, my nephew Tancred or my son will hold Antioch for me and press East. No oaths bind them. Do you know, Caesarissa, I think perhaps I was a fool?" Bohemond shook his head. "I am your father's loyal servant," he told her. "It is disloyal to speak what I truly mean."

He bowed deeply to her and turned away.

Moisture in her palms told her she had dug her nails into them so deeply that they bled.

Three years later, as Bohemond readied his last army, he died. When the news was brought to Anna, she laughed until she wept. Nicephorus had no idea of how to comfort her.

But then, he never had.

1119
CONSTANTINOPLE

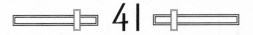

41

The wind off the Horn lent the spring evening just enough of a chill to make a brazier welcome. Its heat took the edge off the night air, while the incense Asherah had sprinkled over the embers soothed the spirit, and the fireglow cast ruddy shadows on the old stone walls of Leo's house. It was too late in the year to kindle the hypocausts: the floors were cool.

Outside the room where Asherah and Leo sat, flowering plants bloomed, an early-spring lavishness for which they had Binah and the years she had tended this house to thank.

Where was Binah now? The last time Asherah had spoken to her, Binah had replied, "Going to and fro in the earth and walking up and down in it." Asherah considered that not just provocative, but over-stated—even if, in Binah's case, "in" the earth described what she might be doing rather better than most. She would have years to wander and explore, probably decades, possibly even centuries be-fore she entered upon a maturity Asherah could not fathom and, she had to admit, did not wish to.

God help the child. It was hard enough for a girl to become a woman: what a creature raised as a woman suffered in trying to be-come an immortal . . . Asherah's mind shied away from the idea. It was hard to think of the child she had raised, the child she would al-ways love, in terms of a word like "goddess." During the years of Binah's service to the daughter of the late Emperor Alexius, God deal mercifully with him, Binah had tended this house well.

Even now, with many of the furnishings packed against their re-turn to Hagios Prokopios in the south, the house held echoes, but no ghosts. Binah had blessed it with the peacefulness she herself lacked. Even the stones radiated contentment.

In private at least, Leo had left off mourning for his cousin Alexius. True enough, last year, when the Emperor's asthma and other illnesses had conspired to overpower once-sturdy flesh and a mind that remained wily until life was extinguished, they had made the journey they had hoped never to make again from Cappadocia to Constantinople. No longer young, they traveled slowly. Even if Asherah abused her powers again to create another horse for Leo that could race from home to Jerusalem overnight, he could never ride that hard.

But he had insisted on traveling to Constantinople. In case Alexius had called for him, Asherah suspected. Ah, the bond between Leo and his younger cousin the Emperor was a paradox that had grown between them for almost two generations. She supposed that only death, and perhaps not even that, would sever it. She suspected, too, that her husband was still Ducas enough to see in the passing of an Emperor a need to be present to secure his interests and his family's.

For Asherah, that meant the Jews of the Empire, of course. Alexius had been too orthodox to indulge them, but he had also been more benevolent than many emperors. His successor, now, would require propitiation, gifts, and assurances of the Jews of Pera's continued obedience.

Ioannes was Emperor now, just as Alexius had always planned. Ioannes, not Nicephorus Bryennius, had had the signet off Alexius's finger. Ioannes had won, although he had not dared accompany the Empress Irene, Caesarissa Anna, and the imperial hordes when they bore the dying Emperor to the smaller Mangana on Propontis where the air was sweeter. For all the good it had done Alexius: the procession of aristocrats hell-bent on pretending that Alexius was not dying had been one of the most grotesque things that Asherah had ever seen.

Ioannes dared not attend his father while his formidable mother and sister took turns tending him, grieving hysterically, and scheming practically to Alexius's dying breath for Anna and her husband to succeed him. What was it Irene was supposed to have said? "Husband, while you lived, you were full of guile, saying one thing and meaning another; you are no better now that you are dying."

After Asherah's own years of dealing with the envies and anxieties of Irene's turbulent eldest child, she could well believe it. Now, Irene, her hair shorn, had taken the name in religion of Xene and withdrawn to the convent of Kecharitomene, while Anna herself . . .

she was at least quiet for now, which was more than Asherah had expected. It was well for the Jews that Kaloioannes was Emperor: Anna had worked with them long enough to have acquired their long, long memories, and she was no friend now to Asherah or anyone close to her.

And so, Asherah thought with a contented sigh, it was all settled, wasn't it? Their packing was almost complete, and only a few transactions in the City demanded their attention before she could extract Leo from this great trap of a city and begin the long, slow journey home. Perhaps they should have accepted Theodoulos and Adela's offer to wait until Leo was ready to leave, but trade must not be restrained, and Adela had already been too long away from Hagios Prokopios, where she ran Asherah's old house as if it were her own keep.

Another caravan awaited. Once they returned home, Asherah vowed, they would *never* travel anywhere again unless, years hence, their descendants saw fit to translate their old bones, like those of Joseph, out of the land of Egypt, out of the house of bondage and to Jerusalem. Given who ruled there now, that didn't seem likely.

Leo, however, didn't see this land as Egypt, and his connection with the caves of their home went deep, terrible pun although that was. Please God, although they had reached and, to Asherah's astonishment, surpassed three score and ten years, they might have joyous harvest years to argue over it and write the results into their wills before they faced that final grief.

Leo had to know that she was thinking about him, worrying about him; he smiled reassuringly at her. His hair and beard were pure silver now, going to white. Nevertheless, in the kindly shadows cast by the firelight, he looked like a much younger man.

Blessed art Thou, O Lord our God, who hast kept us in life, sustained us . . . Best not to say thanks prematurely, she thought, and returned her husband's smile.

"What are you thinking?" Leo asked teasingly.

Quickly, Asherah looked for an answer and found one she knew would please him. "If Sarah saw Abraham as I see you, it was a wonder that she had no children other than Isaac."

Leo chuckled. "And so, you would rather be a mother again than a great-grandmother for the second time?"

Asherah rather liked the idea of Leo as a patriarch. They had a second great-grandchild that they had never even seen from Theodoulos's eldest child. Theo and Adela's youngest had insisted on postponing his wedding until his grandparents came home. Another reason not to have postponed their departure.

"God forbid!" she exclaimed. "It is the turn of my granddaughters—"

"And grandsons, surely?"

"—to get up at night and walk the halls with a screaming infant."

Leo took her hand and carried it to his cheek. "Many daughters have done virtuously, but thou excellest them all," he said, and her eyes filled. Who would ever have expected such riches for the witchy, solitary girl Asherah had been?

"Do you remember how angry I was when you first quoted that?"

"You stormed out, and Tzipporah—"

"God rest her."

"She stayed behind only long enough to sink me with reproaches and the fear that I would never see you again. I remember everything, every one of my days that has you in it as if it passed just a moment ago."

Asherah let her head rest against Leo's shoulder. They were old: no one would begrudge it if they dozed together in the mellow lamplight. She felt Leo kiss her hair, almost as silvery as his after all these years.

Pounding at the heavy barred door made Asherah leap up with a cry. She tried to drop Leo's hand but found her fingers held in the clasp that had sustained her since, years ago, she had watched the destruction of an Emperor.

The road between Susa and Marakanda when bandits had struck. Baghdad. The Rhinelands. Even Jerusalem the Golden. Well, she had had a good life, but there was no need, was there, for Leo to die yet?

"Wait," he told her. Asherah stared at the mosaic on the floor as if each separate shard in the pattern could, at any moment, re-form into a prophecy that only she could read. Out of shards, she and Leo had built up a world of their own. Must it now be shattered?

Again, the pounding at the door, just as she had always feared. She reached for the square of fabric she sometimes wrapped about her shoulders, to cover her head.

"Let me answer it," she whispered. Her, not Leo.

He shook his head at her. "Both of us," he whispered back. "Or neither."

He rose, assisted her to her feet with the manners of the patrician he had always been, and escorted her to the hall. The pounding at the door grew so thunderous Asherah fancied she could almost see it shake. It was well that the Ducas family had built this house like a fortress.

Nordbriht limped into the hall, their devoted old wolf who usually lay by the fire, but still had a tooth or two in his head that would make strangers think twice about harming them. Now he held his ax. It was still well honed, but he carried it with a good deal more difficulty than he had even a year ago.

"Not either of you," he growled. "Go back inside."

Even at the edge of ruin, they smiled at his tone. Obediently, they went back to their seats. Leo reached for a sword he still kept nearby. Asherah had his old obsidian dagger.

"Who's there?" The rasp of command and his Northern accent overpowered the pounding at the door. "Speak up!"

"Is Leo Ducas within? I'm kin of his."

They heard the former Varangian remove the bar from the door and unlock it. Slowly, he limped into the room.

"The Caesar Nicephorus Bryennius," he announced with what curt ceremony he could muster. He was a Varangian, not a majordomo, after all.

Leo rose. He would not willingly bring a man of perilously high birth who came by night, claiming kinship and disturbing the house, before his wife. He was more eastern than many easterners in that regard, in fact. Besides, Nicephorus was the man whose wife had threatened Asherah's life.

"Don't worry, Leo," Asherah said. "Do you want me to withdraw?"

If someone had suggested to the girl I was forty years ago that I would withdraw like a proper wife when Leo might need me, I would have gutted the fool. I've mellowed.

She clapped her hands for cakes and wine to be brought.

"I beg you, lady, stay."

Nicephorus Bryennius held up a hand, barring Asherah's departure. Then he flushed and greeted her and Leo more suitably.

The Caesar was a tall, handsome man of mature years. Known for his tact, his clear writing, and his dignity, he must have been distraught to blurt out a command to a man's wife in that man's own house. He looked about him with guilty fascination.

"What's the trouble?" Leo asked.

Asherah interrupted, "Is it the Caesarissa? She's all right, isn't she?"

Nordbriht himself brought in the wine and cakes, clearly guarding the servants whom he had made his charges as well as their masters. He placed the tray where Asherah might reach it, then took himself off—probably no farther than the other side of the door.

"It's got to be exhaustion," Nicephorus blurted out. "Or maybe grief has turned her mad. You should have seen her when her father died. No one could have done more for him. She practically took over his treatment, chose his food, cooked it, all but swallowed it for him."

"She has always been such a loving daughter," Leo murmured. "I am sorry for your loss, you know that."

"Afterward, when he died, she was like a fury. It wasn't my fault that Ioannes got the Emperor's ring. Alexius was always more than a match for all of us. Since then, Anna's been like a fury. Ioannes didn't even dare emerge for the funeral!"

"Anna has always been ambitious," Asherah put in. "She's always had a grievance against the world. You have just loved her blindly."

"Blind?" Nicephorus asked. He fumbled at the wine cup Asherah handed him and drank the fine vintage far too fast. Silently, she refilled his cup.

"It's gotten worse," Nicephorus muttered. "Somehow, I've got to make things right."

"Son," said Leo, greatly daring, "nothing could make this tangle right. It's been in a snarl since your precious Anna was born and Ioannes after her."

"I want it to be right. Alexius is dead. He's at peace; why can't the rest of the family be?"

Leo drank so that he would not laugh.

If you had wanted peace, you married into the wrong family, Asherah knew he was thinking. Probably, he had a lot of fellow feeling for this Nicephorus. Anna studied him. Binah was right. He lacked the ruthlessness that would have made him an Emperor. If he were stronger, he might have become someone like her Leo.

"I *like* Ioannes," Bryennius muttered. "I swore to serve him as I served his father back when Bohemond submitted himself. Lady, when your daughter was in her service, at least she saw reason! Now . . ." He flushed. "She has gone strange. She reads secretly. She always was a great reader, but now she hides her books, and there is a shadow over her face."

Asherah glanced away. When Binah had left Anna's service some fourteen years ago, Anna had already become more than a dabbler in magic; she had acquired Psellus's library and done her best to coerce Asherah and Binah into remaining her teachers, this time in the sorcery she should have condemned. Leo drew in a sharp breath.

"What else have you noted?" Asherah asked Nicephorus.

"She has always had a sharp wit. But now, her voice is harsh and . . ." He looked at Asherah, then looked away and down in shame. "Sir, must the lady hear this?"

"This is Asherah's house as well as mine," Leo told him.

"If we are to solve this riddle," Asherah said, "I must know all its parts."

"My wife has never been," Nicephorus said, low-voiced, "particularly . . . particularly affectionate. Perhaps because she went too young when, I know, she had no particular desire to wed. Now, however, she is *avid*. I did not know a woman could hurt a man when they . . . when they are together."

Asherah looked down, embarrassed at Nicephorus's shame. "She may simply be trying to exhaust you so that you'll go away and leave her alone," she said. "But she is angry, too. If she simply wanted to seduce you, she wouldn't hurt you."

There were magics in which the joining of man and woman could be twisted for power. Could Anna have sunk so low as to attempt them? Asherah would not have thought she had that much talent, or could have so perverted it. Then, in a long, long life, she had been wrong before.

Most of this coil was Anna's ambition, but part of it was Bohemond's work. Anna, who possessed a full measure of the wit and ruthlessness that had made her father such a strong ruler, had tried to mold Nicephorous. When he had broken in the casting, she had seen Bohemond and, what was worse, he had seen her and read her needs. All of her needs. And then he had frustrated them.

"She wants me at the palace tonight. I know she plans to kill her brother and wants me to wield the sword. I came here instead, so I'd be late. Maybe she'll call off the plot."

"Why did you come here?" Leo asked. His brows went up. "Surely not for protection." He put an arm about Asherah's shoulders as if he had sensed she trembled, still frightened by that apocalyptic knocking. "What do you want of me?"

"I beg you"—Nicephorus Bryennius looked as if he would hurl

himself to his knees—"talk her out of it. You are the only man of her father's generation left alive. You are *family*. Even when we were first married—Anna was scarcely more than a child, too young, I see that now—she used to say you were kind to her."

Leo exchanged a look with Asherah. *Don't go,* trembled on the tip of her tongue. They were almost packed. They could flee tonight, abandoning anything they could not carry with them. Once they reached Cappadocia, let these violent imperials turn upon each other.

Leo rose, and she rose with him. Nicephorus tensed. How had that scrap of a woman so intimidated a man like this?

"My love, I won't go if you object. But if I can prevent another civil war, blood in the streets"—*another Emperor blinded*, she knew he thought but would not say—"I think I must. And it's family."

"I know," Asherah told him. "I would do the same thing." As a matter of fact, she had tried. Please God, let Leo succeed where she had failed.

Leo took her hand and kissed it. Nicephorus shifted from one foot to the other, embarrassed and oddly wistful.

"Will you arm yourself?" Asherah asked.

"It's family!" Leo protested.

"All the more reason. Besides, there are robbers in the streets. Always have been. Sir," she turned to Nicephorus Bryennius. "Take care of him."

Leo grimaced at her concern and reached for his sword. You would have thought he was twenty again. "I'll get my cloak."

And, just like that, he was gone, Nicephorus bowing hastily to her, then trailing him.

42

Asherah stacked the wine cups on the silver tray and tried to calculate how long packing the remaining rugs, cushions, and hangings might take. She had failed to reach a solution three times when Nordbriht edged into the room.

The tall old warrior was shifting his ax from hand to hand as a young maid might twist a lock of hair or a nervous woman her veil or an ornament.

"He didn't take you with him?" Asherah made her voice gentle.

She had long known Nordbriht would follow Leo to Gehenna itself, then hurl himself between his master and the fire. But he had a real fondness for her, as well. "What's the matter, old wolf?" she asked.

Nordbriht looked down at her, then away. That finished Asherah's control. She might be smaller than the women he had grown up among, but she knew her own strength. God knows, it had been tested often enough.

"In the name of God, Nordbriht, if it's about Leo, tell me! Who has a better right to know?"

"What about my lord's rights, Lady?" Nordbriht asked.

Asherah hissed under her breath. The way the big Northerner spoke, anyone would think she bullied Leo as Anna had clearly bullied Caesar Nicephorus. Still, she made herself reply patiently. "I am mistress in this house, but he is master. What rights do you mean?"

"He's old, mistress," said Nordbriht. "A man gets old, he starts to fear the night to come. If not now, then soon. When I was a boy, they told me of an *eorl* who feared above all things that he would die in his bed. There's no honor dying that way. Your heels kick at Asgard, and Hela claims you for her own, down in the ice of Niflheim."

Asherah wanted to laugh or scream. Let Nordbriht lay this farrago of errors before a priest, and he would walk barefoot to Jerusalem in penance. If he didn't have to walk upon his knees instead.

"So, one day, the old man armed himself, sark and sword and shield, and went to the headlands. He called upon the old gods—on the old errors, I should say—hurled himself into the fjord, and the Valkyries came to take him up to Asgard."

Asherah's hands chilled. Leo had no fear of the goddess beneath the earth. He had worn that fear out with Binah's birth. "Nordbriht, if you've got nothing to tell me but pagan nightmares . . . I beg you. You saw them leave. Tell me what you saw before I shake it out of you!"

Nordbriht turned to face her, and she saw the man who had outlived three ring-givers before entering her husband's service steeling himself to report. "He's *feigr*, lady. The light shines about his brow. A man can often escape danger, if his courage holds and it be not his time. But when his Wyrd calls him . . ."

"No." Asherah's hand came up to her lips. "No. It is too soon." *I didn't even get a chance to say good-bye.*

"Lady, I saw the light upon his face. He didn't want me to come because he did not want me to fail to save another master."

Nordbriht's eyes filled, and his face twisted. "Forty years," he said. "A ring-giver out of the old songs." He set his ax aside and stretched out his hands as if offering a comforting embrace, but drew back before touching Asherah.

"We must stop this," Asherah whispered.

"How can we? If it's a man's time, it's his time. My lord is ready to go before the long defeat devours him, life and light together. And," Nordbriht pointed out in a kind of gloomy triumph, "we could never reach the palace before the master and Caesar Nicephorus. By now, the Emperor could be dead."

So could Leo, God forbid.

"I don't believe in your Wyrd, Nordbriht," Asherah snapped. "But I'm no Greek to waste time arguing religion when my husband's life is in danger."

Nordbriht gestured at his lame leg. "Useless," he said. "Useless. I should look for a convenient cliff myself, like the *eorl* in the story. How will we get there?"

His eyes cleared. *Wonderful. Once again, someone looks to me to perform a miracle, when all I want is what I had earlier this evening—firelight, soft cushions, and my Leo beside me.*

Asherah bit her lip. "If I were younger, I could take us there," she whispered. She had not translocated since the disastrous night of Bohemond's assault on the Caesarissa. "But I do not know if I have the strength."

"Lady, I tell you, you do not go alone. I go with you. I'd wager I still know the palace better than you do, and I would die to defend the man who has been friend and lord to me. I've been on borrowed time since he pulled me back from the Salt Sea forty years ago. Besides"—he looked at her levelly—"you know that I would die for you, Asherah."

Honesty, here at the end of all things. Brutal, embarrassing honesty. And, if she had to be honest with herself, not much of a surprise. Asherah lowered her head till her tears subsided. When she looked up, Nordbriht had himself under control, and her decision was made.

"If you consent, I can draw on your strength and we shall fly. It is not like your battlemaid's white horse—what was its name—Grane? Still, I make no promises that we are not unhorsed in midflight. We may none of us survive."

"It is a *chance*," Nordbriht said. "When do we start?"

Asherah reached to the table where she had set the obsidian dagger that Leo had given her decades ago. Once it had served him as a final weapon. Once it had served to cut the birth cord of her foster daughter, deep within the earth.

Nordbriht knelt before Asherah. She held out her arms for the invocation and felt the familiar drain. It went beyond discipline into anguish, beyond anguish into exhaustion, and she staggered. Nordbriht's arms came up and steadied her.

"I told you, lady. Draw on me."

She could feel his immense steadiness, the connection of that sturdy frame to the earth and its creatures.

Again. This time the wards grew bright about her. She knew the way she must go, she could perceive it . . .

Failure.

She reached beyond the wards for the obsidian dagger.

Take thy son, thy only son, Isaac, whom thou lovest . . .

A blood sacrifice. This was no faith she knew, and no faith she should trust. But for Leo—what was her soul without his?

Nordbriht braced himself.

She slashed the black glass across her palm. Blood dripped onto the shards of mosaic—stone and shell and glass—upon the floor, seeping into the matrix that held them all together. She managed not to cry from the pain.

Again, she dared the words of the invocation, felt them vibrate from the crown of her head to the soles of her feet.

Again, failure. Worse yet, these failures sapped what little energy she had.

"Lady," whispered Nordbriht. "I told you, draw on me. Blood has *power.*"

So this would truly be a blood rite: not just her sacrifice but Nordbriht's? Such rituals always carried a price, and blood could lure unholy things, to pounce across the wards if they failed.

"What are you waiting for?" Nordbriht demanded, holding out his arm. He had to know that in some rites, it would have been his throat. Asherah would have died before performing any such rite, as she most certainly would have been damned. She drew a careful slash across his palm, then her own hand. Blood flowed to blood, hot, but annealing before it dripped down to the floor. Again, she drew as deep a breath as she could these years, then chanted the words of invocation.

Above her, greyness opened into light.

Leo, she thought for courage, and hurled herself and her guardsman into the narrow passage. The tli's wings beat overhead as she rushed forward; and she could hear hoofbeats, see the flash of a white winged beast, hear inhuman high girls' laughter beneath the stars that rushed by, traveling far faster than they.

A battlemaid dashed across their paths.

The warrior is mine!

You will just have to wait. Who said that? She or Nordbriht? Their shed blood united them, so Asherah could see the shield maid's face: the chill, strong beauty of the Northern warriors transmuted into divinity. She felt the guardsman tremble.

Warrior, be sure we shall.

On, they plunged. Overhead, the familiar constellations of the stars formed and re-formed. She could even see the shapes of buildings she passed almost every day, quivering with lights that had to mean individual lives, some brilliant and growing, some flickering and fading toward extinction.

The greyness wavered about her—*not to be thrust out, not to be trapped here.* Even here in this realm of pure spirit, she felt Nordbriht's big hands holding her upright. She drew strength from the heat of his blood against her palm, the vitality he poured into her, heedless of his own well-being.

It was too fast! Even in the ether between place and place, Asherah felt her blood chill with the beginnings of terrible fear.

She toppled onto the shining floor, rolled, feared broken bones—*at my age*—and brought up short, not against a wall of porphyry or marble, but against Nordbriht. He was still warm, thank God, but he lay ominously still.

Drained as she had never been, Asherah struggled to her knees at his side, peeling back one eyelid.

He twitched.

"Go . . ." he whispered. "The battlemaids . . . they will wait for me to finish . . . Take him home."

"Home?" she asked. "Did they tell you we'd succeed?"

"Go!" he ordered, his voice breaking. "They'll be in the Emperor's quarters: up ahead, turn left. Guards there—dodge or slay them but in the names of all our gods, go *now.*"

He held up his hand. The cut she had slashed across his palm had already healed. His battlemaid had touched him so that he could go on living so he could, as he said, make an end.

Asherah started down the corridor. Halfway to the turn, she heard a woman scream in rage.

Asherah gathered up her robes and ran like a girl.

43

Could no one do anything right without Anna to order it or do it herself?

She screamed in fury and frustration, then brandished her dagger again. Astonishingly, it kept Ioannes, with his wonderful soldier's training, another of the gifts her father had given him, but not his daughter, at bay.

She and her brother eyed each other, stalking and circling like barbarian duelists. The Varangians spoke of a contest in which two men and their swords rowed out to an island and only one rowed back. Handsome Ioannes, people called the man who had been such a dark, scrawny baby. But now, grey underlay his vivid olive coloring. Finally, he knew enough to fear her.

Where was her pallid brute of a husband? If Nicephorus ever dragged his oversized carcass into these rooms, his fears—and everything else—would be at an end. She would have sworn on the high altar of Hagia Sophia that she had told him when to meet her here and ordered him not to fail her. What a waste of breath.

Ioannes rushed her. Of course, he was a better fighter than she. Alexius had made sure he had had every advantage. Well, Anna had strategies of her own.

She held out her free hand, let her eyes roll back in her head, and, when Ioannes advanced, thinking she was on the verge of a swoon, she gestured. Her hand filled with fire, and she hurled it at him.

His lips parted, then shut. Perhaps she would not need to have Nicephorus kill him or do the job herself. Perhaps she could bind his spirit to her will and not have to spill blood at all. Ioannes could retire to a monastery under another name, and that savage he had wed could just go home, taking her brats with her. Ioannes shook his head as if recollecting himself. No, she could not trust him. His oath would not leave them safe. Only death was safe.

Brother and sister circled each other as they had lifelong, wary, hostile, each searching for the advantage.

Footsteps pounded down the long, long corridor. Anna edged away from the door. Ioannes had been Emperor less than a year, but already they had restored the splendor of this room, which had faded sadly during her father's last illness. Now its air reeked of tension and the powers she tried to summon. All her labor tending her father: she might as well have poured his drugs out upon the mosaics of the floor. No, she must not think of that now. She dared not face her brother with tears clouding her sight.

She had locked the doors, of course, but frightened men, desperate men could break down the door; and if they couldn't, they could summon Varangians . . . who might pause long enough at the sight of "their" Caesarissa menacing their Emperor for her to get in one swift blow. That was all she asked.

Well, not precisely *all*.

Pounding at the door, thunderous and panicked. "Anna, Anna!"

In the name of Maria, Mother of Mercy, *now* Nicephorus arrived!

She screamed again in wordless fury. Bodies hurled themselves against the door, fell, then picked themselves up and tried again. The locks weakened, but the panels gave way before the door. Her husband burst into the room, followed by John Axuch, her wretched brother's Turkish-born familiar, and a tall thin man who carried a sword, but put it up the instant he entered the room. My God, it was Leo Ducas. What right did he have to go on living when her father, a younger man and a better, had died?

"Anna, stop!" Nicephorus cried. His voice took on a coaxing, honeyed tone that might have worked on Bohemond but would not, by Christ's Passion, work on her. She had fire in her eyes. She had fire in her temples. She had fire in her blood.

"We should have been *reversed!*" she screamed at him. "Let you have the breasts and womb and I the—"

Ioannes blinked at the word she used. She rushed at him, dagger ready, but he parried her blow. She half leapt, half staggered back. There was a moment—she knew it—that he could have brought his blade down upon her shoulder, crippling if not killing her.

Damn his forbearance! She screamed again.

Unlike the other men, the old man almost laughed at the obscenities she spat out.

"Child," he asked, "where did you learn language like that? Surely not from my daughter."

"*You!*" Anna screamed. "Old man without enough balls on him to try for the crown himself! Get out of here!"

Leo shook his head, still half smiling. "Your father was my kinsman, and I loved him and swore to be his man. You too swore obedience when your father died. I challenge you"—Leo Ducas might be an old man, but, as he had told her father long ago, he had outworn his fear—"to honor your word. You *do* know what honor is, don't you?"

Oh, he had Purple in his blood too, didn't he? He was quick enough with a barb.

"I'll get the guards," John Axuch said. He eyed Nicephorus Bryennius as if he suspected him of drawing steel and turning on his master. That spineless thing she was wed to shook his head. To her disgust, he was weeping.

Ioannes, reluctant to fight her fair, could not overpower her—at least, she admitted reluctantly to herself, for now. But if the big barbarians advanced on her, they could make short work of picking her up and disarming her.

Make an end, Anna, she told herself.

She drew a deep breath, let the fire that boiled within her well up until she felt as if it would shoot out her eyes, and held out her hands for the thaumaturgy that she had learned from those books of Psellus she had saved from destruction. She could feel the power there, waiting for her to set hand to it as an armsmaster sets a grinding wheel in motion, to build up speed until it is ready to sharpen a blade. An instant longer, and the power would shriek out of her, and she would win. It was just as well that no one else seemed to sense it, or they would have claimed it too, long ago.

Those women had said it was not for her. She would show them that they had *lied.*

Leo Ducas flinched. Well, wouldn't you just expect him to wince at the smell of sorcery? How long had he lived among witches—witches, worse yet, who were Jews or whatever and who oh-so-righteously refused to teach Anna what they knew?

How much did *Leo* know?

"No, girl," Leo said. "What does it profit you if you gain a diadem and throw away your soul?"

He started forward. "My dear, dear child, not that, I beg you. *Anything* but that!"

Leo was old and tired, and he had always been fond of her. She concentrated instead on Kaloioannes. Sooner or later he would slip. Power built up until her long hair, tumbling free of its elaborate hairdressing, crackled about her. She hurled a ball of flame at her brother, who stumbled, dodging it.

Anna leapt at him like a maddened cat, screaming in triumph.

"I think you have done quite enough," a voice spoke in accents so like those of Anna's father that tears blinded her as she struck.

"Anna, NO!"

No? When she finally had her brother at her mercy?

For the first time in her life, she felt a weapon flesh itself in a man's body—living flesh, but not for long.

Leo Ducas screamed in surprise and mortal pain.

"No!" Ioannes started forward. With a fighter's strength, he caught the good old man as he collapsed onto the floor.

Blood had spurted from the wound onto her knife, splashing onto her hand. It was still hot. The room took on the copper reek of bloodshed.

"My God, Anna, what have you done?" Bryennius chimed in after the fact, as always. Her heart chilled; she had meant to kill, but not Leo.

"Oh God, no!" A woman's shriek made them all whirl around.

Christ have mercy, it was Leo's wife, Asherah, appearing out of nowhere just the way she had the night she stepped between Anna and Bohemond, cursed be his name. She dashed past the wrecked doors to fall on her knees at her husband's side. She had a rough dagger in one bloody hand, but let it drop to the floor, where it broke into shards of black glass.

Tugging the veil from her hair—it was almost all silver now and longer than Anna's even though she was an old woman—she wadded it, pressing it against the wound Anna had dealt.

"No good . . ." Leo muttered, his eyes rolling back, his teeth chattering. "Sir, cousin, you . . . you'll take the land . . . promise!"

He snapped the word out as if he were a general commanding Ioannes—or an Emperor himself.

"I promise," Anna's brother said, not that he'd keep it. He touched Leo's hand.

Anna steeled herself as the guards approached: Varangians twice her size and sworn to Kaloioannes's service. A quick blow and she would die as quickly as Leo.

But he had not died yet. Asherah turned his face toward her. Her lips moved almost soundlessly.

Astonishingly, Leo smiled. "It is well," he whispered, "that the last lady I see is so fair."

She pressed his hand, which rested beneath the wadded crimson mess that had been her veil. Not even Aesculapius could have stopped the bleeding from *that* blow.

Kaloioannes leaned forward. Anna saw clearly when he registered on Asherah's tortured awareness. "Speak the words!" she ordered the Emperor. "Speak your Christian words over my husband."

There was nothing handsome about her brother in that moment: he goggled like a frog. A particularly homely, swarthy frog.

"He loved us, he lived among us and for us, but he never abandoned your faith. Let an Emperor pray for him as I cannot!"

She slipped her hand upward to touch her husband's brow. Kaloioannes snatched up his sword. Holding it the way the Franks did when they needed a cross to swear false oath by, he laid it to the dying man's pale lips.

Asherah sighed as if freed of one burden; tears coursed down her face, but she tried to smile for the man she held.

The guards hesitated, then closed in on Anna. Nicephorus shook his head. His face was as white as Leo's. He took Anna by the arm as if he would rather have touched a serpent, which had to be the first time he had ever been reluctant to paw her. A commotion outside made him whirl around. She might have broken free in that instant, might even have evaded the slow-moving guardsmen—but where was there to go?

Not toward the battered door, surely. To Anna's astonishment, a woman she remembered dashed across the threshold, then brought herself up short. *My God, it was Binah!*

That marble-fine skin of hers was unmarred, and she looked no older than she had the first time Anna met her. And she was crying like a terrified child.

"I felt it," she gasped. "What horror is this?"

She hurled herself to her knees beside her foster father.

Leo's eyes focused on her. "My last lesson to you, daughter," he whispered. "Men die. Stay with me." He glanced around. "Theodoulos?"

Binah shook her head from side to side. "No! Theo's got neither strength nor study for this. But Theo! He told me, in Jerusalem, of a wondrous Cup that can restore the dying . . . Let me get it . . . oh, only hold on, hold on . . . Mother, you must make him."

Asherah clutched Leo's hand and huddled in against him more closely. The end, Anna's medical training told her, was very near.

"Wo . . . won't work," Leo whispered. His lips stumbled over the words as if forming them was an effort. "Rainault . . . he said . . . only one miracle . . . to a customer . . . I've had mine."

His eyes turned back to Asherah's blood-smeared face. "I've had *two*," he added.

He looked up at her and smiled. Then his lips and hands went slack. His eyes remained open as if, even in death, he could not bear to lose the sight of her.

Asherah slid bloody fingers over his eyelids and shut them. She whispered strange prayers.

Her eyes met Anna's. In their anguish, Anna began to perceive the desolation she had made of both their lives.

"I . . . I didn't mean . . ." She was stammering like a girl-child, not a ruling Empress.

Asherah shook her head. "No, you never meant to . . . you were just a disaster. Like a child, Anna, who plays with fire and burns down her house with her family within it. A careless and cruel child."

Binah rose with the fluid grace of a leopard. "I told you," she said, approaching Anna, "that if you ever touched my family . . ."

The guards stiffened. Even Nicephorus, whose flesh seemed to shrink where it brushed hers, poised himself against attack. Tears rolled down Binah's face, but the violet eyes were unreddened, the flawless cheeks unmarred by grief.

Anna drew herself up. Binah would be too angry to kill slowly.

"Ah . . ." For a moment, Anna really thought Binah would spit upon the floor. "You disgust me. You may as well live out your life, knowing you have cursed yourself and"—now Binah's voice did break—"destroyed your happiness as surely as you have killed mine." Binah sobbed convulsively. "Ours."

She turned back to kneel beside her foster father, wrapping her arms about Asherah.

Bryennius began to draw Anna away, but recoiled, almost as if being a husband with such a wife shamed him before Asherah. Why did Anna's own husband consider that old woman holy?

Asherah sat holding Leo, smoothing his face into peace. She looked up uncertainly at Binah. "Do you think he was happy? I tried, daughter. God knows I tried. I was cruel at times, afraid and angry, but I've loved him all my life. Tell me he didn't just stay alive for me but really wanted to go, all these years."

Binah grasped Asherah's hands. "He was happy, Mother," she said. "I promise. He was the first man I saw after I was born, and the best. Even now. He was my father—mine!"

Asherah drew a trembling breath and tried to comfort this most paradoxical child of hers. "You must understand, Binah. Let him go. We are not meant to live forever."

Binah was shaking her head.

"My brave, foolish child. See what you have given your love to? I am sorry, child. One by one, we die and depopulate your world."

"You'll all leave me!" Binah murmured like a child. "I'll be all alone, forever!"

"No, my darling. There will be love. Somewhere, there will be love, such as I found with your father. Look for it. Don't fear it, Binah. That's worse than death."

Something crashed into the shattered doorframe. Anna stifled an urge to break into hysterical laughter. *Now* what? Her private revolt was turning into a public disaster, wasn't it? If she laughed now, they would be sure she was mad, and she would never escape them.

The Varangians muttered. One exclaimed in shock at the new-comer, an ancient, bloodless version of himself. Another fingered a silver religious medal he wore around his throat—if it *were* a religious medallion.

"Oh, Nordbriht," Asherah lamented, "we lost him. All your sacrifice . . . and . . . I am sorry . . ." Her voice trailed off into a wail, and Binah pressed her mother's head against her shoulder.

Nordbriht steadied himself against a table that creaked beneath the weight of his flattened palm, on which his entire body leaned.

"Would you have preferred he die in his bed? I tell you, he was *feigr*; I saw the light upon his brow."

Again, the Varangians murmured. This time two of them touched their amulets.

"We should all die so well," a guardsman said. The others nodded.

"I thought you were dying," Asherah whispered.

"So did I," Nordbriht said. "I've been too long in the East. I bargained with the shield maid: didn't you hear? I shall see my ring-giver to his barrow before she takes me up to Asgard. I have her word."

Binah lowered her head and wept. "Another one gone! And when Theo goes . . ."

"You will go on," Asherah told her. "You just go *on*."

Anna felt isolated in the crowd, just as she had been, that summer of her fourteenth year, in the Bazaar, when Leo had rescued her and started them on this spiral downward to his death. *How could you have killed the one man who saw only yourself, your father's daughter, in you?*

"You don't know what it's like!" she shouted. "Since the breaking of my match with Constantine, I've been denied everything that was mine, that should have been mine, because I am *female!*"

She spat out the word as if she hated it as well as herself. Perhaps she did. The thought came as a revelation.

"It's not because you're a woman, Caesarissa," Asherah told her. Her voice froze on Anna's title sarcastically. "You had, you know, a choice. Do you remember when you made it? *I* do. That was when you made yourself the sort of woman who *would* kill a good old man whose only crime was to love you."

She straightened with marble dignity, like Niobe, Anna thought, the instant before she turned from weeping flesh to stone, the tears still pouring down her face.

"You wouldn't use your powers for me," Anna whispered. "But you just tried to bring the dead back to life, a far worse crime."

"For love, Caesarissa. At least, *I* have not sold myself for power," Binah retorted. "What's *your* price?"

"Crime?" To Anna's surprise, Ioannes spoke to her. "I see no crimes. I see nothing but a good man murdered by a traitor. Summon my physician," he ordered one of his guards. "Run and wake him!"

"Is that Gershom ben Gamaliel?" Asherah asked. "He's a skilled lad, but he can't bring back the dead."

"Not for your husband, peace to his soul," said Kaloioannes, blessing himself. "But for you. Leo Ducas was my kin, and you are . . . were his wife. That makes you kin to me as well. I saw how my mother suffered after my father died. What else can I give you that you might possibly want? Name it, and it's yours."

"I want out," Asherah said. "Out of the game for good. Out of the land of Egypt, out of the house of bondage. I want to go home. We were almost ready to leave, my Leo and I, did you know that? Now it is I who will take him home."

"Where will you take him, lady?"

"Where you will never find us!" Asherah retorted. Binah laid an arm over Asherah's shoulder, and the older woman clung to her.

Anna's brother the Emperor bowed his head, then gestured to his guards.

Two Varangians laid shields upon the mosaics of the floor, then lifted Leo Ducas to lie upon them as if they raised a reigning Emperor.

"You permit?" one asked Nordbriht.

He nodded. "It is his right."

Kaloioannes went over to a chest on which he had tossed a gemmed mantle such as their father used to wear in processions. He had just taken it off when Anna had leapt out at him. Now, he draped it over Leo's body.

The Varangians raised the shields. Led by Nordbriht, they carried Leo out, Asherah following unsteadily, her daughter's arm, strong as a pillar, supporting her.

When even the sound of their slow, heavy footsteps died, the Emperor walked over to Anna, sword in hand.

She braced herself for the death blow. Woman that she was, she would die in battle. It was more than she had expected.

She felt a quick, cool breath of wind at her neck, then a lightness about her shoulders as her hair fell away from the blade her brother had used to shear it.

Kaloioannes wiped his hand upon his garments as if, in touching her, he touched the unholy. So it would be the convent for her, not a quick, clean death.

Nicephorus sighed in relief, but kept his face turned away. "Most Sacred Majesty . . ." he began.

"Nicephorus, my father said that when you start talking, you can make black white, and white black. Not now, though, for the love of God. I still have my mother to deal with; I suppose she was in on this too. No! Just leave me alone, the lot of you!"

The Emperor strode from his room, leaving Anna in command of it—but of nothing else, ever again.

THE MID-TWELFTH CENTURY

CONSTANTINOPLE—
ANNA'S CONVENT OF
KECHARITOMENE

44

A prodigy had occurred that spring in the convent of Kecharito- mene, founded by the Basilissa before her untimely death and supported out of filial piety by her daughters. A woman who had taken refuge there gave birth to a child who lived, but never laughed, waved its tiny fists, or cried, whose eyes, terrified women said, held nothing that could be remotely called "mind" or "soul."

Anna had had four children, all disappointments. She frankly didn't see how the women could tell, that early, that the child was not ensouled. And, even more frankly, she did not care.

These days, she cared for less and less. Her mother had died in 1123. Her Caesar—her eyes filled with the tears that came even more easily now than ever before—had died in 1137. Her children had been disappointments. And, as for the people in the palace—even after her brother the Emperor Ioannes had died in 1141, they had still treated her terribly. So, like her mother before her, she had retreated to the Imperial foundation they had endowed at this convent.

Oddly enough, the retreat was not half so bad as the time she had spent in enforced seclusion after her attempt to claim the throne failed. (She winced away from how badly the whole matter had been botched.) Faces flitted before her eyes, and she shut her eyes as if she pulled curtains over loathsome memories: the astonishment and agony in Leo Ducas's death cry; the pallid anguish of his old Varangian shadow and the disappointment on the faces of the Emperor's guards, who had always had a kindness for her; the bloody finger marks on Asherah's face, grown suddenly older than its years; and—her tears spilled from beneath her shut eyelids—the heartbreak and revulsion in her Caesar's face. She had brought her own destruction upon herself, and she knew it.

Nicephorus had acted as if he could not bear to touch her, but he had spent the next years ceaselessly agitating for her release. Her husband, God smile upon him, had always been persuasive. At the last, Anna was persuaded that she must have had a fever that lasted for years: how could she help but love him? He had even persuaded that sycophant of Ioannes, also named John, to refuse her property, which her brother had lavished upon him.

In the end, Anna conceded, she had been freed by love. It was like charity, she thought: it shamed her; and it shamed her worse to reject it. She had thought, once or twice, of sending a letter to the south, trying to find the people she had wronged so terribly and beg their forgiveness. It was not pride that stopped her; it was knowledge. Asherah had wished to disappear, and Binah, skilled in the art, would help her. In the end, too, she knew that the greatest kindness she could give them was silence. The man she had killed would have forgiven her; he had been her kin too, and perhaps the kindest of them.

The years of regret, silence, and prayer passed until, finally, and somewhat to her surprise, Anna found that she had outlived her generation. What use was she now? She might simply have written more bad poetry, but instead, she persevered, working on her history of her father's life. Georgios Tournikos praised it, but he was courtier enough to praise her beauty too. No: if her work had merit, if she had any merit at all, it was that she chronicled her father's life and held up the mirror to the world to show it what a man, a father, and an Emperor should be. She might, like Bohemond, have aspired and fallen greatly, to live with the knowledge that she had failed: but she had her writing, and he—in the end, Bohemond had nothing but an heir who styled himself "prince."

She was tired now. Tired of her work, tired of the consolations of philosophy, of Georgios's flattery, even of her own sorrows. Each morning, getting up for prayers grew harder and harder. Even in the summer warmth, her old bones ached. She could no longer sit and write for hours each day without her fingers spasming and her back aching.

She compelled herself once again to look at the beginning of her history. "*The stream of Time, irresistible, ever moving, carries off and bears away all things that come to birth and plunges them into utter darkness, both deeds of no account and deeds which are mighty and worthy of commendation."* Well balanced and polished, she supposed, but one can escape into the past for only so long before it becomes time to wake.

And she sensed that dawn was near, even for her.

She bent over her manuscript, idly turning the pages. Her eyes fell on words near the end of her book: *"It seems to me that if I had not been made of steel or fashioned from some other hard, tough substance . . . a stranger to myself, I would have perished at once."*

That would, she agreed, have been a gift. *"Living,"* she had written, *"I died a thousand deaths. There is a marvelous story told of the famous Niobe . . . changed to stone through her sorrow . . . then even after the transformation to a substance which cannot feel, her grief was still immortal . . ."*

Truly, it would have been better to be metamorphosed into some unfeeling rock . . . Her memory flickered and fluttered these days, like butterflies in an overgrown garden. How her old attendant Binah's face had frozen with heartbroken rage until her perfect skin looked like marble with tears running down her face. Binah had refused to curse her, and, if Anna remembered properly, one of Binah's curses would have been deadly. Even now, her compulsions held. Anna could not speak of Binah's true nature even to her confessor and could only pray that her silence not be laid to her account as sin.

Perhaps that too was part of Binah's curse? Love had been part of her nature, but not mercy.

There had been times when Anna had wished she had died. Her own scandal was faint now with age. She had outworn not just the scandal, but her time, her strength, her family. Only the doubts were stronger than they had ever been. She was Orthodox, of course. She was not confused about the existence of her soul, despite her worries about its purity. She had come very close to the edge: in the stillness of night, she sometimes still knelt and prayed that she had not toppled over it altogether. Redemption, she must believe, was possible.

After Anna died, then what? She was afraid to face some of the people who had preceded her, surely, into Heaven. Starting with Leo Ducas, whom she had sent there herself. Leo would forgive her; she was convinced he had already. But his wife—his widow—Asherah was, or had been, a Jew, and Anna was no longer fool enough to believe Jews were automatically damned. She had granted no mercy in her long life, but now she longed for it.

Now, this unfortunate child was carried to the convent and set it in an uproar that was totally in violation of its Rule. She would do what she could for it out of pity, and perhaps God would ascribe it to her for good and be merciful.

It was quiet in the convent, here in the hum of late afternoon, broken only by the sounds of this vast household and the booming of the wooden semantrons, calling those who dwelt herein to prayer. She should, she knew, go too. She stared out across the Horn, her eyes seeing not water nor land, but an innocent child, exulting in her escape from the Bucoleon, running off to meet her fate. She had been so fearless then. Now, she was constantly afraid: not of meeting her father or her brother, but the Ruler of All, His eyes burning with flame. What if *He* did not forgive? After all, had she?

No, she could not truly pray, had tried to, but had struggled for years with her burdened soul. She was trying. Today, for example, she had agreed to wait and see the author of the convent's latest wonder: a lady who had written begging for a child, even a sickly one, to raise. They had acquainted her with the story of the convent's prodigy, more the matrix for a child than an actual infant, and the lady had agreed. She would bring the child up—assuming it lived—and worthily furnish it: a noble sacrifice of care and love.

Talk about prodigies! The woman who could do what this woman vowed was the marvel, not some child too helpless even to cry.

"I will see this marvel," Anna had declared in that thin old-woman's voice of hers that she despised for its piping. She sounded like a grasshopper in the evening. She might have sworn to obey Kecharitomene's Rule, but she had long been a rule unto herself and, truth to tell, she rather liked that.

There came a scratching at her door: no doubt, an attendant escorting this living saint of a woman to Kecharitomene's most prestigious inhabitant, a disgraced Caesarissa. After all, she supposed, such a benefactress might wish to see a prodigy herself.

The woman was tall enough, Anna supposed—far taller than she herself, shrunken as she was in advanced old age. She was suitably and soberly dressed, with dark, modest veils that Anna frankly approved of. Too many women these days went about as if they were Franks. Next thing you knew, they would be dyeing their hair just as, in the Western Empire, women aped prostitutes by coloring their hair gold.

Anna murmured something that could pass for blessing or greeting if someone were kindly disposed, and the woman bowed deeply. She folded back her veils. For a long moment, Anna simply stared.

Despite the suitability of her gown and veils, the lady had pinned up her hair with heavy golden butterflies studded with gems. Her skin was white and very smooth, and her eyes glittered like the gems in her hair ornaments. She had the sort of beauty that you did not associate with charity.

In fact, it never did to associate charity with Binah at all. You could not, Anna realized suddenly, blame her. Binah acted in accordance with her nature, and, for all her upbringing, that nature was not human.

The decades had taken Anna's youth and strength and health. She was older than Leo Ducas had been when she had struck him down in error. Binah looked scarcely older than she had the first time Anna had seen her in the Spice Bazaar and she had declared that she would not tolerate any harm to those she loved.

"I could betray you," Anna Comnena said.

"You won't," Binah replied. "Our lives are bound together."

Life and light seemed to wreath Binah as they always did. Like Helen, from whom she had borrowed a name, she was terrible in her beauty.

"Why are you here?" Anna asked. "Did you come and look at me as one might look upon the Emperor's collection of wild creatures?"

Binah shook her head. "I was promised a child to rear. I have come to take it home."

"Her," Anna corrected automatically. Even so close to the final dark before there was neither man nor woman in Christ, she hated to hear of a girl or girl-child slighted. Even if this one had no mind. "Where is the Lady?" she asked.

"My mother Asherah? Long gone," Binah sighed. "She faded after my father's death. Oh, she smiled, holding her grandchildren, even her great-grandchildren, but she lost all interest in life. We tried to hold her, God knows we tried. When it was her time, she went. Simply, quietly, and quickly. She is in God's peace now, and glad, I think, to be there."

Binah smiled bleakly, like water poured out gleaming onto the rocks. "They are together now," her rich voice mourned, "my father and my mother, and Nordbriht lies at their feet."

Anna shut her lips lest she ask "Where?" and be rebuked. Binah, as well as the Jews' God, had taken Asherah and Leo unto herself.

"Why do you seek a child, Binah?" she asked instead.

"My brother and my sisters fade. Even Theodoulos has not that much longer to live." Binah sighed. "I had hoped he might come down the years with me, but he chose otherwise. Even their children and their children's children age and grow away from me. I am alone."

Anna breathed a prayer. Binah looked ironic.

"They always loved you," Anna admitted. "So did I."

Binah looked toward the door. Taking the hint, Anna clapped her hands for the child to be brought.

"In my father's house are many mansions," Binah mused. "If it were not so . . . Only in my case, it is my mother's house, and it too is eternal—for as long as I wish. I am glad you promised me a girl-child."

"The baby has already been baptized," Anna told her former friend.

"I expected no less."

"Since she cannot make promises . . ."

"I understand. Did you stand as godmother?"

Anna sighed. "I was ill that day . . ."

No reason to let Binah know that the sight of a living, mindless creature filled her with horror—another sin for her to confess and for which she would no doubt have to atone on her aching knees.

"Why do you want this child?" Anna asked.

Binah laughed. Anna remembered that laughter. A time or two, it had bewitched everyone in the palace, including (now it was coming back to her) Anna's beloved father.

"Ah, Anna. You always wish to *know*. You always did. It was just that you always wanted to know the *wrong* things, and you do not listen. Did I not tell you, I am lonely? Even my mother had children, but I have had none."

"Am I wrong in worrying about the child?" Anna asked.

"Probably," said Binah. "I will know once I see her."

A woman came in carrying the silent, swaddled infant, solemn as the figure of the Christ Child in icons. Even Anna itched to hold her, little as she had enjoyed her own children.

Binah's eyes glowed enormous in her face. She held out her arms, and the attendant put the baby into them. Binah stared down into the tiny, vacant face.

Her hands achingly tender as they held the baby, Binah looked up. "I thought that the women who told me that the child is only matrix, not human, were deceived. They were right: there is no *nous* here, no *pneuma*, neither mind nor soul."

Anna leaned forward. Georgios Tournikos's visit was long overdue, and she was longing for a good argument about theology—even with such a creature as Binah. Perhaps *especially* with the likes of her. How often, after all, did one get to argue with a goddess?

"Anna." Binah's voice was vibrant, compelling. "You heard my father say that we all get one miracle. One second chance. Perhaps this innocent is yours."

"What are you talking about?" Anna asked. She had begun, useless old stick that she was, to tremble. Something in her blood understood before her mind could fathom it.

Shifting the child effortlessly into the crook of one arm, supporting her head against her shoulder, Binah reached into her sleeve and drew out a shard of black glass.

. . . the obsidian dagger had fallen from Asherah's blood-smeared hand, shattering on the mosaic floor . . .

She drew a delicate line with it upon the infant's finger. It almost flinched. It did not cry.

"Does your heart not ache to see this child thus?" Binah asked.
Anna nodded.

"She need not be. And you need not . . ." A gesture indicated Anna herself, aged, bitter, sorrowful. Trapped from now until death.

Everyone gets *one* miracle. What happens if it goes to waste? Her trembling intensified. To be young again. To be held and cherished and, this time, to grow up without the need for power, the need for approval, the need to be perfect clawing at you.

"If I agree," Anna stammered like a young girl, standing before her mother, "what becomes of me? Am I damned?"

Binah smiled that archaic smile of hers. "Your own faith speaks of second birth," she said. "Lives come and go; earth abides, and I and my children within it. Think, Anna. Think of what you could see! And, if you weary, then, if you wish, Theodoulos's choice can be yours as well."

Binah sighed regret for her brother's mortality, then held out the obsidian shard.

Does she enchant me, that I consider this?

"You will not have to cut deeply," she assured Anna. "Just a nick, and touch your finger to the child's hand."

Anna drew the knife across her index finger. Blood beaded her dry skin. She watched the beads grow, like rubies set into a bracelet. She fancied she could see shadows in its depths, shadows that pooled and moved.

"Quickly, before the cut heals!" Binah whispered.

Anna looked over at the child. So pretty—and she would be loved as few infants ever are.

Tenderly, she touched her finger to the child, as if she were God the Father, instilling life and spirit into clay at the Beginning of the World. Now *that* was a truly blasphemous thought. She suppressed a laugh.

"*Will* it," Binah said. Her lips moved.

Why, she's praying! Anna thought. *I never knew she prayed. Does she pray to herself?*

Her eyes were blurring; the walls were looming up, suddenly unfamiliar; she was falling, toppling into a new world against the strangeness of which warm arms protected her . . .

The wail of a healthy child crying from wind or hunger or fear shattered the holy silence of Kecharitomene.

"The Caesarissa is much too old to welcome noise like that," said a lay sister.

"It was she who asked to see the Lady Helena, who will adopt the child."

Another woman's face brightened. She sank to her knees and blessed herself. "Do you realize that that's the first time we have ever heard that baby cry?"

The women mumbled assent and prayers.

The lady Helena, as they called her, walked out of the Caesarissa's room. Her face was rapt, and she held the child tightly in her arms, against her heart.

"I must get her home," she said. "Forgive me that I do not stay for prayers. Know that you will always have mine."

The women watched her and her new daughter with misty eyes. The baby, they saw, had splendid violet eyes that seemed to peer into every corner as if sight were this baby's best-loved faculty. Those eyes were far too aware for such an infant.

"I think she is small for her age," said Binah.

The infant ceased crying.

"Look, she's smiling!" said the attendant.

Indeed, the baby wore a faint smile like those on the oldest pagan statues that a nun of this Convent should not even think of, so shameful were they.

"I thought," blurted a nun, "that the child was an idiot and had not long to live."

"You," said Binah, "are pledged virgins. The Holy Caesarissa has been a joyous mother of children. She knew better."

The baby's smile widened, almost ironically. Binah wiped her face clean of tears. This time, the baby laughed.

"I understand," Binah said, "that you have already furnished my daughter with the sacrament of baptism. May I know her name in Christ?"

"Anna, of course." After their greatest patron.

"Of course," Binah agreed. "Well, I shall take my little Anna home now. God bless you all."

She bowed her head for their benedictions, holding the child like an icon for their edification and sentimental joy.

The heavy doors to the outer world shut behind her.

"Quick, go tell the Caesarissa she has a namesake," commanded one of the nuns.

The attendant scratched upon the door, then ventured into Anna's rooms. There, collapsed on the floor, she found the husk of an old woman who once had been a princess and dared to claim the throne.

Fluttering above her, dancing in a shaft of light, was a richly patterned butterfly that gleamed as if real gold leaf and gems adorned its wings. As if aware that it was being watched, the butterfly sped toward the window and freedom—flying out across the Golden Horn and into Asia.

The motes that had partnered it seemed to quiver in the stillness. A shower of golden dust fell upon the floor.

Author's Note

The words of the Chinese curse, "May you live in interesting times," could have been invented to describe the second half of the eleventh century. To the West, on the Iberian Peninsula and in North Africa, Christian kingdoms with names like flourishes of trumpet—Castile, León, Asturias—fought one another as well as the Moors, with Rodrigo Díaz de Vivar, called El Cid (1043–1099), among the best-known men of the time. Far to the north, in the space of less than a month in 1066, King Harold, with a somewhat clouded claim on the English throne, won a battle against Haraldr Hardrada, a former Varangian officer, then lost life and kingdom to William of Normandy.

Like Hardrada and the many men who left England, exiled after Hastings, or, who, like William, were descendants of land-hungry Normans, we must look East to the focus of this book to a city of many names. The Norse called it Miklagard; the Emperor who made it his new capital called it Constantinople, or New Rome, and it is often referred to as Byzantium after its ancient founder Byzas.

These Northerners were a turbulent people. As Norse, they terrorized the British Isles and Europe. As Normans, they settled deep in what became France, then turned around and took England. Some went east, like Bohemond of Taranto (d. 1111), who hoped to win an Empire for himself.

He was not alone in that ambition. The Turkmen had eaten their way into Anatolia. The sultans of Rum had penetrated all the way into Nicaea. Michael VII Ducas, who replaced Romanus on the throne, was simply not up to the task and wound up in a monastery.

By 1081, however, one of the most able Emperors in Byzantium's long history, Alexius I Comnenus, had become emperor. In the last decade of the eleventh century, he appealed to the West for help against the Muslims, and, in 1095 at Clermont, what later became known as the First Crusade began.

To Alexius Comnenus, the armies of the West that passed through his city were decidedly more disaster than blessing.

Appalled and wary, he decided to use this mixed blessing as cat's-paws, enriching, betraying, befriending, or abandoning them as his policy guided. His decision, as well as the Westerners' own actions, set up the repercussions that are with us still.

What we now call the First Crusade was an astonishing blend of faith, brutality, courage, and opportunism that had long-lasting repercussions on all sides. Eleventh-century Western armies won victories in Nicaea, Antioch, and Jerusalem, before losing at Harran, the Horns of Hattin, and Jerusalem itself. The Fourth Crusade sacked Constantinople, which ultimately fell in 1453 before the Turkish Empire, which itself fell during the first part of the twentieth century. Even in the 1990s, Saddam Hussein, looking for a word sufficiently harsh to describe the Coalition that opposed him, called the armies from the West "Crusaders."

Many—and many conflicting—first-person accounts of events relating to the First Crusade are available.

Among the Greek sources, preeminent is the *Alexiad* of Anna Comnena (translated by E.R.A. Sewter, Penguin Books, 1969). She is very much the woman who would be Queen—or in Anna's case, Empress. Betrothed as a child to Constantine Ducas, she had every hope of ruling with him after her parents' death. His replacement as heir by her younger brother John, the breaking off of her engagement, and Constantine's subsequent death ended those expectations, if not Anna's hopes.

The *Alexiad* excels in lively portraits—of Alexius Comnenus, of Anna herself, and of Bohemond. The standard source on Bohemond of Taranto is *Bohemond I, Prince of Antioch* (Princeton, 1924) by Ralph Bailey Yewdale. Despite its turgid style, the book is painstaking and helpful. Emily Albu Hanawalt is the scholar who seems to be doing a good deal of the interesting work on Bohemond today.

The West also has many contemporary accounts, both by participants and people who listened to them. To cite a few: Albert of Aix's *Historia Hieroslymitana*, *La Chanson d'Antioche*, Fulcher of Chartres' *Historia Hierosolymitana*, Guibert of Nogent's *De Vita Sua* (he speaks well of the Tafurs), Raymond of Aguilers's *Liber*, William of Tyre's

Historia rerum in partibus transmarinis gestarum. My favorite is the *Anonymi Gesta Francorum*, edited by the great nineteenth-century medievalist H. Hagenmeyer.

Islamic histories of the period also survive. For reference, the reader can begin with Francisco Gabrieli's *Arab Historians of the Crusades* (University of California Press, 1969) for introductions to Ibn al-Athir and Ibn al-Qalanisi. I used some of the works of Bernard Lewis (recommended, *Islam and the West*, Oxford, 1993), Ronald C. Finucane *(Soldiers of the Faith: Crusaders and Moslems at War)*, Hammond *(Latin and Muslim Historiography of the Crusades: A Comparative Study of William of Tyre and 'Izz ad-Din Ibn Athir*, 1987).

My sources for Judaica drew on a variety of texts, including *The Universe of Shabbetai Donnolo* (translated and edited by Andrew Sharf, Ktav Publishing, 1976) for the tli. A book by the more recent Cabbalist scholar Gerschom Scholem, *On the Kabbalah and Its Symbolism* (1965), provided the description of Torah as hidden lady and beloved.

For an account of the Rhineland massacres, I used Robert Chazan's *European Jewry and the First Crusade* (University of California, 1987). Shlomo Eidelberg's *The Jews and the Crusades* (University of Wisconsin Press, 1977) provides translations of the first-person accounts from the Rhinelands.

I had the good fortune to have access to *The Great Chalice of Antioch*, one of a one-thousand-edition series of two folio-size books published by Kouchakji Freres in 1923, featuring an exhaustive description of this chalice, created some time during the first century C.E. and sometimes romantically equated with the Grail.

For history, I relied most heavily on John France's *Victory in the East: A Military History of the First Crusade* (Cambridge University Press, 1994). My principal authority for the Crusades was Sir Steven Runciman's *A History of the Crusades* (Cambridge University Press, first printing, 1951, most recent edition, 1992).

I made, as writers must make, certain choices. For example, most of the time, I anglicized names. Thus, Leo is Leo Ducas, and not Dukas, while Anna is Anna Comnena rather than Anna Komnene. I was inconsistent in my choice of place names. I use Constantinople and Byzantium, but Dyrrachium rather than Durazzo or Durres, Hagios Prokopios rather than Ürgup, Antioch rather than Antakya, Nicaea rather than Iznik.

Because this is a work of historical fantasy, I could indulge myself—within reason—in whatever mischief one might wish had happened.

Although some characters, such as Leo Ducas, his wife, Asherah, their family, and the Varangian Nordbriht, are my own creation (and players in *Shards of Empire*), most other characters are historical personages, among them the Bishop Adhémar (if not his niece), as well as the secular western lords.

My researches turned up extraordinary things such as the tli of Master Shabbetai Donnolo; the information that Andronicus Ducas, traitor at Manzikert and Anna's grandfather, was buried in Constantinople in the Jewish quarter; and the horses of Cappadocia and how they can grow to adulthood overnight.

I am very much indebted to (and bemused by) a discussion early in 1996 of siege tactics on GEnie, a small on-line service that deserves to be better known, and would like to thank Col. William Gross, USAR (Army Corps of Engineers), for the trigonometry of siege warfare at Antioch, Lt. Col. Chet V. Lynn, USMC (ret.), for real-world experience of siege ladders, and the contributions of many others, including Dr. Albert A. Nofi, Flavio Carrillo, Jo Clayton, Di Fadden, Michael Flynn, Pat Fogarty, Tom Holsinger, Richard Kirka, John Lansford, Jerry Masters, Scott Rosenthal, Bill Seney, Josepha Sherman, Eric Taylor, Trent Telenko, Lois Tilton, Mark Turnage, Dr. Harry Turtledove, and many others.

I acknowledge my debts to Claire Eddy for her patience and for insisting over many years of working together that Bohemond and Anna needed a book about them, and to my agent, Richard Curtis, for reminding me of the Jewish heritage of Byzantium.

Above all, I must thank Harvard University's Center for Byzantine Studies at Dumbarton Oaks, which again opened its doors to me. Any misuse of its sources and any errors are totally mine, and in complete keeping with my material's inconsistencies, errors, and passions. After all—and I cannot stress this strongly enough—this book is story, fantasy, a novel—in short, an exaggeration of an exaggerated time.

Susan Shwartz
New York
June 1997